Raised in a farming family in Northamptonshire, England, **Jack Slater** had a varied career before settling in biomedical science. He has worked in farming, forestry, factories and shops as well as spending five years as a service engineer. Widowed by cancer at 33, he remarried in 2013 in the Channel Islands, where he worked for several months through the summer of 2012. He was forced to retire early from laboratory work by ill-health and now concentrates on writing and interests such as gardening, home-improvement, photography and genealogy. He has been writing since childhood, in both fiction and non-fiction. *Nowhere to Run* is his first crime novel and the first in the series of the DS Peter Gayle mysteries.

Also by Jack Slater

Nowhere To Run
No Place to Hide

No Way Home

JACK SLATER

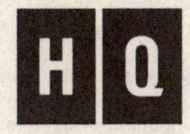

ONE PLACE. MANY STORIES

HQ
An imprint of HarperCollins*Publishers* Ltd
1 London Bridge Street
London SE1 9GF

www.harpercollins.co.uk

HarperCollins*Publishers*
Macken House, 39/40 Mayor Street Upper,
Dublin 1 D01 C9W8

This paperback edition 2024

1

First published in Great Britain by
HQ, an imprint of HarperCollins*Publishers* Ltd 2017

ISBN: 9780008743086

MIX
Paper | Supporting
responsible forestry
FSC
www.fsc.org
FSC™ C007454

This book contains FSC™ certified paper and other controlled
sources to ensure responsible forest management.

For more information visit: www.harpercollins.co.uk/green

Printed and Bound in the UK using
100% Renewable Electricity at CPI Group (UK) Ltd

For Kathy Gale with thanks for leading me, finally, in the right direction.

Chapter 1

Lights glowed through the Yorkshire boarding of the big barn in front of them, gleaming on the cars, pickups and four-by-fours lined up on the wide expanse of the concrete cattle yard.

Detective Sergeant Pete Gayle, crouching in the shadows at the inner end of the short driveway that led to the yard, held up an open hand then closed all but one finger and waved towards the left. He held up the open hand again, then waved two fingers to the right. Eyes roaming the parked vehicles, he waited for the two flanking teams to report.

'Bravo two, in position,' came quietly through his earpiece . . .

'Bravo three in position.'

'Bravo one, received,' he muttered into his radio. 'Alpha. Sit rep?'

'Give us forty seconds,' DS Jim Hancock said quietly from the far side of the big barn, where he and his crew were approaching up an open field that sloped down steeply into the valley beyond.

'Roger. Beta teams, close in.' He raised himself up so he could see into the surrounding vehicles and began to move cautiously forward between them, his two PCs, Ben Myers and Jill Evans, pacing him on the other sides of the vehicles he was moving between.

Behind him, the two police Range Rovers he and his team had arrived in were parked nose to tail across the closed metal gates.

There had been two heavily built men in waxed jackets and beanie hats guarding the gates, but they had been taken by surprise by another team emerging from a house across the road and arrested before they had a chance to warn the people in the barn.

Pete's eyes were constantly on the move as he advanced slowly between the parked cars. Anyone who had stayed behind in one of them, or anyone stepping out of the barn, could raise the alarm in an instant, ruining the element of surprise they were relying on to minimise the possible response of the people inside.

He could hear the murmur of a crowd grow in volume. Male and female voices were raised in excitement. The barking of dogs cut abruptly through the noise. It turned quickly to growling and snarling as the enraged animals saw each other. Pete didn't need to see what was going on in there. He could easily imagine it. Metal sheep hurdles locked together in the middle of the big space, people crowding around, excited, anticipation reaching a peak as the two dogs were led on short leashes from their cages. Muzzles removed, they had seen each other and reacted exactly as they had been raised to since they were pups.

Cash would be changing hands as bets were hurriedly placed before it was too late.

The excited shouting got louder as the hurdles were locked together, the two dogs held at opposite sides of the ring prior to being released.

Pete paused between two expensive four-by-fours in the front row of parked vehicles. He poked his head forward and peered left and right. His carefully raised hand was answered by others at either end of the row. He keyed the radio again.

'Jim?'

'In position.'

'Roger.'

Inside, the two dogs were released. Their snarls changed tone as they met in the middle of the ring. The shouts from the onlookers reached a crescendo.

'Go, go, go,' Pete said into his radio, then ran for the big steel doors.

They were closed with a simple bolt that was accessed from inside and out through a square hole in the right-hand door. Pete flipped the handle and pulled it back, cracking the door open just enough. Ben and Jill preceded him through as the other two teams, having checked for possible exit points along the sides of the barn, closed in. Pete entered, followed by two more uniformed officers who had been chosen for their size. Looking past the crowd, he saw the door at the far side of the barn being closed behind Jim Hancock and his team.

They still hadn't been spotted in the excitement of the crowd.

He raised an air horn in his right hand and pressed the button. A blast of noise erupted, instantly quelling the crowd, though the dogs were still snarling and yelping in the ring.

'Police,' Pete shouted. 'Stay where you are. You're under arrest.'

'Back door,' someone yelled in the crowd.

'No, you don't,' Jim shouted.

'Swamp them,' another voice bellowed as people began running everywhere. A large part of the crowd came at Pete and his team. He snapped out his extendable baton just as a woman in a short black dress squealed and fell towards him, clearly pushed from behind. His instinct told him to save her, but training and practice stopped him. He stepped aside. She screamed, grabbing for his coat as she stumbled, falling, and the man behind her, dressed in a waxed jacket that looked brand new, tried to dodge past Pete on his other side. Pete lifted his baton slightly and pushed it forward between the man's legs. He yelled as his own momentum took him down. With no time for niceties, people going every which way, Pete stamped on the man's crotch and turned, baton raised.

'Hold the doors,' he shouted as his baton impacted with an older woman's arm and chest, almost snatching it from his hand.

'Whoah.'

He allowed the baton to swing and grabbed the back of her coat. She planted her front foot and spun towards him, fist swinging. Pete met her forearm with his baton, hearing the snap of bone, and she screamed, rage switching to agony on her weathered face. He used his foot to sweep her legs out from under her and she fell across the already downed man.

The girl in the short dress was scrabbling to rise at his other side. He swung the baton hard at the tendon just above her right knee. She screamed and fell flat on her face again. He used the baton to deaden her left arm as someone barrelled into him from the side. He tripped over the downed young woman, twisting as he fell and raising the baton. A heavy-set man in a leather jacket and jeans, head shaved but a bushy beard on his lower face and neck, was standing over him, legs spread, fist drawn back and about to swing.

From this angle, there was only one target. Pete raised the baton as hard as he could. The man's eyes widened and he froze for a moment, then puked violently over Pete's jacket and trousers. Pete sat up, the baton held two-handed now as he raised it like a bar, meeting the man's throat and using it to push him across to the side, where he collapsed in a foetal position.

Another man tried to leap over Pete, but he reached up, catching his foot and using his whole torso to yank it backwards. The man yelled and came down hard on his face across the young woman's back, pinning her to the swept concrete floor as Pete gained his feet.

A woman dodged around him and he glanced that way. Saw Jill, tiny though she was, extend her arm, catching the woman across the top of her chest with a forearm block that took her down as if she'd run into a steel bar. He heard the crack of her head hitting the concrete and hoped she wasn't going to be seriously injured by the impact. It was her own fault, but it could ruin Jill's career, justified or not.

He turned his head just in time. Two men were running at him, heads down, arms interlocked in a joint rugby tackle. There was nowhere to go, no time to step aside. He did the only thing he could: dove forward, going up and over them, hoping there would be something other than concrete to land on.

There wasn't.

He twisted in the air, taking the impact on his shoulder. Even though he rolled into it, pain seared through the joint, spreading across his chest and back. Combined with the stench of sick on his clothes, it made his stomach heave, but he held it back and gained his feet again. A punch that had been aimed for his head caught him in the side instead and, despite the stab vest, agony lanced through him. He went to raise his baton, but his shoulder flashed agony. He bellowed, swapped the baton to his left hand and used the handle end as a ram, driving it sideways into his attacker's stomach. The man doubled over and Pete met his face with a raised knee, left hand driving him down harder on it, but the man shook off the impact as if it was nothing.

Whistles and air horns blasting around them, the man reared up and grabbed Pete in a bear hug. He was three inches taller than Pete's six feet and almost twice as wide, and it felt like his whole bulk was muscle and bone. With his right arm trapped inside the bear hug, Pete's shoulder screamed its agony again as his feet left the floor.

One hand trapped, the other holding the baton and his feet dangling useless, Pete brought his knees up around the guy and tried kicking at the backs of his legs, but it was useless. Instinct urged him to grab the back of the guy's head and pull back, but he knew what the reaction to that would be. A headbutt. Instead, he brought the baton down between them, placed it under the man's nose and pushed back hard. The man growled like a big dog as his head was forced back, but his arms didn't give at all. Then he turned his head, but the steel baton lodged under his cheekbone. He turned further and it was across his ear. Pete saw a chance, took a breath that was limited by the pressure on his ribcage, and bellowed in the man's ear as loudly as he could. 'Let go. Now.'

It had the opposite effect.

He felt himself jerked tighter into the crushing embrace. Twisting in the man's grip, he tried to get a knee between his legs, but the big man anticipated the move and blocked it.

Which left only one option.

Pete dropped the baton and clawed his left hand, going for the face. His first and third fingers found the man's eyes while his thumb and little finger gripped the sides of his face. The man tried to twist away, wrenching his head around to the side, but Pete held on. He tried the other way and, despite the pain in his wrist, Pete still held the grip, pressing the two fingers into his eye-sockets. With his eyes squeezed shut, the man wrenched his head this way and that, tightening his grip on Pete's torso even further, but there was no escape. Pete felt the eyeballs give a little under the pressure of his fingers. With a roar, the big man lifted him higher, then slammed him down onto the floor, letting go as he did so and twisting away, body bent as his hands went to his eyes.

Pete took the fall, neck bent to hold his head up off the concrete. Pain lanced through his shoulder again. A quick glance told him he couldn't see his baton, so he rolled to the side, away from the man, in case he recovered more quickly than expected, then gained his feet. He saw the baton on the floor three feet to his left, reached for it, but was beaten by the older woman he'd taken down earlier. She snatched it back away from him, her face twisting into a hate-filled grin.

'Now, Mr Piggy . . .'

Her broad local accent was somehow unexpected, but Pete didn't allow it to affect his reaction. He lunged forward, ducking his head as he grabbed for the wider end of the baton. Felt the top of his head impact her face as his hand closed around the coated steel. The woman screamed, falling backwards as he snatched the baton backwards out of her hand. He opened his eyes to a horrific image. Her hate-filled eyes blazed over a lower face that was slick and red with blood, the mouth open in a snarl of bloody teeth. He caught her still-extended arm and snapped a handcuff onto the wrist, twisting it hard to turn her around and connecting her hands behind her with the cuffs, then shoving her forward so she fell with a scream onto her face.

Pete turned fast, baton raised and brought it down hard across the back of the big man's neck, flooring him. Used a second pair of cuffs to bind his wrists around the top of his leg, then looked up and around.

The fight was over.

The one in the ring, too, he saw. A white bull terrier was snarling quietly as it mauled and shook the body of a brindle dog that was covered in blood.

And beyond, the back doors of the barn stood ajar.

'Shit,' he muttered. They'd hoped for a clean sweep, but it looked like someone, at least, had got away.

He searched the figures in the barn. Couldn't see either Jim or Mick Douglas, one of the city PCs who had accompanied them on the raid. A quick count told him that two other members of the crew were missing too. With the gate blocked off, they must be in the fields and woods between here and the university. He lifted his radio. 'DS Gayle for DS Hancock, over.'

'Oh, come on. Nobody doesn't like fairgrounds.' PC Qadir Hussain waved his hand expansively. 'Look around you. The lights, the smells, the sounds, the excitement: what's not to like?'

His patrol partner, PC Karen Upton, kept resolutely walking. 'The lights, the smells, the sounds,' she said. 'The crowds, the pickpockets, the cons. The whole thing makes me sick.'

Qadir laughed as one overloud pop song gave way to another, the smell of diesel fumes wafting between the brightly lit stalls to briefly overlay the sweetness of candyfloss, the salt of the ocean and the sourness of cooked onions. 'Killjoy was here, eh? Down on Plymouth Hoe.'

'I've got nothing against people having fun. I just don't see it in these places. They're nothing but a legalised excuse for petty crime.'

'Who tipped your pram over tonight?' He glanced across at her as they approached a particularly dense knot of people between a hot-dog stand and a confectionary trailer.

Karen shot him a sour look, her dark eyes fiery in the flickering light of the densely packed seafront fair. 'Nobody. I just don't happen to agree with you. It happens sometimes. Get over it.'

They eased through the densely packed throng and suddenly were in the open. He nodded to the dodgems stand to her left. 'You can't tell me you don't enjoy them, at least.'

She turned. 'OK. There's an exception to every rule.'

'Says the woman who's here to enforce them.'

'What – you're a Muslim in a navy town and you don't appreciate irony?'

Something in her voice as she ended the comment made him glance at her. She was frowning, staring at the expansive ride. 'What is it?' he asked.

'The kid on the back of that yellow car over at the far side. There's something . . .'

He saw the youth she was talking about. He might have been in his early teens. As he watched, the kid jumped off the back of the yellow car, ran a few steps and hopped onto the back of another, one hand to the upright pole that drew power from the overhead grid to drive the little vehicle. Two girls were in the seat, long hair flying as they laughed, one steering while the other glanced up at their new rider. The kid grinned down at her then dropped into a crouch.

Qadir shook his head. 'He doesn't look familiar.'

'I'm sure I've . . . Got it. He's on the mispers list. Comes from Exeter, I think.'

'Are you sure?'

'There was something about his background.'

'He's coming around.'

The young girl was steering the car around the sheet-rubber arena, going with the flow of the multicoloured mass of cars with their laughing and shrieking occupants. They rounded the last corner, heading towards the two uniformed patrol officers. Qadir raised a hand to wave.

'Hey, kid.'

The youth spotted them. His expression changed. He reached through between the girls, grabbed the steering wheel and shoved it over to the side. The car suddenly angled across the centre of the arena, away from Qadir and Karen.

'Shit,' Karen shouted. 'Go that way.' She pointed to the right and set off to the left, jumping up onto the wide metal edge of the ride and running along it as Qadir headed the other way. A family group was standing right in his way. He swung around them, started to run, but the crowd was too tightly packed. He pushed through to the edge of the ride, jumped up and started around it in the opposite direction to his partner. Glancing across, he saw the kid jump free of the car an instant before it hit another one at an acute angle. The girls screamed as the kid jumped over the nose of an oncoming red dodgem car, stepped between two others as they passed and reached the far side. Qadir swung around a group of young guys who were standing in his way and ran on. He made the corner, glanced across again, but the kid had gone from sight.

'Crap,' he muttered. What chance did they stand now, in this crowd?

But the kid had seen them and run. There had to be a reason for that. He couldn't give up now.

The crowd on this side of the ride was a lot thinner. A few long strides and he reached the far corner. He stopped, one hand to the brightly painted corner post as he stared out into the crowded and noisy night, searching for movement amid the milling sea of constantly shifting figures. Something caught his attention at the edge of his vision. His head snapped towards it. A small figure darted into sight and then was gone again, several yards away to his right. He waited. There, dodging through the crowd. He lifted a hand to his radio.

Emma Radcliffe stepped out into the warm April night to the gentle sound of the river at the far side of the pub car park. Minutes ago, that sound would have been torture, but now it was soothing. Restful.

She checked her watch.

Still only twelve minutes since she'd left her broken-down car on the side of the road. She'd wondered if she was going to make it back out of the big pub in time. When she'd got here, she had barely been able to walk without wetting herself. Then, when she sat down and let the flow commence, she'd wondered if it would ever stop. But it had, with three minutes to spare. She shook her sleeve back down over her watch and glanced down the road.

And here it was.

A good thing she was early, she thought, as she stepped forward to the kerb and raised her hand. She had called the cab company as she was stepping away from the bloody useless car, which had just lost power and died on her, out of the blue, and refused to start again. When she said she'd be here, at the Old Mill Carvery, the woman had said fifteen minutes.

The cab drew up beside her, light shining orange on its roof. The passenger window buzzed down as she leaned down to it.

'Pennsylvania?' she asked.

'Hop in.'

Of course, she should have expected him to be Indian. Ninety-five per cent of the taxi drivers in the city were. She opened the back door of the cab and climbed in.

'Buckle up, please.'

'Oh. Sorry.' She'd forgotten the need for that in the back seat, these days. She drew the seatbelt across and clipped it in.

'Right-o.' He slipped the handbrake and eased the car into motion up the long hill out of the city. 'Did you have a good evening?'

'No,' she said. 'I was working late, then my bloody car broke down.'

They passed the little Nissan on the side of the road where she'd left it, but she decided not to comment.

'Sorry. I thought, seeing where I picked you up . . .'

She let the comment go without reply. Silence settled in the car until he flicked on the indicator and it began its rhythmic click. He turned off the main road, heading up the tree-lined lane she'd been dreading.

Emma saw his eyes on her in the driving mirror. In his mid-forties, she guessed, he was stocky and round-faced with lush, wavy hair and designer stubble. He was wearing a denim shirt, but she imagined him in a suit and tie as a bouncer on a night-club door. And his eyes . . . There was something in the way they shone that sent a shiver down her spine. Instinctively, her knees clamped together, her legs turning slightly away from him.

'So, what do you do, to be working so late?' She detected just a slight hint of Devon in his accent and felt somehow reassured by it.

'I was finishing the preparations for a big court case that starts tomorrow.'

'You look too young to be a lawyer.'

She caught his gaze in the mirror again, saw the twinkle in his dark eyes. 'I'm not. I just work for one.'

'Oh, I see.'

The car slowed as they approached a tight right-hand bend with the entrance to a picnic area on the left, the trees growing more densely than ever, branches twining together overhead to give the impression of a tunnel.

'Nice along here, isn't it,' the driver said. 'Quiet. You wouldn't know you were anywhere near the city.' There was something in his tone that didn't sound right.

Oh, God. Had this been a mistake? Which way was he going to turn? Along the road or . . .?

The car eased around to the right.

'Of course, in the dark like this, you don't see it at its best. Looks like something out of a cheap horror film, eh?' He chuckled.

She shivered. 'Hmm.'

'I love those old Hammer ones. Peter Cushing and Vincent Price when they were young. Do you like a horror movie? Bit of a scare?'

The tunnel of bare branches opened out around them, switching to high, dense field hedges. A little farther on, she knew, a gate led in on the right to a field with a wooden building in the far corner where three horses were kept.

'I see enough scary things at work,' she said, forcing herself to think of the grey horse that currently lived in the field. It's big, gentle, liquid eyes, those long lashes. The warmth of its soft skin as she stroked its nose. The almost prehensile mobility of its lips when she offered it a sugar lump or a piece of apple. The image in her mind began to calm her.

'You do criminal cases, then? Killers and rapists and that?'

'Yes.' Although most of the criminality in this city was to do with drugs rather than violence, she thought.

'You must see some horrible stuff, then, eh? Bodies and that.'

'Only in photographs, thankfully.'

The hedge on their left dropped abruptly to a level you could see over. She glanced across, knowing that a flock of sheep and new lambs were being kept in there now. She could see a number of pale blobs dotted about in the darkness.

She frowned. It seemed particularly dark all of a sudden. Glancing across to the right, she saw that the thin sliver of the moon had disappeared, the previously clear sky giving way to a heavy bank of cloud.

'Don't expect you watch much of that true-crime telly then, eh? Get enough of it at work,' he said as they passed two police Range Rovers parked up in a gateway on their right.

'Exactly.'

'Me, I love it. Try and figure out who the criminal is before the detectives get there. I sometimes think I should have been a copper instead of doing this. Of course, it's all down to the editing, I expect. They lead you in a particular direction without saying as much. Let you figure it out for yourself so you feel good about it.'

They were passing houses now. Back in civilisation, as she thought when she drove along here in daylight. Although civilisation was a generous description, considering how rough and poorly kept some of the houses along here were. Detached, edge of town, they should have been smart and expensive, but in truth, many of them looked shabby and dirty and unkempt, as if they were on a building site. Which was one reason she didn't like driving along here. The car got so dirty.

'I expect the idea is to let the public feel better about the crimes they describe,' she said. 'And those crimes are the worst, so, if people feel better about them, they feel better about crime levels in general.'

'Yeah. Hadn't thought of it like that. Same with Agatha Christie and *CSI* and the like, I suppose. People figure out these convoluted plots, they imagine the police must have it easy in the real world. Makes them feel safer.'

'Exactly.' She began to relax. He wasn't as creepy as she'd thought. He actually had some interesting insights. And she was nearly home. Another three or four minutes . . .

'Whereas, the truth is, these days, with the government cutbacks and everything, most criminals get away with it. We have the technology: just can't pay for the staff to use it.'

'Not in a timely manner, at least,' she agreed, as they passed the last of the houses on the narrow lane and the verges opened out wide at either side. Once more, there were woods beyond, but only a small area. She could see the streetlights of Pennsylvania Road just a few hundred yards ahead.

The driver grunted. 'Takes months to get samples processed,

not minutes like on the telly, and, by then, chances are your perp or whatever you want to call them has moved away. Might even have a new identity. Especially these days, with everything being so easy to forge on the computer.' He reached across to the glove box and opened it. She couldn't see what he was reaching for. The headrest of the seat in front of her blocked her line of sight.

Emma glanced at the mirror.

He was staring at her again, instead of at what he was doing. She felt a cold tingle around the back of her neck. He glanced away then, looked down at the glove box and snapped it shut. 'And despite all the technology, all you need is one of these and a bit of intelligence, and you can get away with anything.'

He held up a small, square, plastic packet. A condom.

Jesus! Who did this creep think he was?

'This would be a perfect spot, wouldn't it? Dark. Quiet. Easy getaway. Don't know where the nearest CCTV camera is. There's those houses back there, but that would just add to the thrill, wouldn't it?'

'I . . .' Her throat clogged. She coughed to clear it. 'I'd imagine so.'

He nodded towards the wide verge on his side of the car. 'I mean, you pull over there, nobody would take a blind bit of notice, would they? They'd just assume you were having a bit of nookie. A lovers' tryst.' She felt the car slow as he took his foot off the accelerator.

'I think I'd like you to concentrate on driving,' she said, her voice sounding small and feeble. She cleared her throat again.

'You never done it in a car? You haven't lived, lovey. Can't beat it.'

Panic rose up within her, her breath getting short. This had been a terrible mistake. She'd known it even as she was making the call. Why had she even . . .?

'If you were in the front here, you could change gear for me, if you know what I mean.'

She heard the metallic buzz of a zip and a whimper escaped from her throat.

'Actually, you could even reach through from behind there. Relieve the stress a bit.'

The car juddered and shook and she realised that he'd pulled off the road onto the wide area of grass to the right. *My God!* 'What are you doing?'

The car slammed to a halt. She heard the rasp of the hand-brake, then he was turning in his seat, safety belt off, rising up to climb through towards her.

'No! Jesus, no!' She scrabbled for her bag. 'Please, don't do this!'

His eyes were mesmerising as they came towards her. She shuddered, glanced down at what she was doing. Her hands were shaking in feverish panic. She could barely control them, but then her bag was open somehow. She reached in. Felt the cool round metal and snatched it out. He was halfway through the gap between the front seats, head and torso up against the roof of the car like some kind of human cobra rising up over her to strike. She leaned back, both hands rising defensively.

Chapter 2

Kid was the fourth name he'd answered to in his fourteen years, but he'd accepted it readily. It was kind of cool. Sounded like an Old West hero. A new name for a new life. And he'd been happy with both over the past few weeks. The fair's season started at Easter. He'd wandered in that weekend and somehow stayed. Been offered a bed for the night, in exchange for manning a stall while the owner went off to answer a call of nature that a stomach bug had made both urgent and protracted.

Since then, he'd moved from the stall to a ride, then on to the dodgems. Had thought he'd found his place in life. But now all that was ruined. Had they known he was here? Had they been looking for him? Or was it just chance? Just dumb bloody luck?

He didn't know and now wasn't the time to be thinking about it.

He darted around a couple with a kid of about four and almost ran into a looming, dark figure. Stopped himself just in time, rearing back.

'Hey! Watch it, sonny.'

'Sorry, mate.' He jumped to the left and went around the big man, between two big diesel generators, leaping over the fat, black cables that snaked away from them across the tarmac. Now he was in the semi-darkness of the promenade, between the fair and the shoreline, where few people bothered to go in the dark. He could make some time here, get some distance. He ran headlong eastward, towards where the fair's caravans were bunched in an out-of-the-way corner beyond the naval academy. If he could get there, grab his stuff – not that he had much – and get away, he could hide out for a couple of days or so. Tonight was the fair's last night in Plymouth before they moved on. He could rejoin them in the next town.

'Oi!' The shout came from behind him. A male voice full of authority. 'Stop. Police.'

The kid ignored him, running on at full speed, feet slapping on the paving, breath rasping in his throat. He didn't know how much longer he could keep up this pace, had never been great on stamina, but he had to get away. He couldn't let them catch him.

Heavier feet than his own were slapping the pavement, coming fast behind him. He didn't look back. He knew better than that: just kept going, chest heaving, throat raw, arms and legs pumping. He was almost past the big, pale block of the naval building. HMS whatever-it-was. Bloody stupid thing to call a building. How pretentious and up themselves did they have to be, to do that?

Uniforms. They were all the same. The forces. The fuzz. The lot of them.

Beyond the high stone wall darkness loomed, welcoming and safe. Only a few yards further and he could hide and rest until the coast was clear, get his stuff and be gone before they searched properly for him. He made the far end. Kept going. A dark bulk loomed at him out of the darkness.

'Shit,' he cursed, dodging right. But he was too close to the iron railing along the edge of the prom. He hit it with his shoulder, bouncing off into a pair of arms that snaked around him and clamped tight. 'Whoa. Hold up there, sonny. Not so fast, eh?'

He writhed and wriggled. With his arms trapped, he kicked out instead. The figure barely seemed to register the first couple of blows, but then hissed in pain. 'Damn you, boy. Stop fighting or I'll hurt you.'

'Try it.' He brought his knee up and kicked backwards, his heel connecting with the man's shin.

'Ow! That's it.'

He was lifted bodily off the ground, turned on his side and slammed down to the pavement, a knee coming down over his legs, the shin trapping them so that all he could do was thrash his feet back and forth, but that scraped his right ankle on the paving.

'Shit. Get off me, bastard. Police brutality! I'll get you sacked for this. I'll tell 'em you felt me up.'

Another figure appeared behind him. 'Damn, that little bugger can run!'

'He can bloody kick, too,' the one holding him replied. 'Where's Karen?'

'She'll be along in a minute. Do you want my cuffs?'

'I've got his hands. You could wrap his legs up, though. Little shit.'

'You can't do that,' the kid shouted. 'That's against my human rights. Child cruelty. I'll report you. Both of you. I want your names and badge numbers.'

'We *can* do that, if we decide it's best for your own safety,' said the one holding him. 'To prevent you from coming to harm while in our care. Health and safety: trump card every time, sonny. Isn't that right, Qadir?'

'Yep.'

He felt the cold of metal around his wrist, heard the ratchet as the cuff was squeezed into place.

'What are the charges?' he demanded. 'What are you arresting me for?'

'Resisting arrest.' That was the second one. Qadir. Though he didn't sound like a Qadir. He sounded completely local.

The kid's arm was pulled around behind him. Then the other one.

'And assaulting a police officer,' the guy on top of him added. The second cuff was snapped into place and cinched up.

'But, what were you chasing me for in the first place? You never told me that.' He felt the big guy get up off him. 'For all I knew, you were planning to attack me. Just 'cause you're in uniform doesn't mean you're not some kind of pervert.'

He was lifted bodily by the shoulders of his coat.

'Ankles,' the first one said as he planted him squarely on the ground.

'Hey! You can't do that.'

He felt big hands clamp like iron bands around his ankles. He tried to kick out, to free himself, but was held firm. 'We've already had that conversation. And you lost.' A Velcro strap was wrapped round and round his lower legs and he was stuck.

'What are you doing?' A female voice came from the darkness behind him and relief sang through the kid.

'Where've you been?' Qadir countered, killing the kid's relief in an instant. *Karen*, he thought. *The missing colleague.*

'He was kicking the shit out of my shins,' the first one told her.

'Yeah, but we're not meant to be . . .'

'He ran,' Qadir interrupted. 'He must have a reason. So, he's under arrest until we find out what it is.'

'You chased me,' the kid said loudly. 'What was I supposed to do? I didn't know what you were up to. Could have been anything. Civil liberties, mate. You're bloody taking one.'

'You've got the right to remain silent,' said Qadir. 'How about you use it?'

The kid felt himself pushed from behind, couldn't step forward, so bent at the waist. Then the other one's arm went under his middle and he was lifted bodily off the ground.

'Hey! Put me down, you fucker!'

'If he does, you won't like it. Now, shut up and hold still.'

* * *

'The hunt for missing ten-year-old Molly Bowers ended today, when her body was found by police with a cadaver dog in woodland outside Stoke-on-Trent,' the reporter said solemnly into the camera. 'She'd been buried in a shallow grave, her clothes seemingly tossed in after her like so much rubbish. Detective Chief Inspector Daniel Taft was interviewed at the scene.'

Pete caught his wife's expression and switched channels quickly.

Louise looked at him, her eyes wide and tearful at the tragedy of the case: a young life snuffed out, the body discarded with no more respect than you'd have for an empty milk carton.

It was eleven months, all but two days, since their son had gone missing. At least they knew he was still alive – or had been a few weeks before Christmas, when he'd broken into the home they sat in now with the evening news bringing back memories neither of them needed reminding of. It wasn't as if they ever stopped thinking about him. Pete had taken five months off until a big drugs case had pulled him back to the station and circumstances had conspired to keep him there. Louise had gone back to work as a nurse in the Devon and Exeter Hospital only two and a half weeks ago, having been unable to face it until then.

Pete could guess what she was thinking. Their eleven-year-old daughter was asleep in the room above them as they sat there.

'Annie's as safe as any young girl can be,' he said.

'I expect Molly Bowers' family thought the same, though, didn't they?'

He tilted his head. She had a point. 'You've checked Facebook and so on?'

They had taken on the task of searching for their son after Pete's colleagues had no success. Posters had been put up all around Exeter, in spite of the bylaw against them. Newspaper articles had been published. The local TV stations had done interviews. Missing persons charities had got involved. Social media pages had been set up. They'd done, and were doing, everything they could think of to track down their son.

'I did all that when I came in,' she said. 'I don't understand. I mean, where the hell can a fourteen-year-old boy be, all this time? It's not as if he's big for his age, could be mistaken for an adult, is it? So, how's he still out there?'

They had long accepted that he was missing of his own free will. The evidence was irrefutable. But Louise refused to even acknowledge the possibility that any harm had come to him.

Pete sighed and reached for her hand. 'It does make you wonder, doesn't it?'

The phone chirped on the coffee table in front of him and he reached for it quickly, not wanting to let it wake Annie. 'Gayle.'

With no open cases that demanded overnight action and the dog-fighting case all wrapped up – Jim had walked back into the barn moments after Pete noticed he was gone, leading three other coppers and two handcuffed detainees – Pete was on call for the night. Any case that arose requiring CID involvement would come to him.

'Pete, it's Bob.' *The duty sergeant at Heavitree Road police station.* 'I've just had a call from Plymouth. They've got Tommy.'

Pete felt like he'd been punched in the stomach. 'What?'

'Your lad. He's at Crownhill. He was spotted working on the fair, down on the Hoe.'

'Jesus Christ. Thanks, Bob. I'll give them a call.'

He put the phone down in a daze.

'What is it?' Louise's voice sounded like it was coming through a long tunnel. 'What's wrong? Pete!'

'Huh?' He blinked, staring at her dumbly. 'They've . . .' His eyes closed for a moment as his brain tried to process the informa-tion. Then he opened them, looked at his wife again. 'They've found Tommy. He's . . .'

He stopped as a wail erupted from her throat. He took her hands, stared into her tear-filled eyes. 'He's alive, Lou. He's OK. They've got him in Crownhill station in Plymouth.'

'Oh, my God! Oh, my God. Oh, my God. Oh, my God. He's OK? Where's he been? What's he doing in Plymouth, for God's sake?

21

He's in . . .? What's he doing there? Have they arrested him? What's he done?' She clung to him, pleading for answers that he couldn't give.

'I don't know, Lou. Give me a chance, I'll find out.'

'Dad? Mum?'

Pete hadn't heard Annie's feet on the stairs, but now she stood in the doorway, dressed in her favourite Winnie-the-Pooh nightie. He glanced down and saw that her feet were bare.

'What's all the ruckus about? Have they . . .?' She swallowed, unable to go on.

'Yes, love. They have.' Pete held a hand out to her. 'They've found Tommy. Alive and OK.'

'Oh, God, that's brilliant!' She ran to him, clasping him into a desperate hug. 'Where is he? When's he coming home?'

'I haven't got any details yet, Button. All I know is, he's at the police station in Plymouth. He was working on a fairground.'

'But . . .' She stopped, too confused to even form a question.

'I need to give them a call and find out what's going on.'

She blinked owlishly. Pete took a step back, directing his wife and daughter into each other's arms while he made the call. They clung to each other, both watching him intently.

Pete found that his hands were shaking as he tried to dial the number from memory. Then he couldn't remember the correct order of the last three digits. 'Shit. What's the bloody number? Hang on.' He went out to the hall, found their personal phone listing and flipped it open at the letter P.

Quickly, he finished dialling and held the phone to his ear. It rang once, twice, a third time, a fourth. 'Come on,' he muttered.

There was a click. 'Devon and Cornwall Police, Plymouth. How can I help?'

'Hello. This is DS Gayle, Exeter CID. I'm told you've got my son there: Thomas James Gayle.'

'One moment, sir.' More clicks, half a ring. A different voice. 'Custody suite.'

22

Custody? They've got him in the cells? What the hell has he done? 'He . . .' His voice clogged up and he coughed to clear it. 'Sorry. DS Gayle here, Exeter CID. I've been put through to you from your front desk. I understand my son's there, in the station.'

'Gayle? Thomas James?'

'That's right. What's the deal?'

'He was brought in a couple of hours ago. A patrol officer recognised him from the misper notice, but he didn't come willingly. Hence he's in the cells here. Assaulting a police officer; resisting arrest; possession of an illegal weapon, specifically a knife. We thought that would do for now.'

'Jesus!' Pete shook his head, bewildered. What the hell was going on? What had Tommy got tied up in? 'I was told he was found at a fairground. What's the story there?'

'Seems like he's been with them since Easter. Just mucked in when they needed it, helped out and became part of the setup by default. Saw the chance of a new life, I suppose. It never ceases to amaze me, the number of kids who run away to join the circus or the fair. I don't know what it is about that kind of lifestyle that's so attractive. Seems like a lot of hard work and rough living to me.'

'And the charges. Is there anything we can do there? I'm not trying to get him off because I'm in the job. We need him as a witness in a child-sex case.'

'I knew the name was familiar. You're the one that cracked that big paedophile ring, right?'

'Yeah, that's me.'

In the course of his first case after returning to work, Pete and his team had uncovered a ring of paedophiles that extended from Cornwall north to the West Midlands and east to the Home Counties. Thirty-seven arrests had been made by seven different forces just the previous month, some of them of prominent men in local government and even the police itself.

23

'Well done, mate. I know it reflects badly on the force, but we were glad to get rid of Markham. The bloke was a self-aggrandising arsehole. No more use as a copper than I'd be as a brain surgeon.'

Pete knew he was talking about Chief Superintendent Markham, who'd been in charge of the Plymouth station until his arrest last month in a coordinated series of operations that had closed down the whole ring in one morning's work, organised by his own station chief, DCI Adam Silverstone.

'Well, that's what you get for letting politics into policing, eh?'

'Yeah, along with empire-building, jobs-for-the-boys . . . Still, what can we do, eh?'

'That's right.' *Come on*, Pete thought. *Answer the bloody question.*

'Anyway. As far as the knife, facts are facts. He was carrying. But, the rest of it can go away if it needs to. If he's a witness in a case like that . . . Happens all the time, doesn't it?'

'I don't want him let off just because he's my son,' Pete said firmly. 'If he's got things to answer for, he'll answer for them. But yes, we do need him as a witness.'

'Firm but fair, eh? Only way to be, I reckon. Bit of discipline never hurt anyone. Well, it might have stung a bit at the time, but you know what I mean.' He laughed.

'Yes, so . . .'

'Get your boss to send the paperwork through and we'll transfer him to Exeter custody. Might be worth letting him stay put until morning. Just my opinion.' Pete could almost see the custody sergeant shrug. 'Teach him a bit of a lesson.'

'Right. I'll get onto my chief. Thanks, mate.'

'No worries.'

Pete ended the call, looked up and saw both Annie and Louise standing in the doorway of the lounge, watching him, their expressions, one above the other, identical. He couldn't help but smile.

'So . . .?' They said together.

Pete's smile became a chuckle.

Although Annie's temperament was much more like his than her mother's, she got more like Louise every day, in all the good ways.

He shook his head. 'God, I love the pair of you.'

'But what about Tommy?' Annie demanded.

'Well, I love him too, of course.'

'Answer the damn question, would you?' Louise joined in. 'What's happening with Tommy?'

The smile stayed on Pete's face. 'He's in Plymouth nick. I need to get hold of Colin, get him to arrange a transfer to Heavitree Road and we can go from there.'

'So, he'll be home soon?' Annie demanded.

'Well, it depends on your definition of soon, but potentially, yes.'

She squealed and ran to him, wrapping her slender arms around him and squeezing with all her might.

Louise was less easily pleased.

Looking over Annie's head as she clung to him, Pete saw the doubt in her eyes.

'Why do you need to arrange for a transfer? Has he been arrested or something?'

He tilted his head. 'Yes. When he was spotted he did a runner, and when they caught him, he was carrying a knife.'

'A knife?'

Annie picked up on this and stood back, staring up at him, big-eyed.

'He was working on a fair. I expect he needed it. Tool of the trade, like a farmer or gardener. But when he fought them off, they cuffed him and found it.'

'He fought them off? This gets worse by the second.'

'He was in Plymouth, remember. We don't know how long he's been there. It could be he doesn't know we're not planning to charge him in the Rosie Whitlock case.'

'Hmm.' She seemed to relax at least a little. 'So, you've got to get Colin to arrange things, to get him transferred?'

He shrugged. 'I can't do it, can I? I'm his dad. How would that look to anyone that didn't know the history?'

'OK. So, what are you waiting for?' She nodded at the phone, which was still in his hand. 'Get onto him.'

'It's nearly eleven. He'll be in bed, I'd have thought.'

'So? He'll understand. He's Tommy's godfather, for Christ's sake. Come on. Either ring him or give me the phone and I will.'

'Give me a chance, woman.' He lifted the phone, thumbed in the number from memory and held it to his ear.

It rang twice, then was picked up. 'Hello?' Colin sounded groggy. He had been asleep.

'Colin, it's Pete. Sorry to wake you, but I need a favour.'

Five minutes passed. Then ten. The phone was still silent. None of them was going to sleep until they heard.

'Who wants a cup of tea?' Pete suggested.

'Yes, please,' said a red-eyed Annie.

Louise nodded.

'OK.' Pete headed for the kitchen, put the kettle on and fetched out the mugs. He was pouring boiling water over the sugar and teabags when the phone finally rang. He put down the kettle and headed for the living room.

'Colin?' he heard Louise ask.

Silence. He stepped into the room and she held the phone out to him, her expression blank.

He took it from her. 'Hello?'

'Pete? Bob again. I'm afraid we need you, mate.'

Shit! Now, of all times?

'A body's been found, corner of Pennsylvania Road and Argyll Road.'

'Eh?' Pete frowned. 'I was only up there an hour ago with Jim and the team. What happened?'

'Dunno. Doesn't look like it's linked, though.'

Pete shook his head. He couldn't believe it was merely coincidence. He stared at Louise. The expression on her face said more than a thousand words. How could he leave her here, now, with things as they were? OK, Annie would be with her, but . . . He felt as desperate as she was to hear back from Colin, to know what was happening with Tommy. She was fully aware that they wouldn't be allowed to see him tonight, but they both – *all*, he thought, thinking of Annie – needed to know how he was faring, at least. And her emotional state was still delicate. It was barely any time at all since she'd got her head straight after Tommy's disappearance. How would she cope on her own, now he'd been found?

'Pete?' Bob's voice came over the phone. 'You still there?'

Bob knew the score. If anyone else could have taken the call, he'd have gone to them first. And Pete was duty SIO tonight. He sighed. 'Yes. OK, I'm on the way.'

Chapter 3

Pete saw the flashing blue lights through the trees from a couple of hundred yards away. When he reached the junction, he could see the cluster of police cars, an ambulance and a couple of other vehicles, tape stretched across the end of the side road and a small cluster of onlookers standing around idly.

Hadn't they got better places to be, at this time of night? He stopped the car and climbed out, making sure to lock it as he stepped forward, raising his warrant card to one of the uniformed officers guarding the tape.

The blue and white plastic ribbon was raised for him to step under. He headed for the lamps and the white protective windbreak across the grass to his left. He could see the shape of a car and more uniformed police. A generator rumbled close by. Pete passed the ambulance crew as they were leaving the scene. He nodded, drawing a response from one of them. Closer to the windbreak, which had been erected to mask the view from the public rather than for its nominal purpose, he could see a white-overalled figure working over a body which had been laid out on a tarp.

Having recognised the car back on Pennsylvania Road, he didn't need to see the man's face to know who it was.

'Evening, Doc. How's it going?'

Tony Chambers looked up from what he was doing. 'Peter. You've drawn the short straw again?'

'Apparently. What can you tell me so far?'

'We have a quite vicious attack, clearly aimed at being fatal. The victim was killed with a short, sharp blade – possibly a scalpel or utility knife – and some considerable force. The carotid and the jugular were severed as well as the windpipe. There are traces of inflammation around the eyes and nose which suggest the use of pepper spray prior to the knife attack. You can still smell it when you get close enough. The victim's ID is in the car.'

Pete grimaced. 'Sounds messy.' He looked up at the vehicle. No need to ask if the victim was the driver or the passenger. The blood sprayed across the inside of the glass made it obvious.

'Any idea when?'

'Rigor hasn't set in yet, so less than four hours. Body temperature suggests closer to one or two.'

'OK.' He looked up and around. 'Who found him?'

'Where is he?'

It was past one in the morning. Pete had been out more than two hours. His eyes were sore, his head fuzzy. He was exhausted. How did Louise not look as knackered as he felt?

But she didn't. She'd met him at the door, blocking his way with her body as if unwilling to let him in until he gave her the answers she wanted.

At least now they were in the hall, the front door closed behind him. Pete kept his voice low, not wanting to disturb Annie, who he hoped was asleep.

'For now, he's still in Plymouth. Colin's arranging his transfer but they won't do it until morning and, even then, he won't be coming home for a while. He'll have to go for assessment, be interviewed and so on. And the knife charge won't just go away. He'd be bailed if he wasn't a flight risk, but given his recent history . . .' He shrugged, hands spreading.

Her gaze locked on his. 'We'll be able to visit him, though?'

He raised a hand, indicating she should go through to the sitting room. Following her in, he closed the door behind them.

Tommy would be transferred from the custody of Plymouth nick to that of Exeter, where someone other than Pete – probably Colin Underhill – would interview him. Then he would be transferred again, to a secure youth residential facility where he would be assessed before any further decisions were made about his future.

'My guess is, the best we can hope is that he gets transferred to Archways from Heavitree Road. Once they've settled him in we'll have visitation rights, the same as any other parents. Except, of course, I won't. Not with the case outstanding.'

She rubbed at her forehead, eyes closing, then fixing intensely on Pete once more. 'I need to see him, Pete. Talk to him. Know he's going to be OK.'

'I know. Me, too.' But Pete knew how the system worked. Tommy was involved in a case that he'd worked – a case that was yet to go to trial, thought the date was fast approaching. He wouldn't be allowed to see him, in case of a conflict of interest. 'But at least you'll be able to in a day or two. And he'll be as safe there as he would be anywhere. Those places are designed for it.'

Archways was a secure children's home which happened to be less than half a mile from where they were sitting, here in Exeter.

'God! I feel so . . . mixed up. Happy he's been found and desperate to see him but at the same time scared to death. I'll tell you – if I'd be able to see him when I got there, I'd be halfway to Plymouth by now.'

'No, you wouldn't,' Pete countered. 'You'd *be* there. And so would I, because I'd have used the blues and twos to get us there and sod the consequences.'

Emma didn't really sleep that night. Her mind kept playing back the attack, the moments leading up to it and those that followed. Over and over, she relived it. Could she have done anything different? Should she simply go down to the police station and report it?

Her instinct was to hide. The last thing she wanted was to have to go through it all again, even just verbally. But, was she thinking straight? She felt groggy, her eyes sore and gritty from lack of sleep. She didn't know how many times she'd got up in the night to puke, though by three in the morning there was nothing left to bring up. Her stomach ached from trying. It heaved again now, but she knew there was no point rushing to the toilet. She rolled over, moaning, and grabbed a tissue, holding it over her mouth as she retched painfully.

If she went to the police now, her past, which she had tried so hard to leave behind, would all be brought out into the open. The press would get hold of it. Her colleagues would find out. The persona she'd built since she got here would come crashing down around her.

She couldn't have that.

Emma wiped her mouth with the tissue and clambered out of bed. Took a sip from the bottle of water she'd left on the bedside cabinet last night, swishing it around her mouth before swallowing.

No, she thought: she couldn't come forward.

But, having decided that, what was she going to do about it? What *could* she do? She checked the time. The red numbers on her digital alarm read 6.38 a.m. The buses didn't start until eight and she really needed to be at work by then. She had to get back to her car, see if it would start and, if not, call the breakdown service. Get it going. Get it moved. Otherwise, it would only be a matter of time before someone spotted it and the police came knocking on her door.

But, how was she going to get there? She certainly didn't fancy walking it.

There was only one way.

Could she?

31

After last night, she wasn't sure she'd ever be able to climb into another taxi, but what other option was there?

None, she told herself.

She reached for the phone, about to dial a number she knew by heart.

No.

That, she couldn't do.

She picked up the phone book instead.

Chapter 4

Her tension increased with each passing second. As the seconds became minutes, she barely knew how she managed to stop herself from screaming or running from the flat in a blind panic.

She alternated between watching through the sitting-room window and watching the clock.

Five minutes passed.

The dispatcher had said ten until the cab arrived. But surely, at this time of day, it wouldn't take that long? Maybe she should go down and wait outside. It was a bright and crisp day. No doubt chilly out there, but there was no frost. Perhaps the fresh air would do her good? But she didn't want to be seen pacing out there, and there was no way she'd be able to hold still.

She crossed to the window, looked out. Her stomach lurched, one hand going to her mouth as she turned quickly towards the bathroom.

A taxi was pulling into the parking area out there.

She moaned through the hand clamped over her mouth.

With nothing left to bring up, she swallowed and looked out again.

She could ignore it. Let it go on its way. Have the day off sick.

She sighed. She'd already been through all this. It wouldn't work. She had to go in. Today, of all days, she didn't have a choice.

Stomach roiling, legs like jelly, she picked up her bag, checked its contents with shaking hands and headed for the door.

'Bob. Is Tommy here?'

The custody sergeant looked awkward. 'Yes, but I'm under strict orders. You can't talk to him. Fast-track was adamant. Called me himself. He's got to be processed through as if you didn't even know him.'

Pete's jaw clamped, teeth pressing together hard. 'If that were the case, I'd have him straight into an interview room. He's a material witness in an ongoing case of mine.'

'I know. But, like I said . . . my hands are tied, mate.'

The urge to ignore the station chief's orders and head down the corridor to his son's cell regardless was almost overpowering, but he knew he couldn't. Apart from anything else, there was a powerful electromagnetic lock in the way, the release of which was out of his reach, on Bob's side of the desk. He sighed. 'He's OK, though, is he?'

'Of course. We're checking on him every hour.'

Every hour? 'How long's he been here?'

'Since three. Five hours, nearly.'

'Well, dammit, how . . .' Pete stopped himself, forcing his body to relax against all his instincts. He already knew the answer to the question he'd been about to ask: orders from Fast-track Phil, DCI Adam Silverstone, station chief until he took the next step in his rapid and illustrious rise towards the higher echelons, whether he deserved it or not.

Which, in the opinion of just about everyone who actually had to work with him, he definitely didn't.

He tapped the high counter. 'OK, Bob. Just take care of him, yeah?'

'Goes without saying, mate.'

'Thanks. Can you tell him I was asking after him, at least?'

'Of course.'

Pete nodded to the big man and headed along the corridor towards the centre of the building.

Emma's whole body was quaking by the time she got down the stairs into the foyer. The taxi was parked directly in front of her, just a few feet away from the toughened glass doors that were all that separated her from the outside world at this point.

She stepped reluctantly forward, didn't even think to check her mailbox as she stared hard at the dark maroon car parked sideways on across the entrance. In the deep shadow of its interior, she could just make out the shape of the driver. She frowned. Something didn't look as it should.

Then she realised.

It was a woman.

'Oh, my God!' She couldn't help saying it out loud as relief flooded through her. She pushed through the doors and hurried to the waiting car. Climbed into the passenger seat. 'Hi. Sorry it took me a minute to get down here,' she burbled. 'Had to check the front door three times. You know how it is. I'd lose my head if it wasn't screwed on. At least, that's what my boss tells me.' She laughed.

The driver, curly blonde hair covering her ears, but not enough to hide her big hoop earrings, looked at her like she was crazy, but also a customer. 'No worries. Where to, love?'

Emma had prepared her story. *Don't flunk it now*, she told herself. 'The Old Mill. Early start today. Big party coming in and we've a delivery scheduled this morning.'

The woman put the car into gear and set off towards Pennsylvania Road. 'On a Wednesday? I usually see your deliveries on a Monday and Friday, don't I?'

Oh, shit. Trust me to get a driver that knows more about my alibi than I do. 'Uh . . . yes. That's why we got the party booked for today. But the suppliers phoned last night. They've got some kind of vicious bug going around the depot. Lots of drivers off sick with it.'

Wow, she thought, proud of her quick thinking.

They turned left onto the main road, heading south.

'So, how come you're using a taxi this morning, then?'

Oh, crap. Why had she chosen a chatty persona for this journey?

Pete had made several calls when he got up that morning and, for once, he was the last of his team to arrive in the squad room. As he approached his desk, five pairs of eyes watched him, waiting to see what he was going to say. And about what, he guessed.

Draping his jacket over the back of his chair, he rolled up his sleeves and went straight to the whiteboard where, last night, he had put up the basic information on the new case.

'Morning, all.' He picked up a marker pen, not caring what colour it was. 'Ranjeet Singh, 34, born and raised in Exeter, an independent taxi driver for the last four years, having previously worked for Cathedral Cabs since he got his licence in 2008. He was found, pepper-sprayed and with his throat cut, in the driving seat of his taxi near the junction of Argyll and Pennsylvania Roads at 10.27 last night. He'd been there at least half an hour at that point, though we've no other witnesses as yet. It doesn't appear to have been a robbery, so we need to canvas the area, see if we can find any witnesses, speak to his colleagues and family to try and find a motive and establish a timeline. I informed his wife last night. She was too distressed to give an interview, though, so I said I'd go back this morning. Family liaison's with her in the meantime.'

'Pepper spray, boss?' asked DC Jane Bennett. 'Does that suggest the same thing to you as it does me?'

'Probably. The fact that his flies were undone and the condom – still in its wrapper – found on the passenger seat beside him would tend to support it. But the fact that he's married argues against. And he's got no previous form.'

'That only means he hasn't been charged,' DC Dave Miles pointed out. 'It'll be something to check with his previous employer, if nothing else.'

Pete nodded. 'That's your first job, then. Then you can follow the theme. Find out which ranks he used and talk to the other drivers on them. I'll ask his wife about pre-bookings and let you know what she says. Jane, look for unsolved sex attacks in the city, see if any show signs of a taxi driver being involved. If not, we can eliminate the possibility. If so, you can follow them up. Dick, take Jill with you and interview family and friends. Ben, get a couple of PCs from Uniform and get yourself up Pennsylvania Road, canvas the area for witnesses and so on. The position of the car suggests it had come along Argyll, so concentrate along there initially.' He clapped his hands together. 'Right, people. Let's see if we can get this solved in record time, eh? There's a killer out there. For the sake of public safety and the victim's family, we need to get them off the streets sooner, rather than later.'

Turning to the whiteboard, he wrote up a quick series of notes of who was doing what, then put the marker pen down and headed for his desk.

Stopped in the middle of his first step.

His whole team were still sitting where they had been, staring at him expectantly.

'What? I've given you all assignments, haven't I? Or did I dream that?'

'We're waiting to see what else you've got to say, boss.' Jane glanced at the rest of the team for support.

There were nods from around the grouped desks.

'That's right,' said Dave. 'There's a bloody great elephant in the room here. You going to shoot it or hide from it?'

Pete sighed. It had been inevitable that they'd ask. A function of the team he'd built. Of any good team. They cared. That didn't make him any more comfortable with the situation, though. This was his son they were talking about. His flesh and blood.

He crossed quickly to his desk and sat down, leaning forward on his elbows. 'There's not a lot to tell. You know Tommy's downstairs, obviously. He was spotted working at the spring fair on Plymouth Hoe, stopped and found to be carrying a knife. So they arrested him. Colin got him transferred here because of the Rosie Whitlock case. I expect he'll go to Archways in the short-term. Meantime, I don't get to see him until after Colin's interviewed him. If then. He's . . .' He stopped himself with a grimace. It was no use whining.

'Why Colin?' DC Dick Feeney, the old man of the team, asked.

Pete looked at him. It wasn't yet nine in the morning and his cheeks were already grey with the suggestion of stubble that was just one of the reasons for his nickname of Grey Man. 'Well, it's not going to be me, is it? And what's the alternative? Simon?' He huffed dismissively. DS Simon Phillips had been looking for Tommy for months and come up with nothing. 'Or Fast-track?'

'God save us all from that,' PC Jill Evans said, shaking her head.

'No need,' said Dave. 'The only interviews he'll ever do are the press type.'

'And annual reviews,' Jane added.

'Yeah, and *there's* a good reason not to rush into any promotional opportunities,' Jill replied. 'At least, not until he's moved on up the ladder, out of the way.'

'Well, sitting around here, yakking, isn't going to bring that any closer, is it?' Pete said briskly. 'So, let's get to it.'

He grabbed his jacket and headed for the door, glad of the opportunity to get out of the station. With his son in a cell downstairs, if he couldn't talk to him, he'd sooner be out and about, doing something, keeping himself occupied rather than just a few steps away, dwelling on the fact that he was so close, yet so inaccessible.

He went quickly down the stairs and along the bland concrete corridor towards the back door and the fresh air.

Ranjeet Singh had lived just a few streets from the station, in an area of Victorian terraces. Pete walked there, needing the fresh air and the few minutes downtime to clear his head. Even at this time of day, the street was filled along both sides with parked cars. The Singh household was just a few doors up from the end of the street. The front garden was almost non-existent, but it was clean and tidy. He knocked on the door and it was answered by a uniformed police officer.

'Morning, Sarge.' She stepped aside to allow him in.

'Naz. How's Mrs Singh?'

'Emotional, as you'd expect, but calmer this morning. We've sent the boys off to school. Keep things as normal as possible for them.'

There were two sons, aged five and seven. Pete had met them the night before when both appeared shyly at the top of the stairs, long after they should have been asleep, peering down, big-eyed, at the unusual activity in the hallway, until their mother shooed them away to bed.

It was moments after that that he'd informed her of her husband's death.

'She's in the lounge.'

PC Nazira Mistry was one of three family liaison specialists in the city and the only Indian officer they had. She showed Pete through the door on the left of the hallway. Mrs Singh was on the sofa. The TV was on, the last few minutes of the BBC breakfast programme playing, but she was ignoring it, head bowed as she wrung her hands together.

'Mrs Singh.' Pete extended a hand. Her grip was limp and lifeless, but it stopped her hands writhing together, if only for a short time. 'Would it be all right if I asked you a few questions about your husband this morning?'

She looked up at him, her expression blank as if she didn't understand who or what he was, never mind what he'd asked.

'I need to know as much as I can about Ranjeet, to stand the best chance of finding out who did this to him.'

She nodded wordlessly.

'Are you aware of anyone having made any accusations against Ranjeet of any kind?'

39

She shook her head slowly.

'Nothing? No one's said they wouldn't ride with him again? He doesn't owe anybody any money? There's been no arguments with other drivers or with neighbours?'

'No,' she whispered.

'You understand, I'm just trying to figure out what the motive behind this attack might have been? So that I can figure out who might have done it. This isn't about Ranjeet's character, it's about his attacker's.'

She nodded again.

'So, there's nothing you can think of that might have caused anyone to want to hurt him?'

'No.'

'OK. Do you have family locally? Anyone you can turn to for support?'

Once again, she shook her head. 'Ranjeet's family are here. Mine are in Manchester. His mother and I . . .' She shuddered.

'It's often the way with mothers-in-law, isn't it?' He smiled reassuringly. 'I'll get Naz to give you the details of the local support network, to help you through.'

'Thank you.'

Pete's instinct was to reach out to her, take her hand, but he didn't know how that would be seen in her culture, so kept his hands firmly on his knees. 'I know it won't bring him back, but we will do all we can to find out who did this and bring them to justice, Mrs Singh. That's a promise.'

She stared at him, her eyes brimming.

'I'll leave you with Naz. Again, I'm sorry for your loss.'

Ben shook his head, his short, spiky hair glistening under the strip lights of the squad room. It was mid-afternoon and he had just got in, having returned from Pennsylvania Road. 'There were some people not in, of course. We'll have to go back for them. But so far, we've drawn a blank on the area canvas.'

'There haven't been any taxi-related complaints of sexual assault in the city in the past five years, either,' said Jane. 'But I did find one thing. There was a complaint made against him back in 2008, but it wasn't followed up because the victim refused to come forward.'

'What sort of complaint?'

'A woman came in and told the desk sergeant he'd raped her friend. But the friend refused to talk to us and she was from out of the county.'

'Have we got any details? Names, addresses?'

Jane shrugged. 'Yes, but it was eight years ago. No telling where they've gone or what's happened since.'

'Follow it up anyway. See what you can find.'

'Of course.'

Mrs Singh hadn't mentioned anything about this. Did she know? How long had they been married? It could have happened before they were together, Indian culture being what it was – arranged marriages and so on – but it would be something to check on, he thought.

Dick looked from Jane to Pete. 'Everyone we spoke to reckoned he was always polite, friendly and appropriate. No hint of anything like that.'

'And yet I was told there were two complaints against him with Cathedral Cabs,' Dave said. 'The second one just before he left. Can't say yet whether it was the reason he left, but . . .' He shrugged. 'It makes you wonder, doesn't it? The owner's on holiday abroad; a cruise in the Caribbean. Due back the week after next. But no charges were filed in either case. Both customers just made a complaint to the company and left it at that. I've spoken to the other drivers on the ranks at the bus station, St David's, the Arches. Even went out to the airport. None of them seem to be aware of any issues, but I don't suppose they'd admit it if they were, would they? Bad for business.'

Pete nodded. 'His pre-bookings were done by mobile phone or email. I did an Internet search, but came up empty, and I'm waiting on his mobile phone provider to come through with a full set of records. They set aside their privacy considerations when I pointed out that he wasn't going to give a damn, being deceased.'

Dave leaned back in his chair and stretched, his black waistcoat pulling tight across his stomach. 'So, to summarise: he's one hell of a lucky bugger, with three complaints against him for sexual assaults but none of them followed through. But other than that, as of now, we've got SFA.'

'Except that his last recorded drop-off was at St Thomas railway station,' Pete said. 'And the distance on his meter, if you work back in that direction from where he was found, would put him somewhere near the Old Mill.'

'Which would fit with the timeline,' Dick pointed out. 'Someone wanting a ride home from there.'

'Yeah. The staff weren't aware of anyone, though. Although it's perfectly possible someone used a mobile, of course.'

'And how many of those would have been in or around there at that time of night?' Jane said sourly.

'Loads of them, I bet,' Dave said, looking up from his screen.

'Worst comes to worst, we'll have to find out and track them down,' Pete said. 'Although we can only do that for the ones on contracts, of course. Any pay-as-you-goers will be out of the picture unless they're regulars in there. But that's only if every other line of enquiry falls flat.'

'Thank God for that,' said Ben.

Dave laughed. 'Worried about your workload, Spike?'

'I don't mind working. What I don't want is RSI.'

'Don't worry,' Pete told him. 'Dave will help.'

Dick laughed at the expression on Dave's face. 'Serves you right for taking the piss.'

The phone rang on Pete's desk. An internal call. He picked it up. 'Gayle.'

'Peter.' He recognised DI Colin Underhill's voice. 'I need a word. In my office.'

Chapter 5

'Close the door.'

Colin Underhill sat stiffly in his chair, big hands flat on his desk, his broad face expressionless.

Pete did as he was asked and Colin nodded to the spare chair in the corner. As Pete sat down, Colin leaned forward, putting his elbows on his desk.

'I've been talking to Tommy.'

Pete felt a stab of urgency in his chest. 'How is he? When can I see him?'

'He's fine. And you know the answer to that second question. He's got charges outstanding. And he's a material witness in the Malcolm Burton case.'

'Yeah, but the charges are just trumped up to get him in, aren't they? I mean, he would be carrying, wouldn't he? A knife would be essential for what he was doing.'

Colin nodded. 'But this was a flick-knife.'

'A . . .? Where the hell did he get one of those?'

'He told me he'd had it for years. His words. Bought it on the street when he was ten.'

'Jesus! That's the first I knew of it. Christ!' It fitted with what Simon Phillips's file on the boy suggested, but that had just been on paper. This was real. What the hell had he been getting up to while Pete was out of the way, at work? Had he really become the evil little toerag Simon's file portrayed? And, if so, how? And why?

'I asked him about Malcolm Burton and Rosie Whitlock.'

Pete looked up, Colin's voice interrupting his thoughts. 'And?' Malcolm Burton, schoolteacher and paedophile, had abducted thirteen-year-old Rosie six months ago from outside her school on the day that Pete returned to work after an extended period of compassionate leave following Tommy's disappearance. Pete's investigation of the case had thrown up the fact that Tommy had been intimately involved in Rosie's abduction and subsequent sexual abuse, as well as the death of at least one other victim, ten-year-old Lauren Carter.

'He says Burton picked him up off the street. Took him home. Threatened him and his family if he didn't do as he was told.'

'Well, yeah. We guessed that much, despite what Burton said.'

Colin was nodding slowly. 'Which makes it a classic case of one word against the other.'

Pete leaned forward. 'So, f . . .' He stopped. He was about to say that forensics would give them the truth, but that was equivocal, to say the least. In fact, some of it specifically suggested that Tommy was guilty, although Rosie Whitlock herself painted him as another victim rather than a willing participant. 'Burton's case is coming up in just a few weeks now. What can we do?'

Colin's eyebrow rose. '*We* can't do anything. You can't be involved. Not with Tommy tied up in it. You know that. You need to pull everything together from the case and bring it to me. Sooner the better. I'll review it and take it from there.'

Pete had expected as much. It was standard procedure in situations like this. 'And in the meantime? What happens to Tommy?'

Colin shook his head. 'He's proved himself a flight risk. We need his testimony, plus there's his own possible involvement. He can't be bailed. He'll have to go to Archways.'

'So, he'll be able to have visitors.'

'Louise and Annie, yes.'

Pete sighed, eyes closing. It was what he'd expected. He would not be permitted to see his son again until after he'd testified, but at least his wife and daughter could. And, with Colin on the case, he had no doubt that the best outcome possible would result in the end. Except . . . He opened his eyes. 'Did you ask him about Lauren Carter?'

Lauren had been held with Rosie Whitlock for a time, then killed. And forensic evidence on the body had suggested that Tommy had been directly involved in her death.

Colin drew a long breath and let it out through his nose. 'I asked.'

'And?'

He shrugged. 'Again: one word against another. No way to prove either scenario now.'

'So, we need a confession from Burton.'

Colin grunted. 'Good luck with that.'

'He's a narcissist. He'll do whatever he thinks will give him the best result. He'll have to be told we've got Tommy now.'

'Yes.'

'And he's in the city jail.'

'He is.' Colin's tone was becoming more cautious.

'So, any interviews will be done there. Where they're *not* recorded. Solicitor-client privilege and all that bollocks. I'm sure he'll have found out by now how his sort are treated in prison. And he's looking at a long stretch, whether or not murder gets added to the charge sheet. If he survives, that is – doesn't get shivved in the showers one fine day.'

Colin's lips were pursed. 'What I think you're suggesting is unethical at best.'

'Not politically correct, I'll give you that. But unethical?' Pete shook his head. 'What would be unethical would be to let him get away with murder.'

45

'Either way, you can't interview him again. Not now we've got Tommy. That'll be down to me.'

Pete nodded, holding his gaze. 'I know.'

Pete stared at the big street map of the city on the squad room wall. 'Where had you come from, Ranjeet? Whoever killed you had to be in the cab with you, so where did you pick them up?'

He concentrated on the point where the taxi had been found. Its position and the marks in the grass around it suggested it had come along Argyll Road. The meter, if it was correctly calibrated, suggested a distance of nine tenths of a mile or thereabouts from his last pickup, so . . . He reached up and traced a forefinger back along Argyll, through the woods and out onto the A377. Which way then, though? Into town or out? It looked like a good half-mile remained from there to wherever he'd made the pickup. Going back into town gave him the area around the carvery by the river, as they'd said earlier, the estate on the other side of the main road from there, or down the New North Road into the university or city centre. The other way led towards either Newton St Cyres or Stoke Canon. There were way too many choices. How the hell was he going to narrow them down? He stepped across to the wider map of the area that was pinned up to the left of the city plan.

Both Newton St Cyres and Stoke Canon were too far.

Into the city, then. But, where?

They knew Ranjeet had dropped his previous fare at St Thomas, but that didn't really preclude either direction.

Then he looked closer at the map. Checked the distances.

'Hmm.'

Regalvanised, Pete turned back towards his desk, sat down and flipped his notepad over to a new page.

'You got something, boss?' Jane asked.

'Maybe. We said earlier that his meter might take us back to the Old Mill. But, taking the other fork, it could equally take us up to the clock tower.'

'So . . .'

'You might have been right. About the pepper spray. We might be looking for a prostitute. Or someone Ranjeet assumed was one. There's several bars and hotels round there as well as the railway station just along the road. Maybe he made a mistake and paid for it the hard way.'

Jane nodded. 'Possible, but it'll be hard to prove. Not the most reliable set of possible witnesses round there, especially at that time of night.'

Dave glanced up from what he was doing. 'No CCTV either, apart from Central Station. We did hear from forensics, though, while you were in with the Guv'nor. They found a print that might be significant. Just the one. They said it appeared to be female. And it was on the steering wheel, at what they described as a strange angle. But there were no matches in the system for it.'

'So, no use until we catch whoever it is we're looking for, if at all.' Pete pursed his lips. 'Looks like another late night, then. Thermals and thermos flasks.'

'And here I was hoping to get lucky tonight,' said Dick.

'You'll be in the right place, up by the clock tower,' Dave said with a grin. 'We won't tell your missus, will we, guys?'

'Keep practising, you might get to be a comedian one day.'

Jane laughed and gave Dave a shove. 'I can just see you in your waistcoat and Chubby Brown flying hat.'

'Now, that would have to go on YouTube,' Ben said with a grin.

'Ah.' Dave leaned back, spreading his arms. 'Fame at last.'

'Remember us on your way up,' said Jill. 'You'll want somebody to catch you on the way back down.'

'Meantime, let's concentrate on catching whoever killed Ranjeet Singh, shall we?' Pete suggested. 'We need a witness. And his car wasn't exactly distinctive, so it won't be easy to find one.'

* * *

'Tommy.'

Colin Underhill sat down across the table from him. A big bear of a man in cord trousers and a tweed jacket, he looked like a farmer dressed up to go to town. All it needed was the flat cap and a suntan. Tommy held the smirk back off his face with difficulty.

'Uncle Colin.'

They were not related, but it was what he'd always called his dad's boss and his godfather.

'We've got a problem, son. And getting out of it's not going to be easy, even with me and your dad on your side.'

'I told you – I never even thought of the knife as a weapon. It was a tool, that's all. I used it pretty much every day round the fair. You can ask any of them.'

Colin pursed his lips, letting the air noisily out through his nose. 'I'm talking about the other problem. Mr Burton. Lauren Carter. Rosie Whitlock.'

'But, you said she supported what I told you.'

'She does, but Burton won't. And nor does Lauren.'

'But, she's . . .' Tommy screwed his face up and dropped his head towards his chest. He swallowed, took a breath. 'She's dead.'

Colin grunted. 'That's part of the problem. She can't speak, but her body tells its own story. And the doctor might be a friend of your dad, but he can only describe the facts as he finds them. And there's a couple of those that put you firmly in the frame unless we can come up with something that throws the blame back onto Mr Burton.'

'I told you.' Tommy fixed Colin with a firm, almost angry stare. 'He made me do those things. He made me.'

'He made you strangle a ten-year-old girl?'

'He grabbed my hands, put them around her neck and squeezed. He killed her, not me. He just had my hands between his and her neck, that's all. And I wake up every night, dreaming about it because there was nothing I could do to save her. All I could do was let her know I was sorry.' His face began to crumple with emotion.

'All right, son. I understand. But, what about the rapes? Even at your age, you know a jury is going to believe you can't do that unless you want to. Or, at least, unless your body wants to and your mind isn't off in some other place entirely.'

'Have you . . .?' Tommy swallowed and dropped his gaze. His voice was little more than a whisper when he spoke again. 'Have you seen the videos he made?'

'Not all of them, but yes – some.'

'Well, most of it was faked. Low light. Careful camera angles. Sharp editing. You've seen his darkroom and video suite?'

'Yes.'

'He's good at it. People pay a lot for what he does. He sends stuff all over.'

Colin frowned. 'How do you know that?'

'I helped post them. I saw the addresses.'

'Is there a record of those addresses anywhere?'

Tommy shook his head. 'No. And I don't remember any specifics – just some of the towns and cities that I saw.'

Colin nodded. 'OK. But, back to the matter at hand. As you say, a lot of it could be faked, but not all. In some of it, it's clear you were a willing participant.'

Tommy's hands slapped down on the table. 'OK. So, a few times, I had to let myself get into the moment. If I didn't, he'd beat the shit out of me. Have you seen *those* videos?'

Colin looked horrified. 'No.'

'Well, they exist. They're around somewhere. He'd . . .' Tommy's eyes closed and he let his head drop forward as he clamped his jaw shut, hands balling into fists on the table. He took a couple of deep breaths. Looked up. 'I couldn't stop him.'

He saw Colin's arm move as if he was going to reach across the table, but the big man held himself in check. 'I'm sorry,' he said. 'But Burton's trial's in just seven weeks. We need you willing and able to testify in case his defence team call you. You need to have everything straight in your mind and we need to know the facts in case we need to cross-examine you, to refute any of his accusations.'

Tommy nodded. 'I understand.'

'So, let's move on. Once you got away from Burton, where did you go?'

Tommy shrugged. 'Wherever I could find a place to doss, at first. I stayed around the city for a while.'

'How did you eat?'

'I got stuff wherever I could. It's surprising what you can find, especially if you're not picky.'

'And you broke into your house while the family were out, at least once.'

Tommy nodded. 'Just the once. To get some things.'

'You waited till they were out. Did you know what they were out doing?'

Tommy shook his head. 'I just knew they were going out, so I had a chance to get in and get what I needed.'

'You must have found out at some point, though?'

'What – about the posters? Yeah, I saw one or two a couple of days later.'

'Your dad – a policeman – broke the law to put them up. Why didn't you respond?'

'Broke the law? What law?'

'There's a bylaw against posters in the city. Point is, your dad knew that. He put his career on the line to reach out to you.'

Tommy couldn't stop his face twisting into a grimace. 'Yeah, right. Good old dad. You can always trust him to do the right thing. Even if it's bringing his own son in for rape and murder.'

Colin's head was shaking slowly. 'We wanted you in as a witness, that was all. There were no charges. Your mum and dad just wanted you home.'

'What about what you said before? The forensics. My hands on that girl's throat.'

'Which you've explained.'

'Yeah, but . . .' Tommy slumped forward so his head rested on his folded arms. Moments passed. Finally, he looked up, rubbed his eyes. 'So, you mean . . .? All this time . . . Hiding out in holiday cottages, moving on every few weeks, fishing and nicking to eat all winter. There was no need?'

Colin shook his head.

Tommy slumped back in his chair, head falling back as he stared at the ceiling. 'Fuck.' He looked down quickly. 'Sorry. That slipped out.'

Colin smiled. Then he sat forward. 'But now we are where we are. These charges aren't going away. They've come from Plymouth, not Exeter. So, it's not up to your dad or me. We've got to play the hand we've been dealt.'

'But, can't I make some sort of deal? Testifying against Mr Burton for a consideration on the other stuff?'

Colin shook his head. ''Fraid not, son. Testifying against Burton's in your best interests anyway. You can't have two bites at the same cherry.'

'So, I'm stuck here, whatever?'

'For now, yes. We'll have to see what happens after.'

'And you said Mr Burton's case is coming up in seven weeks. What about mine?'

Colin shrugged. 'It's relatively minor . . .'

'Yeah, but so am I. A minor, I mean. So, they shouldn't keep me in any longer than necessary, surely? For my long-term well-being. Mental scarring and all that.'

Colin's eyebrows rose. 'Have you been reading law books in here or something?'

Tommy shook his head. 'They explained it all when I came here.'

'OK. Well, the juvenile court's separate from the adult one, so there doesn't need to be a delay in one because of what's going on in the other. But, I don't know how soon they'll get to your case. What I do know is that you'll be held on remand until they do.'

'How's that fair?'

Colin shook his head. 'I'm just telling it like it is, son. It can't be any other way in the circumstances.'

Tommy grimaced. 'So, at the end of the day, you want my help but you're not going to help me.'

Again, Colin looked like he was about to reach across the table, but held back. 'I'm sorry, son. If I could, I would. You know that.'

When Colin had gone, Tommy went back to his room. He kicked the door shut behind him and flopped down on the bed, staring at the ceiling. That hadn't gone too badly, he thought. He'd steered the conversation in the directions he wanted without making it obvious. Had said enough to promote his own case without incriminating himself. And he thought he'd managed to come across as a victim – a regretful and unwilling participant in Malcolm Burton's crimes rather than a co-conspirator.

Now, he had just seven weeks to maintain that impression and make sure he could do the same in court with Burton's solicitor badgering him. His story would have to be solid and flawless and he would have to know it backwards, forwards and sideways, to the extent that even he believed every word. He would have to be the little boy lost, the hapless victim, the innocent caught up in things he didn't understand and couldn't control.

Could he do it?

He smiled. The smile turned into a chuckle. He'd been doing it for years. There was nothing new here.

Chapter 6

'Talk to me here, now – it'll take two minutes and you won't lose anything by it. Or we can take it down the station. You'll lose a couple of hours. Maybe a couple of punters.' Pete shrugged. 'I'm not out to spoil anyone's business. I'm just trying to find out who killed a man here in the city last night.'

The girl couldn't have been more than twenty-two, but she looked ten or fifteen years older with the harsh make-up and sneering attitude. Her dark hair was tied back in a high ponytail, her skirt couldn't have been a half-inch shorter without drawing an arrest warrant for indecent exposure, and her naked shoulder-blades above the low-cut vest top were decorated with tattoos that he'd glimpsed when he first saw her a couple of minutes ago on the corner of Queen's Square, one hand on her hip while the other held a cigarette that she was dragging on like it was going out of fashion.

As soon as she'd turned around and seen him, she'd pulled an attitude. She didn't want to talk to him, but she knew he could haul her in if he wanted to.

'All right,' she said heavily. 'What d'you wanna know?'

It was ten o'clock. Trade would be picking up for her any time now. She didn't have time for Pete and his questions and he knew it. He hoped that the fact she was in a hurry would force her to tell him the truth. 'First, were you here last night?'

'Yeah.'

'Do you know a taxi driver by the name of Ranjeet Singh? Drives a grey Mondeo.'

She shook her head with a grimace. 'Nope.'

'Have you seen a grey Mondeo taxi around here lately?'

'No.'

'Sure?'

'Positive. Is that it?' She threw down her cigarette stub and screwed it into the pavement with the sole of her high-heeled shoe.

'No. Is anyone missing from here tonight that was here yesterday? Or anyone here both nights but acting different tonight? Agitated? Nervous?'

'People get agitated when they're coming down off the gear. Or when they've got things to do and some bloke's holding them up.'

'True. We're not picking on you girls because of what you do for a living. We're looking for witnesses, that's all.'

'What, so, if I was a waitress in that hotel over there, you wouldn't be asking me all these questions?'

'Yes, we would. In fact, we already have.'

'And had any of them seen anything?'

Pete smiled. 'The more witnesses we can gather, the clearer the picture we can build up and the more likely we are to get a killer off these streets you're walking.'

'Yeah, well – if they're killing taxi drivers, I'm safe anyway, aren't I? I don't even drive, never mind taxis.'

'So, you don't give a shit.'

She shrugged. 'Like I said, I didn't know the bloke.'

Pete sighed. 'All right. On you go.'

His last hour and a half had been spent in similar conversations with mostly similar girls. A few had been older, a few significantly younger, but all had about the same attitude. It wasn't their problem and they didn't want to get involved in it.

Yet, if something happened to one of them, they'd be up in arms, wanting protection and all sorts. There was no winning with some people. He lifted his radio and keyed the mike. 'If we're all done, let's call it a night. We can scratch one possible pickup location off the list, at least.'

'OK with me, boss,' Dave replied from the far side of the hotel the hooker had mentioned.

'I can't see anyone I haven't already spoken to,' said Jane.

'Nor me,' Dick added.

'Right. Nightcap's on me.'

Forty-three minutes later, Pete turned into his drive for the second time that evening and stopped the car.

'What the f . . .?' He sat stock-still, staring at his white up-and-over garage door. Nearly three feet high, right in the middle of it, caught squarely in the beam of his headlights, was a drawing – a cartoon, really – in pink spray paint that, in places, had trickled into runs. A pig's face stared out at him, underneath it the words 'More bacon, Guv'nor?'

'Who the bloody hell . . .?'

He switched off the headlights and the engine, got out of the car and went up to the garage door. He could still see the image clearly in the light of the streetlamp across the road. He reached out a finger, although, even before he touched it, he could smell that the paint was still wet. Sure enough, his fingertip came away smeared with colour.

'Bastards,' he muttered and marched towards the front door. Letting himself in, he dropped his briefcase in the hall and stepped into the sitting room where Louise was curled up on the sofa, watching TV.

An image flashed into his mind from a few short months ago, when all she seemed to want to do was just that. She'd barely been able to acknowledge either him or Annie. But now she looked up, a smile forming on her lips. 'Hiya. Have you . . .?' She stopped mid-sentence when she saw his expression. 'What is it?'

He held up his finger. 'Spray paint. All over the bloody garage. Someone's figured out what I do for a living and decided to make an issue of it.'

Louise slumped. 'Oh, God. Will it come off?'

'I've got a can of brush cleaner in there. I'll see if I can shift it before it dries. Little sods ought to be made to come back here and bloody lick it clean.'

Louise couldn't help a grunt of laughter. 'I don't think that idea would go down too well with the bleeding heart brigade.'

'Then maybe we ought to go and spray-paint their garage doors and see how they like it.'

'You're a grumpy bugger tonight. Didn't anybody want to play with you or something?'

Pete shook his head. 'I just don't understand people's attitudes sometimes. You'd think they'd want to help get a murderer off the streets. They'd feel safer for it.'

'Yeah, but everybody's too busy these days. Who's got time to sit in a draughty corridor outside a courtroom for a couple of days or more, to help put someone away for not nearly long enough, who's probably never going to be a risk to them anyway, eh? I mean, you can understand it really.'

'You sound exactly like a lot of those girls I've been talking to tonight.'

She shrugged. 'I'm just saying, there's two sides to every argument.'

'Yeah. Like there's two sides to that garage door and a can of brush cleaner on one that needs to be on t'other. I'd best go and deal with it, I suppose.'

'You want a hand?' She nodded towards the TV. 'This is rubbish anyway.'

Pete's eyes widened as he recalled again the time when she'd sit there for hours, staring blankly at the TV, regardless of what was on it.

'Or maybe it's me,' she continued, ignoring his expression.

'I can't concentrate on anything, knowing Tommy's just a few hundred yards away now, and I can't go to him.'

Pete sighed, nodding. 'I know. But tomorrow's not far off. Then you can ring them and set up a visit.'

'It's just so hard. It's almost worse, having him so close, than it was not knowing where he was. The need to see him, hold him, talk to him, be a mother to him is . . .' She shook her head, unable to put her feelings into words.

Pete reached for her hand. 'Come on,' he said, trying to pull her away from the brink. 'We'll do what we can out there, then a drink and bed.'

She blinked. 'Bed? I don't know as I want to share a bed with you after you've spent the evening consorting with prostitutes.'

'Huh. None of them even wanted to talk to me, never mind consort.'

She stood up and took a step towards him. 'Ah. Baby losing his touch?' One hand cupping his jaw, she placed a quick kiss on his lips then squealed as he grabbed her around the waist.

Tommy went from breakfast, which he ate alone, to the common room, where he grabbed a bunch of felt-tip pens – pencils weren't permitted as they were considered sharp objects – and a pad of drawing paper.

He was trying to put an image of Rosie Whitlock onto the paper when his chair was jarred abruptly from behind and a pair of hands clamped down on his shoulders, pressing him down into the seat.

'Watcha, Titch. What you in here for then, eh? That your girlfriend, is it? Ahh. Pretty, ain't she? I'll do her for you when I get out of here, you being too small and all.'

Tommy went completely still. He almost felt relaxed. 'Which order do you want me to answer all those questions in? Forwards or backwards?'

'Smart arse, are you?' The hands left his shoulders and a slap rocked his head. 'Think you're clever, do you?'

Tommy heard several sniggers. There was a bunch of them. Without even thinking about it, he turned the felt-tipped pen in his hand, gripping it tightly. A shiver ran through him as fingers ran through the hair up the back of his head. Then they gripped painfully and began to lift. He rose with them, but his chair got in the way. He pushed it back with his knees, felt it snag on the carpet and begin to tip. Rising further, the chair reaching a steeper angle, he gently, carefully raised one foot off the floor, bringing his knee up until it touched the underside of the table in front of him.

Waited an instant longer . . .

Then slammed his foot up and back so that it hit the underside of the chair, driving it back into his tormentor's stomach. The boy grunted. His fingers disappeared from Tommy's hair. Tommy spun around fast. Several boys were surrounding him, all of them bigger than he was. Their leader was just beginning to recover and straighten up, his pockmarked face twisting into a snarl of rage.

Tommy didn't hesitate. He used the chair again, this time as a step-up, launching himself off its upturned front edge, his other knee driving at the older boy's chest. The impact sent him staggering backwards, the group splitting to let him through. Tommy's free hand grabbed his hair and held on tight, his momentum carrying him over the bigger lad, who stumbled and fell back. Tommy landed on top of him, his knee driving once more into his chest before slipping sideways to leave Tommy straddling him, one hand gripping his hair while he leaned down over him, the other hand holding the felt-tip pen just a couple of millimetres from his left eyeball.

The bigger lad was wheezing beneath him, trying to get his breath.

'Don't blink. You'll have a yellow eyelash,' Tommy said. 'I'm in here for rape and murder. The girl in the picture was one of my victims, but she's going to help get me out of here shortly. It's up to you whether you see that or not. These pens might be soft, but they'll still burst your eyeball if they're pressed hard enough.'

The other boy swallowed. Tommy saw his throat working as he struggled not to cough.

'Now, I'm not interested in joining your gang or any other. I don't need them. See, the difference between you and me is that you're a bully. You want status, attention or whatever. I don't care what anyone thinks of me, so I don't care what I do to anyone. I don't have any boundaries. I could happily blind you. I could rape you. I could bite your ugly nose off. Or I could kill you.' He shrugged. 'Wouldn't make a blind bit of difference to me.'

He grinned suddenly. 'Get it? Blind bit of difference?' He chuckled. 'I could do any of those things without even blinking. Without batting an eye.' He laughed again. 'I've got loads more where they came from. Good, eh?'

'Yes,' the other boy said hoarsely.

'So, you stay out of my way and I won't have to hurt you. Understand?'

'Yes.'

'Good.' Tommy sprang up off him and spun around to look down at him, upside-down. 'And don't try sneaking up on me. I don't give second chances.'

The boy blinked and launched into a coughing fit. Tommy stared into the eyes of the lanky blond kid standing in front of him. The confident grin was gone from his lean face. He looked a lot less sure of the situation now. And, to be fair, it could go either of two ways from here, Tommy thought. He could be left alone, or the kid coughing his guts up on the floor could make a play to reassert his dominance. Which would no doubt bring trouble and pain to Tommy's door, but he was used to both of them. They were almost old friends. 'Out the way,' he said. 'Unless you want some of the same.'

* * *

Tommy looked up from the book he was reading as the door of his room was opened and one of the wardens leaned in and gave a jerk of his head. 'You've got a visitor, Gayle. Come on.'

Tommy didn't move. 'Who is it?'

'Your solicitor.'

Inwardly relaxing, Tommy closed his book and set it aside, swung his feet off the side of the bed and stood up.

He'd finished his drawing half an hour ago, but it hadn't done Rosie justice, so he'd screwed it up in a tight ball and thrown it in the bin, stalking out of the common room and heading back here. Now he followed the warder, a large, heavily muscled coloured guy called Adam, back down the corridor, past the common room to one of the small rooms that were used for visiting.

He tried not to show his hesitation as Adam opened the door and stood aside. He hoped the warden had told him the truth about who it was. The last thing he wanted was some surprise, like his dad sitting there, waiting for him.

He stepped forward nonchalantly.

The chair on the far side of the central table was occupied by a man he'd never seen before. Somewhere between his dad and Uncle Colin in age, he was slim with greying dark hair and a three-piece suit.

'Who are you?' Tommy asked bluntly.

The man tilted his head. 'I'm Clive Davis. I'm your solicitor.'

'Why?'

Davis pursed his lips. 'You've been charged with carrying an offensive weapon. A knife, I understand. We're going to have to attend court. It's a charge that can carry a term of confinement.'

'Prison?'

Tommy heard the door close behind him.

Davis tilted his head again. 'More like where we are here. You're only – what – fourteen? You wouldn't be sent to a conventional prison.'

I've lived worse, Tommy thought. *This past winter.* 'How long for?' he asked.

'It depends on the circumstances. It can be up to four months. Or you could get an official caution or anything between the two.'

'So, they might just tell me off and let me go?'

Davis pursed his lips. 'That's not the way to look at it, but in essence, from a practical point of view, yes. However, it goes on your record, so that if you're charged again it'll be taken into account and you will serve time.'

'OK.'

'So, tell me how you came to be here.'

Tommy shrugged, spreading his hands. 'I was just minding my own business, doing my job, and all of a sudden, this guy's coming after me, so I ran. They caught me and searched me and, next thing I know, they're charging me for carrying a tool of the job.'

'A flick-knife.'

'Well, I'm not going to carry an open blade in my pocket, am I? And penknives can be dangerous. I saw a kid using one once and it folded up on him, got his finger between the blade and the handle. No, thanks. A flick-knife's much safer.'

'But illegal.'

'As a weapon. Mine's a tool. It's essential for the job.'

Davis shook his head. 'It makes no difference why you had it, Thomas. The simple fact is, you shouldn't have.'

'What am I supposed to do then? Bite stuff?'

Davis paused. 'I'm not saying the law is perfect, Thomas, but it is the law and it's there to be obeyed. Your father's a police officer, isn't he?'

'So?'

Davis sighed. 'So, a number of questions arise from that fact. We may discuss them at another time, but the point for now is that you ought to appreciate the necessity of rules.'

'Yeah. They're made for the rulers. To keep the little guys in line.' He sat back, arms spread wide. 'And what am I?'

Davis smiled. 'A very clever and resourceful young man, evidently. But still one who needs to learn when to fight and when not to.'

Tommy's lip curled into a sneer. 'Try living my life. It's one long fight. Always has been.'

Chapter 7

Pete wound up the stop-and-check at just after nine.

'We'll take it up again at lunchtime,' he told the assembled crew when they returned to the cars, parked on a side street just down from Argyll Road, on the opposite side of Pennsylvania. 'That'll catch any late-shift workers. Meantime, I'll get onto communications at Middlemoor and get a couple of signs made up that can be put either side of the junction to pick up anyone we haven't managed to interview.'

'So, what's next other than that, boss?' Ben asked.

'We need to interview as many taxi drivers as possible, for one thing. Find out if there've been any threats, any attempted robberies or other attacks on them and get whatever details we can. I can't imagine this came out of nowhere. There's got to be a history there somewhere. Something significant's behind it.'

'Or it could be about the other way round,' Jane said. 'Taxi drivers attacking customers. Specifically, our victim and those cases we talked about before.'

He nodded. 'That would go with the use of the pepper spray before the knife. Have you got any more on them?'

'When? I haven't had five seconds to spare yet.'

'Right. That's your first priority when we get back then. See what you can dig up. We also need to check the PND, the papers, the Internet. Any other sources anyone can think of. And we can't do any of that from here, so let's get going.'

'Aye aye, Cap'n.' Dave saluted smartly.

'For that, you can go down to the *Express and Echo* and check their archives. Then do the same at the *Daily News*,' Pete told him.

'Oh, cheers.'

Pete gave him a grin. 'It's a tough job, but somebody's got to do it.'

As the day drew to a close, Pete wasn't grinning any more. After two days of hard work on the case, he and his team had got nowhere and frustration was setting in. He recognised it even as it took hold, pulling his mood down and breaking his concentration.

He finished his daily case notes and hit save. 'Right, that's it. Time to call it a night. We'll pick it up fresh in the morning.'

'Sounds like a plan,' Dave agreed. 'Trouble is, where do we go from here?'

'Well, we've got all night to sleep on it. I'm not going to spoonfeed you now.' *And besides, I'm as bloody stumped as you are*, he thought, but kept it to himself. Where *were* they going to go from here?

He'd been to the Devon and Cornwall Police Headquarters at Middlemoor to get a couple of road signs made up, asking for witnesses to come forward. DCI Silverstone was dealing with the press office, as usual. Three sessions of stopping traffic at peak times and questioning the drivers had come up empty, as had visits to the two most likely places for him to have picked up the suspect. Investigation of the victim's past had drawn a blank apart from unsubstantiated rumours from some years ago that couldn't be corroborated because the owners of the company he'd been working for at the time were currently out of the country and no official complaints had been made. Jane had come up empty on the other complaint. The complainant had moved and left no forwarding address, though census records had last put her in Bristol, and the alleged victim had been from somewhere in Lancashire, and there was no trace of her either. Singh's family offered no likely suspects. He seemed, of late, to have a decent reputation. There were no signs of enmity with rivals or colleagues. And as for forensics – there were loads of prints on and in the taxi, but none were identifiable and the same applied to other trace evidence in the vehicle. If they got a suspect, then comparisons could be made, but until then, the lab was no use to them. And there had been nothing in the local papers or on the database that helped either.

It looked like the case was going to come down to possible motives.

It hadn't been a robbery, unless something less obvious than money was the target. No mention had been made of drug traces being found in the car. He would check on that with forensics, but he could probably discount the idea. Was there anything else he might have been carrying in the car? He picked up the phone.

'I thought you were packing it in?' asked Jane.

He looked up and saw that she was standing behind her chair, shrugging into her jacket. He hadn't even been aware of her getting up. 'Just thought of something. A quick call and I'll be on my way. You go on.'

'OK. Night.' She picked up her bag and headed for the door, followed by the others as Pete flipped through his notebook and dialled the number he'd noted down.

It was picked up on the second ring. 'Hello?'

That wasn't the voice he'd expected. 'Naz? Is that you?'

'Yes. Who . . ?'

'It's Pete Gayle. Could you ask Mrs Singh a question for me?'

'Yes, Sarge. What is it?'

'I need to know if he was carrying anything in the taxi that might have given his killer a motive. Something worth stealing, apart from money.'

'Hold on, I'll ask.'

'How's she doing now?'

'Still not very good. Very emotional.'

'Well, it's still fresh for her, isn't it? She must have loved him a lot.'

'Yeah. And yet, I assumed it had been an arranged marriage.'

Pete laughed. 'They do sometimes succeed, you know.'

'Yeah, but . . . I don't know. I suppose I'm closer to the idea than you. It's part of the culture, you know. I've had pressure in that direction myself. It's scary.'

'I bet it is.'

'Anyway, I'll go and ask her.'

Pete heard the clunk of the receiver going down. He waited. After several seconds, the phone was picked up again.

'Sarge?'

'Naz.'

'She says no, there was nothing he'd have been carrying that was worth stealing.'

'OK, thanks.'

He ended the call, one more possible motive eliminated. Something was nagging at the far corner of his consciousness, but he couldn't bring it into focus. Long experience had taught him that, in that situation, it was better to give up for a while than try to force it, but frustration fought with reason, pushing him on. His lips pressed together as he fought to grab hold of the idea and pull it out of the fog, but it was no good – it just wouldn't come.

His hands slapped down on his desk as he stood up. He could do no more of any use here for now. It was time to go home and spend some time with his wife and daughter.

Emma had been sitting patiently in the queue created by the roadworks on Pennsylvania Road for a little over ten minutes. Finally, the lights changed ahead of her and she let the handbrake off and moved forward with the traffic flow. The road was coned down to half-width for about a hundred metres, a long trench dug up the middle of the other carriageway, a roll of bright-yellow plastic pipe waiting on the verge to be laid the next day. Accelerating gently up the hill, she was about two thirds of the way through the narrow section when the Nissan's engine note changed abruptly, faltering and slowing. She pressed her foot to the accelerator, but it made no difference.

'Oh, for God's sake, not now!' She slammed her fists on the steering wheel, dropped the clutch and raced the engine, but still nothing. 'Buggeration, you horrible, horrible bloody car.'

Letting the clutch re-engage, she sat there at the mercy of fate as the car coasted steadily to a halt. A horn sounded from behind her, then another. Another.

'Shut up, you idiots,' she muttered. 'I'm not stopping from bloody choice, am I?'

The engine cut out completely, an awful silence replacing its comforting hum. She sighed, pulled up the handbrake and unclipped her seatbelt. More horns sounded as she stepped out, turned to face the offending drivers and raised her hands in a gesture that said 'There's nothing I can do'.

She heard a handbrake being applied and the door of the car behind hers opened. A man stepped out, tall and good-looking in a dark suit. 'What's the problem? Have you run out of petrol or something?'

Anger flared. 'It's over half-full, thank you. The engine just cut out.'

'Well, try giving it some revs.'

He might be good-looking, but the guy was an arse, she decided. 'I did. It didn't help.'

He sighed pointedly, as if it had to be her fault rather than the car's, then turned and beckoned to the other drivers behind him, motioning with his hands in a pushing action.

A few doors opened. People stepped out of their cars.

'What's the bloody problem?'

'Engine's cut out.' The guy gave an open-handed shrug as Emma's hands were planted firmly on her hips.

It wasn't her bloody fault. Just because she was female . . .

Four other men joined the first one, heading up the hill towards her.

'What's the problem?' one of them asked as they drew closer. He was wearing leathers. She'd seen him pull off his helmet and climb off a big, black motorbike, running a hand quickly through his short, dark hair.

She shook her head. 'I don't know. It just lost power and then cut out.'

He nodded. 'Could be a number of things. Best just push it out of the way for now and call the AA or whatever. You got a membership?'

'Yes.'

'Hop in, then, and steer. It ain't going up that kerb so we'll have to push it up just past the lights and leave it over there, out the way.'

'Are you sure? It seems a long way.'

He smiled. 'Only a small car, though, isn't it? We'll manage.' He glanced at the others. 'Come on, guys.'

She climbed back into the car, looked in the door mirror.

The biker was on the corner of the little car, right behind her. 'Everybody ready?' he asked. 'Right. Handbrake off, love.'

She complied.

The sounds of straining came from behind her. She thought for a moment that she was going to roll backwards, that they wouldn't be able to hold it, never mind move it forward, but then the little car began to inch slowly, hesitantly, up the hill. It was a weird feeling, slowly gaining momentum, the only sounds those of the tyres and the men's feet on the tarmac as she held the steering wheel steady.

After a few steps, gravity seemed to somehow give up the fight and they were moving at almost walking pace. Then, before she knew it, they were approaching the end of the roadworks.

'Steer it over to the side and you can let it roll back up to the traffic lights,' the man behind her called. 'It'll be out of everyone's way there.'

'OK.'

She steered the car across with the angle of the red and white cones, letting the men continue to push her a few yards beyond the temporary lights on their bright-yellow stand.

'There you go,' the man in leathers called and stood away.

She pressed down on the brake pedal.

'Right. Ease it back down to the lights. They're tall enough to be seen over it.'

She checked that the men were all standing clear, then used the far door mirror to guide herself slowly down the line of the kerb until the man raised his hand, calling, 'That'll do.'

She stood on the brake, pulled up the handbrake and put the car into first gear as extra insurance, then stepped out. 'Thank you so much, all of you.'

'No problem.'

'S'all right.'

The others simply nodded and headed back to their cars.

'You sure you're all right now?' the guy who had taken charge asked.

'Yes, thank you. I've got my mobile. I'll just try to sound helpless.'

He laughed. 'OK. Take care.'

'Thank you,' Emma called again as he raised a hand and turned away.

She reached into the car for her phone, brought up the menu and dialled.

By the time the connection was made, the traffic was moving again, the rhythmic hum of passing engines acting as a background to the call.

A female operator answered after just two rings.

'Hello, yes. I've broken down. The engine just died on me. I'm at the top end of the roadworks in Pennsylvania Road, Exeter.'

'Is the car in a safe position?' the woman asked.

'Yes. Some men helped me move it.'

'Are you on your own there?'

'Yes, I am.'

'OK. We'll have someone there with you as soon as we can.' She heard the tapping of a keyboard faintly over the line. 'It'll be about twenty minutes.'

'Thank you.'

She slipped the phone back into her handbag and stood beside the car, on the far side from the passing traffic. She checked her watch. Six-seventeen. She watched the lights change. The downhill traffic started flowing through. The evening was warm, almost muggy, as if a storm could be brewing. She took off her jacket, folded it and put it on the passenger seat. After a few moments, she reached into the back of the car and moved her briefcase to the front passenger footwell so that everything she would want to take with her if he couldn't get the car going again was in one place, ready.

Tommy was in the TV lounge with most of the other eighteen residents, watching the last few minutes of a documentary on the nature of New Zealand, when the single warder who was sitting with them got up and announced, 'Back in a minute. Don't do anything I wouldn't, any of you.'

He stepped out of the room, closing the door behind him.

'Yeah, more like ten minutes,' said one of the other kids. 'Must be them steroids, I reckon. Mess him up something terrible. Bloody bog stinks like hell after he's been in there.'

Several of the others laughed and Tommy joined in as he filed the information away for future reference.

'Should be plenty.' The bully who had attacked Tommy earlier, who he had since learned was called Sam Lockhart, turned in his seat and grinned at him.

Tommy frowned . . .

Had barely had time to form the expression when his seat was tilted suddenly back. His arms and legs darted out reflexively, but there was no stopping it. His grasp slipped from the shoulders of the two boys either side of him and he landed on his back. The lanky blond kid from this morning grinned down at him as some of the others laughed. Tommy slammed a fist up into the lean face, felt his second knuckle impact directly on the tip of the boy's nose. He yelled, darting back out of reach, as Tommy rolled sideways off the upended chair.

In the confined space, he hadn't reached his feet when he was grabbed from behind and yanked backwards. His feet tangled with the chair, almost spilling him again. Then his right foot landed on the front edge of the chair and he pushed hard against it, driving himself backwards into his new attacker, who stumbled, letting go of the back of Tommy's standard-issue polo shirt as he swore.

Tommy turned the opposite way to the other boy, landing on his side and shoulder across the back of two chairs, the occupants of which had sat forward and begun to turn to see what was going on. The padded chair backs dug into his ribs, but not as badly as they would have if they had been wooden. He grabbed them with his upper hand, turning further as he got his feet under him. Someone shoved him from behind, but he righted himself and saw that, as he'd suspected, it was Lockhart who had attacked him.

The bully was pushing himself up off the backs of the two lads he'd fallen against, struggling upright in the tight space between the rows of chairs and the feet of their occupants. Tommy only needed one foot and he didn't care where he put it. He slammed his right foot down, the leg still slightly bent when his heel drove into the top of someone's foot, and he launched himself forward in a dive as the person behind him howled in pain.

Tommy's grasping hands both caught hold of something: the right got Lockhart's belt while the left gripped his right forearm. They went down in a tangle of chairs and legs. Tommy's head bounced off the edge of a chair seat, but he paid it no attention, using his arms and his grip on Lockhart to power himself forward, landing on top of the larger boy, who slammed his head forward in a butt that was aimed to smash Tommy's nose.

His aim was way off. Tommy's move had brought him further and higher than Lockhart had anticipated so that his forehead struck Tommy in the chest.

It was like being hit with a hammer. It stunned his ribcage into inactivity, but survival was Tommy's only motivation now and inactivity would not allow that. As Lockhart's head fell back, Tommy relaxed his arms, falling flat on top of him, at the same time ducking his head so that his teeth hit Lockhart in the face.

Quickly, Tommy opened his mouth. Snapped his jaws closed.

Lockhart howled as his nose was caught between Tommy's sharp front teeth. Tommy squeezed down on the warm skin and cartilage, stretching his lips wide open.

'I thought we had an understanding,' he said through his tightly clamped teeth. 'What did I say this morning about biting your ugly nose off?'

'Get off me or I'll fucking kill you, you little bastard.'

'Promises, promises.' Tommy adjusted the grip of his teeth on the larger boy's nose. 'And, talking of . . .'

'No!' Lockhart shouted.

Tommy bit down hard. He could feel the grease of the other kid's nose. The give of his nostril walls against his tongue and the roof of his mouth as Lockhart howled in pain and terror. Then something wet and warm in his mouth. He hoped it wasn't . . . No, he tasted the iron tang of blood. Kept on bearing down with his teeth as he shifted his right hand from under him to grasp the back of Lockhart's neck, pulling him in so he couldn't escape.

Other hands were grasping and pulling at him, trying to pull him off the other boy. Lockhart's left fist was pounding on his back, but he barely felt it. His whole awareness was focused on what was between his teeth.

'Get off me! Get off me!' Lockhart bellowed. Then he jerked upwards under Tommy, forcing him backwards. Tommy went with him. Used the opportunity to slide his arm around behind Lockhart's neck and lock his hand over his own shoulder, clamping them tightly together as his other hand let go of his arm and came up around his head to grasp his ear.

Tommy gripped the ear, pulling back on it hard. He felt warm blood trickling down his chin.

'Tommy Gayle! Release him at once.'

That wasn't a kid's voice, like all the others yelling around him. But Tommy was committed. He wasn't going to back off now. He ground his teeth, making Lockhart howl even louder. Then a big hand gripped the back of his shirt and another got hold of his jaw, finger and thumb pressing in painfully from either side.

'Let him go.' The voice was as slow, firm and implacable as the fingers pushing into his cheeks, but Tommy was committed. There was no winning here. Not any more. But he couldn't give in. Couldn't show a trace of weakness or pity.

He pulled harder on Lockhart's left ear, twisting at the same time. Lockhart wailed. The blood flowed even more freely from his nose, dripping steadily from Tommy's chin. Agony coursed through his cheeks and jaw.

'Gayle, let go. Now.' The warder's voice was harder, angrier, as he held on relentlessly. 'Give it up or I'll break your damned jaw and where'll that get you, d'you think?'

Tommy saw the chance and took it. Tugging even harder on Lockhart's ear, he opened his mouth and looked up at the warder, grinning, his chin red and dripping with blood. 'Nowhere I haven't been a hundred times before.'

Chapter 8

Pete pulled into his drive and switched off the headlights, glad to be home – and glad there was no new decoration on the garage door. He killed the engine as the front door opened, expecting Annie to come running out and greet him.

He was surprised when, instead, it was Louise who came out, closing the door behind her and standing on the doorstep, arms folded.

He stepped out of the car, took his briefcase from the back seat and locked the silver Ford.

'Lou? What's up?'

Her eyes closed, her face scrunching up with emotion as her arms dropped to her sides. Then she took a breath, opened her eyes and the tears ran down her face as he dropped his briefcase and gathered her into his arms. 'What is it, love?'

A sob escaped from her throat, then she swallowed. 'It's Tommy,' she whispered, clinging to him.

Pete felt icy fear grip his body, freezing him in place like a living statue. 'What about him?'

He wanted desperately to see her face, but she clung even more tightly to him, her bead buried into his shoulder. 'He's . . . We can't see him. I phoned a few minutes ago. He had to be there a day before they allowed visitors. Settling-in time, they said. So I phoned to arrange it for tomorrow, after school. For me and Annie. But . . .' She began to cry again. Conflicting emotions battled within Pete. Love and protectiveness for Louise made him hold onto her, comfort her as best he could, while the need to know about his son raged, *For God's sake, spit it out, woman! What's happened?* But he held on, stroking her hair with one hand while she clung to him, sobbing into the shoulder of his jacket until she finally gulped, shook her head and loosed her grip around his body.

'I'm sorry,' she whispered. 'But . . .'

'What is it, love? What's happened?' he asked gently.

'He's . . . He nearly bit some boy's nose off. On his first day! My God, what have we raised, Pete?'

Some of the contents of the file Simon Phillips had compiled on Tommy while searching for him last year flashed through Pete's mind and he wondered the same thing – as he had done since reading the file, months ago. Yet, his fatherly instinct kicked in behind the doubt, pushing it down, feeding that tiny residue of pride that he would never lose. *Surviving, probably*, he thought. *Knowing what kinds of kids end up in those places and the softly, softly approach they have to use with them, these days . . .*

He almost asked again: what happened? But no one would have the answer other than Tommy and some of the other inmates, he guessed. The staff would just have come upon the end result. Kids weren't stupid – especially, in some ways, the kinds of kids who ended up in places like Archways. It would be a huge mistake to underestimate them, and one he'd learned long ago not to make when dealing with criminals of any age.

'So, they've put him in solitary,' he guessed. It was the ultimate punishment in places like that. 'How long for?'

'A day.' Head tipped forward, she tucked a strand of hair behind her ear. Then she looked up at him, her eyes large and moist. 'How did it come to this? Where did we go so wrong?'

'We can't have gone completely wrong. Look at Annie.'

The girl had been a minor miracle last year, after Tommy disappeared. As Louise had spiralled downhill into a deep clinical depression, so their daughter had stepped up, almost to the point of swapping roles with her mother, taking on responsibilities an eleven-year-old never should have needed to.

'Yes, but . . .' Louise shook her head. 'It's like he's got the Devil inside him. He's . . .'

'He's our son,' he said firmly. 'He's got his problems, but he's surviving the only way he can. He knows the score. He's not daft. He wouldn't have done something like that without needing to.'

'Yes, but . . . to try to bite somebody's nose off!'

'He's been a snotty little bugger for years.'

She stood back, staring up into his face. 'Really? You can joke at a time like this? Jesus! No wonder we've raised a bloody psycho.' She spun away, heading for the door.

Something stirred in Pete's chest. Fear, anger, he didn't know, but . . . 'Don't ever call him that. He might be troubled. He might be *in* trouble, but he's no psycho. Rosie Whitlock will testify to that.' He snatched up his briefcase and followed her as she opened the front door and stepped in.

'Maybe, but that doesn't make this a time for jokes.'

Pete took a breath, regaining control of his emotions as he fought to keep hers from pulling her back into the darkness. 'It worked, didn't it? You've got the fire back in your belly.'

'I'll give you fire in the belly, Pete Gayle . . .'

'Good. You do that. We haven't had a good curry in ages.'

She spun on him, fists raised. 'I swear, you get bloody worse!'

He stepped in close, caught her round the waist with both arms and hugged her tightly. 'Whatever gets us through, Lou.'

He felt her draw in a deep, slow breath and let it out. Then the living-room door opened and Annie burst out.

'Daddy!'

* * *

76

Emma leaned both arms on the roof of the Nissan, drawing in deep, watching the seemingly endless flow of vehicles pass by. Finally, a bright-yellow van with a large logo on the side came through the roadworks. Orange lights began to flash on its roof and she breathed a sigh of relief.

At last.

She checked her watch. 6.38. The woman on the phone hadn't been off by more than a few minutes. It just felt like an age had passed since she made the call. The van passed her then stopped. Reversing lights glowed and it swung half onto the verge before rolling gently back towards her, other vehicles sweeping past like impatient bats coming out for the night's feeding.

The van stopped. The driver stepped out and headed towards her.

'Evening, miss. What's the problem?'

'It just lost power and died on me. There was nothing I could do to keep it going.' She used the remote to unlock the little car. 'It's not the first time it's happened.'

'OK. And what have you found, if anything, that gets it going again?'

'Just time. Let it rest awhile and it's fine. It starts up and off it goes as if nothing's wrong. That's the frustrating part.'

He nodded, opened the driver's door and popped the bonnet catch.

Emma didn't bother to watch what he was doing. She had no clue about what went on in an engine, other than that it required occasional top-ups of oil and water, and no interest either. Instead, she continued to watch the traffic pass by as the uniformed man worked under the bonnet.

The downhill flow stopped again and she glanced down towards the far end of the cones, waiting for the vehicles to start coming through from there. When a voice sounded from a few feet away, she jumped, her head snapping around, expecting it to be the repairman.

It wasn't.

The second car back in the queue had its window rolled down and the driver was speaking to her.

'Sorry?'

'I said, broken down again?'

She frowned as a flutter of fear swept through her chest. 'Excuse me?'

'Wasn't that the same car I saw down by the Old Mill the other night?'

Now her heart was hammering, her breathing rapid and shallow as the fear of discovery froze her brain. What should she say?

But then, she realised, she had no idea who this man was, he didn't have a clue who she was, and she would probably never see him again. She forced a shrug. 'It's not the first time this has happened. I just hope it'll be the last.'

'I bet. Good luck with it.' He wound the window up as the repairman moved from the engine compartment around to the passenger side of the vehicle, opened the door and ducked down to check something under the glove compartment.

Emma was torn between seeing what he was doing and trying to memorise the numberplate of the man she'd just been talking with. If she managed to remember it, she had no idea what she would do with it. What she would be able to do with it. But he was a potential witness. It felt important that she should try. That she should have some information on him.

'There you go.' The repairman stood up with a small object held triumphantly in his greasy hand. 'There's your culprit. I'll test it, but I'd lay odds on it. A dry solder joint in this little bugger'll stop you dead as soon as it gets warm.'

The traffic began to move in the other direction and Emma's glance was torn away by the driver's wave as he set off down the hill. She refocused with difficulty. 'That tiny thing can stop an entire engine?'

'Yep. Just like that.' He stepped across to the back of his van, delved inside for something and fiddled with it for a moment. Then he nodded. 'Yeah. I've seen it before a few times.'

'Do you have a spare?'

He shook his head. 'No, but like you said, give it time to cool down and it'll get you home and back out to a garage, as long as you don't sit in this queue for too long. The Nissan dealership should have them in stock. Take it there as soon as you get the chance. Five minutes and they'll have it replaced and you'll be good as new. I'll just pop it back in for now.'

She let her eyes close briefly as she exhaled, long and slow. So, that tiny, inch-square little metal box had caused all this hassle. It seemed incredible. She opened her eyes at the click of the cover going back into place over the fuse box. 'There you go, miss. I'll wait with you until it gets going. Shouldn't be long. A few minutes. Especially now I've had it out of there for a while.'

Pete passed a troubled night, worrying about all three members of his family when he wasn't tossing and turning, his mind filled with nightmares of cannibal boys, suicidal wives, and daughters who turned into drug-crazed rebels with piercings, clothes that were barely decent and attitudes to match. By morning, he felt worse than he had when he went to bed, and that didn't improve when, after a quick coffee and toast breakfast, he headed out to work.

He took two steps away from the front door and stopped in his tracks.

'Shit.'

He stalked around to the other side of the car and found the situation was even worse.

All four of his tyres were completely flat.

He stepped closer, crouched to look at the nearest one. He could see no hole in it. Maybe they'd all just been let down. Bad enough, but recoverable with a bit of time and effort. He moved to the back tyre on the same side and swore again.

This one had definitely been slashed. Or, more accurately, stabbed, he saw from the shape and size of the hole in the side wall about half an inch from the rim.

He moved on around the car. The third tyre had been punctured in the same way, but the fourth again showed no sign of damage. He unscrewed the valve cap and found a tiny ball bearing inside. Returning to the first tyre he'd checked, he found the same.

So, two suspects? Or one who'd stabbed the first two then chickened out and used a quieter approach? Or, again, maybe stabbing two was all they needed to do, to achieve what they wanted. People only had one spare, after all.

Was this just to piss him off like the painting on the garage door, or was there more to it?

And how had he heard nothing when it felt like he'd been awake most of the night?

He gave growl of frustration, took out his phone and flipped through the contacts list. He would get the tyre people out to replace the two damaged ones and, in the meantime, pump up the other two.

'Good morning. Tyre-Right. How can I help?'

'Hello. I've come out to my car this morning and found that someone's slashed two of the tyres.' He crouched by the nearest one to read off the specifications from the side wall.

'OK. We'll get someone out to you as soon as we can. We'll just need the address and the tyre size.'

As he quoted the address, he was thinking that he'd have to let his team know too. They'd be expecting him a lot sooner than he was going to be able to make it into the station this morning. This was the last thing he needed while he was in the middle of a difficult case.

Or was that the point, the cynical side of his mind suggested as he ended the phone call. Did someone not want him to solve the case?

'No.' He shook his head. That was just too unlikely.

So, who did want to mess with him? He sighed. Unfortunately, the list was a long one. But, he had at least half an hour to kill. He headed back inside. He would call Dave on the landline.

'Hey, boss, what's up?'

It was Jill, not Dave, who had picked up the call in the squad room. His mind pictured the small, slim PC reaching across to pick up the phone on the deserted desk next to hers because Dave hadn't turned up yet.

'Somebody seems to have taken a dislike to me,' he said.

'Hard to imagine, boss.'

He could hear the smile in her voice.

'I know. Isn't it? But, this is the second time they've targeted my house this week. The first was just a spray-can job on the garage door. This time, they've slashed two of my tyres and let the other two down, so I'm waiting for Tyre-Right.'

'Dare I say that using the garage would have saved you the trouble?'

'Not if you know what's good for you, Jill. I didn't have a good night and I'm not having a good morning, so tread careful.'

'Got it, boss.'

'I'll be there as soon as I can.'

'Right, boss.'

Pete put the phone down and turned towards Louise, who was watching him from the sofa.

'So, who the hell is it?' she asked. 'Who's got it in for us now?'

'Un-bloody-believable! Men!'

Tanya plonked herself down in the chair opposite Emma and slammed her handbag onto her desk.

'What about them?' Emma asked, not that she was particularly interested in the younger girl's infamously varied love life.

'Bloody misogynist pigs, the lot of them. Do they all think we're here just for sex and cooking?'

Emma sighed inwardly. She was going to hear about whatever it was that had happened to the office junior, whether she wanted to or not. 'What happened now?'

Tanya flicked her long dark hair back over her shoulder. 'My neighbour couldn't bring me in this morning, so I had to get a taxi. What a bloody rip-off! Six quid! And it didn't save me more than ten minutes over walking it! If it wasn't for these heels . . .' She huffed.

What's that got to do with misogynist pigs? Emma thought. But Tanya hadn't finished.

'Then, to top it off, the bloody taxi driver came on to me. Put his hand on my leg, for God's sake! Jesus, he was old enough to be my dad. And talk about ugly! He had a face like a hammered steak. And he stank of curry. I mean, I'm no racist, but really . . .?'

Emma frowned. 'He put his hand on your leg? What did you do?'

'I just looked at it, looked at him, crossed my legs and my arms and stared him out. He was driving, so he had to look away, and he took his hand away at the same time. But, I mean . . . Where does he get off, putting his hand on me in the first place?'

An image of the man she'd been attacked by popped unbidden into Emma's mind. She shook her head. 'Why would he do that?'

'You're asking me? How would I know what goes on in a head like that? He told me I looked lovely or something, I thanked him – as you do – and suddenly, he was talking about his wife – his wife, mind you – who's gone to India for two months. Some family thing. And how they're not really compatible. Arranged marriage and all that. And he prefers English girls because that's what he was brought up with. *What*, mind you, not *who*. And how I reminded him so much of a girl he'd known when he was my age. And then . . .' She shook her head and fixed Emma with a wide-eyed gaze. 'Then he said, "I wanted her so much, but my parents wouldn't allow it," and . . .' She shuddered. 'Ugh!'

Jesus! Was the world full of rapists, perverts and chauvinists? 'So, have you reported it?'

'No.'

'Why the hell not?' Emma burst out before she could continue. 'He's assaulted you, for God's sake! You can't let him get away with it. What if he does it to someone else? He could go further next time. He might rape someone!'

Tanya sat back in her chair, her dark eyes narrowing. 'Oh, come on, Em! It's a bit of a leap from groping my leg to rape.'

'Maybe, but it's a slippery slope. And if he gets away with the first step, who's to say he won't take the second? And the third?'

'Yes, but . . . we don't know he would, do we? I mean, he's missing his wife at the moment. Once she comes home, he'll probably be as faithful as a puppy and there won't be any more problems.'

Emma stared at her. 'I can't believe you're defending the man.'

'I'm not defending him. I'm just not prepared to make an issue of it, that's all. Nothing happened.' She flicked her hair back again.

'Then why were you making so much of it a couple of minutes ago?'

'God! I wish I hadn't said anything now. I was just venting, that's all. Drop it, will you?' She pushed her chair back and stood up. 'I'm going to get a coffee.'

'OK, what progress have you guys made this morning?'

Pete dropped his briefcase by his chair and shrugged out of his jacket.

'I've managed to get one step closer,' Ben said, leaning back in his chair to look across behind Dick Feeney. 'Got a response from his mobile provider with the tracking data. Looks like we were right at the start, boss. He was out on Bonhay Road rather than round by the clock tower or the university.'

Pete gave him a nod. 'Nice one, Ben. Anyone else?'

'Found that for you, boss.' Jill tossed a catalogue towards him and Pete grabbed it out of the air, looked down at it, then back at Jill with a raised eyebrow.

She shrugged. 'Well, what you said earlier on the phone – I thought it might come in handy.'

'OK. Thank you. But what about the case?'

'We've also got the victim's call log,' Dave said. 'The last one he picked up was from the fare he took to the station. Nothing after that, apart from missed calls coming in. Nothing at all going out.'

'So, whoever he picked up wasn't a pre-booked fare,' Pete said. 'They must have flagged him down.'

'Somebody from the carvery then,' said Dick. 'They've got CCTV, haven't they?'

'Yes,' Pete confirmed. 'But not out the front. Only in the back corridor inside and the car park behind the place.'

'Still, it's a starting point.'

'Anybody needing a taxi won't have gone out the back, though, will they?' Jane argued. 'You've got a car, you don't need a taxi. You haven't, you go in and out the front.'

'Unless you drove there, then had one too many,' Pete said. 'It's a fallback option. And it gives us another place to canvas for witnesses. Anybody who saw anything on Bonhay Road, in the area of the carvery, around the time he passed there. Customers, staff and passing motorists.'

'That would be best handled through the press, wouldn't it?' Dave asked.

Pete nodded. 'I'll have a word with his lordship. But we also need to go out there and talk to people. And we can check for other properties and businesses down there that have CCTV. See if they picked up anything useful.'

'So, what's the Ann Summers all about?' Dave asked, and got an elbow in the ribs from Jane that, for once, he didn't respond to.

'Eh?' Pete frowned.

'The catalogue,' Jane explained. 'It's the only type he knows, poor lamb.'

'What we've just been talking about. CCTV. There've been two attacks on my house this week. A spray-paint job and then my tyres slashed. It's why I was late in this morning. Jill's suggesting I put a camera up out there and catch the perpetrator on it. But, who's to know they wouldn't be watching me put it up?' He looked at Jill.

'So, use two,' she said. 'Overlap them so there aren't any blind spots.'

'Or just figure out who it is and arrest them,' Dick put in.

'Yeah, that's easier said than done lately,' Pete admitted. 'We haven't exactly been idle since I came back, have we? Plus, there's all those we put away before, some of whom might be out by now.'

Dick nodded slowly. 'Good point, well made.'

'Well, on the bright side, we know a few it isn't,' said Dave. 'Malcolm Burton. Neil Sanderson. Gagik Petrosyan. Frank Benton.'

'Tommy,' Pete added and got a nod in response.

'Yeah, but knowing Petrosyan's reputation, it might well be connected to him,' Ben said. 'I mean, the fact that we've got him inside doesn't mean we've got his whole gang – clan – whatever they are. He must have visitors now and then. It wouldn't be that hard for him to still be calling the shots from inside.'

'Ain't you the cheerful little sod this morning,' Jane said dryly.

'He's got a point, though,' Pete said. 'It would bear looking into. He's up for trial soon, same as Burton and Sanderson. He could well be trying the same tactics that built him his reputation and his business.'

'I'll get onto the prison, see what I can dig up,' Dave suggested.

Pete looked at him.

'Well, you can't, can you? It's your house being targeted.'

'OK. Jane, you can come with me out to Bonhay Road then. Jill, get onto the council, see if they've got any CCTV over that way. If they have, give me a ring and tell me where exactly. Ben, check with Graham downstairs to make sure we haven't, then let me know and carry on with what you were doing. Dick, you could go back through our arrest records, see what possibilities you can dig up. Let's get somewhere today, shall we?'

Chapter 9

Emma's mind festered all morning. She could barely focus on what she was doing. How did this bloody man think he was going to get away with being such a perv? Did he think that, just because he was an Indian or Pakistani or whatever, political correctness would prevent any comeback?

Because, if so, he was going to learn a powerful lesson, that was for sure. Whether Tanya wanted to pursue the matter or not.

And Emma couldn't understand why she wouldn't. After all, he hadn't actually assaulted her, so it wasn't as if she'd have to submit to a rape examination or to reliving a major trauma under cross-examination. So, if it was going to potentially prevent further, worse attacks, then surely it was a moral obligation.

She gave up trying at 12.30, closed down her screen and announced, 'I'm off to lunch. I've got to go into town, briefly. So, what was this groper driving, specifically, so that I can avoid him?'

Tanya gave her a sour look. 'You're not going to go and report him, are you?'

'No. I couldn't if I wanted to, could I? I didn't witness anything. I just don't want the same experience, that's all.'

Tanya sighed. 'All right. It was a black Prius with yellow signage on the doors.'

'Thank you. Do you want anything, while I'm out?'

Tanya shook her head. 'I'm fine, thanks.'

'See you in a bit, then.'

Emma knew perfectly well which cab company in the city that signage belonged to. And, although she couldn't go to the police about the matter, she could certainly go to the company.

She picked up her handbag and walked out of the office, across the road and through into Cathedral Square, heading for Fore Street and beyond it to Bartholomew, where she knew the taxi company had its offices, two doors down from the cinema.

Pete had just turned left off Pennsylvania Road, only a few yards short of the queue to the traffic lights, when his phone rang. He hit the button on the car's hands-free system to accept the call.

'Boss?'

'Dave.'

'We've got something on Ranjeet Singh. Could be something big.'

He glanced at Jane, in the passenger seat beside him. She raised an eyebrow but said nothing. 'What sort of big?' he asked.

'Friend of a friend. Singh's Hindu, but he associates with a lot of Muslims. Goes with the job, I suppose. But one of those associates turns out to be a cousin of Mohammed Iqbal.'

Mohammed Iqbal, Pete knew, had been arrested in Plymouth the previous November. He had been one of the main players in the city's drug trade. The city's police had been after him for a couple of years before that, but he had been too slippery – always a couple of steps away from the actual product. But, that morning – the morning Pete had returned to the job after his leave of absence – he had been caught with his pants down. Literally. In bed with a known drug runner: a fourteen-year-old boy with three outstanding warrants against him.

And he had a cousin driving around Exeter.

'Why didn't we know about this bloke?'

'Don't know, boss. But we do now. Should Dick and I go and see what we can find out about him on the streets? Ben can dig up what there is online and in the database.'

'Yes, do that, Dave. We've got a quick interview to do, then we'll be back.'

Reaching the address they were looking for among a row of small, modern houses, Pete pulled over and stopped the car.

The manager of the Old Mill pub and carvery had only been able to give them one thing of possible use: the name of a barmaid who had spoken to a taxi driver on Tuesday evening, the man having come in to ask after a fare to Pennsylvania Road.

'Here we are. Let's see what Mandy Appleton can tell us.' He stepped out of the car and headed briskly up to the front door of the little redbrick house, Jane hurrying to keep up. He pressed the bell-push and a pretty chime echoed from within.

Mandy opened the door in pyjamas and dressing gown despite the hour. Her dark-blonde hair was up in a scruffy bun, and she had no make-up on her girlish face and pink fluffy slippers on her feet.

'Oh.' Her brown eyes narrowed when she saw Pete. 'Sorry. I was . . .'

Pete held up his warrant card. 'Sorry to disturb you. I'm DS Gayle. This is my colleague, DC Bennett. Could we have a brief word? We've got a couple of questions that you might be able to answer for us.'

'Uh . . . yes. Come in.' She stood back, still not entirely recovered from her confusion. 'I was expecting a friend.'

'We won't take long,' Pete assured her.

'Go on through.'

A short, narrow hallway led into an open-plan kitchenette that gave onto a living/dining area with French doors at the back, leading out into a small, plain garden. Pete headed through, followed by Jane.

'Have a seat,' Mandy offered.

Pete waited for her to settle herself in the single armchair, then took the sofa, leaving room for Jane beside him.

'So, what's this about, officer?'

'Tuesday night,' Pete said, taking his notebook and pen from his pocket. 'You were working at the Old Mill.'

'That's right.'

'A taxi driver came in, looking for a fare to Pennsylvania Road.'

'Yes.'

'What can you tell us about him?'

She settled back in her chair. 'Not much, really. He was forty-ish, I suppose. Local, from his accent. Short, thick-set with wavy, sandy-coloured hair. I didn't get his name and I didn't see what car he was driving.' She frowned. 'Cassie asked me about this a little while ago on the phone. Is there some sort of problem?'

Pete pursed his lips. 'A taxi driver was killed that night, up at the end of Argyll Road. We thought there might be a connection, but it was obviously someone else.'

'I saw something was going on up there yesterday. I normally cut through that way to work and back. Saves going into the city centre, especially with the roadworks down here.'

'Well, thanks for your help. We'll get out of your way before your friend comes.' He stood up and had taken just one step towards the entrance when the doorbell rang again.

'Oh,' said Mandy with a shrug. 'Too late.' She hurried past them to the door.

When she opened it, Pete tilted his head, smiling in recognition. 'Hello, Darren. Fancy meeting you here.'

Confusion was followed by fear, then defiance, on the face of the young redhead at the door. 'DS Gayle. What are you doing here?'

Darren was an occasional and reluctant informant of Pete, who he hadn't seen for a few months now, since Darren had put him onto a drug dealer who'd been killed in a car crash before Pete got the opportunity to question him. Pete had wondered at the time if Darren had told anyone else of his interest in the dealer, but in the end had put it down to a strange coincidence.

And here was another one.

'Just leaving, as it happens. But, seeing that you're here, you don't happen to know anything about a taxi driver who got killed up the road from here a couple of nights ago, do you?'

'What? Why would I . . .?' He stopped, shaking his head. 'Don't wind me up.'

Pete pressed his lips together. 'It was a serious question, Darren. Bloke called Ranjeet Singh. Had his . . . well, I won't go into details with ladies present. Suffice to say it was particularly messy.'

Darren looked from Pete to Mandy to Jane and back to Pete. 'I heard someone had died, but I don't know any details,' he said. 'Why would I?'

Pete shrugged. 'No reason at all. Just thought I'd ask while the opportunity was there. Anyway, we'll be on our way. Thanks again for your help, Mandy.'

He stepped forward, passing between them, followed by Jane. Behind them, they heard the door close, but Pete didn't look back until he got to the car. Darren had gone inside with Mandy.

'Darren Westley?' Jane stared at him across the roof of the car. 'She isn't . . .?'

Pete shrugged. 'Opposites attract. Or maybe she's not as squeaky-clean as she ought to be.'

'I can't see it,' Jane said as they climbed in. 'Nice little house. Well kept. And she's only a barmaid. She's not going to be overly flush, is she? Won't have the spare cash to waste on a habit.'

'True. And much as I know you'd like to, I can't see any cause to go back there and search him.'

She grimaced. 'I don't know that I'd *like* to. I might be *inclined* to . . .'

* * *

'Shafiq Ahmed, boss.' Dave pointed to a photo he'd put up on the whiteboard. 'Mohammed Iqbal's cousin. A taxi driver here in the city. Brought up here from the age of three, when his parents came here from Saudi, along with Iqbal's. They stayed in regular touch until the Iqbals were killed in a house fire seven years ago. Gas leak, apparently. More of an explosion than a fire, but it was proved to be an accident.'

'I've just got into Ahmed's Facebook account, boss,' Ben announced.

Pete turned to look at him. 'Right. Check him out thoroughly, then move on to Singh's account.'

'I already covered Singh's. That's how I got into Ahmed's. There was nothing out of the ordinary there.'

'OK. See what their friends throw up.'

Ben nodded and Pete turned back to Dave.

'We spoke to the people at Ahmed's firm and some of the other drivers on the ranks he uses. No signs of anything untoward there. Haven't spoken to his family yet, though.'

'There's nothing official on him,' Ben said. 'And, so far, his Facebook page looks perfectly normal. Family stuff and general stuff that you get on there. And his interests don't show anything out of the ordinary.'

'OK. Keep looking.'

Dave shrugged. 'That's about it, so far.'

'We're going to see Ahmed's wife in an hour,' Dick said.

'We?' Dave asked.

'With your delicate disposition, I'd probably best take Jill.'

'What's the matter with my disposition?' Dave demanded.

Jane laughed. 'Subtle you ain't, matey. And subtle is exactly what it'll need to coax anything useful out of the bloke's wife. She'll be on her guard from the first question.'

'I can do subtle.'

'Yeah,' Ben put in. 'As a brick. There's nothing indicative on Ahmed's Facebook, boss. I'll check out his friends' pages.'

'Right, Ben. While you were finding all that out, Jane and I have been making a few discoveries of our own.' He brought the rest of the team up-to-date on what they had discovered. The taxi driver looking for a fare at the Old Mill. The fact that he was white rather than Indian. And the fact that there would be no useful CCTV footage from the area.

'So, are we saying Ranjeet Singh nicked a fair?' asked Jill.

Pete tilted his head. 'Looks possible. Unfortunately, our witness didn't get any details, so it'll be a case of trawling the various cab companies. Jane, maybe you can do that.'

'Sure.'

There were only a handful of major companies in the city, but an unknown number of one- and two-driver family firms. The council could provide licensing records that would help track them down.

'Meantime, I've got something else to follow up on.'

'What's that then, boss?' Dave asked.

'See,' said Jane. 'Like Ben said – subtle as a brick.'

'How's it going, Bob?' Pete leaned his elbows on the high-topped counter of the custody desk in the basement of the station.

'Quiet, for now. Don't tell me – you're about to spoil all that. Bloody typical.' Bob shook his head, his bald scalp gleaming under the fluorescent lights.

'I don't know where you get that idea from,' Pete said defensively. 'I was just going to ask you to have a play on that computer in front of you, that's all. What's so hard about that?'

'Depends what you want me to play.'

'Hunt the drug gang.'

'I thought that was your job?'

'Yeah, but I need to know if we've done it as thoroughly as we ought.'

Bob nodded, 'Which gang?'

'The Armenian's. Gagik Petrosyan's.'

Bob sucked air through his teeth. 'I hope so, for your sake, mate. If you've left any of them out there . . . They can be some nasty buggers, from what I hear.'

'Which is why I was asking you to check.'

'Eh?'

'Somebody's cottoned on to where I live. The wife's not happy.'

'And you suspect Petrosyan? If it was him, I'm betting you'd know for sure. You'd have had a firebomb through the letterbox or something.'

'I was hoping to nip it in the bud before it comes to anything like that.'

Bob grunted. 'OK. I'll have a shufty through the records.' He turned to his computer and began to jab at the keys with two fat forefingers.

Pete kept his expression even and his mouth shut – Bob was doing him a favour, after all – but this was going to take some time.

Chapter 10

'There.' Bob slid a piece of paper across the desk to him. 'I've got five other arrests related to Gagik Petrosyan. Two of them are currently out on bail, the other three are on remand, along with the man himself.'

In Exeter prison, Pete thought. *Good. Get them acclimatised to it before they're sentenced. They'll know what they've got to look forward to while they're standing in the dock.* 'Thanks, Bob.' He picked up the sheet and looked down at the list of names. One of them jumped out at him straight away. He glanced up at Bob. There was a 'B' next to the name, indicating bail. Davit Achabahian, resident of Exwick, was one of the few people in the world Petrosyan trusted.

'Have you got access to the prison database from here?'

Bob shook his head. 'No. They run an isolated system over there.'

'What, no Internet access? There must be, surely.'

'Yes, but not from any of the computers they keep their records on.'

Pete grunted. 'OK. I'll have to go over there again.'

'Something there, then?' Bob nodded to the sheet he'd just finished compiling.

'Possibly. Davit Achabaihan. It'd be useful to know if he's been in touch with Petrosyan since he's been inside.'

'Well, that don't take a visit. I can call them and ask.'

'Now, why didn't I think of that?'

'Wrong mindset, mate. You've got to think simple and lazy. Like the hare and the tortoise.' Bob picked up the phone and dialled a number from memory. 'Hello. Kev? Yeah. How's it going over there? Keeping you busy enough, are we?' He laughed. 'Yeah, I need a quick favour. Could you have a look in your visitor log and see if Gagik Petrosyan's had any visitors, other than his brief?' He paused. 'OK.' Looking up at Pete, he gave a quick nod. Then he concentrated on the phone again. 'Yes? Ah. That's interesting. Thanks, mate. I'll see you tomorrow night.'

He put the phone down. 'Mate of mine. I play skittles with him at the Hope and Anchor.'

Pete nodded. 'And what did he have for us?'

'Petrosyan's had just the one visitor since he's been in there. Regularly, once a fortnight.' Bob paused, stringing it out.

'Well, it ain't bloody conjugal,' Pete said. 'So, who's the lucky winner?'

'Davit Achabaihan.'

'Yes!' Pete punched the air. 'Thanks, Bob. So, I will be going out, after all. To see what he's been up to while he's been out on bail.'

'I might be seeing you later then.'

Pete gave him a wink. 'You never know, buddy.'

'Yeah, that's the trouble with you lately,' Bob grumbled. 'Keep giving me more and more bloody work.'

Pete laughed. 'Don't go filling the place up while I'm gone, eh?' he said with a slap of his open hand on the counter.

Bob grunted and Pete gave him a wave as he headed back into the station. Before he could go and talk to Achabaihan, he needed to find out where he was.

* * *

'Oh, my God! Tommy!'

Louise ran forward and gathered him up into her arms, crushing him to her in a smothering hug while Annie stood one step back, waiting her turn.

'My beautiful boy,' Louise crooned. 'Thank God you're safe. I've been worried sick about you. We all have. But none of that matters now. You'll soon be home.'

Annie knew what those hugs felt like, how she reacted to them, and she saw no such reaction from Tommy. Her brother accepted the embrace, but Annie could see his face. His eyes didn't close like hers would have and, when he saw her watching, rather than pretend, he scowled at her.

She frowned. What was wrong with him?

She could see the bruises on his face and her heart went out to him, but this was their mother he was holding. And he wasn't reacting in the way Annie would have expected at all. 'What's wrong?' she mouthed silently.

Now he closed his eyes – but not to sink into the intensity of emotion. Instead, to avoid answering her.

Louise was still murmuring to him. One of the staff was standing in the corner of the room, hands behind his back, watching. They had both been patted down as they entered the facility, but she supposed the staff had to be sure they hadn't missed anything. That she or her mother hadn't managed to sneak anything in for Tommy. Parents, especially, must do some desperate things in places like this, she imagined. And yet . . . were all the kids in here like Tommy? As shut off and distant?

Louise stepped back, extending an arm to bring Annie in. Annie hesitated just an instant, then stepped forward. But she could tell as she wrapped her arms around her brother that he had noticed that tiny pause. She hugged him all the same, but he felt almost rigid in her arms. He didn't squeeze her back as he normally would have.

'It's so great to see you, Tommy,' she said. 'We thought we'd lost you. Where've you been?' She stood back, holding him at arm's length. 'We've heard bits of stuff about you now and then, but nothing for ages. Are you coming home soon?'

She turned to Louise. 'Mum? Is he?'

Louise smiled down at her, reaching out to stroke her hair while her other hand rested on Tommy's shoulder. 'Yes, love. It won't be long now. Then we'll all be a family again. Just get this trial thing over, I expect . . .'

'So, where's Dad?' Tommy spoke for the first time.

'He couldn't come today,' Louise told him. 'He's not allowed – not until after Mr Burton's trial.'

Tommy grunted. 'Yeah, right. Too busy working, eh? As usual.'

'No, Tommy,' Annie said. 'Mum's right. It's the rules. He's not allowed because it's his case that you've got to go to court about. He could tell you what to say and stuff.'

'Of course he could – with a warder looking over my shoulder all the time.' Tommy glanced at the man in jeans and polo shirt standing in the corner of the room.

Annie caught the tightening of the man's lips and the frown that flashed across her mother's face at the use of the term 'warder'. They had been told on entry that the staff tried to downplay any association with the prison service – which they were entirely separate from – as much as possible. With the exception of the registered manager and the unit's psychologist and psychiatrist, they were referred to simply as staff rather than any other title or description.

'Well, that's what the rules are, anyway. And it's not for long. Just until Mr Burton's convicted. Then you can come home. Can't he, Mum?'

'That's right, hun.' Louise looked from one child to the other. Annie could see the love shining in her eyes. She looked back at Tommy. All she could see on his face was pent-up anger and resentment. But she had no idea what to do about it. She desperately wanted him to be happy. To be pleased to see both her and their mother. To love them as deeply and obviously as they loved him. But something was stopping him, getting in the way.

She stepped forward again, wrapped her arms around him.

'Come back to us, big bruv,' she whispered. 'We need you.'

'Davit?' the woman on the other end of the line said. 'He's . . .' Pete heard the clicking of a keyboard '. . . At the airport. Dropped a fare there a few minutes ago. He'll probably be there for another fifteen, twenty minutes, depending on arrival times and baggage claim, then he's got a pickup from there to Exmouth. He's working eight to four today, so that'll probably be his last of the day.'

'And does he come back to the office at the end of his shift?'

'No. He uses his own car, so there's no need.'

And no saying for sure that he'll go straight home after, Pete thought.

'So, can you tell me where he's going in Exmouth, so I can meet him there?'

'Umm . . . well, I'm not sure I should, but . . . You want to speak to Davit rather than his fare, so . . .' Taxi and private hire firms tended to want to keep the police sweet as much as possible. There was no telling when it might be useful and Pete was relying on that now. 'He's going to 37 Albert Drive.'

'Thanks.' Pete put the phone down before she could ask any more and checked his watch. It was mid-afternoon. Achabaihan would probably get to Exmouth in about an hour from now, which gave him a few minutes. He stood up and glanced around his team. 'Who wants a coffee?'

'Right. I'm off out for a bit,' he said a short time later. 'While I'm gone I need someone to look into the whereabouts, background, criminal history and known associates – in other words, every-thing we can find – on one Apkar Sarkissian.'

'Bless you,' said Jane.

'What's one of them?' asked Dave.

'It's not a what. It's a who. And it's a close personal friend of our old buddy Gagik Petrosyan. In fact, it's one of the five other people who were arrested in connection with him and one of the two of those who's currently out on bail. The other one being Davit Achabaihan.'

Albert Drive in Exmouth was a street of pastel-painted Georgian townhouses with basements protected by black iron railings. It was one street back from the coast and had yellow lines painted along one side and cars parked nose to tail along the other – mostly expensive ones, Pete noted, as he cruised slowly, looking for somewhere to park his silver Ford saloon.

Number 37 was a pale blue house of three storeys above ground level with white-painted window frames and a high-gloss, dark-blue door. He found a gap in the row of cars and four-by-fours a few doors down and pulled in. Checking his watch, he found he was just four minutes early. He stepped out of the car and locked it, strolled back down towards the house where Davit was due to drop his fare, and leaned on the spike-topped railing, arms folded across his chest.

It was just a couple of minutes later that he heard a car turning into the end of the road. He glanced that way, recognised Davit's Skoda from their last meeting a few months ago, and turned his head away. Keeping a relaxed appearance, he gazed down the street until he heard the car come to a stop a few feet away. He heard the door open and looked around. Saw the recognition on Achabaihan's face and smiled as he unfolded his arms and stepped forward.

Nodding to the passenger, who gave him a look before stepping away, he leaned down to look through the side window, focusing on the driver. 'Hello, Davit. How's it going?'

'Detective.'

'Good thing I ran into you,' Pete said. 'I need to ask you about something.'

The Armenian's expression said he didn't believe for a second that this was a chance meeting. 'What?'

Behind him, Pete heard a house door open and close. They were alone. He dropped the light and easy act. 'Where were you last night between 11.00 p.m. and 6.00 a.m.?'

Achabaihan shrugged. 'Here and there. In bed, mostly.'

'Alone?'

Pete knew he wasn't married from their previous encounter, when Davit had been caught aiding and abetting the fugitive Gagik Petrosyan.

'Of course not. I had three students with me. What you think?'

'I think it's highly unlikely, Davit. But if it's true, I'll need their names.'

Achabaihan shrugged. 'I lose track, you know? So many girls. So many names.'

Pete nodded. 'I see where you're coming from. Trouble is, you start to lose your memory like that, you'll end up taking wrong turns, overcharging passengers. Could lose your licence. And, now that Petrosyan's out of the picture, where would that leave you?'

The Armenian's eyes narrowed.

Pete met his gaze, relaxed and in control. Held it for a long moment until Davit finally spoke.

'I work until midnight, go home to bed. Alone. No witness.'

Pete nodded. 'There. That wasn't so hard, was it? Of course, I will check.'

'Is that it? I have place to be.'

'Almost.'

Pete stood upright, wandered towards the back of the car. As he moved around it, he reached down and popped the boot open. 'Whoops. Sorry about that,' he said as he looked inside.

'Hey! What are you doing?'

Pete looked around the raised boot lid. 'Hand slipped. You'd best close it before you move off.'

He heard Achabaihan mutter something under his breath, then the car door opened and he stomped towards where Pete stood back to give him room. He reached up and slammed the boot lid. 'You see what you want?'

'Don't know what you mean, Mr Achabaihan. Have a good evening.'

Davit grunted sourly and turned away.

Pete stepped back onto the pavement. No point tempting the guy. In fact, he hadn't seen what he'd thought he might. The boot was clear and clean, as you'd expect from a taxi driver. He'd hoped to see a bag in there, perhaps containing spray cans and a knife of some kind.

The car door slammed and Achabaihan roared off down the street as Pete took out his phone and made a call.

'Ben?' he said when it was picked up. 'A quick job for you. Check on Davit Achabaihan's mobile phone records, will you?'

'What's he been up to, boss?'

'That's what I want to find out.'

'Looks like he was telling you the truth, boss.'

Pete stopped, about to pull his chair out, having just got back to the squad room. 'Ben?'

'Davit Achabaihan. We know he's been visiting Petrosyan, but there's no evidence in his mobile call logs that he's been passing on any messages from him. And he was at home from about twenty past twelve last night.'

'OK. And what about the other one? Sissi-what-not.'

'Again, no evidence that he's been involved in anything unfriendly. One conversation with Achabaihan ten days ago, but that's it. Nothing on their social media pages either.'

Pete nodded. Could he discount the pair of them, then? If so, where did that leave him?

About the same place with this as with the cabbie killer, he thought. *Nowhere.*

He looked around at his team, who were all watching him. 'Has anyone got any good news?' He focused on Dave, giving him a firm stare. This was not the time for levity.

'Jane said something about you meeting up with Darren Westley. I checked up on him. Seems like he's been seeing that barmaid for a few months now. They're in regular touch by all the usual methods and he goes over to her place regularly.'

'Is he in touch with anyone else we should know about?' Pete asked, sitting down.

'Not that I could see.'

Pete grunted. 'Maybe she's cleaning him up then. We'll give him the benefit of the doubt for now. What else?'

'We got nowhere on Shafiq Ahmed, boss,' Dick put in. 'He seems to be clean. The wife let Jill and I check his computer, even search the place to see if there was another one. Which there wasn't.'

'OK. We'll have a chat with the man himself, though, just to be thorough.'

Dave set his elbows on his desk, fingers entwining in front of his face. 'Every lead we follow on this seems to dry up after a bit.'

'Then we're following the wrong leads, Dave. Come on. We've got a killer out there somewhere. We've got someone targeting my house. Has anyone checked if any other officers have had the same treatment?'

'Yes, boss,' said Jill. 'It's just you.'

'Then there's nobody better placed than us to figure out who's doing it,' he said firmly. 'Come on, people. Let's make some progress, can we? Anybody got Ahmed's licence plate or cab number?'

'Yeah, both.' Dave wrote quickly on a Post-it and passed it over. 'The phone number there's for City Cars, who he drives for.'

'Cheers.'

Pete grabbed his jacket from the back of his chair and headed out. He would talk to the taxi driver, then, all being well, head across the river. There wasn't time to mess about with catalogues and he remembered seeing a place that sold security cameras and so on in one of the small arcades of local shops in the residential area of Redhills. He wanted the cameras in his hands and preferably installed tonight.

Chapter 11

Pete made the call as he descended the central stairs. A young-sounding woman picked up before he reached the ground floor. 'Good afternoon. City Cars. How can I help?'

'Hello. This is DS Gayle, Exeter CID. Can you give me a current location on one of your drivers, please?'

'Uh . . . Which one?'

'Shafiq Ahmed. I need to talk to him about a friend of his who's sadly died.'

'Oh. Well . . . in that case, I suppose . . .' He heard the tapping of a keyboard as he reached the bottom of the stairs and let himself through into the back corridor. 'He's on the taxi rank on Sidwell Street at the moment. Shall I let him know you're on the way?'

That was the last thing Pete wanted. 'No, best not. It's kind of delicate, you know? Best approached in person. And if he's on a rank, I don't want to cause any unnecessary problems.'

'Oh, OK.'

'Thanks, anyway. I'll see him shortly.' Pete ended the call, hoping she wouldn't contact Ahmed regardless. Not that he suspected the man of anything, but it was always best to catch someone off-guard. You got a much more honest response that way.

Sidwell Street was a narrower continuation of the High Street, leading up to a roundabout on the inner ring road, just past the multiplex cinema. The taxi rank was nearer to the High Street end, outside a supermarket. Pete approached from the city end of the street, coming up behind his target. There were only four cars in the rank when he got there. As he approached, he could see Ahmed's black Prius, second from the front. He pulled up behind the fourth car in the line, a white Skoda saloon, and stepped out. Crossing to the pavement, he drew out his warrant card and showed it to the man in the Skoda as he walked past. A young woman with a pushchair and several carrier bags of shopping had emerged from the supermarket and was approaching the cab at the front of the line. Pete heard an engine start. He passed the third taxi, warrant card still in hand, its leather cover closed.

Ahmed's engine was idling.

In front of him, the young woman opened the rear door of the leading taxi as the driver stepped out to help her. Pete tapped on the roof of Ahmed's car and leant down at the open passenger window.

'Shafiq Ahmed?'

Something flashed in his eyes. 'Yes.'

He held up his badge. 'DS Pete Gayle. I need to talk to you about . . .'

Ahmed's head turned quickly away. His hand flicked the selector in the central console as his foot hit the accelerator and the car's engine roared as it lurched away.

'Shit.'

Pete turned, tucking his warrant card away as he ran for his own vehicle. Jumping in, he started the engine with one hand while the other hit the blues and twos in the front grille and the back window. He slammed it into reverse, shot back a few feet, then launched himself after the fleeing taxi, which was already too far ahead.

If he reached the roundabout before Pete closed the gap, he could go anywhere. Pete would have lost him.

Sirens blaring, engine roaring, Pete sped up the narrow street as the black Prius shot across the crossroads up ahead and on towards the big cinema.

What the hell was the bloke thinking? Clearly he was scared, but why? What had he done, that he would be scared enough to leg it from the police on sight?

There was nothing in his recent record: just the drug conviction from a few years ago. So, was he still dealing? Was that the reason?

Pete crossed the junction with York Road. He had gained maybe thirty yards on Ahmed, but the taxi was still over a hundred ahead of him and fast approaching the Blackboy roundabout. He jammed his foot to the floor. Reaching for the radio, he keyed the mike. 'DS Gayle. In pursuit of suspect Shafiq Ahmed, headed north-east on Sidwell Street. Report any sighting or stop and detain if possible. He's driving a black Toyota; registration . . .' He glanced down and read it off Dave's note as the Prius was still too far away to read the plate itself. 'Driver wanted for questioning regarding the murder of fellow taxi driver, Ranjeet Singh.'

He released the mike and concentrated on the road ahead and on the black cab as it entered the roundabout. He had to try and see which way it went. There were too many options from here. He could go north towards Pennsylvania or Stoke Hill, north-east towards the County Showground and Beacon Hill, east on the Pinhoe Road, or even cut back south through Polsoe or down the Western Way.

The black car vanished from sight into the traffic on the roundabout.

'Shit.'

One option down: he wasn't going north.

Pete slowed as he approached the roundabout, scanning the roads to his right.

There. Was that him? A black car was heading north-east up Blackboy Road. But then the car behind it slowed to turn right, letting it pull away, and he saw it wasn't the right shape.

'Dammit,' he muttered, following the flow around. He had to be going down Western Way then. Pete pushed through the late-afternoon traffic, using his lights and sirens, and accelerated south down the main road.

Free of the bulk of traffic on the roundabout, he pushed the Ford hard. In seconds, he cleared the long right-hand curve and could see down to the roundabout at the end of Heavitree Road.

There was no black Prius.

'Bastard!' He slammed the steering wheel with the flat of his hand. Ahmed must have gone all the way round the Blackboy roundabout. He could have gone back down Sidwell Street or carried on round again and gone anywhere. 'Shit.'

Easing off the accelerator, he killed the lights and sirens and keyed the radio again.

'DS Gayle. Subject lost. Repeat: subject lost. Any unit seeing the car or driver, please report and apprehend. If an excuse is required, use the traffic violation of going twice round Blackboy roundabout. I need officers attending his home address and the office of City Cars urgently.' He quoted both addresses, released the microphone button and used the Bluetooth to make another call to City Cars. The same girl answered.

'It's Detective Sergeant Gayle,' he said. 'Did you speak to Shafiq Ahmed after I called you?'

'Uh . . . no. You said not to. Why?'

He turned left into Heavitree Road. The traffic was queueing solidly down towards the roundabout but his side of the road was clear.

'Because he saw me and sped off. Dangerously. Which makes me wonder why. So, as soon as you see him or hear from him, I want to know about it. Clear?'

'Perfectly.'

'Another taxi driver was murdered four days ago. A man Shafiq knew. When I spoke to you before, Shafiq was just someone I needed to talk to about the victim. His flight now makes him a suspect.' He made the turn into the station car park.

'In a murder?'

'Exactly. So, as I said: as soon as you know where he is, we need to. Failure to adhere to that would make you an accessory after the fact. You'd be charged with aiding and abetting a suspected felon.'

'There's no need for that! I'll call. I promise.'

'Good. 101 and ask for me. It doesn't matter what time.'

'All right.'

Pete ended the call and took his phone with him into the station. Heading through the custody suite, he was stopped by the sergeant on the desk.

'Pete. It just came over the radio. That cabbie you're after – he was seen turning west at Eastgate.'

So, he had gone full circle and back where he came from, using the traffic and the size of the roundabout to hide from Pete. 'Is anyone in pursuit?'

'No, it was a foot patrol that saw him.'

'Gimme the radio.' Pete reached over the high counter for it. 'All vehicles, all vehicles, this is DS Gayle. Suspect vehicle spotted west-bound on New North Road from Eastgate. Stop and apprehend. Repeat: stop and apprehend.' He reached over again and replaced the handset on its clip. 'Cheers, Bob.'

There was little point in rushing out again. The man could have gone anywhere from there.

The radio hissed again abruptly. 'Papa Charlie 4072 for DS Gayle. Did you say black Prius, registration ending yankee Charlie foxtrot?'

Pete exchanged a look with Bob, who passed him the handset. 'Affirmative.'

'Just spotted, headed north into St David's. In pursuit.' Pete heard the sirens just before the transmission cut off.

'Received. On route.' Pete passed the handset back again.

'Change of plan. Again.' He hurried out and back to his car. Starting the engine and the lights and sirens, he headed out as fast as he safely could, passing the traffic queue on the wrong side of the road and heading straight over the roundabout and up past the city council offices towards Eastgate and the New North Road. He was far enough back that he would be able to turn off as soon as the pursuit car told him which way to go.

As if on cue, his radio hissed. 'Subject turned right, right, right onto Cowley Bridge Road. That's northbound on Cowley Bridge Road.'

Heading out of the city, Pete thought. Of course, there were plenty of places he could turn off and cut back, maybe hoping to evade pursuit in the side streets if he knew them well enough. Which, given his job, he should do. Or maybe he was planning a long way around back to where he lived. There was a turnoff just up the Crediton Road that led all the way back down through the area where he lived. He keyed the mike again. 'DS Gayle. Is anyone attending the suspect's address in St Thomas yet?'

He reached the roundabout and turned left past the prison.

'Papa victor zero seven. On route, Sarge. Four minutes out.'

'Keep your eyes peeled. He might be planning to cut back down through Exwick.'

'Received.'

As Pete slowed again for the clock tower, the radio hissed again. 'Subject turned right, right, right into West Garth Road.'

So much for looping back homeward. Pete put his foot down, passing the sixties-looking art college on the left, followed by the technical college. He pictured the black car's location in his mind, streets of seventies- or eighties-built redbrick houses, many with their own garages, looping around and feeding off each other before emerging onto Wreford's Lane.

Pete pressed the Transmit button again. 'Received. Continue pursuit. I'm two minutes behind you.'

Hopefully, Ahmed was going to try to be clever. If so, he'd come unstuck if Pete could get there in time. His sirens seemed to get louder as he emerged onto Cowley Bridge Road, passing the low, brick-built flats on the left. Now he had walls on either side of him, the road feeling uncomfortably narrow at the speeds he was travelling. Cars and vans pulled over to let him through. Moments later, he passed the filling station on his left, a cyclist pedalling past it. He checked the mirror briefly. The cyclist had set one foot to the pavement as he wobbled in the unmarked car's unexpected slipstream.

The radio sounded again. 'Papa victor one two one. We've just turned onto Wreford's Road from Pennsylvania. If he comes this way, we can stop him.'

Pete reached for the mike. 'Thanks, Papa victor one two one.'

'Papa victor zero seven, arrived at target's address.'

'Don't crowd him, papa victor zero seven. Let him stop and get out of his vehicle, then apprehend.'

'Will do.'

Pete touched the brakes gently, slipping down the gears on the approach to West Garth Road.

'Subject turned left, left, into Ridgeway. Now approaching West Garth again.'

Would he meet him at the top of the hill? He made the turn. Keyed the mike. 'Turning into West Garth now.'

'He's gone left, left, towards Wreford's.'

Pete could hear the other car's sirens up ahead now. He put his foot down once more up the hill, the road curving left then right.

'Left, left,' came over the radio again. Would they trap him between two cars on Wreford's Lane? Surely he was planning to head for Pennsylvania and back down into the city?

'Left, left. Subject turned left, left on Wreford's Lane.'

'Shit,' Pete cursed.

He was doubling back.

Pete stopped at the end of a side road, reversed in and turned the car around, heading back down the hill, the way he'd come.

'Papa victor one two one, I can see papa Charlie four zero seven two ahead.'

'I'll be coming up Cowley Bridge Road to meet him,' Pete told them.

'Right, Sarge.'

He slowed at the bottom of the hill. The sirens were a warning to other road users, but you couldn't guarantee their reactions. Seeing it was safe, he pulled out, turning right. Now, hopefully, Ahmed was coming back around in a loop and they could trap him between them.

'Jesus, that was close! Turning right, right, right onto Cowley Bridge Road. Subject nearly got taken out by an artic. Barely missed it. *Shit!* Lorry skidding across the junction: possible jack-knife.'

'Son of a bitch,' Pete muttered. How lucky could this bastard get?

'Whoah! Two northbound cars on the pavement. I see his wheels turning.'

Pete was slowing as he approached the location. He could hear the juddering screech of tyres on tarmac. The lorry's engine roared as the driver tried to pull it back in line. Now he could see the big truck in the distance, trailer bouncing. Car tyres squealed as brake lights lit up, more vehicles mounting the pavement, trying to avoid the struggling lorry. It straightened on the wrong side of the road, then eased back over to the left carriageway.

'Target visual lost. You take the Stoke Road, we'll go left.' He heard the patrol cars continuing the pursuit. Saw the flash of blue lights beyond the slowing lorry.

The road wasn't really wide enough here for the guy to stop without causing traffic issues, but Pete couldn't blame him for doing so. He buzzed his window down and raised a hand in salute to the shocked driver. Passing him, he saw that, although four cars were up on the pavement, the only damage was a crushed bollard in the middle of the road on the approach to the roundabout beyond.

Which had probably helped the driver regain control, Pete guessed. It was still an impressive bit of driving, though.

'No visual on the target,' came over the radio as Pete reached the roundabout. 'Repeat, no visual on the target.'

He recognised which car was transmitting. 'Carry on up the Crediton Road, papa Charlie four zero seven two,' he said into the mike. 'I'll take the left onto St Andrews.'

'Roger.'

'And floor it, both of you. We need to find this guy.'

'Roger.'

'Will do.'

Both marked cars were gone from sight as Pete took to the wrong side of the road again to pass the four cars queueing up to the roundabout, then cut left and over the bridge. Seconds later, he hit the brakes hard and swung left into the narrow, rural lane that cut back south between high hedges and stone walls, broken here and there by field gates and the occasional farm house. He accelerated again, determined not to lose the cabbie. The road swept left and right through dips and rises. Only just over one car wide, passing places were few and far between, the tarmac damp-looking in the shadows of the overhanging trees and uncut hedges. Headlights on to increase his visibility, Pete pushed the car as hard as he dared. Now and then the road straightened out so he could see a couple of hundred yards or more, but he never glimpsed the black taxi. His radio was quiet. The two patrol crews would be concentrating hard, covering ground at least as fast as he was. Faster on the wider main roads.

Ahmed had only a few options from the Cowley Bridge junction. One of them had to spot him and catch him, surely.

The entrance to a narrow track flashed past on Pete's right, then a junction showed ahead. A small roundabout where the road split, the left fork continuing down through St Thomas, where Ahmed lived with his wife and two daughters, the right one looping up the hill and around, ultimately back down to join the

113

main route after passing through a widespread and convoluted area of suburban housing.

Pete slowed the car.

Which way? Would Ahmed go for speed or trickery?

'Shit.'

In the end, he had only one choice. He had to hope the taxi driver had opted for speed. If not, he could be anywhere, but if so, Pete might stand a chance of trapping him between himself and the car waiting for him in St Thomas.

He took the left fork, accelerating hard. Fifty yards further and the road curved left. He saw a bus stop, a woman standing beneath it. He made a flash decision, hit the brakes and killed the siren. Winding the side window down, he leaned over. 'Excuse me. Have you been there long?'

She was in her fifties, he guessed. A large woman in slacks and a dark blouse with tiny white polka dots. She leaned down to see his face. 'Three or four minutes. Bus is due any time now.'

Pete hadn't passed one, so he guessed it must be coming around through the residential area – you couldn't call it an estate and it certainly wasn't a village. 'Have you seen a black Toyota Prius come by? A taxi? He'd have been driving fast.'

She shook her head. 'Not since I've been here.'

Damn!

'OK. Thank you.'

He wound the window back up and drove on more slowly. There was no point turning around to search the maze of streets and cul-de-sacs off to his right. The taxi could be anywhere. He keyed the radio. 'DS Gayle. Any sign of the target vehicle?'

The first reply came. 'Not on the Stoke Road.'

Then the second. 'Crediton Road's clear.'

Bugger. He'd gone to ground somewhere. There was only one chance of finding him now. He keyed the radio again. 'OK. Thanks, guys. Papa victor zero seven, do you still have his house under observation?'

Chapter 12

Annie opened the front door as he locked the car and stepped away from it. 'Daddy!' She was actually bouncing with excitement. Then she paused, eying the package under his arm. 'What's that?'

'A hard disc drive.'

'What for?'

'That's a surprise. And not for you.'

'*Dad!*'

'In. I'll tell you in a minute. How was your day?'

'Good. We sa . . .' She stopped, realising she'd said more than she wanted to.

'You what?' Something had got her excited.

'We . . . I wanted to let Mum tell you.'

He stopped. 'Tell me what?'

She slumped, deflated. 'We went to see Tommy.'

'Brilliant.' He stepped forward and ruffled her hair. 'How is he?'

'He looks awful. Bruised and sore. He won't admit he's hurting, though.'

'Where's your mum?' Pete set his briefcase down at the bottom of the stairs.

'Front room.'

He went through, Annie following. 'Hi, Lou.' He stopped, his memory flashing back a few months to the height of her depression, when she would sit just where she was now, just as she was now, eyes glued to the TV, unresponsive. *Oh, God.* His stomach swooped as fear swept through him.

'Lou? You OK?'

She looked up at him, her eyes haunted.

Pete quickly sat beside her. He took one of her hands in his. It was cool and limp. 'He's back, love. And when everything gets sorted, he'll be home. We've just got to stay tough a little bit longer.' God, he hoped she could! That she wouldn't slip back into the depression she'd suffered before. He looked up at Annie, a question in his eyes.

She shrugged.

'Go and finish your homework, love. I'll come and see you when I've had a talk to your mum.'

She hesitated, looking from one to the other and back again. 'It's OK,' he said. 'I won't be long.'

Her shoulders slumped and she left the room while Pete turned back to Louise, stroking her hand. 'He's nearly home, Lou. And he'll be OK in there. It's one of the safest places he could be.'

'Safe?' She met his gaze, her eyes sparkling with anger. 'You didn't see him. The state he was in. All bruised and battered-looking. He didn't look safe to me. Just the opposite.'

His lips pressed together. 'I must admit, I was surprised by that. They normally keep violence and bullying pretty much at bay. It's one of the advantages of those places. They've got the staff to control it. But they'll keep an eye on him now. I'm sure they will.'

Louise slumped, the brief spark of fire extinguished. She was quiet for several seconds. 'I just can't work it out,' she said finally. 'Where did we go wrong? Tommy's the exact opposite of Annie. I don't understand how that can be.'

He squeezed her hand gently. 'Me neither, love. The only people who might claim to are the psychologists and they don't have all the answers.'

She straightened. 'Then what are we supposed to do?'

Pete pursed his lips. 'I wish to God I knew. I suppose all we can do is show him he's loved and wanted. What else is there?'

The haunted look was back in Louise's eyes as she met his gaze. 'I thought we did that before.'

'Well, we can't very well ask him what he wants or needs, can we? That *would* be a weird conversation.'

'But someone needs to.'

Pete realised with a jolt that she was serious. And she was right. 'Yeah, but who? Send him to a psychologist, he'll think we think he's sick.'

'Humph.' Louise seemed to be climbing out of the slump of depression. 'It needs to be someone who understands stuff like that and can be a sympathetic ear, though. Surely there'd be someone at Archways that'd specialise in that sort of thing?'

'Yeah, but can you see him opening up to anyone there? After what's happened?'

'Well, who else is there?'

Pete thought of Colin Underhill, but he was having to play the bad guy for now, so that idea was dead in the water. Then another name popped into his mind. He glanced at Louise. How would she feel about the idea? Not many months ago, she'd accused him of having an affair with the person he was thinking of. A groundless and false accusation, made in the depths of her depression, but it had stuck in his mind nevertheless.

Louise looked up at him. 'You've gone quiet. What is it?'

'I was thinking. Colin can't do it now. Not with the case and that. And I can't see it being in Dave's skill set. But there's Jane. Tommy knows her. Likes her. There's no axe to grind there.'

There was no reaction, Pete noted with relief. Then: 'Wouldn't she be in same position you are, being part of your team?'

Pete shook his head. 'If she goes as a friend, not a police officer . . .'

'Do you think he'd open up to a woman the same as he would to a man?'

117

Pete's head tilted. 'More, I'd have thought. Feelings and emotions are more of a woman thing, after all. With a bloke, he might not want to let on that he could be vulnerable. It would go against his pride. With a woman, that wouldn't apply – at least, not in the same way.' He shrugged. 'I don't know, but it's got to be worth a try, hasn't it?'

Louise gave a deep sigh. 'Maybe.'

He couldn't tell if her reaction was one of agreement, acceptance or resignation, but at least she wasn't yelling at him. He chose to take it as a good sign. Leaning over, he kissed the side of her head and stood up. 'Annie?' he called.

'Yes?'

Her voice came from the kitchen.

'What are you doing?' he asked as he headed that way.

'Homework,' she said, as if it was a stupid question.

Stepping into the kitchen, he saw her sitting at the table, her back to him, books open and pen in hand. He moved up behind her, wrapped his arms around her and gave her a squeeze. 'So, tell me about it.'

She put her pen down and turned to face him. 'He was like a different person. He recognised us, but he was a stranger, you know? I didn't say anything to Mum, but she must have noticed it too. She was quiet after we came out of there and just went into herself as soon as we got home. Back like she was before. I tried to pull her out of it, but . . .' She shrugged. 'She just wouldn't respond.' She looked up at him. 'He will be all right, won't he?'

Pete nodded. 'He's in one of the best places he could be for now, love. There's people in there – specialists – that can help him get better. Get back to his old self. And he'll be coming home in a few weeks, hopefully.'

She frowned. 'Why "hopefully"?'

'There's something that needs to be sorted out, from when he was found. And it depends what happens in Mr Burton's trial.'

'How can it? It's Mr Burton that's on trial, not Tommy.'

Pete sighed. 'It's complicated, love.'

'No, it isn't. Rosie Whitlock says Tommy helped her get away. That he was a victim too. It doesn't matter what Mr Burton says, if he tries to blame Tommy. He's the adult. Tommy's just a kid. He could make Tommy do whatever he wanted.'

Pete smiled down at her as love flared with a fierce intensity in his chest. 'You're a gem, you know that?'

'Mm-hm.' She nodded.

Pete laughed and placed a kiss on top of her head. 'Don't ever change, girly mine.'

Annie had been in bed for almost an hour. Pete had linked the two security cameras he had purchased to his laptop computer in the upstairs office – he had set them up on the front windowsills for tonight – and he was sitting with Louise, watching a documentary on the wildlife of Madagascar, when the phone rang in the hall. He got up quickly and went to pick it up.

'Gayle.'

'Pete, it's Andy. There's been another.'

He recognised the voice of one of the station sergeants, Andy Fairweather. 'Another what?'

'Taxi driver killing.'

'Where? When?'

'Not sure exactly when, but in the last couple of hours. And where is down by the river. Friars Green.'

'OK, I'm on the way.' He put the phone down and stepped back into the sitting room. 'Work. The taxi driver case I told you about. There's been another one.'

Louise looked at her watch. 'What about St Thomas? It's only a couple of hours or so until you're due to take watch.'

Pete had told her about Shafiq Ahmed and that he had accepted the next watch rota on his house. He shrugged. 'We'll get it covered by someone else, if need be. I'll see when I get to the crime scene, I suppose.'

She nodded. 'Be safe, OK?'

He gave her a smile and a kiss, grabbed his jacket on the way out and headed to the scene.

Friars Green was a modern luxury riverside apartment complex, including boutique shops and manicured gardens, across the river from the old quay. As Pete drove into the complex on Haven Road, minutes later, headlights shone into the back of his car. He recognised their shape and size. For once, he'd beaten the pathologist to the site, if only just. They parked next to each other and walked together towards the group of uniformed police officers that signified the presence of a crime scene.

'We meet again, Peter.'

'Evening, Doc. What have they told you?'

'Just that there's work for me here. Another taxi driver, apparently.'

'Yeah. Same here.' They both lifted their IDs as they approached the blue and white tape that cordoned off the immediate scene. The PC manning the tape lifted it for them and they ducked under. A break in the closely packed officers in front of them showed the dark shape of a car and the yellow light on top of it. A man turned to face them.

Pete nodded to him. 'Mike. What have we got?'

'Deceased male in the driver's seat matches the ID in the car, Sarge.'

'And who reported it?'

'A resident, returning home from the flicks. He's over there.'

Pete looked in the direction the uniformed man was pointing. A man was sitting in the back of a patrol car, the rear door open and another PC standing by him. He looked pale and shaken, even from a distance. He'd probably benefit from a minute or two longer.

'Let's have a look at the victim first.'

The car was parked neatly in a space, about as far from a streetlight as you could get in the parking area belonging to the complex. Looking over Doc Chambers' shoulder, Pete saw that the driver's seat appeared to be in the correct position for him.

He was slumped back in it, his head tipped back against the headrest, a curtain of blood like a bib down the front of his shirt. More blood was sprayed across the inside of the windscreen and over the dashboard and steering wheel. It had dripped down and pooled in the footwell.

Although he was pale from a combination of death and blood loss, the victim was an Indian male.

Another Indian male.

Was that significant? Given that the majority of taxi drivers in the city were of that ethnic origin, if the two deaths were linked, then was it about race or simply about taxi drivers? Or was there another link he hadn't seen yet?

'What's the verdict, Doc?'

Chambers didn't look up from what he was doing. 'Single cut to the throat. No hesitation marks. Like the other one, a thin, sharp blade was used. Unlike the other one, I don't detect any lingering odour of pepper spray, but I have taken swabs and I'll check further, back at the mortuary.'

Even from a few steps back, Pete's sense of smell was overwhelmed by the ferrous stink of blood. It would be easy to miss a lingering hint of pepper spray under that, he imagined. Especially if it had been a while since it was used. 'Any idea how long he's been here?'

'Body temperature and the blood spray would suggest no more than an hour. The meter there might tell you more.' He nodded at the taxi fare meter on the far side of the body.

'Still running?'

'Indeed.'

'Right. I'll go and have a word with the bloke who found him.'

Approaching the patrol car with its rear door still open, he saw that the occupant was probably in his thirties, dressed in a casual but expensive-looking shirt and dark trousers. His dark hair was carefully styled, his pale features clean-cut. He didn't look up as Pete approached. His gaze was turned inward, eyelids half-closed.

Pete nodded to the officer standing by the car.

'I understand you found the body, sir,' he said.

The man registered his presence and looked up at last. He blinked. 'Yes.'

'You live here?'

'Juniper House.' He waved a hand vaguely, indicating the block behind him, overlooking the river and the footbridge across to the old quay with its pub, antique emporium and archway shops and cafés.

'And your name?'

'Danny Byford.'

'So, tell me what happened, Danny. How did you come to find him?'

'I was on my way back from the multiplex. I dropped my girlfriend off at her place, drove back here. That's my car.' He indicated a small Japanese sports model parked a row in front of the taxi. 'I saw the taxi there. When I got out of the car, I noticed the engine was off. I looked over, could see the guy's face – how his head was tilted back. I thought maybe he was asleep or something. I went over and . . .' He gave a shuddering breath. 'I saw why it was only his face I could see from a distance. All that blood . . .! So I called you guys.' He lifted his right hand, which was clutching a mobile phone.

'And you haven't been up to your flat since then?'

He looked confused for a second. 'No. The man on the phone said to stay put, so I did.'

'Did you see anyone else here, before the other officers arrived?'

Danny shook his head. 'No. There've been a few people since. Residents, I suppose. But not before. Why?'

Pete shrugged. 'We have to get as full a picture as we can. OK, Danny. You get off home now. We'll be in touch if we need to ask you anything more.'

'Thanks.'

Danny stood up out of the car and headed away, still looking dazed.

Pete would get the time of his 999 call from the call centre. Then, in canvassing for other witnesses, they could be accurate in finding out if anyone had been seen leaving the area. In the meantime . . . He looked across the square to where a small group of people stood at the police tape. Heading towards them, he let his eyes scan the onlookers, searching for any abnormal behaviour, anyone who looked out of place or nervous, anyone who looked as if they were not simply curious.

As he drew near to the tape, he saw no one trying to slip away in the darkness. 'Evening, folks,' he said, hands raised to include them all. 'If anyone saw anything out of place around here this evening, anything unusual, anyone they haven't seen before, please come and tell me or one of the other officers here.'

As he was talking, the white panel van of the forensics team arrived and disgorged the already white-overalled investigators.

'What's happened here?' a female voice asked from the small crowd.

Pete tried to spot her, but couldn't. 'There's been a death. At this stage, all I can tell you is that it appears to be suspicious. Officers will go through the complex shortly to ensure your safety. In the meantime, as I said before, if anyone has any information, no matter how innocuous or irrelevant it may seem, please do let us know.'

He stepped back from the tape and headed over to the forensics van, where the scientists were donning caps, shoe covers, gloves and masks before approaching the scene. He recognised the plump figure of the chief technician, his glasses gleaming in the intermittent lights from the police cars around them. 'Evening, Harold. How's it going?'

'Detective Sergeant Gayle.'

'I won't delay you, but give me a call when you're done, yes?'

'Of course.'

Pete moved on to where Tony Chambers was just stepping back from the car and removing his gloves. 'Any more news, Doc?'

'Nothing helpful. Just the one injury. No defence wounds. It appears the attacker was in the back seat. The efficiency of the killing might suggest premeditation, but beyond that, we're into your territory.'

'OK. Thanks.' Pete pulled on a pair of nitrile gloves and stepped around the other man to the open door of the victim's car. He leaned in and used his phone to take a picture of the ID hanging from the driving mirror. Checking the door pocket, he stepped back and moved around to the passenger side. Carefully opening the door, he checked the glove box but found only the car's owner's manual, a pen and notepad, and some chewing gum. Next, he photographed the meter, followed by the dead man's watch. The two together would give them a timeframe in which the victim's last passenger must have been picked up.

Looking up, he saw the white-suited forensics team approaching, aluminium cases in hand. He stepped back from the car, taking one last photo of the licence plate on the rear. 'All yours, Harold.'

Pete parked a few yards down from the cab company's office and walked back up. As he stepped away from his car, a crowd of people began to emerge from the old cinema beyond his destination, most seeming to come towards him down the narrow side street, filling the pavement and spilling out across the narrow cobbled roadway as they chatted and laughed, voices echoing off the surrounding buildings.

Pete stepped between two parked taxis in front of the office and eased through the flowing crowd to the open door.

Two men were sitting inside, cups of tea in hand, while a woman perhaps ten years older than Pete, stocky, with rough, smoker's skin and way too much make-up under a thatch of bleached-blonde hair, sat behind a desk with a phone console and radio mike in front of her. She looked up as he entered.

Pete nodded and was lifting his ID from his pocket when he was barged from behind by a guy in his late twenties with his shirt hanging out of his trousers and a girl in a short, sparkly dress hanging on his arm.

'We need a taxi to the university.'

'In a sec, son. You weren't the first in here.' The woman's voice was rougher than her complexion; almost masculine.

Pete held up his warrant card. 'Don't mind me. I don't need a ride.'

She nodded and looked across at the two drivers sitting at the side of the room. 'Amrit?'

One of them shrugged, set his mug down on the window ledge and stood up.

Pete watched him leave, the giggling couple trailing after him, then turned back to the woman. Checking the photo on his phone, he asked, 'Do you know a Sunil Pati?'

'You know I do, or you wouldn't be here.' She thrust her chin at the remaining cabbie across the scruffy little room. 'That's his brother. What's he done?'

'That's what I'd like to find out. Whatever it was, I'm afraid I've got some bad news for you.' He turned to face the seated man. 'Your brother was found deceased this evening, Mr Pati.'

'Deceased?' The man frowned. 'He's . . . dead? How? When? Where is he?' He stood up, his tea forgotten as grief and anger fought for dominance on his face.

Pete lifted his hands in a placating gesture. Glanced at the woman, then focused on the bereaved brother. 'Mr Pati, we're doing everything we can to catch whoever did this and we'll continue in that effort until we apprehend them. But, to make that happen, I need to find out everything I can about your brother, in order to work out why this might have happened.'

The man turned on Pete, rage twisting his face now. 'You think this was his own fault? That he doesn't deserve justice if you can find fault with him?'

'Not at all,' Pete said, struggling to stay where he was. 'As I said, we're going to do everything possible to bring whoever did this to justice. All their motive does is make it easier for us to figure out who they are. One of my officers is talking to his wife now. We'll be speaking to his neighbours, colleagues – everyone we can. It's standard procedure. Now, have a seat, Mr Pati.'

Pete waited until he stopped pacing the small room and returned to his seat. His mug of tea remained on the windowsill, forgotten as he leaned his elbows on his knees, face covered by his hands. The rise and fall of his shoulders gradually reduced as he calmed down until, finally, he let his hands fall between his knees and looked up, grief filling his eyes.

Pete held his gaze. 'So, can you tell me if your brother's had any problems with anyone recently? If anyone holds a specific grudge against him?'

Chapter 13

Back in the squad room, Pete pulled up another whiteboard and started filling in the details of the second victim. Then he paused, an idea crossing his mind. Back at his desk, he switched on his computer and entered the Police National Database. Keying in Sunil Pati's name and date of birth, he hit return on the search page and waited for the system to churn out what it would.

It took only a couple of seconds.

One arrest for possession of a controlled substance, a little over two years ago.

So, was this some sort of turf war? Had the major sweep on local drug dealers a few months ago left a vacuum that was now starting to be filled? He frowned and looked across at the other board. The first victim, Ranjeet Singh, had no known drug connections.

He was reminded of another case he'd worked recently. A university student and his buddy had instigated a clean-up campaign across the city, killing off 'undesirables' of various sorts in ways that attempted to conceal the murders as natural deaths. Was this a copycat? One suspected drug dealer and one possible rapist . . .

He shook his head. No. That was too much of a coincidence.

So, was it a race thing? Both were Indian males. Then again, both were taxi drivers, so it could as easily be about that. Perhaps some kind of revenge thing or, again, a turf war. He'd heard nothing about strife between the city's firms, but it would be worth checking with the licensing office at the local council in the morning as well as with the uniformed branch.

He picked up the phone and dialled the front desk.

'Drummond.'

'Bill, it's Pete Gayle. Quick question. Have you heard anything about any problems between the taxi firms in the city? Any sort of agro?'

'No. Why? You thinking this guy tonight might have been involved in something?'

'Hmm. Just thinking through the possibilities. Another one is the fact that he's got drugs in his background.'

'We swept all that up last November, though, didn't we?'

'Yeah, but we didn't get rid of the demand, just the supply. Somebody's going to fill the gap eventually, aren't they?'

'True.'

'I take it you're not aware of any new sources cropping up lately then?'

'No. Doesn't mean there aren't any, of course. We're always the last to know.' He laughed.

'Yeah. Thanks, Bill.' Pete put the phone down, thinking of Darren Westley. That was his specialist subject, as a rule. He hadn't seen or spoken to the lad in months and now he was going to do so twice in a couple of days.

He stood up, grabbed his jacket and slipped his mobile phone into the pocket. He was stepping away from his desk when his phone rang. He paused. Checked the big clock on the wall at the far end of the room. Who the hell was going to be calling at this time of night?

He sighed, turned back to his desk and picked up the phone. 'DS Gayle.'

'Pete. Bill, on the front desk. I've got a call for you. From Panama.'

'Panama? Who the hell's calling from there?' He knew no one in Central America. He'd never been further west than Falmouth.

'A Martin Devonish.'

'Means nothing to me. OK, put him through. Let's see what he wants.'

'Right-o.'

There was a click, then another. 'Hello? DS Gayle speaking, Exeter CID. What can I do for you, Mr Devonish?'

'It's more the other way round, actually.' Pete instantly recognised the man's local accent, despite the hollow echo on the faint line. 'I've just seen a report on the news about Ranjeet Singh's death. My wife and I own Cathedral Cabs. He used to drive for us.'

'Ah, yes. So, what can you tell me about him?'

Pete recalled Dave's remarks about Singh having a couple of complaints against him; one just before he left.

'Well, most of the time, he was the picture of politeness and professionalism, but there were a couple of occasions when we had cause for concern. After the second one, we let him go. There was never anything official – the customers didn't want to take it that far – but it wouldn't have done our reputation any good if we'd kept him on, so . . .' The man's voice tailed off. Pete could almost see his shrug down the phone line.

'So, what can you tell me about these instances, Mr Devonish?'

'They were about a year or so apart. The first one was a molestation complaint. A young woman reckoned he'd groped her backside as she was getting out of the car. She was angry, offended, but to be honest, the way she was dressed . . . I mean, I'm not condoning or excusing what he did for a second, but it made me wonder at the time if she might have a reason for avoiding the police. Do you know what I mean?'

Pete's mind went back to the previous evening around Queen's Square and the clock tower. 'I get the idea.'

'Then the second one – well, that was a lot more serious. I was amazed the girl didn't want to press charges, but it's their choice, isn't it? At the end of the day, if it goes to court, they've got to go through it all again, but with an audience, haven't they? I mean, I can see why, but it's nasty, really, isn't it? Like they're being victimised – attacked – all over again by the state.'

'What can you tell me about her?'

'She was younger. Fifteen, I think. Indian girl although she was wearing Western clothes. Nothing too revealing, not like the first one. Just typical teenage gear. And this time, he actually raped her. Or at least, she said so. Again, there was no police involvement. She insisted. Got quite tearful about it.'

'OK. Do you remember a name for either of the victims?'

'I asked, of course. Wrote it all down at the time. The first one had a name I thought sounded professional. False. Cindy something . . ..' He trailed off as if he was thinking. 'Cindy Cummings, that was it. The girl had an Indian name, of course. Leela Banerjee. I'll never forget her. She was devastated, poor kid. But she was adamant. Didn't want us to call anyone. Not even her parents. I don't think we'd have even known about it if it hadn't been for the others.'

'Others?'

'Three of them. Two white girls and another Indian one. She'd been on the way to meet them, apparently. They saw the state she was in and marched her straight down to the office, despite the fact she didn't want to come.'

'OK. Any other details on any of them, Mr Devonish?'

'Yeah. One of them was the daughter of another of our drivers. Tony Seger. He's still with the firm. One of the few.'

'How's that?'

'English taxi drivers in Exeter. Most are Indian or Bangladeshi nowadays.'

Pete had noticed the same, but he wasn't going to comment and open himself up to accusations of racism. 'Well, thanks for the call, Mr Devonish. You've been very helpful.'

'No problem. DS Gayle, was it?'

'That's right.'

'Well, best of luck catching whoever did for Ranjeet. As long as it wasn't one of his victims, that is.'

Pete knew what the guy meant, even if he couldn't condone the sentiment. 'Enjoy the rest of your holiday, Mr Devonish.'

'Will do.'

There was a click as the call ended. Pete picked up his notepad and crossed to the whiteboards to add the new information.

Darren Westley was in his favourite haunt – the pool hall on Fore Street.

Pete walked in at ten to eleven. He didn't know what time these places closed, but business seemed to be still brisk. The tables were all occupied and several bystanders with pint glasses in hand were standing around watching. Pete spotted Darren's mop of red hair at the second table from the far end as he leaned down to take a shot. The bar was along the left side of the long, narrow room. Pete headed to the right and eased his way along, close to the wall. By the time he'd passed the five intervening tables, Darren had potted whichever ball he had been aiming at and was in a new position, at the near end of the table, lining up another shot.

Pete slipped around behind a big man with a long, strawberry-blond beard and close-cropped hair, a half-empty pint glass in his hand, just as Darren's arm swung forward. There was the crack of cue on ball, the second crack of two balls hitting, and then the black angled cleanly across to the far corner pocket. It dropped in without touching the sides.

'Nice shot,' he said loud enough for Darren to hear him.

The red-haired youth's head snapped up and around as he recognised the voice. His narrow face took on a frown.

Forty-three popped up on the LED scoreboard above the far end of the table. His opponent had sixteen.

Pete gave him a wink. 'Doing well, Darren.'

Darren's lip curled into a brief sneer. He turned back to the table without speaking, moved around to replace the black on its spot and lined up a red into the left middle. His cue arm swung gently as he readied himself then drove through. *Click, click.* The red rolled towards the pocket, the white ball staying dead still, in position for the black again. Pete watched as the red rolled to the pocket, gently thumped the side cushion and stayed on the table.

'Oooh.' He joined the general groan of disappointment. 'Bad luck, Darren.'

As his opponent stepped up to the table, Darren stalked over to where Pete was standing, his face set in a scowl.

'That's the first ball I've missed tonight,' he said. 'And I seem to remember you don't believe in coincidences, so what does that tell you?'

Pete shrugged. 'Some you win, eh?'

Balls clicked and Darren glanced over his shoulder as the red he'd left over the middle pocket went in, the cue ball rolling swiftly away up the length of the table. He turned back to Pete. 'So, what do you want? You're not here for the beer – or for the snooker, I'm guessing.'

'Something came up a little while ago and I thought of you, Darren. Thought you might be able to answer a quick question for me.'

The click of balls sounded again and they both turned to watch the black drop into the corner pocket again. The dark-haired, clean-cut player came around the table, respotted the black and took position for his next shot.

'Depends on the question.'

'Well, once upon a time, there was this taxi driver here in Exeter. Indian chap.'

Darren grunted sardonically.

'Well, turns out he had a record for drug dealing. Only minor. But a few months after nearly all the dealers in the city were swept up and put away where they belong, all of a sudden he's killed. So, I'm wondering if it's related to his past. Specifically, the drugs. Was he, perhaps, dealing again? Got caught up in a turf war of some sort? You haven't heard about anything like that going on, have you? I mean, there's bound to be some new players coming in to replace the old – fill the gap in the market. No telling who they might be or how ruthless. And I dare say you know better than I do what kinds of crap they cut the drugs with nowadays, to boost the profit margins. They certainly don't give a shit about the customer, do they?'

'*Whoah.*'

'*Shot.*'

Applause rippled around the table as Darren's opponent sank another ball, this one a long shot sending the pink into the far corner pocket, the cue ball bouncing off three cushions to come around for the last remaining free red on the table.

Darren looked from the table to Pete and back again. He could see the game running away from him. He shook his head. Pete wasn't sure if it was in response to his question or simply his presence here and the effect it appeared to be having on Darren's concentration.

'I haven't heard about nothing like that.'

'So, where's the demand getting filled from now?'

Balls smacked together and, from the corner of his eye, Pete saw the bunched reds going everywhere, including one of them into a corner pocket. Darren's opponent leaned over the table, lining up the black again.

Darren stepped in closer to Pete, his voice dropping to a murmur that Pete could barely hear over the general noise of the place. 'Mostly from out of town. Southampton and Bristol.'

Pete smiled. 'You sure you're not protecting your source, Darren?'

'And have you after me for aiding and abetting? Yeah, right.'

Pete slapped him on the shoulder. 'Just pulling your chain, mate. Best get back to your game while there still is one.'

'Thanks.' They both looked at the scoreboard. The bright-red numbers told them that Darren had been overtaken. His opponent was now on sixty-three with the reds spread across the table and only the pink resting near a cushion, making it difficult to play.

'Oh, well. Next frame, eh?' Pete said lightly.

He didn't hear Darren's response as he stepped away towards the entrance.

There was one more source Pete could check with tonight. This one might be harder to track down than Darren, but his information came without Darren's conflict of interest. It wasn't that Pete disbelieved Darren. He had more than enough on the lad to keep him honest. But it never hurt to be doubly sure.

He headed back to the car, climbed in and keyed the police radio. 'DS Gayle. General call. Does anyone have a location on Mick Duggan? I need to talk to him.'

Static hissed over the airwaves for a moment, then a voice cut through it. 'This is PC Collimore. I passed the old garage plot where he was last known to be living about half an hour ago. There was a fire going there.'

'Thanks. I know the place.'

Pete started the engine and headed across to the site where a set of old garages had been pulled down to allow for a housing development that never happened. It had been occupied by a few of the local homeless for months now, living illegally in tents behind the high wooden hoarding. The council had yet to do anything about it, despite several complaints from the surrounding householders. And the police couldn't intervene until either the council or the landowner asked them to.

The narrow, mainly residential street had very few unoccupied parking spaces at this time of night. Pete parked a hundred and fifty yards or so further up the street and walked back. The night was warm, the sky clear. As he neared the site he glimpsed the orange glow of flames between the big boards that closed it off

134

from its surroundings. Slipping through the gap he knew the illegal occupants used, the first thing he noticed was the lack of smell. Last time he'd been here, the place stank. They must have cleaned it up in order to keep the council away.

Over towards the back of the site there were now five tents where before there had only been three. The fire was in front of the one at the far left. Pete could see a figure hunched over it, sitting on an old camp stool. He heard the soft sounds of a guitar over the crackle of flames and glimpsed the long blond beard overhanging the front of the man's jacket.

'Hey, Mick. How's it going?' he called as he stepped closer.

'Who's that?'

The figure put down the guitar and stood up. Pete could see him clearly now in the firelight. He looked as menacing as his voice had sounded, long hair hanging over his shoulders from under his battered and stained cowboy hat.

'Pete Gayle,' he said, stepping closer to the light.

Hands deep in his pockets, Duggan didn't move until Pete got close enough to be seen. Pete couldn't blame him for his suspicion. Around the time they had first met, two of the site's other occupants had been victims of a multiple murderer.

'Oh, it's you.' Duggan visibly relaxed, pulling his hands out of his pockets and straightening up to his full height of just under six feet.

'Haven't seen you for a while. Been keeping out of trouble?' Pete grinned.

'Mostly. What brings you round here at this time of night?' He extended a hand, which Pete shook. The man's hands were hard and calloused, his grip firm.

'Wanted to ask you about something.'

Duggan grunted.

'I'm wondering what's going on in the local drug trade lately. I know you're not into the stuff, but I expect you know a few that are. I need to know a bit about who's dealing nowadays.

Where the supply's coming from, that sort of thing. I've got a murder victim who might be tied into it somehow.'

Duggan was nodding slowly. He stopped at the mention of murder. Looked at Pete sharply.

'Indian bloke. Taxi driver.'

Duggan nodded. 'No links there as I know of. Far as I've heard, it's coming in from out of town since that foreign bunch got closed down. Bristol. Southampton. Bit from Brum, or so they reckon. Lot of Indians up there.'

'Yes. And a lot of them involved in the drug trade. Thanks, Mick.' Pete drew his hand from his pocket and held out a folded note to Duggan. 'Spend it on solids, eh?'

Duggan gave a grunt that might have been laughter. 'Why change the habits of a lifetime?'

Pete clapped him on the shoulder with one hand as he stuffed the note into his coat pocket with the other. 'It's called survival, mate.'

'Yeah, and look where that gets you.' Duggan held out his hands to their surroundings.

'Fair enough.' Pete paused. 'So, what did you do, other than the music? Before this?'

'I was a bus driver for a bit. A postie before that.'

'And you couldn't get back into either of those? Or something else?'

'See me in an interview, can you?' He shook his head. 'I'll stick to the music career, thanks.' He gave a dry laugh. 'At least it keeps the wolf from the tent flap.'

Pete nodded. Duggan was a busker – and a good one – playing a mix of country and blues wherever he could find a place on the city's streets. 'Well, take care, eh? Wouldn't want a talent like yours to go to waste. I'll see you around.'

'Heard they found your boy. Look after him, yeah?'

'I intend to.' Pete raised his hand in a wave as he headed back towards the fence at the front of the site.

It never ceased to amaze him how someone like Duggan could get to hear of all sorts of things, many that didn't concern him in the least. But it could sometimes prove useful.

If there was gear coming down from the Midlands, that could be the link he was looking for. It was certainly something to look into, come the morning.

But in the meantime, what was he going to do about Tommy? As Duggan had said, he had to be there for the boy. To look after him. But, how could he? He was both a suspect and a witness in a case Pete had worked, which was going to court in a few weeks. Even if the knife thing got set aside – which was unlikely – they wouldn't be allowed to share a roof until after the trial, even if Tommy himself wasn't charged, which was still a possibility. And yet . . . Tommy was his son. He had to do something.

He slipped through the hoarding and started up the road towards his car. He was still struggling with the question when he unlocked the car and climbed in. Shutting the door, he took out his phone and hit a speed-dial number.

The call was answered with a dull, sleepy 'Hello?'

'Sorry, Jane. I didn't mean to wake you.'

'Boss? What's up?' She sounded a little more awake now.

'I was going to ask you a favour. I didn't realise what time it was until you answered.'

'Well, I'm awake now. What do you need?'

'It's . . .' He grimaced, suddenly less sure that he wanted to ask her. 'It's a personal thing. I wouldn't ask, but I don't know who else would be better able.'

'OK.'

'It's Tommy. Louise and Annie went to see him this afternoon. He's . . . well, he needs to talk to someone. A friendly face. I know they've got professionals at Archways, but there's no way he'd open up to anyone there. I thought maybe you might be able to . . . you know . . .'

'Spit it out, will you? Jesus! Men! What's the matter with you? It's like trying to have a conversation with a different species sometimes.'

'Steady on. I was only asking a favour.'

'For a clever bloke, you're amazingly dense sometimes, Pete Gayle. Now, bugger off and let me sleep.'

There was a click and Pete was left holding a dead phone.

What the hell?

Chapter 14

Louise was curled up in her usual spot on the sofa, watching a late-night rerun of an American cop show about a mystery writer who'd hooked up with a police unit.

She looked up as he came in. 'You were a long time. How'd it go?'

'Well, the crime scene doesn't look like it's going to give us anything, but I've spoken to a couple of contacts and I might have developed a starting point.' He grinned. 'We might even be able to blame Fast-track for it, indirectly.'

She laughed. 'Now, that would be a turn-up for the books! How come?'

'Operation Natterjack. He killed off the drug trade in the city. At least, the supply side of it. So, the demand needs filling from elsewhere. Places like Bristol and Birmingham, where a good part of it's controlled by the Indian and Pakistani communities. And our new victim has previous for drugs.'

'Mmm.' She was nodding slowly. 'Works for me. I don't think it'll be enough to get rid of him, though.'

'Huh. No, but it's another nail to save up for his coffin. I see there's been no new activity out the front here.'

'Good. Maybe whoever it is has made their point or got bored and given up.'

'Yeah. We can but hope.'

She looked across at him, her expression serious.

'You don't believe it, though, do you?'

Pete grimaced.

Louise shifted around in her seat to face him. 'So, what are we going to do about it? Who do you reckon it is?'

Pete grimaced. 'My first thought was the Armenian – or someone on his behalf, at least. But it seems too petty for them. They're some serious players. And I can't see it being connected to Frank Benton. The most likely suspects seem to be Malcolm Burton and Neil Sanderson, as far as I can see. Or again, someone acting for them or in support of them.'

'Paedophiles.'

He paused. That aspect of it hadn't occurred to him, but she was right. That's what the two men were and that's why anyone else might be acting on their behalf. He had potentially brought paedophiles to their door. To Annie's door. *Shit.* If anything happened to her . . . 'There's no way Annie's walking to or from school on her own until we've got whoever it was.'

'That poor kid's life is being ruined.'

'We'll catch them – whoever they are,' he said firmly. His mind threw up an image of the two security cameras mounted, for now, in the bottom corners of two of the front windows of the house. With no way of knowing who was targeting them or when they might be watching, he'd decided that the weekend would be the best time to put them up on the house. He would make it look like part of his normal maintenance of the property. Maybe clean the gutters or something and screw them into place while he was up there. Or, better yet, as tiny as they were, maybe he could put them up with superglue. That would make it a lot easier to hide what he was doing.

'Mmm.' He nodded to himself.

'What?'

'Just thinking. Planning. If they come back, I've got a way of identifying them.'

'What – those cameras?'

'Partly. For confirmation, though, I'm going to need to get a couple of things from the DIY shop, then have a word with young Ben, see if he can do a bit of jiggery-pokery for me.'

'Oh, yeah?'

He winked. 'Nothing illegal, but it should act as a deterrent and a confirmation at the same time, if it works as I'm thinking.'

Louise pursed her lips. 'There's two words I don't like in there. Should and if. We've already come too close for comfort to losing Tommy. If any harm comes to Annie through that job of yours . . .'

'I know.' Pete's stomach fluttered nervously. 'I wouldn't forgive myself, either. Don't worry. It won't. We won't let it.'

'Yeah, well, that's the thing, isn't it? I do worry. And I will until you catch whoever's been doing that out there.' She nodded towards the front of the house. 'But there's one possibility you haven't mentioned yet as to who it might be.'

Pete frowned. 'Who's that?'

'Mates of Tommy.'

'Wh . . .' He stopped, head tipping to one side. 'Mmm.' She was right. Both incidents had been fairly juvenile. He nodded. Smiled. 'You're not just a pretty face, after all.'

She swung a punch at his shoulder. 'This is no laughing matter.'

'I know. But if it's a choice of laugh or cry . . .'

She drew a long, deep breath. 'Yeah, I suppose.'

It was good she was now capable of either, Pete thought. The only emotion she'd been able to express during her depression was anger. And the only target she'd been able to identify for it had been him.

'Ben,' Pete said as he dropped his jacket over the back of his chair at just before nine the next morning, having come from the graveyard shift at Shafiq Ahmed's place. 'Are you still into electronics and stuff?'

'Yes, when I get the time. Why?'

'I've got a little project for you.'

'What's that, boss?'

'In the car I've got a watering timer, a hosepipe, a sprinkler and one of those security lights with a motion sensor. Is there a way you can combine all that so that the motion sensor can switch on the watering timer and trigger the sprinkler?'

Ben grinned. 'Sounds like fun. Is this for your front garden?'

Pete nodded.

'I'm liking this,' Dave said. 'We need video footage.'

'That can be arranged.'

'Yes!' He slapped his desk.

'I'll have to take it all home, take it apart and do a bit of soldering, but I should be able to make it work.'

'Good. There's one more thing I need to get hold of before I set it up, then we'll see what happens. Meantime, what's anybody got on the case?' He looked from one face to another.

'I've tracked down the Seger girl and spoken to her,' Jane said. 'Holly. She's married now, changed her name to Jennings. Lives in Paignton.'

'And what did she have to say?'

'Pretty much what you were told last night. They had a struggle to get the victim to go to the taxi office. There was no way she was coming here. But when she met them that night, she was bruised, sore and bloody, her underwear was ripped and bloodstained, she was shaking like a leaf, make-up shot, and really just wanted to go home, but couldn't until she'd sorted herself out.'

'All of which confirms her story,' Dave said.

Jane nodded.

'While Jane was onto her, I looked a bit further into the new victim,' Dave continued. 'He's only got the one conviction, but he was better known to us than that suggests. I've spoken to a few local uniforms. He had quite the rep for being able to get

142

whatever you wanted a while ago. Connections in London and Birmingham. After the arrest, though, he went quiet.'

'Learned his lesson, eh?' asked Dick.

'Learned something, at least,' Pete agreed. 'If only how to stay out of our way. We need to follow that up further. See which option's the right one.'

'There's no record of a Cindy Cummings anywhere – surprise, surprise,' Jill said. 'Except the PND links the name as an alias to a hooker who was operating in the city until eighteen months ago. Real name was Monica Parry. Now Devlin.'

'And where's she now?'

'Gone straight. Got married and taken on a pub with her husband. In fact, I think you spoke to her a few months ago, boss. They run the Firkin.'

Pete remembered her instantly. Fiftyish, small and fit with curly blonde hair, a dry, coarse voice and an open, helpful manner. He'd interviewed her about a couple of male students who had been regular customers in there and who had turned out to be the suspects in a series of killings in the city. He nodded. 'That's right. I'll go and talk to her again. Meantime, we need to track our second victim back to where he picked up his last fare. See if there's any CCTV that'll help us identify who it was or pick out any potential witnesses.'

'Talking of identifying suspects,' said Jane. 'Who do you reckon's been targeting your place?'

'Well, that's what the cameras are for,' Pete said. 'To save us having to speculate.'

'I know, but if they don't pick anyone up, or if they do and whoever it is isn't identifiable . . .'

'Well, then we come back to the timing, I suppose. We've got several trials coming up in the next few weeks. Burton. Sanderson. Frank. Petrosyan . . . although it's not likely to be him. Too subtle. And Burton's family and colleagues have all taken a step or two back from him. They've got to, in the circumstances, haven't they? Get tarred with a brush like that, they'll be out of a job pretty quick.'

'Well, I can't see anyone liking Frank enough to risk their careers for him,' Ben said.

'No, but the people he dealt with might,' Jill put in. 'The ones he sold to. There's a lot of money involved there and you cut off their supply. They're not going to be happy about that.'

Frank Benton was an ex-copper, a former member of CID who had been illegally taking and selling the eggs and chicks of birds of prey since before he retired from the force. Pete and Ben had tracked him down in the hills to the west of the city, on the edge of Dartmoor, and caught him almost red-handed.

Pete nodded. 'It's possible.'

'The other choice is Neil Sanderson,' Dave said. 'Not personally, of course, being in the clink, but his associates. The perverts he was sharing pictures with. Again, we've cut off their supply, haven't we?'

'And round we go, full circle,' Jane observed.

'The only way to break out of that is to get some firm evidence,' Pete said. 'And that's what the cameras and sprinkler system are for.'

'So, how's the sprinkler going help?' Dave asked. 'I mean, yes, it'll wet them, but so what?'

'Ah, well,' Pete said. 'It depends what you wet them with.'

'Something that's not going to ruin your lawn, I hope,' said Dick.

Pete grinned. 'It might confuse the bees for a while, but that's all.'

'It'd take a hell of a pump to push honey through a sprinkler system. A fair bit of honey too.' Dave's comment drew a laugh from the whole team.

'That's what I've got to go out to Middlemoor for,' Pete said.

'What, the honey or the pump?'

'I've got something a bit more subtle than that in mind.'

Jane reached across and patted Dave's leg. 'Never mind. You wouldn't understand, Dave.'

'Oi!' He turned back to Pete. 'Come on then, boss. Out with it.'

'UV dye packs.'

Dave grinned. 'Oh, yes. I like that. They won't even know about it until we catch up with them and the proof'll be all over them. Even if they change clothes before we catch them.' He turned to Jane. 'See. Ye of little faith.'

'OK. Colour me surprised.'

'Yeah, and colour them violet,' said Ben.

'So, how's that going to confuse the bees?' Dave asked.

'Bees see ultraviolet,' Dick told him. 'Don't you watch nature programmes on telly?'

'Not the sort that tell you stuff like that, I bet,' said Jill.

Pete stepped out of the Firkin Arms and started down the narrow, shaded alley towards the High Street. Monica Devlin had been as helpful as he had expected, recalling their last encounter. She had confirmed that she'd been attacked by Singh in his cab. He had tried to rape her, assuming that her profession would prevent her from reporting it. She had fought him off, but he'd been right: she had seen no point in going to the police about it. She had, however, gone into the taxi firm's office and made a complaint to them.

Pete hadn't bothered to tell her about Singh's other victims. There was no point. Sadly, she was right. His colleagues probably wouldn't have taken her too seriously as a known prostitute making a complaint about an attempted rape.

He turned a corner and could see down to the brightly sunlit High Street. A group of people walked past the end of the narrow alley. One of them – a girl in her late teens or early twenties – looked towards him as his phone began to ring in his pocket. He pulled it out, saw the number on the screen and answered it.

'DS Gayle.'

'Hey, boss. It's Jill. We've just had another alleged victim of Ranjeet Singh's phone the station. Saw the report in the paper about him, thought she'd be safe to get it off her chest now.'

Pete stepped out into the sunshine on the wide pedestrianised street and stopped. 'So, that's four. How many more are there?'

'Who knows? That could be all of them or there could be dozens out there.'

'And his wife knew nothing about it? I don't buy that. There'd have been signs, surely. And one of the victims her own sister?' Pete was shaking his head.

'She could just have been in denial,' Jill suggested. 'Didn't want to admit to herself that she wasn't satisfying him that way.'

'She didn't strike me as a proud woman. Just the opposite, if anything. Quiet. Recessive.'

'It wouldn't have to be about pride. If she's as recessive as that, it could be more about not wanting to rock the boat. Could be too scared of him. Or it could be a cultural thing. Women out that way are very much second-class citizens. Something like that would be more about family honour than pride as such.'

Pete was reminded of the so-called honour killings that happened within the Indian and Pakistani culture. There was no honour there, he thought. And none here. If she knew about what Ranjeet was doing, it was her duty to do something about it, not just stay quiet and let him carry on. Even if the alternative meant putting herself at risk of reprisals from him. The system could protect her from that. There were places she could go for safety. It surely couldn't be about loving him. How could she, knowing what he was doing to other women? No, she had to talk.

'OK, Jill. We really need to talk to the wife again, don't we?'

'Do you want me to go round there and have a word?'

At this moment, he was more inclined to send Dave, but perhaps that was a bit over the top. He'd tried the softly, softly approach already, though, and it had got them nowhere. 'No, Jill. I'll deal with her.'

'You sure, boss? She is still a victim here. A victim's widow, at least.'

'Yes. But said victim was a serial rapist and she must have known at least something about that. Which, in my book, makes her an accessory.' He ended the call and dialled another number. 'Naz,' he said when it was answered. 'Are you with Mrs Singh?'

'Not at this moment, Sarge. I'm on the way there, though. Why?'

'Because I'm on the way there too.'

'Uh . . . you don't sound like you're in a particularly sympathetic mood, Sarge. What's up?'

'She's been protecting a serial rapist, that's what. And his memory. And we need the truth out of her.'

Chapter 15

'Mrs Singh, I'm not condoning or excusing what happened to your husband. Not for a second. We won't stop looking for whoever killed him until we find them. But the fact is, he was a serial rapist. Wasn't he?'

Distraught, she looked from Pete to Naz and back again, seeking support, understanding, any way out of this latest horror, But there was none. Pete kept his gaze fixed on her, unrelenting. As far as he was concerned, she was as guilty as her husband – of every rape he'd committed since the first one she'd learned of. And in his book, there was no adequate excuse.

'Do you know how it feels to be raped, Mrs Singh? Was he violent or abusive to you?'

Her face crumpled and she began to cry. Tears dripped from her cheeks. She hung her head, wiping at them with her hands.

'You knew he'd raped your sister,' Pete went on relentlessly. 'Didn't you? You told her to go home and not speak of it. Your own sister, Mrs Singh. Where was your sympathy and understanding for her? Was she the first one you knew about? She certainly wasn't the last, was she? You knew what he was doing. When he'd done it. Did it take some of the pressure off you, afterwards? Is that why you allowed him to carry on?'

'Sarge?'

Naz put a hand to his leg, urging him to ease up. To stop.

'No, Naz. This is rape we're talking about. Innocent young women, including her own sister, abused, hurt and terrified. Maybe even threatened with death afterwards. Even if he didn't say the words, they must have feared it. And she could have stopped it. That makes her as guilty as he was in my book. She can sit there and cry crocodile tears all she likes: it won't make any difference. I've got a wife and young daughter. Either of them could have ended up being victims of the man she was protecting. As far as I'm concerned, she's another Rose West, only without the guts, and if she doesn't start talking to us, I'm inclined to charge her as such.' He turned back to the weeping woman. 'So, come on, Mrs Singh. What's it to be? Are you going to talk to us or are we going to take you to jail?'

He waited a beat, but her only response was more tears.

'I can't even imagine what a prison full of women will do to someone who's in there for aiding and abetting a rapist. Myra Hindley was in solitary for decades, for her own protection. Is that what you want, Mrs Singh? Day after day, year after year, sitting alone in a cell, knowing that anyone you meet might be the one to slip a knife between your ribs or knock you down and kick you to death?'

'That's enough, Sergeant Gayle,' Naz protested. 'This isn't an interrogation; it's a torture session, only without the electrodes. I'm going to call the Super.' She stood up and headed for the door.

Pete turned back to the woman sitting opposite him. 'Last chance, Mrs Singh,' he said as Naz shut the door behind her. 'Once she makes that call, I won't have a choice any more. I'll have to charge you.' He reached out to her, but she snatched her arm away from his touch. 'Were you a victim as well? Did he abuse you too? Rape you? Threaten you? It's still rape if a man forces you to have sex against your will within a marriage, you know. If that's what happened, then we can help you. Even now. There are major differences between the way things are done in India and the way they're done in England. We have a system that's sympathetic to victims. That's set up to help and protect them.'

She looked up at him finally, her face a mess, eyes almost wild. 'You cannot protect a person from what's in their own head, Sergeant Gayle. I do not know who Rose West is. Or Myra Hindley. But yes, I am guilty of terrible things against the women my husband attacked. Even my sister. Especially my sister. I love her dearly, but what could I do? I was his wife. It was my duty to protect and support him above all else. Even myself. Yes, he was harsh. He beat me. He took me when I didn't want him to. But he gave me a roof over my head and food in my stomach. There is a price for everything in life, Sergeant Gayle, and that was the price he charged me for my life as I lived it. You think I am frightened of being killed? I would welcome it! I am so ashamed, it would be a blessing: my payment for all the wrong he did to those other women.'

Now Pete was in a quandary. He'd painted himself into a corner. After all he'd just said, he couldn't now turn sympathetic. 'Naz,' he called.

There was a pause. The sitting-room door opened and Naz poked her head through the gap. 'Sarge?'

He stood up. 'Mrs Singh would like to talk to us. Perhaps you could take her statement?'

She held his gaze for a long beat before pushing the door open and stepping inside. 'Sarge.'

'A full and detailed statement, Naz. Dates, names – everything she can remember.' He passed her and stepped out of the room, closing the door behind him as he headed for the small, cluttered kitchen at the back of the house. He hadn't enjoyed pushing the woman so hard. It was not a technique he normally employed. But she couldn't be allowed to stay quiet, as had clearly been her intention.

He found the kettle, checked it was full and switched it on before starting to hunt for cups or mugs.

Of course there were cultural differences between him and the woman he'd just been interrogating, but they didn't alter what was right or wrong, he thought, as he set out three mugs and started looking for tea and sugar. And the overriding fact was that both the woman and her husband were British citizens living in England and, as such, subject to English law, regardless of their cultural history. Yes, he had sympathy for her plight. But his greater sympathy went to the other victims of the man she'd been protecting all this time.

He had just passed the end of Okehampton Street and driven out onto the Alphington Street bridge when his phone rang in his pocket. He tapped the Bluetooth connection icon on the car's screen.

'DS Gayle.'

'Boss, it's Jane. It's about Tommy.'

'What? You haven't been to see him already? I didn't . . .'

'No, I've been too busy here up to now. But I just took a call from Archways.' Her voice changed. Got quieter and at the same time more hollow, as if she were covering her mouth. 'The resident psychiatrist there, a Dr Brian Letterman. He's been talking to Tommy. Standard procedure. Every new in . . . resident . . . gets interviewed by him and another professional to assess their mental state, their specific needs and so on. He's spent most of the morning with Tommy.'

Pete checked the time on the dashboard. It was almost one in the afternoon. 'Good grief. I didn't realise the time had got on like that. So, what did he have to say about Tommy?'

'Well . . . nothing good, boss.' Her voice had returned to normal. 'Are you on your way back in?'

'Yes.'

'I'll tell you when you get here then.'

'Jane . . .'

'Tell you what – I'll meet you downstairs. We can go straight back out.'

'What?'

But she had ended the call. The open tone rang hollowly from the speakers.

Women! Why couldn't they be straightforward and easy to deal with, for God's sake? Why did everything have to be so bloody complicated? It looked like he was going from one difficult situation straight into another.

At least Naz hadn't followed through on her threat. She had been moments away from it, she'd told him afterwards. But listening at the door to see if he was continuing in the same vein, she'd heard the change in both his attitude and Mrs Singh's. She had taken a statement from the woman, given it to him and stayed behind when he'd left a few minutes ago.

And now, here he was heading towards another situation that was being hampered by female sensitivities. Which was completely unlike Jane.

He drew a long breath. What could be so damned bad that she insisted on keeping it from the rest of the team? Surely Tommy hadn't got into trouble again already? If so, what kind of shambolic mess were they running at Archways? The whole point of places like that was that there was a high staff-to-youth ratio so that trouble was avoided and the young folk got all the attention they needed to put them back on the right track before they were released. It was a policy he knew cut the rate of reoffending by a huge percentage, compared with other methods.

The only trouble with it, in this day and age, was that it was relatively expensive in the short-term – and the short-term was all that modern, media-led politics was concerned with. They didn't care what kind of mess they left the Opposition to deal with when they got kicked out of power at the end of their term. Give it few months and the spin doctors would turn it all around and blame the incumbents anyway.

The really sad thing was that people were daft enough that, for the most part, it actually worked.

He swung around the roundabout at the bottom of Heavitree Road and headed up to the station even more depressed than he had been when he'd left the taxi driver's widow.

Jane was waiting outside the back door of the station. She stepped away from the building as she saw him pass the rear corner. He swung into a parking space and switched off the engine as she walked purposefully towards him. He waited until she'd opened the door and sat in the car. With the door closed, isolating them from the world, she turned to face him.

'So, what's all the secrecy in aid of?'

'Like I said, Dr Letterman, who insists on being called Brian, wants to speak to you urgently. He didn't go into detail. Confidentiality. I'm not family, after all. But he wants to speak to you about his findings. Well, it's not going to be good, is it? So, I thought you'd be best talking to him from out here, rather than at your desk.'

'And you couldn't tell me that over the phone and save time?'

'Well, I could have, yes. But you know as well as I do who'd have been listening.'

Dick and Dave, for sure. Possibly Ben and Jill. And a couple of Mark Bridgman's team, as well as possibly whoever had put the call through to Jane. 'OK. I wasn't criticising. I've just had a rough morning, that's all. Have you got the number?'

She took a slip of paper from her pocket and passed it to him, her other hand settling on the door handle. 'I'll leave you to it.'

Pete made the call as she walked back across the car park, her short ginger hair glowing in the sun. It was picked up on the second ring.

'Archways Secure Children's Home. Vincent speaking. How can I help?'

'Vincent, this is DS Peter Gayle of Exeter CID. I'm told a Dr Brian Letterman's been trying to reach me.'

'Right. Hold on a moment. I'll transfer you to Brian's office.'

Again, the call was picked up promptly. 'Brian speaking.'

'Brian. Pete Gayle. Tommy's father. I'm told you want to talk to me.'

'Yes, that's right. Can I call you Pete?'

'Sure.'

'I've spent most of this morning with Tommy, Pete – interviewing him, getting to know him. I do the same with all our young guests. It's part of the process. I have to say, Pete, Tommy's an extremely troubled young man.'

'Well, we knew that much. From personal experience as well as the investigation into his disappearance last year.'

'Yes, well . . . I'd hope, as a father, you'd be aware of his issues, at least to some extent. As should his teachers have been. But I'm not talking about normal teenage angst. Tommy's problems are far more serious than that.'

'He spent five months living with a paedophile, followed by another five living rough. What do you expect?'

'Unfortunately, what I'm talking about goes far deeper and much further back into his childhood than that.'

'What's that supposed to mean?'

The psychiatrist sighed audibly. 'He's suffering from deep-seated abandonment issues, Pete. Very deep-seated. From way back in his youth. These are things that crop up in a small way quite often in eldest children. Their only-child status is abruptly removed by the arrival of a younger sibling. But usually they cope and adapt perfectly well. Tommy didn't. And his feelings were exacerbated by the fact that both his parents had demanding careers. Long hours, variable shifts and so on, leading to irregular parental contact when he needed it most. Not that it would necessarily have helped, of course. I'm afraid, as much as we like to think we know about the human mind, there are things we still don't have all the answers to, and Tommy seems to be suffering from just such a condition.'

Why the hell could these people never talk straight? 'Which is . . .?'

'I'm afraid Tommy shows all the signs of suffering from a psycho-dissociative disorder, Pete.'

'A what? Are you saying he's schizophrenic?'

'No, no. Not at all. It's more of an inability to empathise, combined with a lack of inhibitive functions.'

Impatience and resentment flared into annoyance. 'So he's psychopath.'

'He's . . .'

Pete could hear the other man struggling to express himself adequately. 'He's what, Brian? Straight answer to a straight question. What, in your opinion, is wrong with my son?'

'Basically, there's a wiring problem in his brain, the causes of which we don't fully understand. It could be genetic, it could be caused by something in his environment, or lacking from it, during his formative years, or it could be a combination of the two. We don't know. What we do know is that there is a wide spectrum of severity of such issues. The vast majority of people with these types of disorder live perfectly normal, productive and fully functional lives. The few at the extreme end of the spectrum are too damaged to be able to do that reliably and safely. Again, there is a range of severity. Some people live normal lives until they're triggered by what's termed a "stresser" into displaying symptoms of the disorder. Others seem to simply grow into it. And still others have problems from a very young age. Tommy seems to lie somewhere between the last two categories, as far as we can tell. Is there anything you can remember from his younger years that gave cause for concern?'

Pete closed his eyes, his teeth clamped together as he struggled not to yell at the man. He drew a breath. It didn't work. He tried again, fighting to calm himself. 'I asked a straight question, requiring a straight answer, Brian,' he said. 'When this conversation started I told you not just my name but my job title, in case you didn't already know it. Part of that job entails interviewing suspects and assessing their reactions and responses. So, bearing that in mind, along with the fact that we're talking about my son, do you imagine for one second that I'm going to accept you acting like a politician?'

'I'm sorry. That wasn't my intention at all. I simply wanted to make it clear what we're dealing with here.'

'And in that you've failed miserably. Let me put it to you this way: is Tommy Gayle a psychopath? Yes or no?'

'Well, that's not a description we like to . . .'

'I don't care what terminology you prefer this week,' Pete snapped, anger masking his fear of the truth. 'Yes or no? Is he or isn't he?'

'In the sense that you're using the expression, I have to say that, in my opinion and that of my colleague, Adrian Stewart, who is a highly respected psychologist and national expert in his field – yes, Thomas Gayle does suffer from what you call psychopathy. But I also have to say, it's not an easy diagnosis to make and it is treatable, with a high degree of success in younger subjects.'

'Treatable how?' Pete was imagining brain surgery, shock therapy and heavy-dose drugs that reduced people to little more than vegetables.

'It depends on the specifics of the individual case. Some require drug therapies for concurrent disorders, but for the antisocial behaviour issue itself, behavioural therapies are, for the moment, the only reliable treatment.'

'Behavioural therapies?'

'Professionally led group sessions, individual psychotherapy sessions. It varies from case to case.'

Pete remembered the police psychologist he'd had to see a number of times at Middlemoor for several weeks after his return to work. He had gone into their sessions expecting them to be a thorough waste of valuable time, but by the time they'd concluded his fourth and final one, he had felt a lot better about both the psychologist herself and the process. And yet, he knew they had been shown to be a waste of time for adult psychopaths. 'And you say these sessions have been proved to be useful?'

'In younger subjects, yes. There's been shown to be up to an eighty per cent success rate.'

'And how long does that take?'

'Again, there are variables, but it's not a quick process. The brain is a delicate instrument. You can't go at it with a hammer and tongs.'

'I wasn't going to suggest you could, Brian. What I had in mind was that Tommy's not going to be there that long.' It was a bloody good thing this conversation wasn't happening face to face, Pete thought. He'd have beaten the bloody idiot to a pulp by now.

'That's true. As it is with the majority of the young people I see here. But, I do work beyond these walls and a large part of that involves people I've met within them. The same applies with Adrian.'

'And you firmly believe you can help my son?'

'Yes, I do.'

'But you need permission from my wife and myself.'

'Exactly.'

Pete grunted. 'I'll speak to her and we'll get back to you.'

He put the phone down and sat still as his brain absorbed what he'd been told. *Doctor* Brian Letterman was saying Tommy was a psychopath. That he had a wiring problem in his brain that, though it was treatable while he was still young, meant he had no ability to feel empathy and, beyond that, actually enjoyed causing pain and distress to others.

He shook his head. That couldn't be true. Not Tommy. His son. Yes, there was such a thing as justifiable retribution, and there was no reason, in Pete's book, not to feel a certain satisfaction in achieving that. But cruelty for the sake of it? No. He'd never seen anything like that from Tommy. Never heard about it either, apart from the things he'd read last year in Simon Phillips's report on him, compiled as part of the investigation into his disappearance.

But that report had included testimony from several people – teachers, kids, and even one or two parents of other kids. It had even included quotes from Annie. So was he simply in denial? Was he refusing to believe what was in front of his face just because it referred to his son? His boy? The product of his own efforts as a father?

As insufferable as he was, was Brian right?

Pete drew in a long breath and let it ease gently out.

Was Tommy mentally ill? Or was it all just a product of the time he'd spent with Burton, preceded by the bullying he'd suffered and finally reacted against at school?

Bullying that, as a father, Pete acknowledged, he should have seen the signs of and dealt with long ago. That was his guilt to bear. He'd let Tommy down.

Well, he wasn't going to do that again. Now and for the rest of time, he would be a father first and a copper second. But that didn't answer the question. Was Tommy mentally ill? Or was he just suffering from the stresses he'd gone through in his short life?

Pete wasn't a psychologist or a psychiatrist. He didn't know all the ins and outs of the mind's complexities. But he did know his son. He'd raised him. Lived with him. Watched him grow. Perhaps not been there as much as he might have – or should have – but . . .

They'd had some good times together, some fun times. Fishing in the upper reaches of the Exe and further down, beyond Topsham. Playing football in the park on weekends. Trips to the beach and so on.

But then, as his mood began to lift with the pleasant memories, another, darker one flashed up, bringing him back down with a grimace as he recalled a trip to Exmouth when Tommy was the same age as Annie was now. They'd been on the beach. Annie was playing in the sand in front of them, happily building the biggest sandcastle Pete had ever seen while Tommy ran down to the sea for a swim. He'd been spotted by a bunch of lads. Four of them, Pete remembered. They had crowded towards him, calling out. Pete had been sure he'd heard the term 'piglet' used and had been about to intervene when Tommy suddenly lashed out. In a lightning-fast series of moves that Pete had had no idea he was capable of, he'd headbutted the closest one, smashing his nose, kicked another in the crotch hard enough to fell him, punched a third one in the throat and faced up to the last one, daring him to come get some of the same.

When Tommy advanced on him, the lad had run, but what had worried Pete at the time was that, on returning from the chase, rather than avoiding the other lads, Tommy had walked up to them, stomped on the head of the one he'd kicked, grinding his face into the sand, then kicked the one holding his throat hard in the kidneys before grabbing the one with the bloody nose by the hair and dragging him, yelling and struggling, into the sea.

At that point, unsure what Tommy was planning and with Louise shouting beside him, worry had abruptly morphed into fear and Pete had finally reacted. He ran down to the surf as Tommy dropped his victim face-first in the shallow water.

'Tommy!' he'd shouted as he ran. 'That's enough. He's learned his lesson. Leave him be.'

Asking Tommy about it later, Pete had learned that a teacher had given the boy lessons in self-defence after seeing him getting picked on on the playing field one day.

Shaking off the memory, which he'd pushed aside for years, putting Tommy's actions down to youthful disregard for consequences and overreaction to long-term bullying, he phoned the Royal Devon and Exeter Hospital, using the direct-dial number for the ward Louise was working on. When the call was eventually picked up, he immediately recognised the voice on the other end. 'How the hell do you get away with leaving a phone ringing for that long before you pick it up?'

'Pete? Is that you?'

'Yes.'

'It's called having more important things to do. You want Lou?'

'Please, George. How you doing?'

'Too bloody busy by half. Apart from that, not so bad, though. You?'

'Running round like a headless chicken. Just had a call about Tommy, though, so needs must.'

'Oh, right. Hold on, I'll get her for you.'

The phone clattered on the desk as she set it down, and moments later there was a scrape as it was picked up again. 'Pete? What's up? George said you wanted to talk about Tommy?'

'I was just talking to the resident psychiatrist at Archways. Bloody waste of oxygen. He and his colleague there have decided Tommy should go in for therapy sessions, which they'll continue after his release, and they want our permission.'

'Hang on. Therapy for what? What do they reckon is wrong with him?'

Pete winced. He'd been hoping to steer her past that question. She was definitely back on the ball – which, while being awkward at that moment, was a huge relief in the larger scheme of things.

He sighed. 'Antisocial Personality Disorder.'

There was a moment's silence as she absorbed and translated that. Then: 'Never! No way! Just ask Rosie Whitlock. She wouldn't agree with that for a second.'

'I know. But that's what they're saying.'

'And will he know we've agreed to his entering this treatment?'

'Ultimately, yes. But in the immediate term – I don't know.'

'Well, I suppose, if it works, it won't matter if he finds out afterwards. But it definitely wouldn't help for him to be told right off the bat.'

'So, you're OK with it, on that understanding?'

'Well, I don't agree with the diagnosis, but even if it's partly right or close to right, we've got to give him every chance we can, haven't we?'

Pete was nodding in agreement. 'Right. I'll call him back then. Go round there if I need to.'

* * *

'So, it turns out Mrs Singh knew a lot more than she was letting on,' Pete said as he joined the rest of his team at their desks. 'I've made a copy of her statement for each of you.'

He handed them out and sat down, reading it thoroughly for the first time himself while they brought themselves up-to-date.

Dave looked up first. 'So, was this a revenge attack then? For one of these women? Or by one of these women?'

'It could be. Either way, I'm convinced it was a woman who did it.'

'Why?' Jill demanded.

'The pepper spray, for a start. It tends to be women that carry that stuff. For self-defence. Then there was the condom on the passenger seat. Still in its wrapper, granted, but why would it be out on display like that if he wasn't intending to use it?'

'To threaten?' Dick suggested. 'Or brag?'

Pete nodded. 'OK. Maybe. Then there was the fact that the child locks were set. And the way he treated his wife.'

'So, if we accept that it's a female perp, are we talking revenge or self-defence?' Jane asked.

'The pepper spray and condom point towards self-defence,' Pete replied. 'But they're not conclusive.'

'Well, for all the hours I've spent on the PND, I haven't come up with any likely suspects for a revenge attack,' Jane admitted. 'Although that doesn't mean it wasn't one. It could be a victim who never reported it. Like the two you were asking Singh's widow about.'

Dave was shaking his head. 'I don't get it. Why wouldn't you report something like that?'

Jane turned to face him. 'Have you any idea how many attacks are not reported every year in this country? Not just rapes, but assaults in general?'

'If they're not reported, how would I?'

'Well, it's a lot. A hell of a lot. And, as for why, would you want to sit there in court and have some smart-arse barrister trying to

161

embarrass and confuse you in front of everyone, accusing you of lying while he forces you to relive the whole thing in every painful, terrifying and shameful detail?'

'But if you're telling the truth, you'd want the guy punished and off the streets, wouldn't you?'

'What – to save some hypothetical person you don't even know? And put yourself through Christ knows what kind of hell in the process? Where would your priorities lie, do you think?'

'Well, if you're right, there's no question about where hers are. We've got two victims that make that perfectly obvious.'

'Yes – now, when it may be too late, in her eyes, to go back and do anything about it legally. Maybe she's been threatened again – or felt threatened. Or she could have seen something. But, for whatever reason, it could be that now she regrets letting her attacker get away with it and wants to put that right.'

'This is all speculation,' Pete said. 'What can we do to find out if any of it's true?'

'Catch her?' Dave suggested.

'Clever-dick,' Jill muttered.

'No, that's him over there.'

'I said clever.'

'Oi!' Dick protested. 'What happened to respecting your elders, Titch?'

'Respect's like common sense,' Dave told him. 'It's out of fashion these days. Is there any CCTV at that second crime scene?'

Pete nodded. 'Yes. It's being collated at Middlemoor as we speak. There's seven different possible sources.'

'Seven?' Dick exclaimed.

'The benefits of living in a yuppy paradise,' Dave said. 'They're paranoid somebody might nick one of their hard-earned Rolexes.'

'By the time that amount of footage gets searched, the bloody thief'll have got old and retired. And most of it's damn near useless, anyway.'

'At least it can give us the basics,' said Jane. 'Male or female. Black, white or brown. That's more than we've got now.'

'I've been working on the second victim's last pickup point,' Jill put in. 'Wherever it was, it wasn't pre-booked and the meter doesn't narrow it down much either. Subtracting the time we know the car was stood idle still gives a possible range of up to eight miles. It depends on the precise arrival time.'

'Which the CCTV will give us when it comes back from HQ,' Dick pointed out, picking up his phone. 'I'll give 'em a nudge, shall I?'

Pete nodded.

'The only thing I have been able to get is his mobile phone records,' Jill continued. 'Nothing useful in terms of calls, but it does give us a series of timed locations I can put on the map to see what that tells us.'

'Well, that'll be a start,' Pete said as, beside him, Dick began speaking to someone on the phone.

Moments later, he ended the call and looked up. 'They've got something.'

Chapter 16

'Who's they?' asked Dave.

'Middlemoor. The CCTV team.'

'Got what?' Pete asked.

'Footage of the taxi stopping, down at the Friars Green apartment complex, and a suspect getting out of it and walking away.'

'Walking?' Dave queried.

Dick tilted his head.

'That takes some bottle when you've just killed somebody. Any identification?'

Dick shook his head. 'Only that she's female. Dark clothes. Peaked cap. No facial shots.'

'Which way did she go?' Pete asked.

'Over the footbridge towards the quay.'

'So, Graham should be able to pick her up downstairs. Did they give you an exact time?'

'She went out of sight of the Friars Green cameras at 9.42.'

'Are they sending us over the footage or stills from it?'

'The file's too big to email, so they're going to burn it to disc and send it down here, but they said they'll pop a couple of stills across in the meantime. You might have them by now.' Dick nodded at Pete's computer.

Pete wiggled the mouse to bring up the screen and clicked into his email account. The latest message, one minute ago, was from Middlemoor HQ. He opened it up and found two picture attachments. Downloading both, he opened them, sent them to the printer and peered at them side by side on his screen. One was a grainy sideview, obviously a blowup from a distant shot. The other was closer, a back view as she walked towards the footbridge. The detail was better, as was the lighting, but it told him little that the other one didn't.

'Slender. Youngish-looking. Job to say how tall she is from these. She's white, though, not Indian. Hair looks to be up under the cap so you can't see its length, but it's dark. If you get them off the printer, Ben, you can all have a look. I'll take a pair down to Graham and see what he can find for us.'

Ben hadn't regained his seat when Pete's phone rang. He picked it up. 'DS Gayle.'

'Pete. It's Andy. I just got a call from Mick Douglas, over in St Thomas.'

'Yes?'

'The target's home to roost. No telling how long for, mind.'

'OK. Tell Mick not to let him leave in the car. We're on the way.' He put the phone down. 'Let's go. All of you.'

Chairs scraped. Ben dropped the printouts on Pete's desk. It wasn't until they were out of the squad room and heading for the stairs that Jane asked, 'Where are we going, boss?'

'To arrest Shafiq Ahmed, all being well. Mick Douglas has got eyes on. He's gone home at last.'

Pete turned off the sirens as soon as they passed the railway station on the far side of the river, but left the blue lights flashing in the grille and on the parcel shelf. A second later, he heard Dick do the same in the car behind him. He checked the mirror. Dick had left his blue lights on too. He reached for the radio.

'DS Gayle for PC Douglas. What's his status, Mick?'

'Still inside as far as I can tell. The whole family's in there. Kids got home a couple of minutes ago.'

'OK. We're a minute away.'

'Roger.'

He keyed the radio again. 'Dick, you take Dave and Ben around the back. We'll take the front.'

'Will do, boss.'

Pete turned left off the main road and killed the blue lights. They were now in an area of mostly Victorian housing – terraces and semis interspersed with more recently built houses, private garages and business premises. Pete went straight over a small crossroads. Behind him, Dick turned left. He would take the next street across so that they could come in from behind the house. Pete pulled over to give him a chance to make up the extra distance then started forward again, driving steadily down the road, between parked cars on both sides. Checking the door numbers, he judged they were getting close now. A stretch of pavement showed on the left, with nothing parked in front of it until, at the far end, the back of a black Toyota with a yellow taxi sign on the roof. He pulled in, parking tight up behind the taxi, and keyed the radio. 'Which door, Mick?'

'The blue one, just by the front wing of his car.'

'Roger. Where are you, Dick?'

'Just about to leave the car. There's an alleyway through from here. Looks like another one crosses it, down between the back gardens.'

'Perfect. We'll give you thirty.'

'Roger.'

Pete counted down in his head, then reached for the radio. 'Dick?'

'In position, boss.'

They opened the doors and he keyed the radio one last time. 'Go, go, go.' Then, with doors slamming, they were running for the blue front door. Pete stepped through the gate. The garden was barely three feet from front to back. He hammered on the door. 'Police,' he shouted. 'With a warrant. Open up.'

Voices sounded from inside, high-pitched and panicked.

He hammered on the door again. 'Open up now.'

He heard the click of the latch. The door cracked open, a female face peering through the narrow gap, surrounded by bright pink and gold silk.

'Mrs Ahmed?' He showed her his badge. 'Police. Open the door. We've got a warrant.' Closing his ID wallet, he shook out the warrant sheet with one hand while pushing the door with the other. She stepped back, letting him open it.

'Where's your husband?'

He glimpsed two small faces peering from a door further back on the left.

'He's . . .'

'We know he's here. He was seen arriving and his car's outside. Where is he?'

She blinked rapidly. 'Upstairs.'

'Jane. With me.' He hurried past the woman and up the narrow stairs, Jane's lighter feet sounding behind him while Jill stayed downstairs with the wife.

'Shafiq Ahmed,' Pete called as his head rose above first-floor level. 'Police. We've got a warrant for your arrest.'

There was a door in front of him at the top of the stairs, another off the landing to his left. Glancing around, he saw a third behind him. No movement from behind any of them.

'Shafiq Ahmed. Police. Come out now.'

He reached the top of the stairs. Still no sound except from below, where Jill was talking to Mrs Ahmed. He reached for the handle of the door in front of him. Shoved it open.

Bathroom.

At the far end, the shower curtain was down and pulled around. Pete stepped in, snatched it aside. Nothing.

Behind him, Jane had gone to the nearest bedroom. He heard the door slam open. As he turned back, she called, 'Clear.'

'Clear,' he replied.

The front room then. He stepped past her, heading for it. Three long strides and he was reaching for the handle when it opened in front of him.

'Shafiq Ahmed. You're under arrest.'

Pete stepped forward, pushing the door wide.

'Turn around. Put your hands behind your back.'

Ahmed complied, thoroughly cowed. Pete cuffed him and, with Jane leading the way, followed Ahmed back along the landing and down the stairs, right hand clamped tight around the rigid centre of the cuffs.

'What is the charge?'

Pete heard the question coming from the wife, rather than from the man in front of him.

Jill replied, her voice low.

Ahmed himself said nothing as they took him outside. Jill shut the door after them and they crowded around him as they walked him the few feet to Pete's unmarked car. Jill sat in the back with him while Jane reached for the radio as Pete started the engine.

'DCs Feeney and Miles. Stand down. Repeat: stand down. Suspect in custody.'

'Received,' Dick's voice came back.

'That was easy,' she said to Pete.

'Yeah. Too easy.' He stopped the car and reached into his jacket as his eyes went to the man in the seat behind him. 'Take this with you and search the place. Top to bottom. Attic, cellar, garden shed: the lot.' He handed her the warrant and reached for the radio. 'DC Feeney from DS Gayle. Hold fire. You can all help Jane search his place.'

'Roger.'

Jane took the radio from Pete. 'Come round. I'll meet you out front.'

'Will do.'

She handed the mike back and stepped out of the car. 'See you later then, boss.'

Pete gave her a nod.

The man they had arrested still hadn't spoken. As Pete reversed the car then swung it around in a three-point turn, he glanced in the mirror again. Ahmed was looking down at his lap.

'Cat got your tongue, Shafiq?'

Ahmed looked up and met his gaze. His eyes were dull and empty-looking as if he'd withdrawn from the world.

'Nothing to say? Nothing to ask?' Pete persisted as he drove away down the street.

Ahmed blinked then looked away out of the side window.

Pete shrugged. 'Best read him his rights then, Jill.'

'Boss.' She turned to face the man beside her. 'Shafiq Ahmed, you've been arrested on suspicion of the unlawful killing of Sunil Pati, contrary to common law. You do not have to say anything . . .'

Ahmed reacted at last. His head came up, eyes frantic. 'What is this? I've killed no one. Especially not Sunil. He was a friend.'

'. . . but it may harm your defence,' Jill went on as they passed the cross-street.

'No. No. I did not kill Sunil. When did he die?'

'. . . if you do not mention when questioned . . .'

'Between ten and eleven last night.' This time it was Pete who interrupted her, answering his question.

'. . . something that you later rely on in court.'

'Then I can prove I am innocent.'

'Anything you do say may be given in evidence.'

'How?' Pete asked, slowing the car as he approached the main road, signalling right towards the city centre.

'I was working until midnight. The car will tell you. And my phone. Its GPS.'

'Do you understand the rights I've quoted to you?' asked Jill.

'I am telling you, I did not do this!'

'But do you understand the rights I quoted?'

'Yes. Please. Call the office. They will tell you.'

'So, why did you do a runner when I came to speak to you this morning? To the extent of breaking the law as you did so?'

'I was . . . That was you?' He shook his head. 'I thought . . .'

'You thought what?'

Ahmed sighed. 'That you were someone else.'

'Well, whoever you thought I was, there's no excuse for dangerous and reckless driving. And there's no denying it either. I was behind you, remember. And dash-cams don't lie.' He pointed to the one at the base of the windscreen.

'But my job! My family. I must earn money to feed them. To house them.'

'You should have thought about that before you took off like a bat out of hell up a busy shopping street, putting people's lives in danger, shouldn't you?' Pete wasn't going to give him any quarter. Not at this stage. He needed him on the defensive. 'Where is your phone?'

'At home. In the bedroom. I was changing.'

Pete reached for the radio. 'DS Gayle for DC Bennett.'

'DC Bennett. What's up, boss?'

'Pick up the suspect's phone while you're there, Jane. And check the GPS history on it. He claims to have been elsewhere when Pati was killed. Have you found anything yet?'

'Still looking, boss.'

'OK. Keep me posted.'

'Roger.'

Pete looked in the mirror as he approached the roundabout at the bottom of Heavitree Road. 'So, Shafiq. Is there anything you want to tell me? Because if you've been a bad lad, we'll soon find out. And deals aren't made after the evidence comes in.'

'Dear, oh dear, oh dear.'

Pete shook his head. He was sitting across from Shafiq Ahmed in Interview Room Two on the ground floor of Heavitree Road police station, DC Jill Evans beside him, the digital recorder running. 'And here we were assuming you were innocent until proven otherwise. Looks like we've proved it, doesn't it?'

They had known before they set out to arrest Ahmed that he hadn't killed Sunil Pati: he was not a white female. But they needed to question him about Pati and he was certainly guilty of something, so the killing was as good an excuse as any to put the squeeze on him. And now Jane and the boys had found exactly what he was guilty of. Stashed in the false bottom of his wardrobe, they had recovered wads of cash and everything needed, including the product itself, to package and distribute cocaine.

'I am telling you, I killed no one,' Ahmed insisted.

'What happened? Did he find out about the drugs? Threaten to report you to us? Or did he know all along? Was it a falling out among thieves, as it were?'

'No! I told you. He was a friend. He knew nothing of this thing.'

'And what about your wife? She must have known about it. Was she an active part of it or did she just sit back and allow it to carry on?'

'She is nothing to do with this. She knows nothing.'

'She does now, even if she didn't before – which I find hard to believe,' Jill added. 'What's going to happen to your kids now, with both of you inside?'

'My . . .? No! You cannot. My wife knows nothing. She was no part of this. You cannot charge her.'

'Oh, yes, we can,' Pete told him. 'It was happening in her home. She must have known about it, even if she had no active part. That makes her an accessory. She could get a couple of years. Which puts your kids into the system. And, as felons, you won't get them back.'

'You cannot do this. You must not do this!'

'Then tell us what we want to know.'

'Oh, God.' He put his head in his hands, took a deep breath. Then another. 'Sunil was . . .' He looked up at Pete. 'He was my source of the drugs. He knew people in Birmingham. In London.'

'So why was he targeted?' Pete demanded, leaning forward, his elbows on the table between them. 'Did he not pay his suppliers? Did he shortchange them? Or was it something else? Because this was a murder. It wasn't just an attack that went too far.'

'I do not . . .' He stopped, brows knitting into a frown.

'What?'

'He was a friend also of the other man who was killed. Ranjeet Singh. *He*, I have heard bad things about.'

'Such as?'

'With women. He would . . . What do you say? Come on to them. Be forward. Even . . .' He shook his head with a grimace. 'An evil man when he thought he could get away with it.'

'But what's that got to do with Sunil Pati?' Jill asked.

'They were friends. I would meet them sometimes. I saw how they looked at women. How they talked about them. I wonder if, perhaps, Singh encouraged Sunil in that direction.'

'You wonder or you know?' Pete asked.

'I have no proof. Just looks. Comments. Laughs. Like that.'

'Was there ever anything specific?' Jill asked. 'From Sunil himself?'

Ahmed shook his head, then stopped. Fixed his gaze on Pete. 'There was one time. He had taken a young woman home. Helped her in with her shopping. She had a very short skirt. He made comments about . . .' His voice trailed off.

'About?' Pete pushed.

'Her body. He had followed her up the stairs. Looked up. You know.'

Jill leaned in. 'You're a very shy man for a drug dealer, Mr Ahmed. Is that all you can tell us about Sunil? Or would you prefer to talk to Sergeant Gayle on his own?'

He looked from one to the other and back again. 'There is . . . Yes, please.'

Pete looked at her. Raised an eyebrow.

'Very well, Mr Ahmed. I'll go and get a coffee. Do you want anything? Sarge?'

Pete shook his head. Ahmed didn't respond, so Jill stood up and left them alone.

'For the tape, Detective Constable Evans is leaving the room,' Pete said. 'Now, Shafiq. Man to man. What else is there you can tell me about Sunil Pati and his dealings with women?'

'My wife. You will not charge her?'

Pete tilted his head. 'If we find no evidence she's handled the drugs or the cash, then no.'

Ahmed's eyes closed, then opened again, meeting Pete's gaze. 'Sunil told me once that he had . . . had sex . . . with a young white girl. School-age. Fourteen. He had other friends. I do not know them. But they were involved in that thing. Grooming. They had connections, I think, to somewhere . . . Peterborough. Leicester. Where this was a big thing.'

'And when was this?'

'Couple of years ago.'

Pete sat forward again, his stomach twisting. 'Do you know who any of these friends were? Or any of the victims?'

Ahmed was shaking his head. 'I think some may have been relatives. Cousins. I told him: this is wrong. He seemed . . . not sorry, but he never spoke of it again.'

'And you didn't report it?'

'Report what? A rumour? A man bragging about something he shouldn't have?' He shrugged. 'I have been in prison once. And you must understand – this is normal where we come from. India. Pakistan. Bangladesh. All these places. Girls are married as young as eleven or twelve. Sometimes younger.'

Pete felt the anger heating his brain and clenching his jaw. He fought it down. 'It may be normal there, but you're not there. And there's a saying: "When in Rome . . ." This is England. I don't care who you are or where you're from – you choose to live here, you abide by *our* laws, not those of your home country. The same as I would expect to abide by your laws if I was to live there.'

'Of course. I know this. I told him. I have children.'

Pete smiled. 'I have to say, there's a certain irony in that, coming from a convicted felon, Shafiq.'

'What I have done does not harm children, Sergeant Gayle. I simply fill a niche in the market. If there was no demand . . .' He shrugged.

At least that last part was true. 'All right. How about that coffee now? Or tea?'

'This is getting bloody worse, not better,' Dave complained. 'Instead of narrowing the suspect field, we've widened it.'

'Well, at least we've restricted the drug supply in the city even more,' Jane said.

'Yeah, with the help of whoever killed Sunil Pati.'

'Saves trying him,' Dick pointed out.

'Yeah, that's not really the attitude we're supposed to be taking here,' Jane said.

'Practical, though. Especially with all the cutbacks and such,' Ben put in with a nod to Dick.

'You're too young to be so cynical,' Jill told him.

'He's not as young as he looks,' Dave said.

'Regardless . . .' Pete interrupted the exchange. 'We've got a white female suspect. She's not likely to be working with a bunch of Indian drug dealers. So, it's either a people-trafficking thing connected to Sunil Pati's paedophile friends or it's about payback for sexual assault and rape.'

'How likely is it that one person's been attacked by two different taxi drivers, though?' Dave argued.

'Not very,' Pete admitted. 'But have you got a better solution?'

'Maybe one of them was on behalf of a friend,' Jill suggested.

'Or both of them,' Ben added. 'And it doesn't need to be a friend.'

'What – we've got a hitwoman in the city now, have we?' Dave asked. 'You've been watching too much telly, Spike.'

Ben shrugged. 'If it's good enough for one, it's good enough for both.'

'In the meantime,' Pete said, 'having just spent half an hour in the dark with Graham, what I can say without having to speculate is that she knows the city. She walked over the footbridge, across the quay and up Lower Coombe Street to South Street. From there, she went into Cathedral Square. And vanished.'

'Great,' said Jane.

'How long after did you keep looking?' asked Dick.

'Until midnight.'

'And no likely candidates at all?' Dave asked.

'A few possibles, but none we could confirm.'

Dave steepled his fingers under his chin. 'Clever girl then. Must have gone into one of the pubs or restaurants. Changed in the toilets.'

'I wonder how many of them have security cameras?' Jill said.

'Not all, I bet,' said Pete. 'But we might get lucky.'

Dave pushed his chair back. 'Not from here, we won't.'

Jane looked at Pete. 'You want me to go with him? Make sure he doesn't try to have a drink in every place he visits?'

'What do you mean, try?' Dave demanded as Pete gave her a smile and a nod. 'There aren't that many round there.'

'Must be half a dozen or more, even without the Clarence,' Dick said, referring to the old hotel that had burned down some time before.

Dave pointed at him triumphantly. 'There. That's not too many for an evening.'

Jane laughed and slapped him on the shoulder. 'I've seen you after half a dozen, matey. You're no good to man nor beast.'

'Are you casting nasturtiums at my alcoholic capacity, Red?'

Pete's desk phone began to ring. An external call.

'Get out of here, the pair of you,' he said. 'And make sure you come back with something more than a bloody hangover.'

'Aye aye, cap'n.' Dave threw him a salute and headed out the door, Jane slipping her coat on as she followed him.

Pete picked up the phone. 'DS Gayle, Exeter CID.'

'Pete, it's me,' Louise cut in, her voice tearful and desperate. 'Annie's been attacked.'

Chapter 17

Pete pulled into his drive with no memory of how he'd got there, his mind a whirling turmoil of raw emotions. He ran from the car to the front door, fumbled the key from his pocket and leapt through the opened door. 'Lou? Annie?'

'Upstairs,' Louise's voice came back to him.

As his feet pounded up the stairs, he heard a sob from Annie that intensified the fear twisting his gut to the point where he had to reach out and grab the banister to stop himself from stumbling, but he kept going. He made the top of the stairs in four huge leaps and crossed to Annie's open bedroom door.

She was lying on her side, legs curled up, hands covering her face. Louise was sitting on the edge of the bed, her back to the door, trying to comfort her, but Pete could see his daughter's whole body shaking with sobs he could barely hear. He stepped up behind Louise, reached out to touch Annie's ankle.

'It's all right, love,' he said gently. 'I'm here. You're safe. Nobody's going to hurt you.'

Her crying grew louder and Louise leaned down, taking her in her arms. 'Oh, baby. Come here now.'

Her slender arms wrapped tightly around her mother's neck and Pete glimpsed her face, red and crumpled, wet with tears, half-hidden by her dishevelled hair as she buried it in Louise's neck.

'We're here for you, love,' he told her as she sobbed out her fear and anguish. 'Always and for ever, whatever happens.'

He stepped around Louise and knelt beside her, stroking Annie's back, smoothing her hair while, with his other hand, he held Louise. He was unaware of time passing while they stayed there, Annie crying on her mother's shoulder while they both tried to comfort her until, at some point, she began to calm down, her shaking easing, her sobs growing more gentle.

'There you go. Easy does it,' he crooned.

Annie pulled back from her mother's shoulder and turned away, pushing herself down into the pillows, her body curling into a foetal position, facing away from them. They still stayed with her, each with a hand resting gently, reassuringly, on her flank and shoulder. Louise met Pete's gaze. She saw the question in his eyes and her lips tightened. She'd told him very little on the phone and would tell him no more here, now, with Annie in the room. But he could see for himself, she was still wearing her school uniform and her clothes appeared to be intact, undamaged.

Thank God.

If some paedophile had assaulted her, he didn't know what he'd do.

Yes, he did, he realised instantly. Police or not, he'd go after the son of a bitch and beat him to a bloody pulp. There would be no quarter, no mercy. He'd kill the pervert with his own two hands and to hell with the consequences. He felt his jaw clamp tight as the rage started to take hold. But there was no need. No point. She was OK. He let the breath ease out of him. 'Who's for a cup of tea?'

Louise nodded. Annie didn't react as Pete stood up and headed for the stairs.

By the time he'd made three steaming mugs and brought them upstairs, Annie was no longer crying, as far as he could tell.

He set her mug on the bedside cabinet and handed one to Louise. 'There we go. Get that down you. You'll feel loads better.'

Louise stroked Annie's arm. 'There. You rest, love. We'll be just downstairs.' She stood up, meeting Pete's gaze, and they stepped out. Annie was quiet as they headed down the stairs and into the sitting room.

'What happened?' Pete asked as they sat down.

Louise drew a breath. 'She didn't tell me much. A bunch of lads surrounded her, pulled her into the cut-through from Sycamore to Hill View and made all sorts of threats. Grabbed her and . . .' She shuddered. 'Poor kid was terrified.'

Pete couldn't help picturing the scene, although he didn't want to. 'Who were they? Did she say?'

Louise shook her head. 'Older, she said. Tommy's age or so. But they'd taken their ties and blazers off and she didn't recognise any of them.'

So, they could be anyone. From anywhere.

'Did she say anything else about them?'

Louise shook her head. 'Just broke down and cried. Pretty much as you found us.'

Pete's jaw was clamped tight, his teeth pressing together almost painfully. 'This has got to stop. Now. Whoever it is and whyever they're doing it, it can't carry on.'

'What are you going do?'

He took his phone from his pocket, hit a speed-dial number. It was picked up on the first ring. 'Boss? What's happened? Is everything OK?'

'Bring Dick with you out to Sycamore Drive, Jane. There's a path leads through to the next street over, Hill View. I need you to search the end of it, see if anything's been left there by mistake, and knock on all the doors around there, see if anyone saw anything this afternoon. A bunch of lads, specifically.'

'So, what's happened?' she asked again.

'Annie was ambushed on the way home from school. Nothing

179

too serious was actually done to her, but it could have been. And the threat was there. Poor kid was terrified.'

'Right. We're on the way.'

'Thanks, Jane.' He put the phone away and looked at Louise. 'I don't care who they are or how old they are. This was sexual assault and they're going to be charged with it. All of them – or at least as many as we can identify.' He glanced up towards Annie's room. Felt Louise's hand settle on his arm and met her gaze.

'Leave her be for now,' she said gently. 'Let her rest and recover a bit.'

His brow tightened. 'I wasn't going to . . .'

Her grip tightened. 'I know. I'm just saying. Let her tell us in her own time.'

Pete was going to protest again, but stopped himself. She was right. The priority had to be Annie – her wellbeing. Much as he wanted to get out there and catch the little shits – and needed all the information he could get as soon as he could get it to that end – he couldn't put her through any more than she'd already endured. He relaxed. Reached for his tea and took a gulp.

Louise smiled. 'She'll tell us as soon as she's ready.'

'I know, but . . .' Pete shook his head. 'I feel so . . . helpless. And responsible.'

'She's asleep,' Louise said as she stepped into the kitchen sometime later, Annie's mug in her hand, the tea cold and untouched. Pete took the mug from her, tipped its contents down the sink and put it in the washing-up bowl with the others.

'Probably the best thing, for now. Let her recover a bit, calm down and so on.'

Louise sighed. 'What are we going to do, Pete?'

'We're going to find out . . .' The phone rang in the hall, cutting him off. Louise spun around, took three long steps and snatched it up.

'Hello?' She paused. 'OK. I'll get him.'

180

Stepping back into the kitchen, she held out the cordless handset. 'It's Jane.'

Pete quickly wiped his hand on his trousers and took the phone from her. 'Jane?'

'Hello, boss. We've checked all the surrounding houses and the first thirty feet or so of the alley.'

'And?'

'One witness, but he couldn't ID the lads. Didn't recognise their uniform ties and blazers, but he said they certainly weren't from the local school.'

'Did he give you a description of them?'

'Just a bunch of lads. Eight or nine of them, he said.'

'Not the lads: the ties and badges.' *Eight or nine? No wonder she was traumatised.*

'Sorry. Red and gold ties and dark-green blazers was all he could tell from across the road.'

Pete released his pent-up breath. 'We know where that is, don't we?'

The public school Rosie Whitlock attended; the young girl who had been abducted and raped last November, whose case Tommy was involved in.

Jane hesitated. 'Risingbrook? Why would kids from there pick on Annie? Or was it random? Has she said any more?'

'No. And she's asleep now.'

'There is one other thing, boss.'

'Yes?'

'In the alley. There was a single fresh-looking fag end in the grass and a crumpled-up packet. Don't suppose it'll help us find a suspect, but it might confirm it if we find one by another method.'

'Nice one. All we need now is a big enough book to cause head injuries with when we throw it at them and we'll be set.'

She laughed.

'Thanks, Jane. I'll see you tomorrow.'

'Yeah. Night, boss.'

'Has she got something?' Louise asked as he ended the call.

'A description and some DNA.'

'DNA?' she asked, horrified.

'A cigarette butt. And the packet it possibly came from.'

Louise slumped with relief. 'God, I thought for a second . . . Ugh!' She shivered. 'And they came from Risingbrook?'

He nodded.

'It's a long way off their turf, isn't it?'

The big public school was over half a mile away, towards the city centre. 'Yes. I'm guessing that's why Jane asked if she was targeted or if it was random.'

'How would she know that?'

Pete tilted his head. 'Depends what they said to her. If they used her name. Or mine. If they knew where she lives.'

The door behind Louise opened. 'They knew. They asked if I liked the artwork on the garage door the other day.'

'Annie.' Pete stepped forward as Annie came into the room and Louise turned to face her. 'Are you OK, love?'

She gave a slow blink that passed for a nod. 'Thirsty.'

Louise gathered her into her arms as he said, 'I'll make you another cup of tea. How's that?'

She gave him a nod and what might have been a smile.

'Don't worry now, lovey,' Louise was saying to her. 'It'll all be OK. Your dad'll sort it out.'

With her arms wrapped around her mother's waist, Annie looked over at Pete. 'They said you'd cut off their supply so I was going to replace it, only better.'

'Supply?' Louise looked from Annie to Pete and back again. 'Supply of what?'

Pete shook his head with a grimace. He didn't want to think about that now. 'We'll look into it tomorrow. Did they say anything else, Annie?'

'No. That's when I got away from them.'

'You got away?' Louise leaned back, holding her at arm's length. 'From eight or nine of them in a narrow pathway?'

Annie nodded. 'I did what Tommy taught me. The leader looked round at his mates, so I kicked him in the nuts, punched one of them on the nose, poked another in the eye, then jumped through the gap they'd left. The rest were too shocked to stop me until it was too late so I just ran as fast as I could.'

'My God, Annie.' Louise crouched so that she was on eye-level with Annie. 'That was so . . .'

'Brave,' Pete cut in. 'We're so proud of you. And your mum's right. You don't need to worry: it won't happen again. I'll make sure of that.'

Pete dropped Annie at the bus stop with her friends in the morning then went straight to Risingbrook School. The road outside was crowded with cars and four-by-fours, uniformed students trickling through the gates singly and in groups. Pete drove into the wide expanse of the grounds and up the tarmac drive to park outside the doors of the main block. He locked the car and strode in. There was a reception desk to his left. He recognised the woman standing behind it, her dark hair pulled back in a bun, black-framed glasses perched on her nose.

'Detective Gayle. What can we do for you this morning?'

'Your photographic yearbooks,' he said, knowing from last year that they kept them. 'I need to borrow three of them. Current years seven to nine.' Kids were passing behind him, chattering and laughing, their voices echoing in the big entrance hall.

'Of course. I'll fetch them out for you. You won't be able to take them away, of course.'

Pete grimaced, sucking air across his teeth. 'That could be a problem. I was hoping to keep things unofficial for the sake of the school's reputation. If I have to come back with a warrant, that'll be out the window.'

'The . . . What do you need them for, Detective?'

'It's in regard to a sexual assault that took place in Whipton yesterday afternoon. A witness identified the perpetrators as coming from here by their uniforms. They wouldn't be able to identify the individuals involved, but the victim would. If she can do that from the yearbooks, they can be dealt with as individuals before the press get hold of anything and start shouting it about all over the place.'

Her naturally stern features closed into a frown. 'There's no need for threats of press involvement, Detective. I'll need to speak to the head, of course, but in those circumstances, I don't see why he'd object.'

'You misunderstood, Mrs Paxton. I wasn't making threats – just pointing out a possibility that I'm trying to avoid on your behalf.'

'Hmm.' She clearly wasn't convinced. 'Give me a moment.'

She turned away and picked up the phone on the desk behind her.

Oh, well, Pete thought as she dialled. *Another Christmas card I won't be getting this year.* He leaned on the counter and waited while she spoke in low tones.

Putting the phone down, she turned back to face him. She was still looking more sour than usual when she said, 'The head has agreed to allow you to take the three yearbooks away with you. I didn't pass on your – *suggestion* – about the press.'

Pete smiled. 'Thank you. And thank him for me, would you? I'm sorry if I was a bit less tactful than usual.'

She pursed her lips and turned away, heading through to a back office. Moments later, she returned, three thick folio-sized books in her arms. She put them carefully on the counter. 'Apology accepted, Detective.'

'Thanks. I'll get them back to you as soon as I can. Depending on how ready the victim is to go through them, of course.'

She drew a long breath. 'Was she . . . badly hurt?'

Pete shook his head. 'Not as badly as a couple of the lads, from what I gather. Not that that's going to affect the charges.'

'Good. And quite right too.'

Pete picked up the books. Maybe he would be getting that Christmas card, after all.

Pete saw Dick and Ben's computer screens as he approached his desk. Both appeared to be going through indoor CCTV footage. 'Any joy yet?' he asked.

'Nothing yet,' Dave answered. 'She actually had seven possible places to choose from at that time of night. We've started by going through all of them for the few minutes around the time she was last seen on the square, to find which one she went into. There's none of a girl with a cap like she was wearing out there, but a few with similar jackets. We've eliminated the blondes and the one redhead to begin with. Got down to four: two of them in the same pub – the one in the alley going through to Fore Street. Trouble is, that time of night, they're all heaving, people coming and going all the time. But we're trying to identify each of the possibles as she leaves, to make sure she hasn't changed her appearance. We're getting there.'

'How've you got on, boss?' Jane asked. 'And how's Annie?'

'She's all right, considering. She insisted on going to school today. I dropped her off. I'll be picking her up too. And I'll be out at lunchtime. I got the yearbooks from Risingbrook to show her – see if she can pick out any of the lads.'

'She wasn't actually . . .?' Jill hesitated.

'No. But the threat was there.'

'But why?' Jane wanted to know. 'What was the point? Surely, it wasn't . . . A whole gang like that. I mean . . .' She shook her head, at a loss.

'Apparently, they were the same ones who put the graffiti on our garage door and did my tyres. And they said to her that I'd cut off their supply, whatever that means. So, she was going to replace it, only better.'

'Eh? What's that about?' Ben demanded, looking up from his screen.

Pete shrugged. 'What have we put a stop to recently? Drugs is the main thing, isn't it.'

'But that wasn't down to you. You were in here.'

'Except for the Armenian.'

'The dog fights, the other day?' Dave suggested. 'That's a lot more recent. Might make it more relevant.'

'There's Frank with his eggs and chicks,' Ben said. He had been with Pete when he arrested the former CID officer a few months before and had been the prime victim of his bullying before he retired.

'I can't see lads that age being into falconry,' Pete said, 'legal or otherwise, no matter how privileged their backgrounds.'

Ben shrugged.

'There's one other possibility,' Jane said carefully. 'Do you remember Chris Mellor?'

Pete frowned.

'Becky Sanderson's boyfriend.'

Becky Sanderson was Rosie Whitlock's best friend. Her father was currently awaiting trial on child pornography charges and she had been sexting with her boyfriend until it emerged that others had seen the pictures she sent him and they broke up. 'Yes, I remember.'

And they told Annie she'd have to replace their source.

'If that's what this is about, there's going to be hell to pay. I can promise you that.'

Dick shrank the video playback window on his computer screen and slumped back in his chair. 'Nothing.'

Pete looked up from what he was doing. 'That's everywhere then.'

'Yep. All four of the girls we picked out emerged eventually from the pubs in the same clothes they went in wearing.'

'So, it has to be one of those you left out. The blondes and the redhead.'

'I'd go with the redhead,' Dave said. 'You can never trust them. Ow! Physical violence, boss!'

Pete looked from Dave to Jane and back. 'I didn't see anything.'

'What? Blatant abuse, that was.'

'And thoroughly deserved,' Jill put in from his other side.

'Who asked you, Titch?'

This time, Pete did see the response as Jill jabbed him in the ribs.

'Hey! I'm getting picked on here,' Dave protested. 'Sexual harassment.'

'You should be so lucky,' Jane said.

'I've said so for years, but you will stick with that husband of yours.'

'Since when did that stop you?' Dick demanded.

'Never,' Jane put in. 'But my knee would.'

'Well, seeing that you're such an expert on redheads, Dave, you can check the one you spotted on the footage while Dick and Ben check on the blondes. I'm going to Whipton. By the time I get back, hopefully one of you will have identified a suspect. Meantime, Jane and Jill can follow through on Ranjeet's alleged victims. Check identities, histories, alibis for the times in question, etc, etc.'

He had slipped into his jacket and was reaching for the door handle when Dave exclaimed, 'Ha ha! Told you. It was the redhead.'

Chapter 18

'Show me.'

Pete leaned over Dave's shoulder, staring at his screen.

Dave leaned back, pointing with the butt end of his pen. 'There she is. Left-hand edge of the screen.' He edged the video forward slowly. 'Disappearing off the edge of the picture.'

'OK.'

The image was reasonable quality but had a yellow tinge to it from the artificial lights that darkened the young woman's hair to a chestnut-brown.

Dave let the video run at normal speed. 'Wait for it. Wait for it. Wait for it. There!' he declared as a young blonde in a summer dress emerged from the side of the picture and walked across at an angle.

'How the hell d'you make that connection?'

'Simple. Blondie didn't go into the toilets in the ten minutes before the redhead did, and the redhead didn't come out in the ten minutes after.'

'Fair enough,' Pete nodded. 'Check a further five minutes before and after, then get as good a printout as you can of her face and let's see if we can identify her.'

'So, she switched from dark to red to blonde?' Ben clarified. 'That's a bit elaborate, isn't it?'

'Says one thing clearly, though, doesn't it?' Dick said. 'If she's set up that complicated a plan to evade us, it definitely wasn't a spontaneous attack.'

'She set out with intent,' Dave agreed. 'Almost . . .' He shook his head quickly.

'Almost what?' Pete asked.

'Almost professional.'

'Here we go again,' Jane protested. 'A female hitman in Devon? Dream on, matey.'

'Have wig, will travel,' Dick said dryly.

'Not many people would dump a whole outfit, including a leather jacket, like that,' Ben pointed out. 'That wasn't cheap, I bet.'

'Well, one of you get over there and see if you can recover it then,' Pete said. 'The whole outfit, if possible. We might get some DNA that way. And get going on that picture of her. Police National Computer, Missing Persons, DVLA, Passport Control. Everywhere you can think of and more besides. Also, send all three images to HQ, get a composite done with the dark hair from Cathedral Square and the face from the pub cameras. Then all three pictures can go to press liaison for putting out to the papers and TV. "Do you know this woman?" – that kind of thing. Well done, Dave.'

'*Dad!* There's no need to check up on me at lunchtime too.'

She came round the corner with her arms full of books from her last lesson of the morning – one of dozens of kids flowing out of the main block, past the reception desk where he was waiting.

Pete grinned. 'Hello, love. I'm not here to check up on you. I'm here to spoil your lunchtime. Sorry.'

'What's up?'

'I went to the school where those lads came from and got the photo yearbooks.'

'But how did you know where they came from?'

He ruffled her hair. 'I'm a detective, remember?'

'*Dad!*'

'So, are you up to looking through some pictures, see if you can pick any of them out? They're just standard school photos.'

'How long will it take?'

'That's up to you, love. I'm here now to save you missing classes and, at the same time, get things in motion as soon as I can, but at the end of the day, you're the most important one here.'

She blinked. 'OK.'

He felt a swell of pride, but still didn't want to push her. 'Sure?'

She nodded.

'Come on then. They're in the car.' He reached for her hand, but she avoided his grip. Then he realised: they were in school. Among her friends. Disappointment vanished and he couldn't help a quiet smile. Much as he hated the idea in some ways, she was growing up.

He gave the teaching assistant who had fetched her a nod of thanks and led the way outside, holding the door so she could slip through under his arm. They crossed the crowded and noisy tarmac to the tall metal gates and slipped through them. He had parked a few yards up to the right. She saw the car and led the way. Pete unlocked it with the remote so she could dump her books on the back seat and climb into the front, where he'd left the yearbooks standing upright at the side of the footwell. He slid into the driver's seat and picked up the big books, laying them on his lap to pick out the first one for her to look at. The middle one. He passed it across.

'Take your time, love. You either see them or you don't. If you recognise any, just point them out and I'll make a note, OK?'

'Mm-hm.' She nodded and looked down at the leather-bound album in her lap. 'Risingbrook? That's where Rosie Whitlock went, isn't it?'

'That's right.'

'And that's where they were from?'

'According to a man who saw them before you got there.'

'That doesn't make sense. What could they have against you?'

He shook his head. He didn't want to go into that with her if he didn't have to. She was his baby girl. She didn't need to know about stuff like that.

She looked up at him for a moment, then shrugged and opened the album. Began to flip through. 'There's nothing like this here,' she said, glancing over at the school gates.

'I bet. It's an expensive school these have come from.'

'Doesn't make the kids any better,' she said.

Pete laughed. She wasn't just incredibly brave, but perceptive beyond her years too.

She continued to flip slowly through the pages, examining every face for some time before stopping suddenly. Staring. Pete saw her lips tighten, her brow furrow, little lines appearing between her eyebrows, just like her mother's. Love swelled in his chest. Then she looked up and met his gaze, her eyes large and serious.

Her little finger pointed to one of the images on the page. 'He was there.'

'Sure?'

She nodded.

'OK.' He made a note of the subject's name. Annie studied the remainder of the pictures and turned the page.

It hadn't even fallen flat onto the previous ones when she froze. 'The leader. The one who did all the talking.'

'Which one?'

She jabbed a finger at the photo in the top-right corner of the new page.

Pete made another quick note. 'Are you OK, love?'

She nodded decisively. And pointed again. 'He was there too. And him.'

Pete wrote down the names.

Annie turned the page. Looked carefully and turned it again. It was several pages later that she stopped again. 'That's the one I poked in the eye.'

Pete grinned. 'That's my girl. I'll soon spot him then, eh?' *And she'd said last night that she did what Tommy taught her. He'd shown her how to defend herself. That wasn't the action of a psychopath.*

She looked up at him again. 'What's going to happen to them?'

Pete's throat clogged. She cared about what would happen to a gang of boys she'd never met until they attacked and threatened her. This girl was incredible. 'They'll get what they deserve,' he said.

'But . . .'

'Don't worry about it, love. You've done really well.'

'Will they get expelled?'

He laughed. 'I should certainly hope so.'

'Then . . .'

'They won't be coming here. They're too old. And before they go anywhere else, they'll be in bigger trouble than that.'

She stared solemnly up at him. He reached over and kissed the top of her head. 'God, I love you! Do you want to pack it in now, go and have your lunch?'

'I haven't found them all yet.'

'You've done plenty, love. I can take it from here.' He took the big book from her lap, easing it closed. 'Go and have a bit of time with your mates. I'll see you later.'

'OK.'

He gave her a hug. She hopped out of the car and fetched her books from the back seat. 'See you later,' she called as she ran back through the school gates and into the playground.

Pete didn't start the car until she was gone from sight.

'The outfit's with forensics,' Dave said when he returned to the squad room a short time later. 'The whole lot was there. Jacket, blouse and trousers.'

'How did she manage to go in there in a blouse and trousers and come out in a dress without it looking all crumpled?' Ben asked.

'Simple,' Jane told him. 'You wear the dress under the blouse,

use elastic or something to tie the skirt up over your stomach and let it hang from there.'

Dave shook his head. 'Poor lad's got no idea.'

'What, and you have?'

'I'm in touch with my feminine side.' He gave Ben a wink. 'I touch her every chance I get.'

'Have you ever heard the term misogynist?' Jill asked.

'Is she one of those Romanian gymnasts?'

'You'll never win with him,' Jane told her.

'But it's fun watching her try,' Dave said.

Jill shook her head. 'While the ladies' man here was out and about, we had another suspected victim of Ranjeet Singh's phone in, boss. This one was molested two and a half years ago as he helped her get her luggage out of his boot. He claimed it was an accident, but it seems pretty suspect. He touched her bottom as she bent to pick up a case he'd dropped.'

'And then, a few months later, he raped someone,' Pete said. 'It speaks of progression. An intensifying of his behaviour. A gradual buildup of courage, perhaps?'

'Yeah. If courage is what you'd call it.'

'You know what I mean. Anyway, we could do with finding some more recent victims. What about the girl's identity? Have we got anywhere on that?'

'No matches on the PNC,' Ben said. 'Nor the Missing Persons database. Not that I expected one on there. DVLA and Passport Control don't keep photo records in a searchable form, unfortunately. I did check with the university, though. They do. But no luck.'

'So, we've got a picture of her, but we can't get an ID.'

'Not legally, boss.'

'And although we've got her face and the CCTV can give us her height and so on, we don't even know her hair colour for sure,' Dick pointed out.

'You're a bright and cheerful bugger, ain't you?' said Dave.

Dick shrugged. 'Facts is facts, like 'em or not.'

'Well, I don't, so I suggest you do something about it,' Pete said. 'Jane, you can come with me. The rest of you: I want to know who that woman is and, more importantly, where she is.'

Jane switched off her computer screen and stood up. 'Where are we going, boss?'

'Back to school. See if we can learn a few things.'

'Thomas. Take a seat. How are you today?'

The psychiatrist waved a limp hand to the chair opposite him. Tommy didn't bother to reply as he sat down. The look on his face would say enough, he imagined.

'I was sorry to hear about what happened to your sister yesterday.'

Tommy's sneer curled into a snarl.

'I can't imagine how angry you must have felt when you were told about it.'

Tommy clamped his jaw closed, his mouth pressed into a thin line as he stared at the man with his thinning grey-blond hair and AC/DC T-shirt, which he must have thought made him look cool, but didn't suit him at all.

'Perhaps we should start by talking about that. I know you've suffered some bullying at school, but when it's your sister on the receiving end and there's nothing you can do about it, that must be extremely frustrating. I have to say, I'm quite amazed you've managed to maintain control today, in the circumstances. Well done for that.' He leaned forward, smiling. 'Very impressive, after the other day. Have you spoken to Sam yet?'

He'd been ordered, on coming out of solitary, to talk to the kid who'd attacked him and settle their differences.

'No.'

'It needs doing by the end of today, Tommy. Otherwise the manager will have to get involved.'

'Has Sam been told that? Because he started it. I was just defending myself.'

'I think you went a bit beyond that, Tommy. And rules are

there to be adhered to. Which, in this case, means you need to make the effort to speak to Sam.'

'And if I'd let him beat the crap out of me, like he wanted to, then he'd be coming to apologise to me?'

'You realise Sam's going to be scarred for life, don't you?'

'It'll remind him not to be a bully then, won't it?'

Brian sighed. 'I've been reading a report on you this morning, Tommy. It was compiled by one of your dad's colleagues, DS Phillips, when you went missing last year. There'd been incidents of violence before that, it seems. Some of the kids in school tended to steer clear of you – were afraid of you.'

'Yeah, well, that's better than the other way round.'

'But why the need to be feared? What do you gain from it?'

'It gets me left alone, doesn't it? Stops them picking on me.'

'You were bullied?'

'What do you think?' Tommy spread his hands. 'I'm not exactly big for my age, am I? I'm fourteen. What do I look? Twelve?'

'There's a difference between standing up for yourself and seriously injuring someone, though, Thomas.'

'Yeah. Stand up for yourself, they try again. Hurt them enough, they stay away from you.'

'That's a harsh conclusion for someone so young.'

'It's reality.'

'How long have you felt this way?'

'I don't. It's a way to avoid feeling. That's the point.'

'But we all feel, Tommy. That's what life is about. The pleasure and the pain.'

'Yeah, well, I prefer to do without the pain, thanks very much.'

Brian's gaze wandered off into the distance. 'I seem to remember a song that said you can't enjoy the sunshine without a little rain. Can't remember who it was by.'

'There's a lot of songs out there that are full of crap. Written by people on drugs or not in the real world for some other reason. Truth is, if you don't give a shit, you can't get hurt, can you?'

'It's a rather sad way to live, though, surely? To miss out on life's pleasures, just to avoid the pain.'

'You don't miss what you've never had.'

'Oh, come on, Thomas. You must have had some good times in your life. You have a loving family, unlike many of the young people I see in here.'

Tommy snorted. 'Yeah, right. My dad's too busy with work to notice me, my mum's not much different – in and out at all hours on shifts. And they've always preferred my sister anyway, ever since I can remember. Then I go to school and most of the kids are bigger than me, so who are they going to choose to pick on, do you reckon? So, no, I don't recall much in the way of good times.'

'And yet, you showed empathy for Rosie Whitlock when you helped her escape. You had nothing to gain from doing that.'

Tommy grinned. 'Didn't I?'

Brian paused, looking at him carefully. 'Did you? You put your own safety at risk in order to allow her to escape. You talk about dealing with young people who are bigger than you. Malcolm Burton's an adult. Much bigger and stronger. You couldn't hope to win in a fight with him. So, what could you hope to gain?'

'She got away, didn't she? So she's going to testify. Against him and for me. Even if I get charged, I've got that on my side. Plus, with her free and clear, I had a better chance of getting him not to hurt me.'

Brian nodded. 'You're a clever young man, I'll give you that. But did you really think that through in the heat of the moment? Or is it a conclusion you've reached since?'

'Well, that's the thing, isn't it? If I was a psycho, I'd have thought about it afterwards. But if not, I might have come up with it at the time. Depends how fast I think in stress situations, right? And to be fair, I'm pretty used to stress situations. With the amount of times I've been in them with the other kids at school. Until I decided to fight back.'

'You *decided*?'

Tommy smiled again. This was fun. He was getting the guy more confused every time he spoke. 'Or it could be I just saw red one day and flipped out. Scared the kid into not coming near me again.' He shrugged. 'If that was the case, I'd have seen the effect it had and used it again next time. And the next. I mean, if they were going to hurt me anyway, I'd have had nothing to lose, would I?'

'So, which way did it happen, Thomas? Did you make a decision? Or did you "flip out"?'

'Which would you prefer? Which one would suit your purpose best, Brian?'

'This isn't about me, Tommy. It's about you. All I'm trying to do is get to the truth, so we can hopefully improve your life, going forward.'

'"Going forward?" Do you mean "from now on", Brian?' Tommy shook his head like a disappointed teacher. 'All this pointless jargon – it's pathetic. Why can't you just say what you mean in plain English?'

'You prefer plain speaking, Tommy?'

Yes! Got him! 'Better to say what you mean than wander all around it, talking crap that nobody understands anyway.'

Brian tilted his head. 'Except when being blunt could be hurtful.'

Tommy grimaced. 'Best to know where you stand, good or bad, I reckon. I never saw the point in fannying about.'

'Say what you mean, do what you want, and to hell with the consequences?'

'Something like that, yeah.'

'And when what you want doesn't suit someone else's needs?'

Tommy shrugged. 'They have to lump it, don't they?'

'By that standard, the same applies in the other direction, though, doesn't it? If someone bigger or stronger or faster or louder than you wants to do something that doesn't suit you, then you have to lump it.'

'Fair's fair.'

'Except, in that direction lies anarchy and war.'

'Well, there you go.' Tommy spread his hands. 'I'm being green. All these environmentalists keep saying there's too many of us on the planet.'

He saw Brian's eyes close and knew he'd won. A few more sessions and Brian wouldn't know which way was up.

Chapter 19

'Thanks for these.' Pete laid the three big books on the counter in front of the receptionist. 'They were very useful.'

She looked horrified. 'You've identified the boys from them?'

'Some of them, yes. I'm hoping that someone here will be able to help with the rest. Who associates with who – that kind of thing.'

'Yes, uh, I'm not . . . That is . . . I know most of the students by sight, of course, but not necessarily by name.'

'Fair enough. I've got a list of names and which year they're in. You just point me towards the head and we'll take it from there.'

'Of course. This is awful. Our students involved in something like this. I wouldn't have believed it possible.' Her eyes closed behind the dark-rimmed glasses and she gave a shudder. Then, picking up the phone, she dialled an internal number.

'Mr Grayson, it's Cynthia. Detective Sergeant Gayle is here again with a colleague. They need to speak to you.' She paused. 'Yes, that's right . . . Very well.'

She put the phone down and looked up at Pete and Jane. 'He'll be out in a moment.'

'Thank you.' Pete turned sideways on to the counter, leaning an elbow on it while he watched the comings and goings around him, students moving this way and that, in groups and singly.

He was surprised at how serene and civilised it all was, in comparison to other schools he'd been in – including the one he'd attended as a child.

True to his word, Richard Grayson came around the corner to Pete's left just moments later. Pete straightened, recognising the man from their previous meetings over the Rosie Whitlock case.

'Sergeant Gayle. Good afternoon. What can I do for you?' He extended a hand which Pete shook.

'This is my colleague, Detective Constable Bennett. I've got a list of names of some of your students, Mr Grayson. Part of a gang. To start with, I need you to help me identify the other members of that gang, if you can. Or at least, the most likely other members.'

'We don't have gangs here, Detective Sergeant. We don't tolerate such things.'

'Well, whatever you want to call them, we're talking about a bunch of eight or nine lads, students here, who associate with each other closely enough to trust each other implicitly, in or out of school. Anywhere else, that would be called a gang.'

'Very well. If you'd like to follow me . . .' He held out a hand and headed back the way he'd come.

His office looked out over the wide lawns at the front of the school. It was large, book-lined and neat, with the feel of an old boys' club room: dark wood, high ceilings, green leather and dry conversation. Pete almost expected Grayson to offer them a glass of port or fine whisky. Instead, he showed them each to a chair and took one opposite them.

'So, how serious was the assault these boys are being accused of?'

'The seriousness of the assault itself is not the point, Mr Grayson. The threat was there. The intent was there. It was just the quick thinking and courage of the proposed victim that prevented it going further and these sorts of actions are not going to be tolerated on the streets of Exeter. Not by anybody.'

'I quite understand, Detective Sergeant. Which boys have been identified?'

'They're all year nine. Fourteen-year-olds. The victim is eleven. He read off the names from his notebook.'

Grayson nodded slowly. 'Yes, they're all friends, apart from Toby Ronaldson. He doesn't fit the picture.'

'So, who else would be in the group?'

'Maybe Toby's a friend of a friend,' Jane suggested.

Grayson hesitated. 'The other members of that group would include Jonathan Hughes, Matthew Bates, Christopher Mellor . . . actually, Jonathan's a friend of Toby Ronaldson.' He drew a breath. 'I'm not sure I can think of any others, but with the five you had, that gives you eight. You said there were eight or nine.'

'Is there anyone else we could ask? Anyone who might have a more precise idea of who they might mix with? Just in case we've missed anyone.'

'They're all members of either the rugby or boys' hockey teams for their year. Samuel Fisher would be the one to expand on what I've told you, if anyone could. He's the games master.'

'OK.' Pete waited for him to continue.

'He's out with a class of year sevens at the moment. Soccer.'

'Is there someone who can take over from him? We really need to get this tied up as quickly as possible.'

'Uh, yes. Miss Peterson will be out with the girls and they each have an assistant.'

'Good. How do we find him then?'

'I'll . . .' He hesitated again, then seemed to reach a decision. 'I'll take you myself, Detective.'

'So, Sam – do you mind if I call you Sam? – what can you tell me about a bunch of lads I've been told are close friends, including Jonathan Hughes, Chris Mellor, Matt Bates and Dan Childs?'

Pete leaned forward in his chair, elbows on his knees. They were in the staffroom, which was otherwise unoccupied at this time of the afternoon, the games master, in his purple tracksuit with navy edging, sitting opposite the two detectives.

'What can I tell you about them? In what sense?'

'What are they like as a bunch? Who else is part of their group? What interests do they share off the sports field?' He shrugged. 'Anything you can think of.'

Fisher drew a breath. 'OK. They're a decent enough bunch of lads, as a rule. A bit rowdy when they're all together, but that's nothing unusual at that age, is it? I don't know much about what they get up to off the sports field – outside my purview, I'm afraid – but I know they hang around with a few of the other lads. Roger Hopkins, Adrian Ellis, Hugh Paige, Mickey Hall and, occasionally, Toby Ronaldson – although he's a bit more on the sidelines, if I'm honest. He's got a couple of friends in the group so he gets included on that basis, but he's not a core member, if you know what I mean.'

Pete nodded his understanding. 'There's often one like that, isn't there?'

'Exactly. So, what's this about? Why are the police taking an interest in the lads?'

'We're conducting enquiries into an incident that some of them have been identified as being present at.'

'I see.' He smiled, relaxing.

'So, how would I find out where they are now?' Pete asked.

'There's an overall timetable on the school server. I can look it up on the computer over there, if you like.' He nodded towards a desktop machine in the corner, opposite the sink and coffee machine.

'Thank you. That would be very helpful.'

'No problem.' He stood up and crossed to the small table that held the computer, switched it on and waited for it to boot up. With Pete and Jane looking over his shoulders, he called up a document from an extensive list on the screen and scanned quickly down and across until he found what he was looking for. 'There we are.

Most of them are in 9F. The remaining three are in 9B and C. So, art, English and physics.'

'You wouldn't be able to take us to them?'

He shrugged. 'My current class is only for another ten minutes, so why not?'

'Excellent. Thank you.'

'Anything for the man who recovered Rosie Whitlock, Detective.'

Pete tilted his head. *That's not where this conversation was going until you thought we just needed them as witnesses, Sammy Boy.* As Fisher led the way towards the door, he raised an eyebrow at Jane, who gave him a slight shrug in return. She'd noticed it too.

'Young Mr Mellor. We meet again. Take a seat.'

Pete leaned back in his chair, indicating the one across the table from him while Jane sat to one side, notebook and pen in hand. Pete had borrowed the room next to Grayson's office, which he said was often used for meetings with parents. The school nurse sat in the corner near the door, taking the role of responsible adult.

Chris Mellor stood stiffly just inside the room, the door closing slowly behind him. His eyes had flicked to Pete as he entered, then slid away and refused to return. He edged forward.

Pete waited for him to sit, maintaining his relaxed attitude. The kid was terrified, as well he should be. 'You know why we're here, don't you?' he said when Mellor had finally perched himself on the chair.

'No.'

'There are that many possible reasons, are there? Have a guess.'

'Becky? Her pictures again?'

'I hope not, for your sake. Who's the leader of your merry little band?'

Mellor frowned, glancing up at Pete.

'You're all out there, waiting in the corridor. Or, I hope you're all there. With Mr Fisher to keep you entertained while you wait. So, you know which merry band I'm talking about. Who's the

203

big cheese? The one who calls the shots? The one everybody says "Yes" to?'

Mellor shrugged. 'Jonathan, I suppose.'

'And which one's he? What does he look like?' Pete already knew the answer, but he wanted to make Mellor talk and a subject he'd already spoken about was the easy route towards that.

'Tall, dark, ripped.'

'Tall, dark and handsome, eh?' Pete glanced at Jane. 'Just what the girls all say they want. So, why does he take you all off to Whipton, chasing eleven-year-old kids?'

What little colour Mellor had in his face drained away. His eyes closed. He seemed to stop breathing. Then he began to tremble.

'Yes, Chris. *That's* why we're here. And don't try to tell me you weren't there because she's already picked you out. So, why? Eh? What was it all about? What did I take away your source of?'

Again, as soon as he'd been given Mellor's name, Pete knew the answer, but he wanted the kid to admit it, to talk to him.

Mellor's jaw began to tremble. He clamped it shut. Finally, he looked up at Pete and held his gaze. 'I'm sorry,' he whispered.

'What was that?'

Mellor flinched as Pete sat forward, arms on the table. He'd made sure there would be a table between him and the kids, just in case his rage boiled over and he did something he'd regret. He knew himself well enough to know it was a possibility, faced with the kids who had ganged up on his daughter, aiming to terrify her or worse. 'Can you repeat that, Mr Mellor? I didn't quite catch it.'

The boy's mouth twisted. Pete wasn't sure if it was a sneer or he was fighting back tears. 'I said I'm sorry.'

'You're sorry. What are you sorry for, Chris?' He felt the anger building, a tirade bubbling just under the surface, aching for release, and forced himself to hold it back.

'For . . .' His gaze slid away again. 'What happened with your daughter.'

'You're sorry for what happened with my daughter. Well, thank you for that, Chris. Which part of what happened with my daughter are you sorry for?'

'Huh?' He looked up again.

'What, exactly, are you sorry for? The crowding, pushing, terrifying, or the threats? Or just for getting caught and identified? And you still haven't answered my previous question. Why Annie? What were you going to make her replace, that I'd taken away? Replace, only better – wasn't that the phrase used?'

Mellor's jaw was clenching and relaxing as Pete spoke, clenching and relaxing as he fought with his emotions. He glanced up. 'I didn't . . .' He stopped himself.

'You didn't what?'

Nothing. Eyes closed, jaw clenched, Mellor sat there, breathing deeply.

'You didn't what, Chris? You know your parents are going to be told about this, don't you? And that's the least of it. Expulsion. A trial. And never mind a young offenders' institute. This is an adult crime, Chris. You'll be tried for it as an adult. Adult prison time with blokes two and three times your size who've seen nothing but big, hairy apes with tattoos and stubble for months or years. Imagine that, Chris. Not enough warders to protect you. What do you think'll happen to a fresh young lad like you?'

'Sergeant . . .' the nurse started.

'I didn't touch her,' Mellor shouted. 'I didn't touch her, OK? I never intended to. It wasn't my idea. It was just . . .'

'Just what, Chris? What were you going to do? Take . . .?' Pete stopped, turning away in his chair, his throat clogging with emotion. This was his little girl, who he loved so dearly, he couldn't bring himself to say or even imagine what their intentions might have been.

He took a deep breath.

'Answer the question, please, Chris,' Jane said. 'What was the plan? And whose was it?'

'We were just going to scare her. Make sure it got back to . . .' He glanced guiltily at Pete as he turned back to the table, resting his elbows on it, face in his hands. 'But then, somebody suggested we go further. That we . . . Then other people started chiming in and it all got out of hand. I'd have . . . I wouldn't have let them . . . I swear.'

'So, what was it all about?' Jane asked. 'What triggered the whole idea?'

He sighed. 'We had those pictures of Becky and Rosie last year. Then they were found and . . . got rid of. It was . . .' He drew a long, shuddering breath. 'Some of the lads wanted more of the same.'

Pete's fists slammed on the table. Mellor jumped in his chair. Jane put a hand on Pete's arm. 'Boss. Maybe you should step out for a minute? Get some fresh air?'

His first instinct was to snap back at her, deny the need, reach over the table and grab hold of Mellor's lapels, drag him forward and plant a headbutt straight on his nose. He could almost feel the words in his throat and Mellor's jacket in his fists. But his brief satisfaction wouldn't give Annie the justice she deserved, or ensure the safety of the other young girls in the city. He closed his eyes, pulled in a deep breath, held it for a moment, then stepped away from her and around the table.

The whimper of terror from Mellor was almost drowned by the scrape of the nurse's chair and the gasp from Jane. Pete ignored them all, strode purposefully towards the door, snatched it open and stalked away down the corridor.

When he turned into the main reception, it was crowded with a milling throng of kids, shoes clattering on the bare wooden floor, but they seemed to part before him like the sea before the prow of a ship as he marched purposefully through. He stepped out of the dark and oppressive interior, into the afternoon sunshine, took out his phone and hit a speed-dial number.

'DC Miles, Exeter CID.'

'Dave. Get yourself down here to Risingbrook. Pronto.'

Jane was right. He'd thought he could do this, but he'd been wrong. It was too close. He'd end up hurting someone if he stayed. And protocol dictated, responsible adult or not, Jane could not do the interviews alone.

Chapter 20

'Mum. Annie.'

'How are you, darling?' Louise asked as she took a seat across the small, round table from her son, who was already waiting for them, Annie moving to one side and pulling out a chair between them.

'OK, considering. Had a nice chat with Brian earlier. The psychiatrist. It is true that you and dad had to sign to give him permission to talk to me, right?'

'Well, technically, yes. It was part of the package. Giving them the right to deal with you as they see the need.'

'So, you think I'm a psycho.'

'No!' she protested. 'Not at all. Like I said – it's just part of the process, that's all.'

'I've seen the file. There's no point trying to sugarcoat it when it's already half-chewed. You think I'm dangerous.'

'No, we don't. We know you've got problems and we accept that they may be at least partly our fault, but dangerous? No. We've never thought that.'

'Well, that's big of you – accepting part of the blame. Maybe. I am your son, after all. You brought me up to be what I am.'

'What are you doing, Tommy?' Annie broke in. 'Why are you

being like this? We've come to see you, to show you we care about you. Mum doesn't deserve this.'

'What, it's just Dad, is it?' He turned on her. 'She's an adult. She makes her own decisions. Signs her own name. They both think I "*need help*".' He wiggled his fingers in the air to form quotation marks. 'And what about you? What do you think? Do you think I need help, little sis? Am I like those kids who came after you in the alley? Or worse?'

She sat back, horrified. 'You're my brother, Tommy. Why would you even bring that up? Of course you're not like them!'

'Aren't I? What were they after, eh? What did they want with you? The same as I had with Rosie and Lauren?'

'Tommy!' Louise broke in as Annie burst into tears. 'How could you? How could you say that to your own sister?'

He turned back to her, his eyes glittering. 'Easy,' he said. 'I'm a psycho. That means I don't give a shit.'

Louise's face crumpled. 'I can't deal with you when you're like this.' She grabbed Annie's hand and stood up, heading for the door.

'That's it,' he called after them. 'Walk away. Easy now, isn't it?' He leaned back, crossing his legs under the table, hands clasped in his lap as he watched them go.

Step three to building the reputation he wanted in this place. By the time he was finished, they wouldn't have a clue what to make of him.

'We've had two more of Ranjeet Singh's victims phone in, boss,' Jill said as he dropped his jacket over the back of his chair. 'One was raped in the back of his cab after a night in Mamma Stone's. She'd asked him to take her out to Woodwater Lane. He went past where she wanted and up onto Pyne's Hill. Stopped along Ludwell Lane and climbed in the back with her. Used the child locks to stop her getting away. This was last November, while we were working the Rosie Whitlock case. She didn't report it because of all the press coverage of the attacks on young girls – thought that was more important. Then, when that was all over, she figured it would be too late.'

Pete sat down at last. 'Did you tell her we'd have made the time anyway – that that's what we're here for?'

Jill shrugged. 'Yeah, but what can you do? Can't charge him now, can we?'

'What about the other one?'

'Last July, while you were off. She asked him to take her out along Pinhoe Road. Lives up Venny Bridge way. He pulled into a side road by the old playing field. Assaulted her and dumped her out there, half a mile from home with no purse, no phone and not a stitch on. She was so traumatised by the time she got home, she couldn't bring herself to report it and have to talk through it – relive it – with anyone, never mind in court. Still doesn't go out after dark, she said, or on her own.'

'So, how the hell did she get home?' Ben asked.

'Walked until a woman stopped to offer her a lift.'

'Naked? Up Pinhoe Road? I bet she got plenty of attention, didn't she?'

'That was part of the problem,' Jill said.

'I expect it was,' Pete agreed. 'But it supports our theory of why he was killed.'

'Doesn't tell us who by, though,' Dick put in.

It wouldn't encourage most people to find out either, Pete knew. But he also knew his team. They might not be too politically correct at times, but they were thorough and they all believed, as he did, that the law was the law, regardless of the circumstances.

'What about those pictures? Have we heard back from Middlemoor yet?'

'Nothing yet,' Dick told him.

'Right. I'll give them a chase.' He picked up his phone and dialled Headquarters' switchboard. 'DS Gayle, Heavitree Road,' he said when it was answered. 'I need to talk to the forensic artists.'

'Hold one moment.'

'Forensic art and photography.'

'DS Gayle, Heavitree Road. One of my team sent you some pictures of a suspect with the aim of getting a composite done, including the hairstyle from a distant shot and the face from one of the closer ones. Any joy yet?'

'It's coming along. Just tidying it up, then we'll send it across. Ten, twenty minutes. No more than that.'

'OK. Thanks.' He put the phone down. 'Is Fast-track in his den?'

'Yep,' Dick said.

'Right. I'd best give him an update then, before we get the pictures back from Middlemoor. They'll be sending them across shortly.'

Louise caught up with Annie fifteen paces down the corridor, still running as fast as her little legs would take her.

'Annie! Stop.' She grabbed her arm, trying to slow her down, but Annie was having none of it. She was crying desperately, wailing her distress to anyone in earshot. She tried to snatch away from Louise, but her mother was stronger, more determined. She held on as they slammed through a connecting door, still running. Louise slid her grip down Annie's arm to her hand, but let her run. They were almost at the reception now. Just one more turn. She tried slowing her steps, grasping Annie's hand tightly, but she was dragged forward by her daughter's headlong flight from the horror of what her brother had said.

Not just what he'd said, Louise thought, but the way he'd said it. He'd really appeared to mean it. He didn't want to see them. Didn't want them coming here. It was like he was abandoning them all over again. She could understand Annie's distress. Felt the same way herself. After all they'd done as a family, trying to find him, to bring him home . . . And his response? First, months ago, he'd broken in while they were out and burgled the house. Now, when they'd finally found him, almost got him home, he was pushing them away as if he wanted to utterly disown them.

Why?

She couldn't understand his rejection any more than Annie could, in truth. It was just that, as an adult, she had marginally better coping mechanisms. At least, she did now.

Last year, for a long time after Tommy disappeared, it had been the other way round. Annie had coped far better than she had, to the point where, despite her resentment of the fact, their roles had almost swapped over in some respects. Annie had been a complete gem. She had kept the family, and Louise as a person, together through the worst times.

She glanced at the receptionist as they hurried past, tipping her head in a shrug. *What can I do?* Then they were slamming through the double doors of the entrance, down the wide, curved, stone steps to the gravel drive. Feet crunching on the pale grit, Annie kept running until Louise was finally able to pull her back and slow them down.

'Enough, Annie. Stop now.'

Annie spun around, burying her head in Louise's chest, still crying disconsolately as she wrapped her arms tightly around her. 'Why was he like that, Mum?' she sobbed. 'Why did he say those horrible things? We're his family!'

'I don't know, love. I wish I did.' She held Annie tightly, trying to comfort her. 'But there are people here who can figure that out and do something about it. It's what they're trained for. It'll be all right in the end. You'll see.'

'But he was so nasty! It was like there was somebody else in Tommy's body. Like he was possessed, like in those nasty movies.'

'How do you know about movies like that? They're not supposed to be for kids.'

'Of course I know about them, Mum. I don't watch them. I don't like them. But I know about them.'

'What do you mean, you don't like them? How do you know?'

'From the adverts, of course. What's that got to do with anything?' She leaned back, staring up at Louise, her face wet with tears and so young and vulnerable that Louise's heart almost broke with love.

She smiled, pulling her back into a tight hug. 'Nothing at all, love. But it got your mind away from Tommy for a few seconds.'

'Come.'

Pete opened the door to the station chief's office and stepped in.

DCI Adam Silverstone was sitting behind his desk, immaculately uniformed as usual, his hat on the coat stand in the corner of the room, his desk neatly arranged with a small stack of files to his left and one open in front of him. He looked up. 'Peter. What can I do for you?'

'Just thought I'd best give you an update, sir. Things are moving a bit quick now, one way and another.'

'Good,' Silverstone nodded. 'What's the latest?'

Pete took a breath and went quickly through the latest developments. 'So, we're going to need to make a statement to go with the pictures,' he concluded. 'If we can get them out there tonight, they might make it onto the news programmes – the ten o'clock, if not the six. And the twenty-four-hour channels, of course. Plus, they should make tomorrow's papers. Singh was a despicable individual, but we can't be seen to let his killer get away with it. There'd be an outcry in the Indian and Pakistani community, accusing us of racism and all sorts.'

'Yes, obviously. All right, then. I'll draft something and be ready for when the images are available. Meantime, I'll give press liaison a call. Thank you, Peter.'

Pete knew better than to expect anything more from him, so he turned and reached for the door handle. He was opening the door when Silverstone said, 'Let me know what Jane and Dave come up with at Risingbrook.'

Pete's eyes widened in surprise. It was a good thing he was facing the other way, he thought, as he paused. 'Sir.'

Stepping out of the station commander's office, he closed the door behind him and returned to the squad room.

'The pictures are back, boss,' Ben said as he crossed towards his desk. He nodded towards the printer. 'Just came through.'

Pete stepped across and took the three A4 sheets from the printer tray. Each one filled the page. They were a bit blurry at that magnification, but definitely identifiable, and the third – the composite – looked as real as the others. They'd done a good job. 'Great. Forward them to the DCI, will you?' He sat down at his desk. 'He'll take it from there with the press.'

'Thought he might,' Dick said.

'You want to be careful,' Jill told him. 'You'll get a reputation as an old cynic.'

'Too late,' Ben said. 'At least for the old bit. They don't call him Grey Man for nothing.'

'Ah,' said Dick. 'That's just the blokes. The ladies call me Christian.'

'Yeah,' Jill laughed, getting the *Fifty Shades* reference. 'You wish.'

Pete's phone rang. He picked it up. 'DS Gayle.'

'Pete. It's Andy.' Pete recognised the uniformed branch sergeant's voice. 'There's been a third one.'

A wave of cold washed through Pete's body. He knew what Fairweather was talking about. He still had to ask the question, though. 'A third what?'

'Cabbie killed in his car.'

'How? When?'

'I don't know. What I *can* tell you is where and when he was found. I've just dispatched a couple of uniforms to the site. We were notified by a 999 call exactly four minutes ago. The body was found on Colleton Crescent by a solicitor returning to his office from a meeting. He parked in front of the taxi and saw the blood as he walked past it.'

Pete checked his watch. It was twenty-four minutes to four. Broad daylight. He knew Colleton Crescent from a case he'd worked a few months before. In fact, he'd visited the solicitors' office up there and made a significant discovery involving that case. He recalled the big, bluff, grey-bearded man who'd helped him view their CCTV footage. What had his name been . . .? He couldn't remember now, but it would come back to him, he was sure.

'OK. I'm on the way.' He put the phone down and stood up. 'Victim number three,' he said, answering the question implied by Dick's raised eyebrows.

Dave gave Jane a look as the latest of the boys left the room, closing the door behind him. 'Really?'

'What – you're asking me? Mr Feminist.'

'Jesus, come on! I enjoy a laugh, but these kids are sick.'

'After that, I'm feeling a bit queasy myself. I reckon it's time we had young Mr Mellor back in here. He's had enough time to calm down after the boss's little outburst.'

They had decided to let Chris Mellor off the hook for a while and talk to the other lads instead when Dave took over from Pete.

'OK.' He got up and went to the door. Opening it, he stuck his head out and said, 'Chris Mellor.'

He had made it back to his seat before Mellor entered the room, closing the door behind him. 'Yes?'

'Time to finish what we started, Chris,' Jane said. 'Come and sit down.'

Hesitantly, he stepped forward, glancing at the nurse in the corner as he approached the chair in front of the two plain-clothes police officers. He sat down, hands gripping the sides of the seat.

'No need to be nervous,' Jane told him. 'We're just here to get to the truth, that's all.'

Dave laughed. 'What, and that's supposed to relax the kid? Come on – that's exactly what he's afraid of. Isn't it, Chris?'

Mellor blinked, confused.

'So, one thing that's confused me for ages,' Dave said to him. 'When you and Becky broke up last autumn, it was over those pictures of her, right? She didn't like that your mates had seen them. But, if you didn't show them – which we believe you didn't, by the way – where did they get 'em from? Because we know it wasn't from her phone.'

'It . . . You'd have to ask them. I didn't even know they'd got them, at first.'

'So, how did you find out?'

'I caught Matt and Jonathan giggling over them. When I saw what they were looking at I went ballistic. I asked where they'd got them from, but they wouldn't tell me. Just wanted to know if I'd seen as much of her as they had.' His fists clenched at his sides, his face reddening as the anger took over.

'But you found out in the end,' Dave reminded him.

'Yes. After Becky had already dumped me. I told her it wasn't me, but she wouldn't have it. There was no other source that made sense to her. Or me, for that matter.'

'So, where did they come from?'

'Mr bloody Fisher!'

The outrage on his face was unquestionably real and still as fresh as the day he'd found out.

'Mr Fisher? The games master?' Dave confirmed. Coming from Mellor, this was hearsay. It couldn't be used in court. But it did confirm what the other lads had told them and it kept Mellor talking, feeling the righteous indignation that would hopefully persuade him to say more. 'How did he get hold of them?'

'Turns out, he's a pal of her dad.' His lip curled in disgust. 'That's where they came from.' He met Dave's gaze. 'How perverted is that?'

Dave heard a tiny noise come from Jane's throat beside him. The irony was not lost on him either, but he managed to suppress his reaction. 'You're saying Mr Fisher got pictures of Becky from her dad?'

'Yes. And just for a laugh, Jonathan grabbed his phone one day while he was out on the field and uploaded all the photos from it to his own Dropbox account. And when he saw what he'd got, he . . .' His face twisted in anguish. 'He shared them with everyone.'

'Everyone?' Jane asked.

'Well, the gang, I mean. Everyone that matters!'

'And does Mr Fisher know about all this? That you lads went into his phone and got these pictures?'

Chris shrugged. 'Don't know. He's never said anything, as far as I know.'

Dave shared another glance with Jane. If he knew, the man would certainly have had some kind of reaction. He'd have been terrified they might get out.

'So, what was your problem with Detective Sergeant Gayle?'

'I didn't have one. But he cut off the source of the pictures, didn't he? Arrested Becky's dad.'

'Hang on,' Jane cut in. 'How many times have you lads grabbed these pictures off Fi . . . Mr Fisher's phone?'

'A couple. They seemed to be sharing them until . . .' He shrugged.

'But Neil Sanderson was arrested six months ago. Why wait until now to go after DS Gayle?'

'We weren't waiting. We knew who he was. It just took ages to find out where he lived. He's not in the phone book or anything. It was only after that we found out he had a wife and daughter. So, somebody said maybe we could find out where she went to school and . . . It all took time.'

'So, how did you find out?'

'I don't know. I wasn't involved in that part of it. I just went along on the day. But when I saw what was happening, I backed off. I swear. The girl will tell you. And when she kicked Jonathan and nearly put Matt's eye out, well, that was it. She ran and we started to chase her, but then some old fart came around the corner with this bloody great dog, so we legged it.'

Jane drew a breath. 'Just one more question. At what point did you all know what the plan was that day? That you were going to have Annie Gayle "replace the source" of those pictures, only better, as someone said to her?'

Dave looked at her, horrified. This was the first time he'd heard that. He heard a noise from the school nurse and glanced across. Her face was pale with shock, her expression of wide-eyed horror in the process of changing to one of outrage. He raised a calming hand to her and returned his gaze to Chris Mellor, who was looking down, shame-faced. 'Really?'

'It came up while we were waiting for her. Like I said – we were just going to scare her. Make sure it got back to her dad. But then someone started making suggestions of what else we could do. One thing led to another. People were joking around, trying to outdo one another. It all got out of hand and, by the time she showed up, it had progressed to that.'

That's what you call progress in places like this, is it? Dave thought. 'I think you'd best give us a minute, Chris.'

Mellor looked unsure.

'Off you go. Wait out there with the others.'

He stood up and left the room.

As the door closed behind him, Dave saw the nurse struggling to stay in her seat.

'My God,' she said. 'I could strangle every last one of them! I've never heard anything like it. And to think, they're boys from this school!'

Dave turned to Jane. She was shaking her head in disbelief. 'They were after Annie, who's just eleven years old, to . . . Jesus! They might be rich and well-educated, but they're bloody animals!'

Dave tilted his head, sucking air across his teeth in agreement. 'I think we've been here long enough. We've got all we need except for the van.' He reached into his pocket and pulled out his mobile phone. Hit a speed-dial number.

'Exeter police station. How can I help?'

'DC Miles, CID. I'm at Risingbrook School. I need transport for nine suspects, all underage.'

'Nine? Get out of it. Don't take the piss.'

'Oh, I'm not, mate. I'm completely serious. And the sooner, the better.'

Chapter 21

On the left side of Colleton Crescent stood a row of Georgian-style houses that had been converted to office-based business premises, including the solicitors' Andy Fairweather had mentioned. They looked out across the narrow road to a strip of parkland bordered, on the far side, by dense shrubbery and small trees that ended abruptly in a vertical drop down to the stone-paved quay over forty feet below.

Five months ago, a man who Pete had spoken to as a witness in a multiple murder case had been thrown over that edge to his death. Again, it had been broad daylight, the quay below full of tourists and shoppers. Now, as Pete rounded the gentle curve of the Crescent and entered the straight section, he was greeted, up ahead, by an array of blue flashing lights atop four patrol cars parked just beyond the far end of the row of houses, where they were replaced for several yards by a high wall.

The patrol cars were double-parked along the narrow road, effectively blocking it. Pete pulled up behind them and stepped out of his unmarked Ford, taking his badge from his pocket to hold it up for the uniformed constable standing guard a few feet away, at the end of a line of blue and white police tape that had been strung around the scene. The constable nodded and lifted the tape for him. Ducking under, Pete approached the scene.

The second patrol car in the line had its back door open, a uniformed constable standing beside it. As he approached, the constable turned and Pete recognised a familiar face. 'Mick. What have we got here?'

'A bloody mess, Sarge. And the man who found it.' He stepped away from the car, indicating the back seat. 'Nathaniel Pearson, solicitor with Pearson, Queensbury and Rollinson.'

Franklin, Pete thought, suddenly recalling the name of the man who'd helped him with CCTV footage, last year, of two killers and their next victim driving past this very point.

He stepped forward, held out his hand to the slender fifty-ish man in a dark pin-stripe suit who was sitting in the patrol car, his complexion pale and sweaty. 'DS Gayle,' he said. 'I had the pleasure of dealing with a colleague of yours a few months ago. Dan Franklin.'

The man shook his hand, his grip surprisingly firm. He gave Pete what could have passed for a brief smile, but looked more like a grimace. 'Pleasure. Yes, I remember. That homeless chap that got tossed off the top over there. Very . . .' This time, it was definitely a grimace.

'Tragic?' Pete suggested, knowing that wasn't even close to what he'd been thinking.

The lawyer looked up, meeting his gaze. 'Quite.'

'So, tell me, Mr Pearson – what happened here? Every detail, relevant or not, if you don't mind.'

'Very well.' The thin man drew a breath. 'I'd been to see a client. There was a parking space along here when I got back, so I pulled in.' He leaned forward, pointing along the road. 'That's mine. The Aston. And as I was walking back, I saw that the taxi, there, was . . . Well, the inside of the windscreen was sprayed red. You could tell it was on the inside. The direction of the light shone off the glass. That's why I didn't spot it until I got up close, I suppose. I could see there was someone sitting in the driver's seat, but it was a taxi, so you'd expect that. Then I saw the . . . What do you call it? Blood spatter. And then, through it, I saw that the front of his shirt was red and he was slumped, as if he was asleep. That's when I realised what I was looking at. I ran into the office, called 999 and here we are.'

'You saw no one else out here, before or after?'

Pearson shook his head.

'Walking or driving?' Pete insisted.

'No one, Sergeant.'

'OK. We'll let you get back to your work then, Mr Pearson. I'll come in with you, see if your CCTV can be helpful again.'

Dave and Jane looked at each other in silence.

The school nurse, sitting across the room from them, recrossed her legs. Dave looked over. 'We've done with the interviews for now, Nurse. I think you can probably get back to your usual jobs.'

'Very well.' She stood up.

'Thank you,' Jane said as she left the room.

Quiet settled over them again. They were both shocked by what they'd learned in the last hour or so, both processing it in their own ways. Then Jane's green eyes snapped into focus. 'Fisher. Did he really get the pictures from her dad?'

'We can't ask him. Not at this stage.'

'No, but . . . ultimately, there are only two possible sources and I think we can discount Becky herself.'

'Yeah, but did they come directly or indirectly?' He paused, eyes lighting up with inspiration. 'We've got the means to eliminate or confirm the first option.' He pulled out his phone again and dialled quickly.

'Ben,' he said when it was picked up. 'Have you got the records from Neil Sanderson's phone and computer handy?'

'Yes, they're on my PC. Why?'

'Could you have a scan through them? See if you can find any contact with a Sam Fisher. He's a games master here.'

'OK. I'll call you back.'

'I really hope he finds something before the vans get here,' Jane said as he put his phone away again.

'Detective Sergeant.' The big, grey-haired man held out a meaty hand. 'Good to see you again.'

'You too,' Pete said as they shook. 'Seems I need your help again. One of the partners here, Mr Pearson, found a body down the street.'

'I heard.' He shook his head. 'Hell of a thing.'

'Yes, so . . .'

'Come on through. We'll have a look, see if the cameras picked anything up.'

'Thanks.'

Franklin led the way across the wood-panelled reception and through a door. 'Start about forty-five minutes ago?' he suggested as he headed down the corridor.

It was now about twenty-five since the 999 call had been made. 'Yes, that should cover it.'

'If not, we can go back a bit further.'

He opened a door on the right and stepped in, switching on a light. Pete followed. The room was small – little more than a cupboard really – with a desk, single chair, computer and three hard drives whirring quietly on a shelf. 'Sorry. I'll get another chair.'

'Don't worry. I spend enough time sitting down. It won't hurt to stand up for a while.'

'Are you sure?'

Pete nodded.

'OK. We'll get started then.' He powered up the computer, then brought up a program that gave him a split screen, all three feeds appearing to be live in windows that, between them, filled three quarters of the screen.

'Right.' He tapped in a time and hit Return. The pictures jumped.

'We can pause at any point or fill the screen with any one of the pictures for a better view.'

'Great.'

The videos began to run in real time. Nothing happened for a few seconds.

'Hang on,' said Franklin and hit a key. The times in the bottom left of each window sped up. 'That's better.'

Still nothing happened on any of the cameras for a while. One of them was showing a neatly maintained garden at the back of the building with three tables surrounded by chairs on a stone patio. Another was showing an inside view. Pete recognised the corridor they had walked down. The third image was looking out from the front door of the building. Cars were parked across the mid-ground, the narrow park across the road showing in the top of the image. This was the one Pete was concentrating on.

A car sped past, right to left. He couldn't tell make and model at that speed, but it was dark-blue. The taxi out there was white. Another car followed it, larger and black. A figure stepped up to the door and entered. Male. Older and balding. As he went from sight, Pete caught the flash of a passing vehicle behind him, pale in the sunshine. 'There. Was that the taxi?'

Franklin hit a key and the images froze. He hit another and they began to creep backwards. A white car reversed into view, frame by frame. The right shape. It edged further backwards until they could see the whole of its roof. No taxi sign. Pete slumped. 'No. OK.'

Franklin hit another key. The car vanished once more, the time ticked forward until a dark car passed. It looked like a black Audi to Pete. Then another pale one. This time, Pete was sure. 'There. That's him.'

The big man ran the footage back, filled the screen with the single image and let it play in real time. The white taxi rolled past, going slowly. Pete was sure he could see a figure in the back, behind the driver, but the camera angle gave him only their lap and the torso up to a couple of inches above the side window on the far side of the car and that was in shadow. 'Stop there,' he said, leaning down beside Franklin to peer at the screen. The image froze with the driver half out of the frame. Staring hard at the figure in the back, all Pete could say for sure was that they seemed to be slim and female and there was a hint of redness about whatever they were wearing.

He stood up and made a note of the time from the image. 'OK. Carry on.'

The picture moved on, the car going out of view. Franklin sped it up to four times natural speed. They waited to see what would happen next. Seconds passed. Another car went past, this one a pale-green saloon. The time readout in the corner of the screen advanced steadily. One minute. Two. Three.

A woman stepped out of the building, closing the door behind her and turning away to the right. 'That's Jacqui,' Franklin said. 'One of the secretaries.'

'Uh-huh.'

Another minute passed. And another. The time readout was quickly approaching the point when . . . 'There's Nate.'

The grey Aston Martin flashed past near the top of the screen.

'And no sign of our killer,' Pete said. 'She must have gone the other way.'

'Looks that way.' Franklin hit the Pause button.

'Can you burn me a disc, though? I don't know how useful it'll be, but best to be safe.'

'Yes, no problem.'

'Thanks.'

Pete waited while it was done then took it with him as he left the building. By then, forensics had set up along the road and the coroner was in attendance. He walked along the pavement. As he approached, Doc Chambers stood back from the car and waved two white-overalled assistants in with a gurney.

'Hello, Doc. What can you tell me?' asked Pete.

'Good afternoon, Peter. Looks like the same perpetrator as the other two. The same single slash across the throat from behind. Same pepper spray. This time, the car wasn't locked, unlike the first one, so your suspect would have been able to simply step out of the back and walk away, probably without a mark on them.'

Pete sighed. 'And the victim?'

The driver of the taxi. ID still in the car. Hardeep Randrashan. Thirty-nine years old, resident of the Exton area. Cause of death was the cut to the throat. No signs of other injuries, defensive or otherwise.'

'So, another apparently preplanned and targeted attack with the victim given no chance to defend himself.'

Chambers nodded, his bristle-cut grey hair glittering in the sunshine. 'That's about the size of it.'

'Cheers, Doc.' Pete turned to the forensics team. 'Have you found anything useful, guys?'

The team leader – for once not the tall and portly Harold Pointer, but a slimmer, older man with a goatee beard – turned to face him. 'Possibly. We'll have to wait and see.'

'What does that mean?'

'There were a few hairs. A palm print on the roof above the back door on the driver's side, a bit of red thread that appears to be dyed rather than bloodstained. No fingerprints in the back of the car or on the outer door handle, which I would say is highly unusual at this time of day for a taxi. Whether any of it's relevant or not, though, remains to be seen.'

'The lack of fingerprints certainly is,' Pete judged. 'Not that it's helpful. This is the third victim in a few days, so I'd appreciate it if you could put a rush on the results. We're going to have chaos on the roads round here if we don't put a stop to it soon.'

'We'll check the red thread and the palm print as soon as we get back and let you know any results ASAP.'

'Thanks.' Pete extended a hand. 'DS Pete Gayle.'

'Yes, I gathered.' The man shook his hand. 'Terry Thatcher.'

'Pleased to meet you. What's happened to Harry?'

'Couldn't stand the pace.' Thatcher smiled. 'Said you work him too hard. Took a few days off.'

'I must remember to take the piss when I see him again,' Pete said, returning the smile before walking away along the road in the direction the suspect must have taken when leaving the scene. The wall on his left enclosed a large, mature garden with trees and large shrubs that overhung it in places. Not far around the bend, the suspect would have had to turn left up Melbourne Place to get out onto Holloway Street. She could have gone either way from there. Left towards Western Way or right, out towards Topsham. But was she on foot or in a car? He stood on the corner, pondering the problem. She could have driven here, walked to the main road and caught a bus somewhere, then got the taxi to bring her back. Or she could have done it the other way around – parked somewhere else, got the taxi to bring her here, then caught a bus back to her car. Assuming, of course, that she didn't live within walking distance of where he was standing.

One thing he did know: there were no CCTV cameras around here, run by either the city council or the police. The nearest would be on Holloway Street or further, so they would be no help at all. All he could say for sure at this point was that she had walked in this direction from the point of attack and he thought she might, possibly, maybe, be wearing a red dress, with or without a jacket over it. He took out his phone. Dialled the squad room.

'Ben,' he said when it was picked up. 'Can you do something for me?'

'What's that, boss?'

'Check for CCTV cameras on Holloway Street and, if there are any, look for a woman in a red dress, possibly with a jacket over it, coming from the direction of Melbourne Place within the last forty-five minutes. And if there's nothing, go back a couple of hours from there.'

* * *

After an emotional trip across the river to inform the latest victim's wife of his death, Pete returned to the station intending to go through the footage he'd obtained from the solicitors' office – until he stepped in through the back door and found the custody suite full of boys in school uniform, being herded by Jane and Dave.

'What the hell's going on here?' he demanded.

'Hello, boss,' Dave greeted him. 'Blitzkrieg. We've established the facts, so we're booking the whole damn lot of them. A bit like the old shoot 'em all and ask questions later plan. Except we're not allowed to shoot 'em, sadly.'

'How many have you got here? It looks like half a class.'

'All nine. We've also established the source of the images that you so inconsiderately deprived them of by arresting Neil Sanderson. We've got a bit more work to do before we can make that arrest, though. Ben's working on proving the link.'

'He didn't say anything when I spoke to him a little while ago.'

'Ah.' Dave tapped the side of his nose and winked. 'Sworn to secrecy, see. Don't want to go off half-cocked, do we?'

Pete looked around him. 'What's this then?'

'Shotgun tactics.'

Pete grunted. 'As long as it hits them all equally.'

'Equally and permanently: that's the plan.'

'Right. I'll go see what Ben's up to then.' He continued along the corridor and up the stairs to the squad room. Dropping into his chair, he looked around at the other three members of his team. 'So, what have you got to tell me, any of you?'

Chapter 22

'There's been no red dresses or skirts on Holloway Street in the past three hours, boss.'

'I wanted good news, Ben, not bad.'

'Did you see Dave and Jane on your way in?' Dick asked.

'Yes. With half a classful of young boys from Risingbrook.'

'Well, we've got some bad news for them too. There's no direct link from Sanderson's phone or computer to any device registered to Sam Fisher.'

'Sam Fisher, the games master?'

Dick nodded.

'Why would there be?'

'Supposedly, they're mates. And that's where Dave and Jane were told the lads got the pictures of Becky from. Borrowed his phone one day and uploaded his photo files. Just as a lark, at the outset. But then they saw what they'd got and . . . Well, you can imagine. Teenage boys.' He shrugged.

'So, Fisher had pictures of Becky taken by Sanderson on his phone, but they weren't sent to him by Sanderson.'

'Unless one of them's got a pay-as-you-go stashed away somewhere.'

'Which you kinda would, if you were sending stuff like that back and forth, I'd have thought,' said Ben.

They all looked at him.

He began to look as if he was going to blush, but then he pushed it back. 'Well, you would, wouldn't you? I mean, you wouldn't use a device that you carry around all the time and could get caught with. Not if you've got an ounce of brains anyway.'

'Fisher did,' Jill said.

'Well, yeah, OK. But he is a games master.'

'So, are we saying we think Sanderson's got another phone stashed away somewhere?'

'Either that or one of them uses a coffee-shop Wi-Fi or the local library or something.'

'Which is entirely possible,' Jill pointed out.

'Yeah. Unfortunately,' Pete agreed. 'Can we track their movements at all?'

'Depends,' said Ben. 'If they're carrying GPS-enabled smartphones or laptops, then yes. There's a log kept of the locations devices like that go to, whether they're used or not. I'm not sure how long the data's kept for. I dare say it varies. But we could be lucky. Especially with phones. As long as we've got the number, we can find the provider and get the tracking data from there.'

'But with a pay-as-you-go, we wouldn't have the number. That's the point, isn't it?' asked Dick.

'Yes, but as long as they've got their normal phone with them as well, we can track that. Then any contact can be traced to a location they're at, at the time. I'm assuming we're looking at more than one relevant contact?'

'Best ask Dave or Jane,' Pete suggested, switching on his computer. 'I don't know if they'll appreciate the interruption at the moment, though.'

'So, what's with the girl in the red dress?' Dick asked. 'There was a movie about that, wasn't there?'

Pete took the disc in its plastic case from his jacket pocket and waved it in the air.

'Where'd you get that?'

'Same place I got the footage of Hardy and Parker with Alfie Bowens.'

'Ah. Nice one,' Dick nodded.

Pete logged in and slipped the disc into the drive. It whirred like a super-charged hoover for a moment, then went quiet as a media-player window popped up automatically on the screen, waiting for him to hit Play.

His eyebrows rose when he saw that Franklin had given him the whole afternoon's footage from the front-door camera. That could be very useful. He enlarged the window to fill the screen and hit Play as, two desks to his left, Ben said into his phone, 'Jane? Quick question. Do you happen to know roughly how many times Sam Fisher downloaded those pictures onto his phone? Was it just the once, or was there regular contact, or what?'

Pete concentrated on his screen as Ben listened then said, 'OK, thanks,' and put the phone down. The silence lasted only a few seconds before Jill broke it.

'So? What's the answer?'

He glanced up. She was staring at Ben as if he should have told her without prompting.

'The lads only know of a couple of times, so it wouldn't be probative on its own. We'd need some supplemental evidence to make it stick. Some way of saying it was definitely him, not someone else who just happened to be there at the same time on those two occasions.'

'Well, if the images are still there, wouldn't they have data attached saying when they were downloaded?' she asked.

'The point is, we need to know at least some of that in advance, to get a warrant to check the phone in the first place,' Dick told her.

'Aah.' Jill shook her head in frustration. 'And the boys' testimony wouldn't do it?'

231

Dick shrugged. 'They're under arrest themselves.'

'Yeah, but they weren't when they first said it, were they?'

Dick tipped his head.

'Can't hurt to try,' Pete said. 'Draw it up and see.' *Then, maybe, he could concentrate on the footage on his screen.*

A car went past the front door of the solicitors' office and he hit Pause, reversed the image slowly until he could see the driver.

Pete's phone rang abruptly. *Jesus! Can I just get a little bit of peace here?* He picked it up. 'Gayle.'

'Peter.' It was DCI Silverstone. 'Would you mind coming through to my office?'

The calmness in his voice was ominous in itself, but Pete was too wrapped up in what he was trying to do to take any notice of that. 'What, now, sir?'

'If you don't mind.'

The phone clicked dead, precluding any further discussion.

'Fast-track,' he told the others. 'Don't know what he wants, but he's a bloody nuisance while I'm trying to go through this stuff.' He left the image on his screen as he got up and headed for the door. He wouldn't be long, he hoped.

Moments later, he knocked on Silverstone's door.

'Come.'

Pete stepped in, closing the door behind him. 'Sir?'

'These arrests at Risingbrook, Peter. At what point were you intending to tell me the identity of the victim involved?'

Shit! 'Everything's in my daily report, sir.'

'I see. And just so that I know, bearing in mind that your psych eval came back with a clean bill of health just three months ago, how long have you had this urge to get fired from the police force?'

Here we go, Pete thought. It was almost a relief to be returning to normality. *He'll start yelling in a sec.* 'I've got no desire the leave the force, sir. A situation arose. I dealt with it the only way I could at the time and, having started, it was natural to continue.'

232

'It felt natural to continue,' Silverstone repeated carefully. Then he erupted, hands slamming on his desk. 'And what about the regulations, Detective Sergeant? Which we both know you're fully aware of, having had this conversation before. What kind of example do you think this sets for your junior officers? And what kind of reputation do you think it'll create for this station? For this force? Eh?'

There it is. Priorities confirmed, Pete thought. 'The aim is for zero tolerance and prompt, efficient action. Sir.'

'Zero tolerance can only work if it includes everyone, Gayle. Police and civilians. What the Devil am I going to do about this? I'm getting sick of cleaning up your messes, do you hear? If anything like this happens again, you'll be back in uniform or kicked off the force entirely before you can think of an excuse. As it is, I have no alternative but to instigate disciplinary action through Professional Standards.'

Pete had half-expected this, pretty much from the outset, but he wasn't going to let anyone else investigate an attack on his own daughter. What kind of message would that have put out? One of weakness, he knew. One that would have left Annie at more risk than ever if it emboldened her attackers.

'Well? What have you got to say for yourself, Detective Sergeant?'

Nothing you'd want to hear, he thought. 'Nothing, sir. Thank you.'

'Is the case done and dusted?'

'The lads are being processed as we speak, sir.'

'Then get out of my sight.'

Pete turned towards the door without speaking.

'And Gayle . . .'

'Sir?'

'You are on borrowed time. I suggest you spend it wisely and imagine you're walking on eggshells every moment you're on duty.'

'Sir.'

He left the office, heading back to his desk. Sitting down, he found he'd been gone long enough that his computer screen had gone black. He wiggled his mouse to bring back the image.

'So, what did Fast-track want?' Dick asked.

'I don't know how much more I'm going to be able to manage to use this computer this afternoon,' Pete said.

'Eh?'

'I've got such a sore wrist, from where he slapped it for not handing off Annie's assault.'

'Jane did warn you, boss,' Jill said. 'She told me.'

'Yes, she did. But what would any of us do, eh? Faced with an attack on our own kid that's reported directly to us? Is it just me?'

'No, boss. You're right. We'd all do exactly the same. Those of us that have kids, that is. Which Fast-track hasn't.'

'And that's a good thing for the kids,' Dick said. 'We just have to hope, for the sake of the country, that it stays that way.'

'Didn't there used to be such a thing as compulsory sterilisation?' Jill asked.

'Yeah. It was got rid of by the European courts,' Dick answered. 'With a bit of luck, once we get out of the EU, they'll bring it back. Especially for the likes of him.'

'In the meantime, I've drawn up the warrant request, boss. Should I take it through?'

'Probably best,' he said. 'I don't think he'd want to see me again this afternoon.'

'Right.' She stood up and headed for the door, the quiet allowing Pete to concentrate on his screen.

The still image showed the back two thirds of a small black Vauxhall hatchback. The driver, judging by the silhouette, was female and slim, but that was about all he could tell. One thing he did know was that there hadn't been a car like that along Colleton Crescent when he was up there. But it was a one-way system around there. It could have been heading for one of the two other roads off Melbourne Place. He took a screenshot, if only for elimination, and let the footage run on. There was no movement on the road for a while. Then two cars passed, one close behind the other. The first was a four-by-four, the second a little city car of some sort. He paused the image and wound it back. Going slightly past the point he needed, he let it run forward again, frame by frame. The medium sized four-by-four edged into shot. Dark-green, it looked like a Toyota. The driver came into shot. A man. Balding, Pete could see the gleam of light on his scalp. He edged the footage onward, the first vehicle passing out of shot. Just a few feet behind it, the little rounded city car came slowly into view. Cream or white – Pete wasn't sure – with a driver who was clearly female. The ponytail was a giveaway, if nothing else. She appeared to be wearing something dark, but he could tell no more than that. He paused the image, took a screenshot just in case, and let it run on.

Suddenly, he doubted that this was going to be as helpful as he'd thought. Still, he had to keep going, now he'd started.

The door opened to his left and he glanced up. It was Jill returning from Silverstone's office. She waved a piece of paper and smiled. 'Got it.'

The relief surprised Pete as it swept over him. 'Thank God for that, at least. Take Dick with you and get it served, ASAP.'

It took Pete almost another hour to go through the footage from the solicitors' on Colleton Crescent and when he'd finished he had a list of five vehicles on the pad at his elbow. He turned to Ben. 'How many cameras did you find on Holloway Street?'

'Two. One in each direction halfway up from Bull Meadow Road.'

'So, the uphill one will cover the end of Friars Walk.'

'Yes.'

'Good.' Pete referred to his notes. 'I want the footage from two o'clock to two-forty-five.'

'OK. Give me a minute, boss. I'll put it on a data stick for you.'

Pete took the DVD out of his computer and slipped it into its plastic sleeve, which he put in his desk.

'Here you go.'

Ben passed across a thumb-drive. Pete plugged it into the USB port on the front of his machine. He waited for it to boot up, downloaded the file from it onto his hard drive and removed it from the port, passing it back to Ben. When the program was ready, he pressed Play, then Fast Forward and concentrated once more on the screen in front of him.

The entrance to the little estate that included Colleton Crescent was in the top-right section of the screen. Pete focused on that part of the image, waiting to see what vehicles would emerge from it, which way they would go and if he could read the numberplates or see the drivers.

He had been concentrating hard for a little more than five minutes when the door to the squad room opened and Jane walked in, followed by Dave.

'All tucked up safely in their beds, boss,' she announced. 'Charges filed, parents and solicitors called. Busy day tomorrow.'

'Busy enough today,' he replied. 'We've got a third victim.'

'Shit, this is turning into a spree,' Dave said, sitting down at his desk.

A message popped up in the bottom corner of Pete's screen. He had a new email. *I hope it's good news, for once*, he thought as he clicked on it. A new window opened over the paused CCTV image. The press liaison office was copying him in, as SIO, on what they had sent out to the press. The three images of their suspect and the accompanying text were attached. He read it through, hit Reply and sent a quick note back: 'Spot-on. Thanks.'

He was never going to please Adam Silverstone, but it couldn't hurt to keep as many as possible of the other members of the force onside.

He closed the email and settled in once more to examining the CCTV footage. Moments later, the pale, rounded nose of a small car showed in the junction he was looking at. It pulled out, coming towards the camera. Pete was sure it was a Nissan Micra. As it approached, he got a look at the driver. Female. Hair pulled back into a ponytail. The image was too blurred to use for identification but it was, at least, indicative. He glanced down at the front of the car. The registration plate was not sharp either, but it was visible. It looked like it could probably be enhanced to the stage of being readable.

He took a screenshot and saved it into the same folder as the others, then let the footage run. A car he didn't recognise emerged from the junction, turning away from the city centre. All went quiet for a while. Then another came out, heading towards the camera position. It was still in shot when a dark four-by-four emerged, turning away. As it crossed the road, Pete recognised the shape and hit Pause, staring at the screen. The driver was on the far side of the vehicle, but the sun was with him. It looked like a female. Long, dark hair. Was that a flash of red as she lifted her arm? He edged the image backwards a couple of frames. Yes. It looked like it. This could be her. There was no way he was going to get a registration number, though. It was too far away.

'Where's the first camera on Topsham Road?'

Holloway Street became Topsham Road a short way beyond the Friars Walk junction.

'The first one's out by the Priory High School, boss.' Predictably, it was Ben who had the answer.

Pete grimaced. There were a lot of side roads going off before that. She could have gone anywhere. 'That's no help then.' He took another screenshot, for what it was worth, and moved on. More vehicles came and went, but none he recognised from the short list he'd compiled from the Colleton Crescent footage. He'd stopped the video and closed the window on his screen when Jill flounced in, hips swaying wildly, waving a clear plastic evidence bag in one raised hand. In the bag, he could see a mobile phone.

Behind her, Dick Feeney held the door, smiling.

Pete sat back in his chair. 'Fisher's?'

'Yep. Complete with a file full of pictures of girls who are far too young to be photographed in the ways they have been.'

237

'Including Becky Sanderson?'

She nodded. 'And Rosie Whitlock.'

'Did he have anything to say for himself?'

'Denied all knowledge,' Dick said. 'Says they must have been put on there by some of the lads.'

Pete drew a breath. 'Well, the phone will show where they came from and where they were sent to, but not who was doing it.'

'What, so he gets away with it?' Jane demanded.

'I didn't say that.'

'Well, how are we going to prove it was him that downloaded them, then?'

'The dates and times of the downloads will be attached to each image. If we prove where the phone was at those times, we might well be able to prove who was there with it. Witnesses. CCTV. Other phone data.'

Jane relaxed, mollified.

'I wonder how helpful Sanderson might be if he thought it would shave a bit of time off his sentence,' Dave said.

'Might be worth finding out.' Pete shut down his computer. 'Meantime, I've got some other stuff to look into. I'll see you all in the morning, bright and early.'

'Lou?' Pete closed the front door and dropped his briefcase on the floor.

'In here.' Her voice came from the kitchen. Another bad sign.

'What's happening? Where's Annie?'

She stuck her head around the corner as he slipped off his jacket and hung it on the newel post at the bottom of the stairs. She indicated with a tilt of her head that he should come through.

Pete complied. They kissed. 'So, what's going on?'

'She's in bed. Upset. Not those lads again,' she said quickly, not knowing what progress the team had made on the case that day. 'It was Tommy.'

'Tommy? Why? What's the matter with him?'

She shook her head and sighed. 'I don't know. He was really off with us this afternoon. Like he wanted to drive us away. It . . . it got to her badly. She cried all the way home.'

Pete sighed. 'I expect she's still suffering with the attack by those lads as well. That wouldn't have helped. She's a brave kid, but even she can only take so much at once.'

'She told me you went to see her at lunchtime with a load of pictures or something. Had her pick out some of the lads that were involved. That was a bit soon, wasn't it? She'd hardly got over the trauma and you wanted to bring it all back for her?'

'That was the last thing I wanted, Lou. But it was by far the best hope of getting them ID'd – and we did.'

'So, what now? You ask permission from their rich parents to talk to their privileged little lads and slap them on the wrists?'

'Not quite. While they're in the school's care, they're the school's responsibility – not the parents'. So, yes, the parents have been informed, and no doubt some of them, if not all, will have hired solicitors. But the lads themselves are all down in the basement at Heavitree Road for the night. All nine.'

'Well, that's all fine and commendable, but what happens tomorrow, when their expensive solicitors get them out of there? They go straight back to normal routine and the next thing you know, they're waiting to ambush Annie all over again? She'll have nightmares for the rest of her days, poor kid.'

Pete was shaking his head. 'They're not getting off that easy, Lou. We've already got confessions from some of them. They're not going back to Risingbrook – none of them. They don't tolerate behaviour like that there, no matter how rich the parents are. And most, if not all, will be remanded. Charges like that demand it.'

'What, so they'll be going to Archways instead? How long do you reckon it'll take them to figure out Tommy's Annie's brother, eh? Then what'll happen?'

'They won't be going there. For one thing, *because* Tommy's there. And for another, the place is already almost full. They'd damn near fill it again. There's nine of them, remember.'

'So, where else will they go? I can't see rich kids like that going to your standard borstal.'

Pete grinned and reached out to squeeze her shoulder then draw her into a hug. 'They're not called borstals any more. They're young offender institutions nowadays. And they cater for all sorts – rich and poor alike. There's no class segregation at Her Majesty's Pleasure.'

'Good. That might scare a bit of respect into them. But the sooner you explain all that to Annie the better, if she's awake.'

'Yes, you're right.' He stood back, holding her limp hands in his. 'I'll go and check on her.' He squeezed her fingers briefly and turned towards the stairs.

Chapter 23

'Christ,' Pete muttered as he came into sight of the Heavitree
Road police station.

It looked like the place was under siege. There were cars everywhere. Both pavements were completely blocked, the road constricted
to a single-vehicle width so that traffic was queueing in both directions to get through. Orange hazard lights were blinking everywhere.
About three quarters of the parked vehicles had taxi lights on their
roofs and most of the rest had council licences on the backs – private
hire cars. No doubt the remainder would be press, he thought, as he
drove closer. He saw a few men with cameras dotted about.

At least the TV crews had yet to arrive.

Even the half-dozen parking spaces in front of the building
were full, he saw.

And this was all for him. Because he had yet to catch whoever
was out there killing taxi drivers.

Fast-track was going to be absolutely apoplectic. His blood
pressure, when he saw this, would set a new world record. Pete
smiled. It would almost be worth being the brunt of his venting
to see how red the man's face could actually get.

He turned into a side road and drove slowly along until he
found a place to park, locked the car and walked down towards

the station. Further down the road, uniformed officers were trying to ease the congestion by diverting traffic off the main road. There would be a couple of others, he guessed, guiding them through the smaller streets and out onto the Topsham Road.

One of the two officers on duty at the junction – the one directing the queueing vehicles into the side road – was a familiar face.

'Morning, Mick.'

'Sarge.'

'Have we got all the numberplates?'

'Oh, hell, yeah.' He tapped his body-cam. 'They're not getting away with this. We weren't going to give them all tickets. We wouldn't have survived the riot. But we can always send them enforcement letters after the event.'

Pete gave him a wink. 'That's the ticket.'

Mick cringed. 'So, what are you doing about the reason for all this?'

'We're working on it.'

Mick continued waving the traffic around the junction as they spoke. 'Yeah, but are you getting anywhere, Sarge?'

'Between you and me, Mick, I sometimes wonder the same thing.' Pete clapped him on the shoulder and walked on towards the station and the chaos that surrounded it.

Pete wasn't the first of his team into the squad room, despite its being a Saturday. Ben, Dick and Jill were already at their desks when he walked in. He put down his briefcase and sat down. 'Somebody tell me there's some good news,' he pleaded.

'Fast-track's not in yet,' said Dick.

'It doesn't help what we're working on, but I'll take what I can get.'

'In relevant news,' Jill said, tossing a newspaper across towards him. 'He did do his job with the press. And Jane and Dave are downstairs, interviewing.'

'Ah. Excellent.' Pete picked up the paper. It was folded open to page three, the top half of which was filled with the three head-shots of their suspect with a large-print headline: *Have You Seen This Woman?* The article went on to state that the three images of her were from the night Sunil Pati, victim two of what they were predictably calling "the cabbie killer", was murdered and left in his taxi in a backstreet of the city. It described what they knew of Pati, which thankfully didn't include his involvement with drugs or child sex, then speculated on why the murders might be occurring. The journalist had ended the piece with the statement that the police were struggling for leads but wanted to speak to the woman in the pictures urgently, in case she had any relevant information.

Pete turned the folded paper back over to look at the pictures. He looked across at Jill.

'This is on page three. What's the cover story?'

She grimaced. 'You weren't supposed to notice that, boss.'

He unfolded the paper and was in the process of closing it to see the front page when the door opened and DCI Silverstone barked, 'Detective Sergeant Gayle. My office. Now.'

Pete looked up, but the door was already closing. He finished rearranging the newspaper and glimpsed the headline: *Third Taxi Driver Murdered. In Broad Daylight.* He pursed his lips and tossed the paper back to Jill. 'Here we go again,' he muttered. 'Find me some evidence while I'm gone, will you? And tell Louise I love her if I don't come back.'

Silverstone's door was closed. Pete knocked. The DCI's voice was a lot less calm than it had been the day before when he snapped 'Come'.

Pete entered.

'Sir.'

'Have you seen the chaos out there?' He waved a hand towards the front of the station.

'Yes, sir. Uniform are diverting traffic down onto the Topsham Road, to come into the city that way.'

'Well, they shouldn't bloody well have to. It's a bloody disgrace. Especially right outside a bloody police station.'

'No, sir. But they are taxis. They need licences to operate and those can be revoked.'

Silverstone looked up at him in horror. 'Are you suggesting . . .? That would cause absolute uproar.'

Pete tilted his head. 'Depending how you handled it, sir.'

'No. No way, Detective Sergeant. I'm not having my station accused of something like that. Where are we on these damned killings? We need to appease them somehow. Get rid of them that way. Is there anything you need in the way or resources?'

'The latest one has given us some more information, sir. We're following up one or two leads.'

'Such as?'

'There were a couple of suspect cars that went by the site that we need to track down. We've got the registration on one, but not the other as yet. And we're waiting for a couple of things from forensics. A palm print and a bit of trace evidence. And your interview yesterday's out there now, so hopefully that'll produce something. At least it shows we're making the effort.'

'Making the effort is not good enough, Peter. Looking out there this morning is enough to demonstrate that.'

'I know that, sir. I'm just saying, we can't be accused of sitting on our laurels for any reason.'

'Discrimination, you mean?'

'Exactly.'

'God.' His gaze turned inward as he contemplated yet another possible stain on his reputation.

'Is that all you wanted, sir?'

Silverstone looked up. 'What? Yes. Get to it, Detective Sergeant. And get me some results. Pronto.'

'Sir.'

Pete returned to the squad room. Jill was putting down the

phone as he walked in. Dick still had his in hand and Ben was concentrating on his computer screen.

As Pete sat down, Ben looked up but Jill beat him to the punch. 'That was forensics. Terry Thatcher?'

Pete nodded.

'The palm print's come back negative and the red fibre is cotton. They're still dealing with other evidence from the car, but he said you wanted results on them ASAP.'

'That's right.'

'I've been going through the file data on these pictures from Fisher's phone, boss,' Ben said. 'It looks like there've been five separate occasions when he downloaded them. Correlating the dates and times, they were all early evening on weekdays and he downloaded between ten and twenty in a session.'

'That's a lot of pictures,' Jill said.

'Thank you,' Dick said and put his phone down.

'So, we need to question Fisher about where he was on those dates and at those times,' Pete said. 'But first, Jill, get onto Risingbrook and see what they have to say about them. Would he have been there? Would he have been on duty if he was? What would be going on in the school, generally, at those times on those days? If we can tie him down that way first, then question him, he'll have no wriggle room.'

Dick was watching him, waiting for a chance to speak.

'What have you got, Dick?'

'That was a bus driver I was just talking to. He saw the paper this morning and recognised the face. Said she was a redhead when he saw her. It was yesterday afternoon. She caught his bus from Holloway Road. He thinks she got off at St David's, but he can't be certain. He noticed her because of her red hair and red skirt and the fact that she seemed to be in a bad mood. Fiery, he thought. She had a leather jacket on that was done up to the neck and a large, black shoulder bag.'

Like the one the girl in Cathedral Square had, Pete thought.

And she'd been a redhead when she went into the pub. So, was that her true colour?

He looked at Dick. 'Buses have CCTV onboard nowadays, don't they?'

Dick nodded.

'So, call him back. Get the number of the bus he was driving and then get onto the company. Get us that footage.'

'Right, boss.' Dick picked up his phone again and started dialling.

Moments later, Jill put hers down and looked across. 'The resident kids, which is about sixty per cent of them, have their dinner in the timeframe we're looking at, boss. There's a staff rota to supervise them. I asked about the specific dates. Fisher wasn't rostered for any of them, so he could have been anywhere, onsite or off.'

'OK. Next question then: where was his phone? And where were the lads we've got downstairs? We need to ask them, check for corroboration and we need the phone GPS records. All ten.'

'Blimey. That's going to take a while,' Ben said. 'These phone companies ain't quick and I'd lay a good bet that, between ten of them, there's going to be several providers to deal with.'

'Best get to it, then,' Pete said. 'Where's Fisher's phone? We'll start with that.'

'Here it is, boss.' Jill held it up, still in its evidence bag.

'Pass it over. I'll get that in motion. Give Jane or Dave a ring downstairs, tell them to get permission for as many as possible of the lads' phones. Any that don't give it, tell them they'll be charged with aiding and abetting a paedophile – see if that helps. And after they've got permission, ask each of the lads where they were on those dates, at those times.'

'Right, boss.' She nodded.

Pete took the phone from her, turning it over in his hand. On the outside of the evidence bag was written the phone's make, model, number and provider, the name of its owner and the date, time and location of its seizure. He brought up the Internet on his computer and found the service provider's web site. With the

Contact Us page open in front of him, he picked up his phone to dial their number.

The girl who answered sounded Scottish and gave her name as Kirsty.

'Hello. This is DS Peter Gayle of the Devon and Cornwall Police, Exeter CID. I need the GPS data from a suspect's phone. I've got the details here and the warrant number.'

'OK. I'll have to call you back, to verify you are who you say.'

'Of course. Quick as you like, though, please. This is very time-sensitive.'

'OK, sir.'

The phone clicked dead. Pete hung up. He waited, hand poised over his desk phone. Seconds slipped past. How long did it take to dial a damned number? They could look him up, the same as he did them. Then, to be put through from switchboard or the front desk . . . Finally, it rang. He picked it up. 'DS Gayle, Exeter CID.'

'Call for you, Pete.'

There was a click. 'Hello? DS Gayle speaking.'

'Ah. Yes. This is Kirsty. If you give me the number of the phone, the name of its owner and the warrant number, I'll see what I can find for you.'

'What, now?'

'You said it was time-sensitive, Sergeant.'

'I did. Thank you.' He read out the information she wanted.

'OK. Hold on.'

Faintly, he heard the tap of a keyboard over the line. A pause. More tapping. Silence again. Then: 'Hello? DS Gayle?'

'Yes.'

'I've got the information you wanted in front of me. Should I read it out or fax it across?'

'Just to be safe, can I say both?'

She laughed. 'OK. Four of the time periods you asked about, the phone was in the same location.' She read out the GPS coordinates.

'On the second occasion, though, it was somewhere else.' More coordinates. 'What's your fax number there? I'll send a paper copy through.'

'Right.' He gave her the number. 'Thanks, Kirsty.'

'No problem. Goodbye, Detective.'

Pete put the phone down and called up a map of Exeter on Google Maps. Moving the cursor over the map, it took him seconds to find the two positions. When he saw the second one, he chuckled out loud. 'Oh dear, oh dear, oh dear. What a silly bugger you are, Mr Fisher.'

'What's up, boss?'

He glanced up. All three of his team members were looking at him. 'What's Fisher's address, Jill?' he asked.

'14 Middletown. Why? He didn't, did he?'

Pete nodded. 'Just the once, but yes, he most certainly did.'

'The dozy sod,' Dick said, shaking his head. 'And him a bloody teacher? No wonder the country's gone to shit.'

'Well, stupidity isn't an arrestable offence,' Pete said. 'But I think we should bring him in for questioning.' He jerked his head. 'Come on, Ben. Let's get you away from that screen of yours for a bit.'

As they headed through the downstairs reception area, Pete saw out of the front window that DCI Silverstone was standing at the top of the steps outside, addressing the crowd of angry-looking taxi drivers and the surrounding members of the press, which now included a couple of TV crews.

'Oh, shit.' He stopped in his tracks.

'Watch it, boss,' Ben said from close behind him. 'I nearly ran into you.'

Pete turned aside to the front desk, where the big, grey-haired sergeant stood watching through the window with a half-smile. 'Bob, have you got a pool car you could lend us for half an hour?'

'Eh?' His attention returned abruptly from the outside of the station. 'Uh . . . all we've got this morning is a patrol car. And that's going to be needed in twenty minutes.'

'Give us the keys. It'll be back in nineteen. Promise.'

Bob gave him a sideways look. 'In one piece?'

'Of course. Unless you dither about.'

Bob rolled his eyes. 'OK. I'll hold you to it, though.' He reached under the desk and lifted up a set of keys. 'Car 57.'

'Thanks.' Pete grabbed the keys from his outstretched hand. 'Come on, Ben. No time for dilly-dallying.' They hurried through from the public area into the back corridor, through the custody suite and out the back door. Pete glanced around the car park behind the station. Several patrol cars were there, as usual. But where was 57? He was checking the big numbers on their roofs.

'There,' said Ben, pointing across to the left.

The car was a big Vauxhall. It was parked facing into the car park, near the entrance.

'Right. Let's go.' Pete led the way at a brisk pace. He unlocked the car with the remote, hopped in and had his seatbelt fastened before Ben had his door open. With less than the usual number of cars in the car park, swinging the big saloon round was easier than it might have been. He completed the move in one big sweep, lined it up on the short drive down the side of the building and put his foot down, waiting until he was almost at the front of the station before he hit the blues and twos. Sound slammed back at them from the wall just a couple of feet from the side of the car as they shot into the open and down to the main road, where Pete turned right, away from the fray in front of the station, and accelerated away towards the city centre.

Middletown was a short crescent overlooking one of the riverside parks between the city centre and the Old Mill. A short, dead-end road, lined on one side with a hedge that bordered the park and on the other by a short row of semi-detached houses, built in the early twentieth century, of dark brick with half-timbered upper floors. This was not a cheap address, Pete knew.

He sped through the light Saturday morning traffic, using the lights and sirens until he got to within a hundred yards or so of the end of the cul-de-sac. Then he turned them off. Turning into the crescent, he found that the houses, having been built before anyone but the wealthiest had cars, had no garages, or even drives, so both sides of the crescent were lined with parked cars. He drove slowly along to the far end, checking numbers as he went, turned the big car around and came back the few yards to Fisher's address, where he double-parked, blocking the road.

'Right, let's see if he's in.'

They stepped out of the car and approached the gate to the large, neatly kept front garden. There was a high wooden fence with a gate at the side of the house.

'You take the back, just in case,' Pete said as he opened the black-painted gate. They split up. Ben went from sight around the side of the house and Pete heard the sound of a latch opening and closing. He counted to five then rang the bell.

The discreet chime had faded to nothing and Pete was starting to wonder if the man was in when a shadow moved behind the door and it swung open. Fisher was in shorts and T-shirt, a light sheen of sweat on his skin as if he'd been working out.

'Detective. What can I do for you?'

'We need to have a talk, Mr Fisher. Down at the station.' Pete nodded towards the car. 'If you wouldn't mind.'

Something seemed to shut down in Fisher's eyes. 'Do I need to call my solicitor?'

Chapter 24

'That's entirely up to you, sir. But think on this: as we stand here now, your job's over. They're not going to keep you on at Risingbrook. They can't. But you've still got your freedom and your life as you know it. You could go somewhere else and get another job.' *As long as it's nowhere near my kids and, preferably, nobody else's either.* He forced his expression to remain neutral as he fought the disgust that twisted his stomach, hoping Fisher would just think he was letting that sink in.

'But once we charge you, that's gone,' he continued, when he could be sure of keeping his voice even. 'You'll be on the sex-offenders register. There's the likelihood of prison with all the risks that entails for someone on those sorts of charges. Will you get bail in the meantime? I don't know. But would you want to gamble on it? I wouldn't, in your shoes. On the other hand, if you cooperate with us, this is your chance to get out from under, get ahead of the game, put your case before the boys and their expensive barristers drop you any deeper in it than you already are.' Pete spread his hands. 'It's completely up to you, but I know which way I'd go.'

Fisher didn't react for several seconds. It was almost like he'd gone into suspended animation. He was a few inches shorter than Pete, but well-built. Powerful. With that and the element of surprise, he might think he could get past him and away. Pete readied himself for a fight. But then Fisher seemed to slump. He took a step back.

'All right. Let me just grab a tracksuit.'

He turned away and headed back into the house. Pete followed.

Fisher mounted the stairs, Pete close behind him. The door opposite the top of the stairs was open, light flooding in. It was laid out as a gym with a rowing machine, exercise bike and set of weights. A maroon tracksuit was draped over a wooden towel rail beside the weights rack.

As Fisher reached for it, Pete was two steps behind him at the top of the stairs.

Fisher put on the tracksuit top. His arm went out again towards the trousers. Suddenly, he bent at the waist, reached beyond the towel rail and snatched up a foot-long dumbbell. Twisting, feet spread, he swung the heavy metal back towards Pete, hoping to catch him off-guard. But Pete wasn't there. He'd paused outside the doorway. The dumbbell slammed into the wall, punching a hole in the plasterboard. Fisher growled, stepping forward fast as he snatched the heavy weight free and lifted it like a weapon.

'Boss?' Ben's voice came from the kitchen.

'Upstairs.'

Fisher was too short for Pete to get inside the move. Space was cramped. There was only one way to go. He stepped back and to the side, grabbing for Fisher's top, pulling him forward. Fisher was already swinging the dumbbell, its weight, combined with his own, pulling him off-balance. The metal struck the banister in front of him. Wood splintered. He yelled. Pete saw what was about to happen and his other hand came around, grabbing for the back of Fisher's vest, trying to swing him around to the side, but his weight and momentum were all wrong. The vest ripped. The dumbbell clunked on the wooden floor. Fisher's shoulder hit the already-damaged banister. It gave way. He went down hard, three-quarter turned back towards Pete, his torso hanging out over empty space. Horror filled his eyes as they met Pete's but then he was tipping, legs flailing in the air. His arms cracked against the banister spindles at his sides, but they were already split and ruined.

Pete went down to one knee, grabbing for his leg, but pain ripped through his shoulder from the damage it had taken at the dogfight the other night and Fisher's skin was slick with sweat from his recent workout. The leg snatched away and Fisher bellowed as he tipped backwards, arms and legs flailing. Pete dove forward, flat on his belly across the landing, reaching over the edge despite the agony spreading into his neck and chest, but it was too late. Fisher started to flip end overend, but the fall wasn't far enough. He'd tipped about fifteen degrees past the vertical when he hit the floor headfirst. Pete paused, watching for movement.

'Are you all right, boss?' Ben had one foot on the bottom stair, his hand on the banister as he stared up at Pete, then down at the broken body just two steps from him.

'Yeah.'

Pete got to his knees and stood up, holding his injured shoulder as he focused on Fisher's inert body, the neck bent at an odd angle.

The ribs moved, relaxing in a slow exhalation.

Pete reached for the banister, then thought better of it. Took a step back instead, to lean against the wall beside the doorway.

'What happened?'

'I tried to grab him, but all I got was a handful of vest. How is he?'

Ben blinked and looked down at the prone games teacher. He stepped away from the stairs, reached for the side of the man's neck with two fingers and paused. 'Nothing. He's gone.'

Pete was suddenly reminded of Frank Benton and the fall he'd taken in the woods to the west of here when, again, Pete and Ben had gone out to make an arrest and their suspect had tried to evade them. At least Frank had survived.

He started down the stairs, a steadying hand to the wall at his side. Reaching the bottom, he sat down heavily, pulled out his phone and dialled 101.

'Exeter police station. How can I help?'

'Bob, it's Pete. I'm not going to get your car back in time. Can you send the pathologist down here to Middletown? We've got a DB for him.'

'See, I knew you couldn't be trusted. Do you want forensics as well?'

'No need. Accidental death. I witnessed it. So did Ben.'

'Shit. Sorry, mate. I'll get onto the pathologist.'

'Thanks.' Pete hung up and looked up at Ben, who was standing by the front door, watching him.

Ben gave him a lift of the eyebrows.

Pete could guess what he was thinking, but it was too soon to say it. 'You could have a peek around for a computer and see if you can get into it,' he suggested. 'No need for a warrant now.'

'Right.'

'It's getting so we can't let you out on your own, boss,' Dick said, giving Dave a wink as Pete and Ben stepped into the squad room. 'What have you been up to now?'

'Saving the taxpayer the cost of a trial and board and lodging for fifteen years or more. And you?'

'On your desk, boss. A shiny new set of pictures of our suspect. From the bus CCTV and the cameras outside St David's station.'

Pete sat down, glanced through the sheets of glossy A4 and looked up with a frown. 'So, she was walking away from the station, not into it or over to the taxi rank?'

Dick tipped his head. 'Peg Wright's in the camera room today. I got her to see what she could find on the city cameras. She picked her up at the clock tower on a camera outside Central Station, then going north on the High Street. And in a queue at the bus stop on Sidwell.'

'Bus going to where?'

'According to the taxi company, the County Cricket Ground,' Dave said.

'I don't suppose there's any cameras out there, unlike the footie ground?'

Dave shook his head, lips pursed. 'Nope.'

'But the season doesn't start for another six weeks or more,' Ben said.

'That's the point, I expect,' Jill retorted. 'She wouldn't want to be seen getting into the cab, would she?'

'Well, if she wants to hide, why go around in a bright-red skirt or dress? And we know she's got wigs. Why be a redhead when she could blend in more as a blonde or brunette?'

'Have you ever tried wearing a wig?' Jane asked. 'They're hot and itchy, especially in warm weather.'

'And the dress, skirt, whatever it is?'

Jane shrugged. 'OK. That, I can't explain.'

Dave looked from one to the other. 'Have you never heard the saying "Red dress, no knickers"?'

'Oh, you would, wouldn't you?' said Jill.

'I'm just saying – maybe that's the point. To encourage those kinds of thoughts in the cabbie she picks up. Like a test. See what response she gets.' He shrugged. 'I don't know.'

'Deliberately provoking a reaction,' Pete added.

'Which would make her a hunter, not just an opportunist or reactionary killer,' said Ben.

'Well, we did say it seemed to be turning into a spree,' Jill said.

'Yeah, but what triggered it?' asked Jane.

'If we knew that, we'd have her in custody by now,' Dave pointed out.

'You're not just a pretty face, are you?' Dick said.

'Not just or just not?' Jane shot back.

'Oi!' said Dave as Pete's phone rang.

He picked it up, missing the retort. 'DS Gayle, Exeter CID.'

'Pete, it's Louise. I just got a call from the hospital. They're desperate. They've got three nurses off sick on CDU tonight. They're desperate for cover on the twelve till eight.'

'OK. Don't worry about it. It's Saturday. I don't suppose Fast-track's going to want to overdo the overtime anyway. I'll cover you for this afternoon so's you can get your head down for a few hours and, if all goes to plan, we can pick things up here again on Monday.'

Considering the amount of time she'd had off following Tommy's disappearance, he could see how she'd want to do all she could to try to make up for it. 'I'll see you later.'

'Thanks, love.'

He checked his watch as he ended the call. It was ten-forty. He had an hour.

'Something up, boss?' Jane asked.

'Louise. She's picked up an extra shift. Needs me home at lunchtime.'

'Best get cracking then, hadn't we?' said Dave.

'You haven't told me yet how you got on with the boys downstairs.'

'Mostly, we didn't. The parents had them tied up with solicitors before their heads hit the pillows last night. A few of them decided to talk to us anyway, if only to provide alibis for the times we asked them about, when those pictures were downloaded onto Fisher's phone. And when you put it all together, they effectively alibi the others too. They're all resident, so, two of the times, they were in the dining hall. Another one was during a hockey practice session, which clears four of them. Another was during a rugby match against a rival school, so the other five were on the pitch and the hockey players were on the sidelines. With witnesses.'

'You'd have thought Fisher would be too,' Pete pointed out. 'That's hardly an alibi.'

'It is for the five on the pitch, boss,' Jane said. 'And if we accept that it was only one person doing the downloading, then the two events clear all of them.'

'*If* we accept that premise,' Pete emphasised. 'Which no solicitor would.'

'While they were playing with the kids downstairs,' Jill said, 'I was onto the school for his work schedule, going back to this time last year. They emailed it to me a few minutes ago. So, if we can pick out the uploads to Dropbox from his phone records, we can match them against where he should have been at those times and, possibly, who should have been with him.'

'More significantly, if we can pick out those uploads, can we identify the account they were sent to?' Pete asked.

'*We* can't,' Ben said. 'But, Dropbox should be able to. We'd need a warrant, I expect – privacy issues and all that. But given the exact dates and times and the source, I'd have thought they could track them. I don't know how long it would take, mind.'

'OK. You and Jill can deal with that next then. The computer issue can wait for Monday. I'll go back to the school and ask about that. He hadn't got one at home,' he added for the benefit of the rest of the team. 'But the two priorities now are to tie at least some members of the gang to those pictures and to identify our mystery redhead. Any chance of accessing any of their phones?'

Jane shook her head. 'Not without warrants, boss. And we haven't got enough, individually, to get them.' She shrugged. 'It's not part of the conspiracy against you and Annie.'

'Of course it bloody well is. It's the reason for it. They've admitted that much. And we've got Chris Mellor's testimony that they had them, which is a criminal act in itself.'

'Don't tell us,' Dave said. 'Tell him in there.' He thrust his chin at Colin Underhill's empty office and the DCI's beyond it.

'There's times,' Pete said, 'when I could happily take a lump hammer in there and use it to try to beat some sense into his thick, obstructive skull.'

'On the upside,' Dave said, 'There wouldn't be any witnesses. That's guaranteeable.'

'I don't know about that. I can think of at least one person who'd take the opportunity,' Pete replied, thinking of his fellow DS, Simon Phillips, the man who'd been tasked with trying to find Tommy and who he'd had more than one disagreement with since returning to active duty. He had no doubt at all that Phillips would take any chance he was offered to end his career. But . . . 'Hold on. Mellor's already confessed. So, do we need a warrant for his phone? It's material evidence in support of that confession.'

'Yes, but we'd still need a warrant or permission to access it,' Jane said.

'Permission from whom? Him or his parents?'

She shrugged. 'Either, I expect.'

'We could promise him a deal if he cooperates. I know he's a horrible little shit, but he's a follower, not a leader. I was inclined to believe him when he said he stayed back out of the way. He did nothing to stop what was happening, but . . . much as I don't like it, it would get us the warrant for whichever one he got the pictures from. That would be a start and you never know – it might be the ringleader.'

'Probably would be,' Dave said. 'I can't see there being too many steps in a path like that.'

'So, let's give it a try. The kid first. Then, if there's nothing doing there, try his parents. Jane, you played the good guy with him. It's down to you.'

'Gee, thanks, boss.'

'Peter.' The shout came from the direction of DI Colin Underhill's office at the far end of the squad room, but it wasn't his voice. Pete looked around to see the dark, uniformed figure of DCI Adam Silverstone poking his head through the door. 'My office. Now.'

No please, Pete thought. *That's not a good sign.* He stood up. 'Here we go again.'

'Your headmaster must have got sick of the sight of you, didn't he?' Dave asked.

'Not at all. I was a good lad.'

Dave laughed. 'What happened?'

Pete shrugged and headed for the door. Glancing across the squad room, he saw that most of the other officers were studiously working, but one or two looked up and met his gaze.

Simon Phillips had his head firmly down, but Pete was sure he could see a smirk on his face.

He stepped out into the corridor and headed along to Silverstone's door. He had knocked only once when the shout came from within. 'Come.'

He entered. He hadn't even got the door closed when the DCI demanded, 'What the hell happened?'

'Sir?' Pete turned to face him.

'Don't act thick, Detective Sergeant. It doesn't suit you.'

'Thank you, sir.' Pete stood stiffly in front of his desk.

'Well?'

'Do I take it this is about Samuel Fisher, sir?'

Silverstone's lips tightened. He made a noise in his throat that was almost a growl.

'He fell, sir. He took a swing at me with a dumbbell, missed, and the momentum carried him forward, so he went through the banister at the top of his stairs. I tried to catch him, but couldn't. Ben saw it all.'

'Hmm. For which you should be duly grateful. Otherwise, you'd be out of here, pending an investigation.' Silverstone exhaled noisily. 'Why is it that whenever anything significant happens in your day, I have to hear about it from someone else?'

'We're kind of busy, sir. There was nothing to be done about it and a hell of a lot else to do, so I just got on with it.'

'A man's died, Detective Sergeant. In your presence. While you were attempting to arrest him, if I'm not mistaken. You can't just ignore it. The press certainly won't and neither will Headquarters.'

'We'll fill out the necessary forms, sir. But, like I said, we've got a lot on. A killer out there on the streets who we're struggling to identify, never mind apprehend. We haven't got time to waste on things that aren't urgent.'

'You haven't . . .' Rage suffused Silverstone's face. He planted his hands on his desk and came up out of his chair. 'What the Devil do you think this is? The Wild West?'

'I don't, sir. But it's getting a bit like it out there for the city's taxi drivers, so we need to find whoever's going after them before the papers start calling it that. This city – this county – relies on the tourist industry. We get a reputation for that kind of trouble, it won't do anybody any good.'

'Damn it, Sergeant, do not presume to lecture me.'

'I'm not, sir. I'm just answering your question.'

'Get out!' Silverstone shouted.

'Sir.'

Pete didn't need telling twice. He turned to the door and was reaching for the handle when Silverstone snapped, 'Sergeant.'

He turned back. 'Sir?'

'Where are you going?'

Pete frowned. 'Back to my desk, sir.'

Silverstone paused, looking almost confused. Then he blinked. 'In future, I want to be informed immediately when something of this level of significance occurs. Do you understand?'

'Sir.'

Silverstone nodded towards the door. 'Go.'

Pete stepped out. As he walked back down the short corridor he was shaking his head. The DCI seemed to be losing it. It seemed, at times, like he couldn't handle the pressure. Exeter was a city, a county town, but at the end of the day, it was a small, friendly and generally peaceful place. If he couldn't cope here, he had no chance in somewhere like Manchester or London. They might call him Fast-track, but Pete was starting to wonder if he was on the fast-track to early retirement on health grounds.

We can but hope, a small voice at the back of his mind said. But in truth, Pete wouldn't wish that kind of ending on anyone's career.

He was reminded of what Louise had gone through for months after Tommy's disappearance. She had come out the other side eventually, but only with the support of her family. Himself and Annie. He didn't know what Adam Silverstone's home situation was – the man kept his private life strictly private – but he didn't suppose it was anywhere near as solid and supportive as his own.

'Christ, don't we even get a break on the weekends in here?'

Brian smiled. 'That's the one way in which these establishments are still rather Victorian, I'm afraid. Sunday is a day of rest, but that's all you get.'

'All we get or all you get?' Tommy asked.

'All the specialised staff get.'

'So, what about us inmates?'

'What do you think, Tommy?'

'I think I'm here for nothing much more than a misdemeanour in the first place, that's what I think. Carrying a knife. I needed it for the work I was doing, for Christ's sake. What are they going to do – arrest everybody who works on a fair, on a farm, in a warehouse or anywhere else you need a knife?'

Brian sighed heavily. 'You know perfectly well it wasn't the fact you were carrying it – it was the type of knife you were carrying. Why are we going around in circles, Tommy? What are you trying to avoid talking about?'

Tommy laughed. 'If I told you that, I wouldn't be very good at avoiding it, would I?'

'So, there is something. We haven't talked about your family life yet, have we? What's your mum like? She's been in every day to see you here. She must love you very much. Tell me about her.'

'Why?'

'So, I can try to understand what's brought you here.'

'What's my mum got to do with that?'

'She played a major part in your formative years, Tommy. Of course she's relevant.'

'How do you know? She might have been at work all the time.'

Brian's head tilted to one side, his gaze focusing on Tommy. 'Was she?'

'She's a nurse. What do you think?' He folded his arms across his chest.

Brian nodded slowly. 'Nurses tend to be very caring people. I imagine she'd have tried her best to be there for you as much as possible.'

Tommy said nothing, holding a blank expression on his face as he waited for the psychiatrist to fill the silence.

'Didn't she?'

Tommy shrugged, maintaining his silence.

'How much younger is your sister?' Brian asked next.

'Three years.'

'And how do you get on with her?'

'OK.'

'Has that always been the case?'

'Dunno.' He shrugged.

Brian leaned forward, elbows on his knees. 'What is it that you're afraid of, Tommy?'

He frowned.

'You've heard of doctor-patient privilege? Whatever you tell me is just between you and me. Nobody else can know about it.'

'Well, what's the point then? What's all this for?' He waved a hand at the room they were in – Brian's office and consulting room was large and bright, even with the vertical blinds closed. The desk was pale wood, like the shelves that covered half of one wall and were filled with books – not all of them psychiatric tomes. There were children's books too, on the lower shelves.

'To figure out why people like you are here, Tommy, and try to help them improve their lives and hopefully not come back.'

'People like me? What's that mean? Criminals? Perverts? Killers?'

Brian paused, lips pursed. 'I don't think you see yourself that way, do you?'

'You think I shouldn't? After last year with Malcolm Burton? Lauren and Rosie and the others?'

'Others?' Brian frowned. 'What others?'

Tommy smiled. 'You only knew of those two? Don't they tell you anything?'

'Clearly not everything. How many were there?'

Tommy sucked air. 'Let's see now . . . There was one from Bristol. A little blonde, she was. Then there was one from a fairground. Same fair as I was working at until the other day, actually.' He met Brian's gaze. 'I got to know her parents. Nice couple. They run a rifle range. No clue who I was, of course. I'm not sure if they reported her missing or just looked for her themselves. A bit like gypos, fair folk are. Keep themselves to themselves. Ideal targets, in that sense.' He scratched an itch on his cheek. 'Even if they do report stuff, the police don't like them. They tend to be seen more as suspects than victims. The first one was actually a gypo. They were camped out on a back lane near the airport. There's a wide bit of verge by a bridge. Just chance, really. We were driving by and I saw her splashing about in the brook. I looked closer and she was naked, so Mel pulled over for a better look. Beautiful. So pale, with long, black hair. Don't know where her parents were but we watched her for a bit. Then, seeing there was no one else around, we took her.'

'Just like that?' Brian couldn't quite hide his horror.

'Well, she struggled a bit, but yeah. I held her. Mel drove. I think it scared him a bit, going through the city with her, in case she kicked up or got away. I thought we were going back to his place with her, but then he went straight through and out to the barn. That was the first time I'd been there. I said I thought she'd be cold there, but he didn't care. Said she could burrow in the hay if she had to.'

Brian drew a breath. 'What . . . what happened to her?'

'She died.' *What do you think happened to her?* he thought.

Brian paused, absorbing that. 'And how old was she?'

263

Tommy shook his head. 'Dunno. Nine. Ten. Something like that.'

'So, slightly younger than your sister, Annie?'

'Yeah, I suppose.' Tommy shrugged. What had that got to do with anything?

'But you didn't connect the two in any way in your mind?'

Tommy looked at him incredulously. 'No. Why would I? She was a gypo. They're not like us. They're like . . . well, wild, you know?'

'I don't think I do. Perhaps you could explain it to me?'

Tommy looked at him like he was an idiot. 'Gypos,' he said. 'They live in tents and caravans. Don't pay taxes or go to school or anything. They're separate. Different. Like . . . savages or something, only living here in our country, using our roads and hospitals and stuff.'

'So, you resent the fact that they take from society without contributing to it?'

Tommy shrugged. 'Plus, they nick stuff and cause trouble. And they stink. That's why we didn't take her clothes with us. They reeked.'

Brian's eyes widened in horror. 'You didn't . . .?'

Tommy's lip curled. 'Have you ever smelt them? It's disgusting. You can't bloody breathe, you get too close to them. No way we were having that in the van. We wouldn't have taken her at all if she hadn't been in the river, getting clean.'

Brian seemed to collect himself, rebuilding his professional façade. 'So, you took her between you, took her to the barn. Then what?'

'Mel used, like, a thin chain to tie one of her wrists to a loop in the wall. We left her for a few hours, then went back and started on her.'

'Started on her? What do you mean?'

'Pictures. Video. On her own, with Mel, then with me. He didn't have actual sex with her.'

'But you did?'

264

'Not the first day. She was still too wild.'

'So, how did you deal with that?'

'No food or water the first day. No food the second. It's like with dogs: you chain them up and starve them, they soon learn.' Tommy grinned when Brian failed to respond. 'I bet you'd like to do that with some of us, wouldn't you? Chain us up and starve us like they used to do in the old days. See if you could turn us around that way instead of wasting all the money places like this cost?'

'Places like this exist because methods like that don't work, Thomas.'

Tommy laughed again, shaking his head. 'Of course they do, Brian.' He reached out to pat the psychiatrist's leg like a kindly father with a slow child. 'Cruelty will change a person's outlook far quicker than kindness, any day.'

Chapter 25

'So, it's just you and me this afternoon, kiddo. Home alone. Unsupervised. What do you reckon we should do, eh? Picnic on the sitting-room rug? Go to the pictures and stuff our faces with popcorn? Slob out and drink beer with the footie on the box?'

'*Dad!* I'm not six and I'm not sixteen. Eighteen. Whatever. Plus, I hate football and so do you.'

'OK. All true. But, if your mum's going to go off and leave us, I've got to try and make her regret it, haven't I?' He winked at Louise, who was watching the exchange. 'Computer games then. That Wee thing. What can we do with that?'

'Nothing you'd want to.'

'I could pop into town and get a couple of steering wheels for it and thrash you at Formula One.'

'That's not the Wee. It's PlayStation. And they cost a fortune.'

'Hey! Who's the adult here?'

'I sometimes think it's me,' Annie said with a sigh.

Pete reached out and ruffled her hair. 'And you might even be right. But you don't know what I have to contend with at work. It's like dealing with a class of eight-year-olds sometimes. I need to have a playtime when I get home to get over it. And anyway, what do we have kids for, if not to play with?'

'To perpetuate the bloodline,' she said imperiously.

'Oooh! Get you!' He grabbed her and tickled her ribs until she squealed and wriggled out of his grasp. He looked up at Louise, who was standing in the doorway of the sitting room, 'What are we raising here? She's far too clever for us to handle. She must be some sort alien. A cuckoo bird that was dropped into our nest while we weren't looking.'

'You speak for yourself,' she shot back. 'I certainly noticed her arrival. I remember screaming for that epidural like it was yesterday.'

'So does that doctor, I bet,' he retorted. 'The names you called him . . .'

Annie was looking from one to the other now, wide-eyed and serious. 'Does it hurt that much, having a baby?'

'Only when they grab on tight in there 'cause they don't want to come out,' Pete joked.

'*Dad!*' Annie's face scrunched up in disgust.

'No, love. It's not that bad,' Louise said. 'We're just joking. Now, I've got to go and get some sleep. Look after him, will you? Make sure he doesn't get into any trouble?'

Pete took the cordless phone into the living room when Louise went to bed so that, if it rang, he could grab it quickly and minimise the chance of it disturbing her. He and Annie were curled up on the sofa, watching a rerun of *Crocodile Dundee* on TV when it rang. He hit the button to answer it before the first ring was complete. 'Hello?'

'Boss? It's Jane. We've got a name. For the redhead.'

One of many they'd get over the next several days, no doubt, following the publication of the photographs. 'What's special about this one?'

'The face matches. The caller told us to look at the Facebook account of an Emma Radcliffe. She's a legal secretary here in the city. They said to look at the pictures from their Christmas party. And sure enough, in a couple of them, there she was. Standing alongside Emma. And she's named in the caption for one of them. Tanya Cunliffe, age twenty-three. I've looked her up. She's got no record. Lives up Copplestone Road, off the Cowley Bridge Road.'

'Best bring her in then, before she sees the papers and does a runner.'

'If she hasn't already. Are you coming?'

'Do you need me to?'

'I just thought you might want to, boss.'

'Maybe so, but I can't, can I?'

Annie looked up at him, then stretched up to whisper in his other ear. 'You can go if you need to. Mum's still here.'

He smiled at her, squeezing her hand as he shook his head. 'I'm sure you can handle it, Jane.'

'OK. Just thought I'd better check with you first.'

'I've got to let you out on your own at some point, haven't I? Ready for when you're all grown-up and flying the nest.'

'Yeah, I think that might be sooner for some of us than others, boss.'

Pete laughed. 'I can't think what you mean, Jane. Be safe, OK? Remember, if it's her, she's potentially armed.'

'I've seen the crime-scene photos. I'm not likely to forget that in a hurry.'

'Good. Go get her then.'

'Will do.'

He hung up the phone, putting it back on the arm of the sofa.

'You could have gone, Dad,' Annie said seriously. 'I'm used to being here with Mum when she was poorly.'

He gave her a hug. 'I know, Button. But there's no need. They're only going to bring a young woman in for questioning. And they are all grown-up, when it comes down to it.'

'That's not what you said before.'

He laughed. 'I know. We all need to act like kids some of the time, though. And I'd far rather be sitting here with you than running round the city after some girl who might or might not have something to do with a case I've been investigating.'

She resettled herself on the sofa, tucked in tight against him. 'I should think so too.'

'She lives in those flats just up from Glenthorne Road,' Jane said to the rest of the team.

'Which floor?' asked Dick.

'First.'

'So, a couple of us out the back in case she legs it,' Dave suggested. 'You and Ben go to the front door. It's not like you're there to arrest her. Just ask a few questions. If she comes quietly, great, but if she refuses, we call in the Taser team. We know she's got pepper spray and a Stanley knife she's not afraid to use as a weapon, so it's no good getting heroic with her.'

'That works for me,' Jane confirmed. 'Ben?'

'Yeah, of course.'

'So, me and Jill at the back and you stay with the car in case she gets past us?' Dick aimed the suggestion at Dave.

'Actually, no,' said Dave. 'Knowing what a warren it is round there, I'll bring the bike. I can follow her better if she nips through one of the pathways.'

'Good idea,' Jane said. 'Let's do it.'

'I'll stop off and have a word with the sarge downstairs,' Dave said. 'Make sure there's a Taser team available if we need them. I can soon catch you up.'

'Remember you haven't got blue lights on that beast of yours,' Jane retorted, heading out of the squad room.

'Why change the habits of a lifetime?' Dick said with a grin.

Fourteen minutes later, Dave rolled the big Norton to a halt outside the metal roller doors of the garages beneath and behind the block of flats where their subject lived. He cut the engine

269

and pushed the kickstand down, flipped up his visor and gave Dick Feeney a nod.

Dick raised his mobile phone to his ear and spoke into it as Dave took off his helmet. Dick's silver Ford was parked in one of the bays opposite the garages, Dick standing beside it while Jill, in uniform, stood next to one of the garage doors, out of sight from the flats above.

Ending the brief call, Dick slipped the phone back into his pocket. 'Now, we wait and see what happens.'

The three-storey block had been built into the steeply sloping ground so that the garages filled the lower floor, opening at the back, while the living accommodation opened from the upper side, on the first floor. They would hear nothing from there unless something significant happened. All they could do was wait.

'Like being in the Army, isn't it?' said Dave. 'Hurry up and wait.'

'Yeah, except you wouldn't last five minutes in the Army,' Jill told him. 'You'd get slung out for insubordination.'

Dave shrugged. 'That's one reason I never joined.'

'What's the other?' asked Dick.

'Oh, there were several. I like my comforts, for one. And decent grub. All this sleeping in dormitories, eating out of tin cans and slogging over Dartmoor in all kinds of weather isn't for me.'

'You old softie,' said Jill.

'We ain't going there again, are we?'

'All right: wimp.'

Dick's phone buzzed in his pocket. He lifted it out and answered it. 'Yes?' He listened briefly. 'OK. You want to try again, give it a minute or two, in case she's in the shower or on the bog?' He listened again. 'Right.' Putting the phone away, he looked at Dave. 'No answer.'

He nodded. 'I gathered.'

'She's trying again in a minute.'

'Might as well, now we're here. Have we got any details on her? Has she got any family in the city? Known associates? Anything like that?'

Dick shook his head. 'Nothing I know of, but I didn't take the call about her. I can ask Jane.' He reached into his pocket.

Dave grimaced. 'Best leave it until we know she's not in.'

Dick nodded and they lapsed into silence.

They waited another couple of minutes or so until Dick's phone buzzed again. He took it out. 'Yes?' Giving the others a brief nod, he listened. 'OK. One more for luck? What's she drive, anyway? OK.' He ended the call again.

'Still no answer. Her car's not out here, but it could be in the garage. No telling.'

'You think?' Dave asked, looking across at the roller doors with their padlocks through the handles. 'Wouldn't take much to get in there and check. She'd never know if she's not here.'

'See, I always knew you'd had a dodgy childhood,' Jill said.

'You don't know the half of it.' Dave winked. 'Shall I?' he asked Dick.

Dick shrugged. 'Up to you, mate. I'm having nothing to do with it.' He looked around carefully. 'I can't see any cameras round here.'

'Always helps,' Dave said. 'Which one is it?'

'Number three. The brass lock.'

Dave swung his leg clear of the bike and left it standing, helmet hanging from the handlebars while he approached the garage door, unzipping the front of his leathers. He reached inside and came out with a small leather key wallet. Kneeling before the garage door, he extracted a couple of thin strips of metal and inserted them into the padlock, wiggling and jiggling them until it snapped open. 'There you go. Piece of piss.'

Dick nodded. 'Go on then. Have a look and lock it up again.' He glanced around to make sure the coast was clear and Dave quickly rolled the door up far enough to see under it.

'Nothing.' He pushed it down again. 'Are you sure this is the right one?'

'Yes.'

'Right then.' He snapped the lock back into place. 'Might as well wait for Jane to call us, in case the car's in for service or something. Then we can clear off.' He straddled the bike again so that he could see both Dick and Jill, at either side of him. This was going to be a wasted hour. And on a Saturday too.

Then Dick stiffened against the side of his car.

Dave noticed the change in him. 'What's up?' he asked.

'*Don't* turn around. Stay put, both of you,' he said quietly. 'She's just walking up the road.'

Dave shifted on his seat. 'Are you sure it's her?'

'I said don't look. Yes, I'm sure. I might be older than you, but my eyes aren't failing yet.'

'The thing is, are hers? With Jill stood there in uniform . . .'

'At least she's in the shadows. As long as she doesn't move, we should be OK.'

Dave grunted. 'We hope. But then she'll get up there and see Ben.' He took out his mobile and hit the speed-dial number for Jane.

'Hello?' she came back on the first ring.

'Target approaching up the road on foot.'

A tiny pause, then: 'OK. Thanks.'

The line was cut.

The urge to put his helmet on and turn the bike around was almost overwhelming, but he resisted. He didn't want to make the suspect look towards him and possibly spot Jill. 'Is she still in sight?' he asked Dick.

'Yeah. Will be for a few more seconds. I'll tell you when you can move.'

'I bet you say that to all the girls.'

'They don't call me Grey Man for nothing.'

Dave almost laughed aloud when he saw the expression on Jill's face. The struggle she was going through not to say anything was obviously immense. But he held his tongue and waited. And waited. More than a minute passed before he said, 'Surely, she must be out of sight by now.'

'Yeah,' said Dick. 'I was just enjoying the quiet, for a change.'
This time, Jill couldn't hold in the snigger.

'You know I'm going to get you back for that, don't you?'

Dick nodded. 'I know you're going to try. But what the hell? It was worth it.'

A shout sounded distantly from beyond the redbrick building. They looked at each other, the banter forgotten – all business now. Dick nodded. Dave crammed his full-face helmet onto his head, kicked up the stand and turned the ignition. The big bike rumbled into life. He tapped it into gear and swung it around towards Feeney.

Which way would she run?

Left would bring her down past them, right was up a fairly steep incline, and the only other choice was down past the far end of the block and onto the narrow path that led through past the old folks' home towards the lower university buildings on Glenthorne Road. If she expected them to be on four wheels, that would be a prime choice. It was an easier run than going up Copplestone, although there were other paths going off further up there, he knew. Still, panic needed speed and speed meant downhill.

Then Jill shouted. He glanced over his shoulder. She was pointing to his left. He'd been right. He saw the girl, red hair flying, her pale coat flapping around her legs. She'd lost the two shopping bags she'd been carrying. She ran full-pelt down the slope beyond the bollards at the far end of the garage and parking area, heading for Glenthorne.

Dave gunned the engine and sped after her. He saw her glance over her shoulder as she heard his engine, her eyes wide and wild. Then she was running as fast and hard as she could, concentrating on making ground. He took the bike through the bollards and down onto the tarmacked pathway. She was running straight down the middle of a wide, straight path. What she thought she'd achieve, he had no idea, but she wasn't getting away from him.

He gunned the engine and quickly closed the gap between them. Pushing his visor up, he yelled at her.

'Police. Stop before you hurt yourself. You're not getting away.'

She ran on. The tarmac was just wide enough for two pedestrians. Either side of it was a strip of grass and weeds at least as wide. He had plenty of room to pass her whenever he chose and more than enough time before the path emerged onto the road ahead.

'Show some sense, for Christ's sake,' he shouted over the rumble of the now nearly idling bike. 'Stop.'

This was stupid. What was wrong with her?

But on she ran. He could tell she was panting now. If she went on much longer, he didn't know how he was going to get her back to the car. At least she wouldn't be able to run away when he did get to that stage.

'Damn it, woman, will you pack it in?' he snarled. Then saw her arms whip out to the side. She grabbed hold of a light pole at the entrance to a side path on their right. Both hands locked around it. Her feet left the ground as Dave cursed and slammed on the brakes, kicking the bike into neutral.

One of her feet hit the petrol tank by his knee, the other caught him squarely in the ribs. It was like being hit with a sharp-edged block of wood. He yelped and grabbed for her feet, but the bike was tilting under him. She wriggled and kicked. He couldn't fight her and the bike. He lost his grip on one ankle.

She got a foot to the ground, kicked out again with the one he was still grasping. His hand slipped on the smooth nylon of her tights and her heel slammed into his upper arm, then flicked up so he had to pull his head back sharply to avoid being hit in the face.

He got the bike stable under him, kicked the stand down, but by then she had broken free and hit the ground running in a new direction – down the side path that led to the main road, which they'd been running parallel with. Staggered metal barriers stood across the end. Designed to stop pushbikes, they were certainly going to stop him getting the big Norton through there.

'Bitch,' he swore, grabbing the ignition key. He snatched it out and was off the bike in an instant, but she had already gained ten yards or more and was off and flying again. He swung through the barrier and set off in pursuit, running hard.

The path was only a few yards long. She was dressed in a short skirt and tights with a thin top under a lightweight mac. Dave was in heavy bike leathers. He drove himself hard but had gained no ground by the time she reached the far end where another pair of metal barriers partially blocked the path. She angled left then lunged across to the right. Her right foot hit the wooden fence, pushing her upwards, arms spreading so that her coat flew out, bat-like as her left foot hit the top of the barrier. Then she was turning in the air, coat swirling around her. She literally hit the ground running, vanishing from sight to the left, along the Cowley Bridge Road.

'Shit,' Dave muttered. He wasn't going to match a move like that, with or without the leathers. He took the opposite approach, angling right to slip through, using the thickness and padding of the leathers as protection. He hit the fence to the left with his shoulder, bounced off, right foot going out, boot sole gripping the ground, pushing him off, but she'd already gained another ten yards on him.

As he pounded after her along the busy road, she glanced back over her shoulder. A few yards further, Dave's long legs were holding ground, but he was not yet gaining. She glanced back again and abruptly veered out across the traffic, narrowly missing an oncoming car. The driver behind it slammed on the brakes, tyres squealing on the tarmac as the car fishtailed. Dave glanced back, but a big lorry was coming towards him, too close for comfort. As he turned back, he saw her vanish into the entrance of another pathway, this one leading down to the river.

'Damn it.'

He stopped, panting, and leaned back against the high wall that ran along this side of the road. Pulling out his phone, he hit a speed-dial number.

'Dave?' She'd recognised his number.

'I lost her. She dodged the traffic and nipped down to the river.'

A pause, then: 'OK. Meet us back here at the flats.'

He put the phone away, pushed off from the wall and started walking back the way he'd come.

Chapter 26

They were waiting for him by the garages, standing in a group beside Dick's car. He stopped the bike, killed the engine and pulled off his helmet.

'All right?' asked Jane.

Dave grunted.

Jane held up a dark leather shoulder bag. 'We haven't got her, but we've got the evidence we need. The wigs aren't in here, but the pepper spray and the Stanley knife are. And it looks like there's going to be blood inside it, even though she's cleaned the outside. We'll leave it to forensics to open it and prove that, though.'

'So, where now?' Dave asked.

They all had smartphones. He didn't expect they'd been idle while they waited for him.

'Her parents live in Brixham,' Jane told him. 'She's got an aunt and uncle here in the city. No other family we know of.'

'Friends?'

She shook her head.

'She's not been on our radar and doesn't use social media,' Ben told him.

'So, what are we waiting for? Where does the aunt live?'

'Exwick,' Dick said.

Dave grimaced. 'She could make that on foot from here, across Station Road. Any idea where her car is?'

'Believe it or not, the tyre place down there by the Esso garage.' Dick thrust his chin in the direction of Cowley Bridge Road.

'Well, let's go then. We don't want her picking it up while we stand here chatting.'

'I told them to put a delay on it, if she comes in, and call me to say my car's ready.'

Dave relaxed. 'Old age and treachery, eh?'

Dick winked. 'Gets 'em every time.'

'So, are you or Red going to wait there for her while the rest of us go to the aunt and uncle's?'

'I will. I spoke to them.'

'Right. I'll follow you then, Red.'

'Does that thing go that slow?' asked Dick.

Dave bobbed his head. 'Not often.'

Nancy and Derek Manning lived in a small cul-de-sac off a side road that led up into the hills off St Andrew's Road, not far from the church. Dropping back down to the main road, they headed towards the city centre, turning right just before St David's to cross the railway lines and the river into Exwick, using the same route as their suspect would have taken, just minutes earlier. Dave was hoping to overtake her before she reached her relatives' house, but there was no sign of her by the time they reached the main road through the old village.

Jane turned right in front of him, then left up the narrow hill towards the address she had found.

The cul-de-sac was fairly new, the houses of dark brick and tile, with attached garages and tiny front gardens, but the edge-of-woodland feel of the place was pleasant. Jane pulled into the short drive of the house they wanted, in the bottom corner, and Dave parked the bike across the back of her bright-green Vauxhall. By the time he had his helmet and gloves off and the key in his pocket, the others were out of the car and Jane was approaching the front door. She rang the bell and they heard it chime from within. In moments, the door was opened by a man in his late fifties, tall and slender, his hair and jaw almost as grey as Dick Feeney's.

'Yes?' He frowned slightly at the number of people crowding his doorstep.

Jane held up her warrant card. 'DC Bennett, Exeter CID. Sorry to arrive mob-handed, but we were all together at another location. Could we come in?'

'Well . . . yes, I suppose. What's this about?' He stood back to allow them access.

Jane stepped forward, glancing around.

'To your left,' he said, showing her through.

The rest of the team followed. A small, plump woman with white hair and something about her that just said 'style' to Dave was on the sofa to their right as they stepped into the large lounge.

'Hello. Mrs Manning?' said Jane.

'Yes.'

'These are the police, darling,' her husband told her.

'That's right.' Jane extended a hand. 'Jane Bennett. These are my colleagues, PCs Evans and Myers and DCs Feeney and Miles. It's about your niece, Tanya. Have you seen her today?'

'No. Why? Is she all right?' Her concern was instant and genuine.

'Yes, she's fine as far as we know. But we need to talk to her fairly urgently and she's not at home, so we wondered if she might be visiting.'

'No. As I say, we haven't seen her since last weekend. She's very busy at work.'

'Where's that?'

'She works for a solicitor in the city. Hamilton, Bayliss and Cunningham on Southernhay.'

'I know it,' Jane nodded. 'A good job, then.'

'Very.'

'Have you got her mobile number? We could give her a ring,

see if we can arrange something sensible instead of chasing round randomly.'

'What's so urgent anyway, Detective?' Derek asked, moving around to stand beside his wife. 'We can tell her to come and see you next time we speak to her.'

Jane grimaced, sucking air through her teeth. 'Yes, it's kind of time-sensitive, though, I'm afraid. We think she might have seen something that could help us catch a dangerous suspect.'

'Dangerous? What kind of suspect are we talking about here?' he demanded.

'We can't say too much. Ongoing investigation and all that,' she said apologetically.

'Yes, well . . . I suppose, if it's that important . . .' He glanced down at Nancy.

'In the book under the phone,' she said.

'Right. Hold on.' He headed out to the entrance hall, coming back moments later with a small, indexed book, which he flipped open. 'Here we are.'

'Thank you.' Jane took it from him and made a note of the number she needed. 'We won't keep you any longer,' she said, handing the book back to him. 'Sorry to have bothered you both.' She nodded to Dave to lead the way out.

Outside, with Derek standing on the doorstep, she tossed the notebook to Dave. 'Here. You'll be back quicker than we are.'

He nodded his understanding, tucked the notebook into a zippered breast pocket of his leathers, and pulled on his helmet and gloves while the others piled into Jane's little car. By the time they had slammed the doors closed he had the Norton started and was lifting the kickstand. He swung the bike around in the road and roared away, heading for the station.

By the time they got back, he would have a trace organised on Tanya's mobile, which, hopefully, would give them a location in double-quick time.

* * *

Alone in the squad room, Dave picked up his desk phone and hit the button to accept the incoming call.

'DC Miles, CID.'

'Communications, Middlemoor. We've got a location on that phone you wanted to trace.'

'Blimey, that was quick.'

'Well, it wasn't difficult. It's at the registered owner's home address.'

'Eh? It can't be. She did a runner from there not an hour ago.'

'I don't know about that, but the phone's there and has been all day.'

Dave sighed. 'She didn't take it with her then. That's a pain. OK. Thanks.'

He put the phone down, put his elbows on the desk and wiped his hands down over his face, sighing heavily. With no clue as to where she'd gone, they were going to have to put a twenty-four-hour watch on her flat. Fast-track wasn't going to like that – not that that was Dave's problem. It would be down to the boss to present him with that little gem. The joys of being in charge. Or, at least, climbing the ladder.

In many ways, Dave was glad to stay down at the bottom. He might get shat on now and then, but at least he couldn't be blamed for anything.

The door opened and Jane led the rest of the team in.

'What's up with you?' she asked straight away.

'What do you mean?'

'You look like a camel that's just chewed a lemon.'

'Well, thanks for that, I'm sure,' he said, as the others laughed at the image.

She sat down and turned her chair towards him. 'So, come on. Spit it out.'

'That trip to her aunt and uncle,' he said. 'It was a waste of time. She left her bloody mobile at home.'

'She didn't?'

'She bloody well did. It's been there all morning. I just got off the phone with comms.'

'Shit.'

'Funnily enough, that's exactly what I was thinking when you walked in.'

She peered at him, not sure which way to take the comment, then obviously decided to give him the benefit of the doubt. At least, she didn't hit him.

'So, what now, Einstein?' he asked.

'Well, now, she could be any bloody where, couldn't she? With a friend, on her own in town, gone to her parents' or just on her toes.'

'Well, as helpful as that is, what are we going to do about it?'

This time, she kicked him. 'Why ask me? I'm not in charge here and nor am I the oldest.'

'No, but you are the brightest.'

'That's just on the *out*side of her head,' Dick said.

Jane grabbed a marker pen from the mug on her desk and threw it at him. 'Come on then, Gramps. Show us your wisdom and experience.'

'Well, the first thing we've got to do is put a watch on her place, isn't it?'

Dave snapped his fingers and pointed at him. 'Exactly what I thought.'

He saw Jane look across him to Jill. 'And fools never differ,' she said.

'OK, smart arse,' he retorted. 'Let's have your brainwave.'

'If she's gone to her parents', she won't have taken the bus because they don't run until teatime. So, we should check the cameras at Central Station. If she was going somewhere *else*, she might have used a bus, so we'll have to check the bus station too. And St David's again, seeing as it's the closest to where she was when you lost her.'

'Hey. Don't rub it in, Red.'

She grinned. 'I'm just teasing. Now who can't take a joke?'

'So, we split up again?'

'Yes. You take Central, Dick can have St David's, I'll go to the bus station and Jill can go downstairs, see what Peg's got. That leaves Ben to call the Guv'nor and ask him to arrange the stakeout.'

'Oh, thanks,' Ben piped up.

'Be grateful you can call Colin, not Fast-track,' Dick said.

'Or DI Underhill to you,' Jane reminded him.

'Yeah. Cheers for that. How come I get to do it, anyway? Dave ought to, really. He lost her.'

'Yes, Spike,' Dave said. 'But, at least I was chasing her in the first place. And besides, you're the junior. It's part of the learning process. When you grow up to be big and strong like your Uncle Dick, then you can pick and choose what you do or don't do.'

'Right, Dad.'

Jill laughed. 'Don't call him that – you'll have him panicking. All those years of back-pay on child support . . .' She shuddered with mock horror.

'He hasn't paid for any of them yet. I can't see him starting now,' said Dick.

'Don't even jest, mate.'

'Come on, kids,' Jane said. 'We've got a suspect to find before we retire. Which will be sooner in some cases than others.'

'Right, Mum.' Dave kicked the lever under her chair so that the seat dropped sharply beneath her.

She swatted at his leg. 'You bugger. Stop doing that.'

'Got to bring you down to size somehow,' he quipped.

Tommy's gaze took in the dining room in a quick sweep as he entered. There were three tables in here. Everyone ate together – staff and young people alike. The theory was that they would all mix and mingle, so everyone would get to know each other and, after a while, get to think of the whole group as family.

It was a good theory.

Except that it was born out of the same utopian dreamworld as communism – in both senses of that word. Back here in the real world, there were inevitably gangs and tribalism, leaders and followers, weak and strong. Certain people were drawn to certain others for various reasons. Like tended to congregate with like. The usual gang were grouped together on the middle table.

A couple of staff were sitting with them for the sake of appearances and to keep an eye on them. Most of the other staff were at the table nearest the kitchen. And on the one to his right as he walked in were the outcasts. The misfits. Again, a couple of staff sat with them, for the sake of form, but there was no conversation going on there like there was at the other two tables, and while the other two were crowded, this one had every other seat empty, with even more space at the far end, where Tabitha Grey sat isolated, separated from the others by three chairs on one side and four on the other.

At fifteen, she was a beautiful girl on the cusp of womanhood. Her height would never allow her to grace a catwalk, but she had the grace he thought it would take, along with large, liquid-brown eyes, a button nose a lot like his sister's – the reason, he presumed, that their father had given her the nickname – and rosebud lips that made her look almost doll-like with her soft, round cheeks and immaculate complexion.

But it wasn't her face that he wanted to look at. He glanced down. Beneath her T-shirt, he could see that she was bra-less, as always. He knew this was not her choice. She was a suicide risk. She was not allowed anything that could possibly be used in that way. There was no belt on her shorts. She wore slip-on shoes and ankle socks. Even her long, straight, brown hair was not tied back.

She fascinated Tommy and had done since he'd arrived here.

He fetched himself some food. A handful of sandwiches, a piece of cake, a dish of trifle and a mug of tea. He wasn't really interested. Then, tray in hand, he went to sit down. He wasn't the last into the dining room, but close to it. There were two seats left at the first table, only one at the second. He strode past both. Passed the third table with its every other seat vacant until he came to Tabitha's end. He set his tray down across the angle from her. Close, but not next to her.

This was even better: he could face her. Look directly at her.

He pulled out the chair and sat down. Nodded to a couple of the others, but said nothing.

Tabitha didn't even look up from her food.

That was OK with Tommy.

He picked up a sandwich and took a bite. It turned out to be egg and cress. He chewed slowly, glancing at her but not staring. He'd only spoken to her in group sessions before and then only a couple of times. It wasn't like they were friends.

He finished his sandwich, put his elbows on the table and looked directly at her. 'So, what's a pretty girl like you doing in a place like this?'

When she looked up at him, her face was a picture of incredulity.

He grinned. 'Gotcha.'

She tossed her head and looked down again.

'Seriously, though,' he persisted. 'Why are you here?'

'Tommy.' The cautionary tone came from one of the staff, halfway down the other side of the table. Gavin, Tommy thought he was called. 'We don't talk about our past here.'

He shrugged. 'Just making conversation.' Turning back to Tabitha, he said, 'You don't have to answer if you don't want to. I'm interested, that's all.'

'Why?' Her gaze locked with his and it was not friendly. 'You want to be a psychiatrist when you grow up?'

He laughed. 'Shit, no.' He glanced at Gavin. 'Sorry.' Swearing was not permitted here. 'No way,' he continued. 'I'm just interested in why a girl as gorgeous as you would be in a place like this. I mean, it must give you all sorts of advantages in life. The way people make assumptions, based on looks.'

'Like you are, you mean? You think I'm pretty, so therefore I'm a nice person?'

'Aren't you?' he persisted, despite her obvious wish that he wouldn't.

'No, I'm a first-class bitch.'

Tommy shook his head. 'You wouldn't know where to start.'

'What? I don't look the type?'

'You're too sensitive. Trust me: I've known some nasty types. As nasty as it gets. And you don't have it in you.'

She looked down at her food again. 'Why don't you just leave me alone?'

He pursed his lips. 'Good question, actually. I don't know the answer. Why would you want to be left alone, though? Don't you find it depressing?'

'Maybe I like being depressed. Maybe it's my natural state: where I feel most at home.'

'Huh. What's so good about being at home?' He picked up his spoon and took a mouthful of trifle. Grunted. 'This ain't bad. Want some?'

She looked up, frowning, and Tommy flicked a piece of jelly at her. Her eyes flashed wide in shock as she tried to dodge, but the red blob hit her on the cheek.

'Tommy!' Gavin exclaimed.

'You shit,' Tabitha cried, picking up a piece of peach from her dish of peaches and cream.

'You went the wrong way. I was aiming for your mouth.'

'Yeah, right.' She threw it at him.

'Tabitha!'

They both ignored Gavin.

Tommy ducked sideways. 'Haha! Missed me.' He took a spot of cream on the tip of his spoon and flicked it at her. She squealed as it landed in her hair and took a much larger blob of cream from her own dish, launching it at him. He let it hit him on the cheek, scooped it off with a finger and reached out to dab it on the end of her nose. They were both laughing uproariously.

Tommy picked up his trifle bowl and raised it.

Her eyes widened in horror. 'No!'

He started to swing it forward, then scooped it around at the last moment, shaking his head. 'Whoa. Waste of good trifle.'

'Bastard!'

'Only by practice, not birth,' he said, putting the bowl down. 'And you're not supposed to swear.'

'You're not supposed to throw food either.'

'Yeah, but rules are made to be broken, eh?'

'Not here, they're not.' That wasn't Gavin; it was his friend, a big black guy whose name Tommy could never remember. Something weird and old like Aloysius. He ignored the comment.

So did Tabitha. 'Only if nobody's looking.'

'Where's the fun in that?'

'Oh, now we're learning. You like an audience, do you?'

'Not necessarily. I just believe in being me, no matter who likes it or doesn't.' He leaned closer and dropped his voice. 'Although it is fun to try and confuse them, so they can't figure out who the real you is.'

He glanced down the tables to where Brian sat on the far one, talking with the registered manager.

'Who, Brian?' she asked. 'How hard is that? He does his best, but he's a bit budget-version, isn't he? Government-grade.'

'Third rate, you mean?' He picked up his spoon and took a mouthful of trifle. 'Yeah, but I like to keep my hand in.'

'You like manipulating people then?'

He spread his arms. 'Look at me. I'm not going to force them into much physically, am I?'

'How old are you?'

'Fourteen.'

'So, when's your birthday?'

'Tenth of March.'

'So, I'm a year and a half older.'

Tommy nodded. 'So, if we went out, I'd be a toyboy. Never tried that before.'

'And who says you're going to now?'

'Well, you didn't say "No chance", so I can still hope.' He winked. 'Anyway, you never answered my question.'

'Which one?'

'What's a pretty girl like you doing in a place like this?'

She took a bite of brown-bread sandwich and munched for a moment. 'I didn't think it was a serious one.'

'Of course it was. I wouldn't be that corny without some point to it.'

'Really?'

'Hey!' he sat back, offended.

She grinned. 'Just joking. I saw you the other day with those kids who were bullying you. Would you really have bitten his nose off?'

He chewed for a moment and swallowed. 'That would be telling, wouldn't it?' He leaned forward to whisper. 'Yes, but I'd have spat it out afterwards. Too gristly.'

'Ew!'

He laughed at the horrified look on her face. 'Come on then. I've told you mine.'

'You know the stated mission of this place,' she said.

'Yes.'

'Well, I'm in the second group – the ones that are a risk to themselves rather than others.'

He nodded, then shook his head, all at once completely serious. 'I can't imagine that.'

'Oh, come on.'

'No, seriously. It's such a . . .' He shuddered. 'Such a waste. Whatever could . . .? Never mind. I'd like to talk to you more, but not here. Maybe later?'

She nodded. 'OK. As long as you're not going to throw any more food at me.'

He grinned. 'I don't make promises I can't keep.'

Chapter 27

It was an hour later when they congregated in the squad room again.

'I don't know where she was going. She used a ticket machine and paid in cash and she was in a damn great queue of people, but she certainly went somewhere from Central Station. I saw her go in, but not come out,' Jane reported when they had all taken their seats.

'One major possibility from there is her parents' place,' Dave said.

'Yeah, but it's only one of many,' Ben argued.

'So, we need a trace on her credit card, bank card and so on,' Dick put in.

'For which we need a warrant,' Jill pointed out.

'Talking of which, how'd you get on, Ben?' Jane asked.

The youngster of the team slouched back in his chair. 'The DI passed it on to Fast-track and he got onto opps support at HQ. It's in place.' He checked his watch. 'Should be starting any time now.'

'Well done, lad,' said Dick. 'In that case, we know who to send for the warrant, don't we?' He sent a wink in Dave and Jill's direction.

'I saw that,' Ben said sharply.

289

'No, you didn't,' said Dick.

'How do you know?'

Dick turned to face him. 'I might look young for my age, but I wasn't born yesterday.'

Jill laughed. 'Who the hell told you that little lie?'

Dick shook his head. 'You know how to put a fellow down, don't you?'

'She ought to,' Dave said. 'All the practice she gets on me.'

'The Guv'nor's done one thing for you this afternoon,' Jane said to Ben. 'He'll be OK doing another, rather than have someone else onto him like we're ganging up or something. And it is related. If one method doesn't track her down, the other one will.'

'All right, all right,' he said, picking the phone up and dialling from memory. There was a pause while all of them watched him. 'Guv, it's Ben again. That watch we put on earlier – Jane's found evidence that she went into Central Station but didn't come out again. Can we get a warrant drawn up for her bank and credit cards? See if we can track where she went?' He glanced up, saw everyone watching him and dropped his gaze, picking up a pen as he listened. 'Yes, Guv. Of course.' He made a note on his pad. 'OK. Will do. Thanks, Guv.' He put the phone down and started writing. After a moment, he looked up. 'He's getting it sorted.'

'Well, considering where we've got to and the fact that only one of us needs to stay alert, I reckon its beer o'clock,' Dave said. 'Anybody with me?'

The dark-red beanbag rustled as Tommy sat in it and pulled his legs up, crossing them like he remembered doing in junior school assembly.

One thing he hadn't done there was nestle himself back comfortably with his hands linked behind his head as he gazed openly at a pretty girl. But he did that now.

Tabitha was sitting in an easy chair in the furthest corner of the TV room from the other kids, who were clustered in front of the big screen, watching something – Tommy had no clue and no interest in what, as long as it kept them occupied. Her plimsoled feet were curled up under her as she concentrated on a book that she was reading.

'Hiya,' he said.

She glanced up.

'What are you reading?'

She held up the thick paperback. *Clan of the Cave Bear*, he read. The author's name – Jean Auel – beat him, though. He frowned. 'How the hell do you pronounce that?'

'What?'

'Her name. Jean Owell?'

'I think it's more like All.'

He grunted. 'Weird. Why not use a simpler one? She'd do a lot better if people knew how to ask for her books, I'd have thought.'

She closed the book, keeping her thumb in the page she'd got to. 'She doesn't need to do any better. She's sold millions. They even made a movie of this one.'

'Is it any good?'

'The book or the movie?'

'You've seen it?'

She nodded.

'So, why read the book?'

'Don't you know anything? They often change the story so much in the movie version, it's completely different. In this case, the movie was utter crap. But the book's really good. It really gets you into the character's mind. You feel every scratch, every ounce of her loss when her parents die, every awful moment when she's picked on and victimised by some of the people who take her in.'

Tommy pursed his lips. 'I never got into reading really. Not like that.'

'So, what do you like doing? Other than winding up psychiatrists and biting people's noses off.'

291

'Dunno, really. I don't like sports much. I like to swim, but that's all, in that sense. And I like to shoot. I picked that up working on the fair.'

'You're from a fair family? That must be really cool.'

He shook his head. 'No. I just worked with them for a while. I'm from just down the road. My mum's a nurse. Don't really talk about my dad in this sort of company.'

She frowned. 'What sort? Nobody's listening.'

He hesitated, keen to open up a little more to this girl who seemed like a kindred spirit, but not sure yet if he could trust her. But then, anyone who hurt him, he could hurt back. How many times had he proved that in his life? He met her gaze. 'He's Old Bill.'

Her eyes went wide. He thought for an instant she was going to repeat it loudly. 'Really?' she said instead.

'Yeah. Really.'

'And you're in here? God, what an embarrassment that must be!'

'Thanks.'

'I didn't mean it that way. And you say *I'm* sensitive?'

'Yeah, well. You are,' he said, glad of the chance to change the subject. 'I could tell before, but what you said about that book confirmed it. So, what's the issue? With you, I mean. How'd you come to be here? You're not common like the rest of us, are you? You're accent: it's expensive.'

'Expensive?' She giggled. 'That's the first time I've heard it called that.'

'First time you've talked about it with a pleb like me, I bet, isn't it?'

'I suppose so.'

'So, what's the story? If you don't want to tell me, just say and I'll shut up about it.'

She sighed deeply. 'No, it's . . .' She paused reflectively. 'I was . . .' Looking up, she met and held his gaze. 'Abused. At home.'

He sat up abruptly, arms coming down at his sides. 'What, you were . . .?'

'No, no. Just . . . My father died when I was seven. My mum took up with this guy when I was ten. She'd had another boyfriend before that, but it didn't last. But with this one – Richard – they soon got serious. A few months and he moved in. Then, all of a sudden, he was acting like he was my dad. Which, of course, he wasn't and I wasn't having it. Even if Mum wanted him to take Dad's place, I knew he never could. Anyway, eventually he turned nasty. Not when Mum was around, but when we were alone. I fought back, which made things worse. He'd hit me. Once, so hard that he knocked me across the room and I smashed a vase that my dad had bought for Mum's birthday just a few weeks before he died. I was horrified. And Mum, of course, believed him when he said it had been my fault. Another time, he locked me in the wardrobe and left me there for ages. Which, being claustrophobic, was utterly horrible. I went mad. But it made no difference. He let me out finally, about an hour before Mum came home, made me tidy everything up, and then, when I told Mum what he'd done, he said I was exaggerating and, again, she believed him. So, after a while, it was like he hated me and she sided with him, so I was alone in my own home. What was the point of that? I had no one to turn to, so I turned to the garden shed and my dad's toolbox. There was a Stanley knife in there. They're very sharp. So, I sat in the corner of the shed, in behind the lawnmower, and cut my wrist.'

She held up her left arm to show him the scar: a single, thin, pink line almost the full width of the inside of her wrist.

'It was so sharp, there was no pain. Not at that stage. Even the blood took a few seconds to realise it had an opening it could come out of. Then it was like I'd opened a zip in a bag of sauce. It came out like a red curtain. I hadn't gone deep enough to cut the artery. I didn't know you needed to. Anyway, I just sat there and waited to die, but after a while, it started to sting like crazy. It really hurt. I started to cry and I suppose they must have heard me. Mum found me and took me to hospital. But it was like something had switched in my brain. Once I'd had the idea, I couldn't get rid of it. Still can't. The peace. The thought of being with Dad again.'

Tommy had been with her until then. He frowned. 'You believe in that stuff? Life after death? Heaven and Hell?'

She blinked. 'I'd . . .' Something shifted in her expression. 'Don't you? If there isn't anything afterwards, what's the point of all this pain?'

'Why should there be a point? Life is what it is. You do what you can to be happy, to get what you want out of it. Some people manage that, others don't. Circumstances don't let them.' He shrugged. 'What else is there?'

She stared at him with a profound sadness. 'God, that's so depressing.'

'No, it isn't. It just means life's what you make it, as long as you get a few breaks. You want to be happy, you figure out what you want and go for it. You want out of your family life, you do what you need to, wait for your moment and get out.'

She looked horrified. 'But I don't want to abandon my mum.'

'How's committing suicide not doing that?'

She threw herself back in her chair. 'Oh, you don't understand!'

'I don't understand? I understand plenty – believe me.' He felt anger stir inside him. 'I understand perfectly well what it's like to be picked on. To be alone. No support anywhere. You get your feet under you and support yourself. You're fifteen. You leave school next year. A couple more and you'll probably go to uni. You'll be free and clear. Able to do what you want. Your life will be yours. And in the meantime, what about this stepdad? Does he make your mum happy?'

'Yes, except when . . .' Her voice trailed off.

'Well, leave them to it then. They deserve each other by the sound of it. Their problems aren't yours. If you've got a goal in life, you concentrate on that.'

She stared at him, her eyes wide and haunted. 'All I've ever wanted is my dad back.'

294

'Well, I'm sorry, Tab, but that is the impossible dream. All you can do is make sure he'd be proud of you.'

Tears dripped from her eyes as she held his gaze, not attempting to brush them away. 'How did you get to be so . . . wise?' You're so young and . . .'

'What? Little?' He grinned. 'They say good things come in small packages.' *Not that I've ever been called a good thing*, he thought. But he felt like one at that moment as she smiled through her tears and reached for his hand.

'Thank you,' she said.

'What for? I only sat and talked.'

She shook her head. 'For the connection. I haven't had that for so long.' Her other hand came across, enveloping his in both of hers.

Ben leaned back, arms up over his head, stretching his spine and resting his eyes for a moment. He'd been concentrating on his computer screen for what felt like hours. He'd pack it in soon and go home. The warrant had come through quickly on Tanya Cunliffe's bank and credit cards, but it had got him nowhere. She hadn't used either since this morning, while they were waiting for her at her flat, when she'd bought milk, bread and a few other essentials at the filling station on Cowley Bridge Road.

All of which had gone to waste when she threw the two carrier bags at him and Jane before she ran. He remembered the milk running down the steps towards her front door, the groceries spread across the brick pathway. What a waste, he thought with a sigh.

Right. One more job to do, then he'd pack it in for the night and probably meet some of the others in the pub. He flipped open his notebook and picked up the phone to dial.

It took just three rings before it was answered.

'Hello?' a male voice said.

'Is that Mr Cunliffe?'

'Yes.'

'This is PC Myers with Exeter CID. Can I ask, have you heard from or seen your daughter, Tanya, today? Only, we've been trying to reach her and haven't been able to.'

'Yes, we gathered that. My wife's sister rang earlier.'

'Nancy Manning? Yes, we met her and her husband at their house.'

'That's what she told us.'

'So, have you seen Tanya? Or heard from her?'

He hesitated. 'What's this all about, Officer?'

Ben remembered what Jane had told the Mannings. 'We need to talk to her in reference to a death that occurred near where she works a couple of days ago. We think she might have seen something significant.'

'I see.' Ben could hear the relief in his voice. 'Actually, she was here this afternoon. She stayed for two or three hours, then left. She had a bad stomach. We tried to get her to stay, but she wouldn't. Said she'd be better at home.'

'So, she headed home again? What time did she leave?'

'Around five-thirty.'

'OK. We'll try her at home again then. Thank you.'

Ben put the phone down and went back to his computer screen. Bringing up the Internet, he checked the train timetable. He knew they ran hourly between Brixham and Exeter. The timetable showed him that the northbound trip departed at five past the hour. He checked the time at the bottom of the screen. It was five to seven.

'Bloody hell,' he muttered. He'd had no idea it was anywhere near that late.

He pulled out his phone, called up the contacts list and hit the button for Dave's phone. Moments later, it was answered.

'Hello?'

Ben could hear music and voices in the background. 'Where are you?'

'Ben? We're in the Bell. You coming?'

'Are you all still there?' The Bell was a small, redbrick Victorian pub a few hundred yards up from the station, on the opposite side of Heavitree Road. It was a regular police hangout.

'Yeah, why? You worried about being seen out with me and Dick?'

Ben ignored the jibe. 'Can any of you get to Central Station in the next nine minutes?'

'Are you having a laugh? We're all on the sauce, mate. Why?'

'Because Tanya Cunliffe's due to arrive there in the next few minutes.'

'Shit. Get some uniforms there. They can pick her up. You'll have to call the boss and get him to come in and talk to her. None of us can do it.'

Ben hung up and used his desk phone to call downstairs.

'Fairweather.'

'Hey, Sarge. It's Ben Myers. I'm upstairs. Have you got anyone in close proximity to Central Station right now?'

The sergeant blew out air and said, 'Hold on.' Moments later, he was back. 'Nearest is Sophie and Jenny. They're currently on Fore Street. Why? What have you got?'

'The suspect whose flat we've got surveillance on up by the university is on a train due to arrive there in the next six minutes.'

Fairweather laughed. 'You'll be lucky. You'll just have to hope the surveillance crew pick her up. I'll radio them, tell them she could be on the way.'

'All right. Thanks.' He put the phone down. Another chance missed. And no chance of getting out of here in the next half-hour either. He knew the boss was at home with his daughter, but he'd want to know the situation. He picked up the phone again and dialled.

'Boss,' he said when it was answered. 'It's Ben. Just phoning with an update. We know where Tanya Cunliffe is, but we haven't got boots in the vicinity at the moment. What we have got is surveillance on her place and Sergeant Fairweather's letting them know she's en route, so hopefully they'll apprehend her when she gets there and bring her in.'

'Are you still in the office?' From his tone, he'd already guessed the answer.

'I had a few bits to sort out. I was just going to get going when I found out where she was.'

'Are you on your own?'

'Uh, yeah. The others were all here until a little while ago, but they cleared off when we'd got as far as we could with everything.'

'So, why . . .? Where are they now?'

'In the Bell.'

The DS sighed. 'I'm going to need to come in at some point, aren't I?'

'Well . . . what would you do with Annie? Your wife's at work, isn't she? I could get the DI.'

'No. It's my case, it's my responsibility. Just call me, yes?'

'OK, boss.'

Where the hell was she?

It was about a fifteen-minute walk from the station and she should have got in there twenty-seven minutes ago. Had she decided to go somewhere else instead of coming home? Had she spotted them as she was approaching and slipped away?

PC Don Sherratt hadn't been happy at taking on this assignment in the first place, but if some pillock had caused them to lose her . . . He reviewed their positions in his mind. Was there any way she could have seen any of them? It was dark. Had been for a while now. Streetlights twinkled through the shifting branches and new leaves of the trees around them.

He had a team of three other officers with him. Jess was behind a big, glossy-leaved rhododendron at the far end of the block, overlooking the path down to the back end of the garages and beyond them towards Glenthorne Road, in case the target came that way. Young Harry was on the far side of Copplestone, up towards the bend, crouched behind a car on someone's drive. Jake was tucked back in the entrance to one of the big houses, a short way back from the entrance to Glenthorne so he could come in from behind her if it proved necessary. And himself: he was in the shrubbery opposite her door. They'd left the car a couple of hundred yards up Copplestone Road, in one of its side-shoots, so it was well out of sight.

He couldn't see how she could have spotted any of them. So, where the hell was she?

Pete held out as long as he could, but eventually he could wait no longer: he had to make the call. He got up from the sofa and headed out to the hallway. Annie sighed behind him and he smiled. Had he been that easy to read?

He picked up the phone and dialled.

'Exeter police. How can I help?'

'You can put my mind at rest, Bill. It's Pete Gayle. Have you heard anything from the stakeout at Tanya Cunliffe's place yet?'

'No. Well, yes – I've heard. But no – she hasn't turned up there.'

'But it's over an hour since she got into the railway station. Where the hell's she gone?'

'The pub? The cinema? A restaurant? A friend's?'

'Yeah, all right. As long as she doesn't go attacking another bloody cabbie on the way home, afterwards . . .'

'We can't very well put a warning out about picking up lone females, can we?'

'Huh. OK. I suppose we'll have to maintain the surveillance and just wait and see then.'

'Yes. It's not like you to be impatient.' The desk sergeant's tone made it almost a question.

'Like I said – I don't want her attacking anyone else while we're looking for her, that's all.'

'I'll keep you posted.'

'OK. Cheers, Bill.' Pete put the phone down feeling as frustrated as when he'd picked it up. But there was nothing else he could do. He went back to Annie and the movie they'd been watching.

'Do you feel better now?' she asked as he sat down beside her.

'No. And I won't until she's caught.'

'They say patience is a virtue.'

He looked down at her. Her gaze was fixed on the screen across the room, but the way she was holding herself told him all he needed. 'They also say children should be seen and not heard.'

'That's *so* outdated.' She was still staring at the TV. 'Young people need validation, you know.'

Pete laughed and ruffled her hair. 'I know exactly what young people need, my girl.'

She looked up at him, big-eyed, her expression saying "Really?" though her mouth stayed closed.

'Discipline,' he said. 'Respect for their elders and betters.' He grabbed her around the ribs and started to tickle her.

Annie squealed and wriggled, trying to escape, but he held her down easily.

'Dad! Stop!' She laughed and giggled, gave up trying to get away and instead fought back, tickling him in the ribs, then the back of his neck.

Pete's head snapped back as an electric sensation shot through him. 'Ow! I'll have you for that.' He intensified his attack, one hand holding her while the other darted this way and that, fingers wriggling. She squealed again, gave up trying to tickle him and instead grabbed his nose between a small thumb and forefinger. 'Beep, beep.' He intensified the nasal effect on his voice. 'That's the way to do it. Where's my truncheon?'

He stopped tickling and sat back.

She held on, pulling his nose around towards the TV. 'Con-cen-trate,' she said slowly, then finally let go.

'Ooh. I could so tan your backside for that, young lady.'

'You wouldn't dare.'

300

'Huh! Don't you believe it, missy. How long has this got left?'

'Twenty minutes. It's just getting to the best bit.'

'OK. See the end, then its bedtime.'

'For who? It's only just gone eight.'

Pete grunted. 'Well, it feels a sight later.'

'That's because you're not paying attention. You're fretting over that suspect.'

He nodded. 'You're right. I am. How'd you get to be so damn clever, at your age?'

'Hmm.' She pursed her lips as if pondering the question. 'It can't be genetic, so it must be from school, I suppose.'

He gave it until just short of midnight. He couldn't wait any longer. He picked up the phone and dialled. It rang three times before being picked up.

'Hello?'

'Jill. It's me. We're going to have to make an early start in the morning. She hasn't gone back to her flat, so we need to stakeout that, the tyre place and her office between us. You and Dave take the flat. Make sure you're out of sight. I'll call him and tell him in a minute. Get there for seven-ish, maybe a bit before.'

'OK.'

'Night, Jill.'

He ended the call and made the next one. This time, it was picked up more quickly. 'Miles.'

'Dave, it's me. The target's not come home to roost. I've just spoken to Jill. Told her to meet you at the flat just before seven and get set up to observe.'

'Right, boss.'

'Night.' He pressed the red button a second time. He would get Dick and Jane to stakeout the tyre place. He and Ben could take the solicitors' office on Southernhay, where she worked. At least there, if she hadn't turned up by nine-thirty, they could

301

get back to the squad room and start trying to track her down another way. In the meantime . . . He dialled again.

'Transport Police. How can I help?'

'Evening. This is DS Pete Gayle from Heavitree Road. We've got a suspect who might well be a flight risk, so we need to keep eyes open for her.'

'OK . . .'

Pete explained the details briefly.

'Right. We'll do what we can. Don't know how effective it'll be, though, if she's as good at disguising herself as you reckon.'

'OK. Cheers.' Pete hung up and dialled the station again. 'Bill. Tanya Cunliffe's bank card and credit card. We've got a warrant and we checked earlier, found no activity since this morning, but we need to keep an eye in case she uses one to book a train or a plane – anything to get her away from here. Can you do that?'

'Yeah, if you give me the details.'

'I'll get Ben to give you a ring in a minute.'

'Right-o.'

'Thanks.'

Four more calls and Pete had done all he could. Except relax – and he wouldn't be able to do that until Tanya Cunliffe was in a cell at Heavitree Road police station.

Chapter 28

By five past nine, Pete and Ben were sitting in the reception area of Hamilton, Bayliss and Cunningham, solicitors, on Southernhay Road. He had used the police radio to check with Dave and his phone to speak to Jane, but neither had any news for him. He and Ben had stepped into the tall, old building as soon as the door was unlocked. He had shown the receptionist his badge and explained the situation, then they had taken a seat on the dark-red leather of the built-in seat that went all the way around the bay window. Unwilling to allow the receptionist to overhear their conversation, Pete had kept it to a minimum. They had flicked through the out-of-date magazines on the coffee table in front of them. Ben had been doing things on his smartphone that related to the investigation, but there had been no sign of Tanya Cunliffe arriving.

At half past nine, a tall, slim man in a tweed suit and brogues that shone brighter than any military boots Pete had ever seen came through a side door, glanced at them and leaned over to speak quietly to the receptionist. She nodded. 'Yes, sir.' And he went away.

She picked up the phone and dialled. Held on for several seconds, but there was no reply. She frowned and put it down.

Stillness returned to the room. All Pete could hear was the ticking of a clock and the passing traffic through the old, single-glazed window behind him.

Then his phone rang in his pocket.

He took it out, glanced at the screen and hit the green icon. 'DS Gayle.'

'Pete. It's Andy Fairweather. We've got a bite. She went into the HSBC on the High Street and withdrew five hundred pounds.'

'When?'

'Four minutes ago.'

'Cheers, Andy. Can you put me through to Graham?'

'Hold on.'

There was a click, then a ringing tone. It was picked up on the second ring. 'CCTV observation room, Graham speaking.'

'Graham, it's Pete Gayle. Four minutes ago, our girl withdrew some cash from the counter in the HSBC. Can you see if you can spot her coming out and see where she's going?'

'OK. I'll call you back.'

'Thanks.'

He ended the call. The temptation to get up and get going was almost overpowering, but they didn't know where she was headed yet. If she came here and they'd just left, he'd be kicking himself.

'Boss?'

'Hold tight, Ben. No use going off half-cocked.'

He waited, phone in hand. Moments later, it rang again. He thumbed the icon and raised it to his ear. 'Yes?'

'Pete. She came out and headed north and turned up Castle Street.'

Where there were no cameras.

'Bugger. OK. Thanks, Graham.' He ended the call and looked at Ben. 'She's dropped out of sight. And she hasn't got her mobile with her, so we can't track her with that. Come on – we're wasting time here.' He stood up. Crossing to the reception desk, he handed the girl a card. 'If anyone here hears from her or sees her, give me a call, yes?'

'Of course, Sergeant.'

He paused, holding her gaze. 'We're trying to get a killer off the streets here, understood?'

'Perfectly.'

Pete nodded. 'Thanks for your help.' He turned to Ben. 'Right, let's go.'

Outside, he walked briskly up the road towards the courthouse, where he had parked.

'Get on that phone of yours,' he said to Ben. 'Contact every car-hire firm in the city – there can't be more than a handful. Get them to delay her and contact us as soon as she shows her licence.'

'Right, boss.'

So, her car was contained, he had a watch on the train stations, car hire would be out of question. If she was planning to leave the city, that just left the bus services. And there was nothing he could do about them. There were too many pickup points in too many directions. He just had to hope CCTV would pick her up again.

With Ben speaking quietly into his smartphone at his shoulder, Pete took out his own phone and hit a speed-dial number. 'Jane,' he said when it was picked up. 'Get onto the aunt and uncle, will you? Emphasise that we need to speak to Tanya urgently and they should contact us as soon as they hear from her or see her.'

'OK. You got something? You sound like you're in a hurry.'

'She's in town. Last seen going into Castle Street with five hundred quid in her purse. While you're on with them, ask if they know any of her friends, get any contact details you can and follow them up.'

'Right. See you later.' She rang off.

Pete would call her parents himself, but he wanted to do that from the squad room.

Back at his desk, while Ben got onto social media and started searching for Tanya's friends, Pete opened his notebook and reached for the phone.

The line had not even finished its first ring when the phone at the other end was snatched up.

'Hello?'

'Mr Cunliffe? This is DS Gayle from Exeter CID. I'm calling about your daughter, Tanya.' He heard a gasp on the other end. 'Have you seen her or heard from her today?'

'Umm . . . Why? What's the problem?'

'We're still trying to reach her. I gather one of my colleagues spoke to you last night about this. We need to talk to her urgently.'

'DS Gayle, you said?'

'That's right. Peter.'

'We've been trying to reach her as well. I told your colleague she was here yesterday. She left in a bit of a state and we haven't been able to get hold of her since.'

'A bit of a state?' He already knew this from Ben, but the man might say something more if he let him.

'Well, she was sick. Threw up. She blamed it on a bad Indian the night before, but she seemed OK when she got here: sat out on the patio with us, chatting and looking at the local paper. Had a cup of tea. Then, all of a sudden, she muttered something and ran indoors, heaving.'

'These things can come on quickly, can't they?'

'That certainly did. She hadn't said anything. Didn't even look peeky. Just "Oh, God", and off she went. When she came back, she said she'd go home, but we haven't been able to get hold of her since.'

'Have you tried her friends? Other family members? She might have changed her mind, decided she'd be better with someone than on her own.'

'I thought of that, but there's only Nancy and Derek, family-wise, and I don't really have much idea of who her friends are these days.'

'OK. Well, we'll keep you posted if we track her down. Can I ask you to do the same for us?'

'Of course. I suppose you can't tell me anything about why you want to talk to her?'

Pete blew out air as if reluctant. 'Have you seen anything about these taxi driver deaths in the city? Or did Tanya mention them?'

'Only what's . . . Funnily enough, that's what we were talking about when she got sick yesterday. There was a bit in the paper about the last one. Bloody shame, eh? To have his daughter raped at fourteen, then, barely two years later, this happens. His poor wife must be in a right state. The girl too.'

'That's right.'

'But Tanya was only just saying she didn't know about that when she rushed off to the bathroom, so how can she help you?'

That gave Pete pause. 'She didn't know about what?'

'I don't know. She just said something like "Oh, God. I didn't know that", didn't finish what she was saying – just took off with her hand to her mouth.'

'I see. Right, well, I'll talk to you soon, hopefully.'

'Yes. Thank you.'

Pete ended the call and looked across at Ben. 'Anything?'

Tanya's social media presence was limited to Facebook and an old Twitter account she hadn't used for several months. She had only a handful of Facebook friends and her homepage showed that the one she corresponded most with was a work colleague, the girl whose account had given them their original break in the case: Emma Radcliffe.

Pete looked her up.

Her address was towards the top end of Pennsylvania Road, in one of the side roads that led off to the east, a short way up from the murder scene at the end of Argyll Road. Pete thought about where Tanya lived, off Cowley Bridge Road. Had she been on her way across to Emma's that night?

But she had her own car. Why take a taxi? Unless . . . He couldn't imagine that someone capable of murder would worry about driving with a dodgy tyre or two, so perhaps she hadn't been in the taxi. She could have been following it, seen the attack take place. The physical evidence from the back of the taxi confirmed that an attack – or at least a sexual encounter – had taken place in there, although that same evidence left a large question mark over the presence of the condom on the front seat. Had he intended to use it, then given up on the idea in the heat of the moment?

Irrelevant. Focus, he thought. The important point here was Emma's potential proximity and therefore her possible involvement – although, how she would connect to the other two cases, he had no idea. Still, one thing at a time. While they were at the solicitors' earlier, he had picked up a card. He took it out now and laid it beside his keyboard, picked up the phone and dialled the number on it.

'Good morning. Hamilton, Bayliss and Cunningham. How can I help?'

Pete recognised the voice of the receptionist. 'Kerry, this is DS Gayle. I need to speak to Emma Radcliffe, please.'

'One moment, please.' No hesitation, completely professional, he noted.

The line switched to a buzzing ringtone and was picked up again on the second ring. 'Mr Cunningham's office. How can I help?'

'Is that Emma?'

'Yes. Who's this?'

'My name's DS Gayle. I'm with Exeter CID. I've been trying to track down a friend of yours and I wondered if you might be able to help.'

'I see.' Her tone had become more cautious. Reticent. 'Which friend are you looking for?'

'Tanya. Tanya Cunliffe.'

'She's not in this morning. I . . . I'd have thought she'd be at home, though she hasn't phoned either, so I couldn't say for sure.'

'Well, I'm afraid I can. And she's not at home. Have you got any other thoughts on where she might have gone?'

'Um . . . No. She's not exactly a party girl. If she's not at home, then . . .'

'Yes?'

'I'm afraid I'm at a loss, Detective.'

'OK.' He paused, letting her relax. 'And you haven't seen her over the weekend?'

'Um . . .' She hesitated, her brain clearly working, trying to decide what to say.

'It doesn't put you in any trouble if you have, Miss Radcliffe,' he said. 'I'm just trying to figure out where she might have gone, that's all.'

'But . . . well . . . yes. She stayed with me last night. She'd come home from her parents feeling ill, thinking she'd be better off at home, but then she decided she wanted company. Or at least that's what she told me. I left her at home this morning. She said she was still poorly, wanted to stay in bed a while longer. I told Mr Cunningham when I came in this morning.'

'Is it him she works for?'

'She's the office junior. She works for all the partners – whoever needs her at the time. Why?'

'Because I thought one of the partners was looking for her this morning. Tall, thin gent in tweeds.'

'That's Mr Hamilton, the senior partner. I thought Mr Cunningham wold have passed it on. Obviously not. He does get absent-minded sometimes, when he's engrossed in a case. I'd better do it myself, before she gets in trouble, hadn't I?'

'Right. Thanks for your time, Miss Radcliffe.'

'Goodbye, Detective.'

Somehow, I don't think it's goodbye, Pete thought as he put the phone down. *I think I might be talking to you again, Emma Radcliffe.*

He stood up and plucked his jacket from the back of his chair.

'I'm off out for a bit, Ben. Keep trying on the Facebook thing and let me know if you find anything.'

'Right, boss.'

An hour later, Pete was back at his desk and no further forward. He had been up to Emma Radcliffe's flat. It had been easy to find, looking out over the road and down the hill towards the city centre. But there had been no one there. A neighbour had told him that the red-haired girl had left about half an hour after Emma. She'd seen her walking away towards Pennsylvania Road.

He'd seen a bus stop a little further down as he was driving up so, presumably, she had used it to get into town, where she'd gone to the bank. Why she hadn't used the cashpoint at the Co-op on Union Street, just a couple of hundred yards from the flat, he had no idea, but she had chosen not to. Or maybe she didn't know it was there.

'Any joy, boss?' Ben asked as he sat down.

Pete grimaced and shook his head. 'Might as well call the others back in if she hasn't shown up yet. You found anything?'

'Nothing useful. I've checked with everyone I could while you were out, but no one's seen her.'

'OK, get hold of the others and bring them in.'

'Will do.' Ben picked up his phone and began to dial as Pete logged into his computer.

Emma Radcliffe, he thought, unable to shake off the proximity of the first attack site to her flat. *Who is she?*

A work colleague of Tanya Cunliffe: he knew that much, but no more. And yet, he had a feeling he should. He logged onto the Internet and looked up Hamilton, Bayliss and Cunningham. Their About Us page included a series of staff photos with names and job titles underneath. Emma Radcliffe was listed as a legal secretary, aged twenty-eight. She was an attractive girl with long, dark hair and a smile that seemed to light up her face. Pete closed the website and logged into the PNC, inputting the details he had for her. There were no matches. Not unexpected. He looked next for her census records. No matches.

'Huh?'

He tried again with the same result. Then he checked the DVLA. She had a driving licence, issued in 2012. Change of address? Maybe. Next, he sought out a mobile phone account. Again, it was set up in 2012. He got onto the local council site to check for poll tax records. She had moved into the flat in 2013. Before that, she had been renting a place in the student quarter, not far from Tanya Cunliffe's place, for just short of a year. And before that . . . nothing.

'What the hell?'

So, where was she before 2012? This looked extremely odd. He sighed. 'Oh, well.' There was only one thing for it. He had her address now, plus her mobile and landline numbers. He'd have to go and see her. And the sooner, the better. He picked up the phone and raised it to Ben, who was talking to Dave. 'I'll call Jane.'

She picked up on the second ring. 'DC Bennett.'

'Jane, it's me. Call it off and come back in, the pair of you. I think she's done a runner. Meet me in the car park out the back here, soon as you can. We're going back out.'

'OK. We're on the way.'

Pete filled Jane in on the situation as they walked down Heavitree Road towards the Western Way roundabout.

There was no point taking the car: it wasn't far and they weren't intending to arrest anyone.

Crossing the ring road, they walked up the hill towards the Civic Centre, the pavement wide and open, dotted with young trees that were just breaking into leaf. The air was cool, but the sky was a clear blue, the sun bright.

'So, what are you thinking?' Jane asked as they passed the big, modern building – one of many that had been constructed after

311

large parts of the city centre were destroyed by German bombs in the Second World War.

'I don't know,' he admitted. 'But it's suspicious. And when you combine it with how close she lives to the attack site and the fact that she works with our main suspect, I'm inclined to insist on some answers.'

'Ooh. So, am I coming along as the required token female or to keep you in line then?'

Pete looked sideways at her. 'Have you been talking to Naz?'

'No. Why? What would she tell me if I did? You haven't been following in Dave's footsteps, have you?'

On the far side of the road, they were passing the end of the street where Neil Sanderson, who they had arrested and charged with possession and distribution of indecent images of minors – specifically and chiefly, his own daughter – last November, had worked.

'Not at all,' he said. 'I was just a bit more stern than she approved of in dealing with Mrs Singh after I found out she'd been covering up for her husband.'

'Tut, tut. Bad boss.' She waggled a finger at him in mock reprimand as she turned the corner and led the way down Southernhay East, past the yoga centre.

A couple of minutes later, they turned into the old building that housed the solicitors' office. Pete held the door for her and they stepped in. The receptionist looked up, a professional smile starting to appear.

'Hello again, Kerry. This is DC Bennett. We need a word with Emma Radcliffe, if you could either point us in her direction or get her down here for us.'

Chapter 29

Emma took them along a narrow corridor towards the back of the old building, where a conference room allowed them privacy. They sat around a large table that overlooked a small flagstone garden.

Leaning forward, Emma steepled her fingers then laid her hands flat on the polished wood. She sat back in her chair, moved to cross her arms, but then stopped herself. Finally, focusing on Pete, she asked, 'So, what's all this about, Detective?'

He leaned forward, notebook and pen at hand on the table. 'As I said earlier, we're trying to find your colleague, Tanya Cunliffe. I know you told me earlier you don't know where she is. But towards that end, we need your help to corroborate a couple of things.'

She frowned slightly, sitting up primly. 'All right.'

'First of all, where were you before 2012?'

She blinked. Her hands disappeared from the table to grip her knees as the rest of her body went completely still. 'What do you mean, Detective?'

Pete allowed a trace of a smile to widen his lips. 'You know exactly what I mean, Miss Radcliffe. If that's your name.'

Her gaze flicked across to Jane and back.

'You can trust DC Bennett. I do. Completely.'

'And what about you, Detective Sergeant?'

Pete smiled.

'With DS Gayle's reputation and his clean-up rate, he could have been a DI long ago, miss,' Jane said. 'I've worked with him for several years now and it's my belief that the reason he isn't is because he doesn't back down and he doesn't give up.' She glanced across at him. 'Even when he should sometimes.'

Pete tipped his head in an appreciative shrug but said nothing, waiting for the young woman to make her mind up.

After what seemed like a long silence, she sighed. 'Very well. I need your phones, radios, whatever, switched off and on the table.'

'OK.' Pete took out his phone, switched it off and set it on the big, highly polished table. Jane followed suit, then added her chest radio. They sat back, waiting.

Emma looked from one to the other and back again. 'What I'm going to tell you does not leave this room, agreed?'

'Agreed,' Pete nodded.

'OK,' said Jane.

Emma's jaw clenched. Her arms stiffened as her hands squeezed her knees. Her eyes closed briefly. Then she opened them and took a breath. 'When I was a child, I was in care. My parents were killed in a car accident. I was around four at the time. Well, a few years later, the home was taken over by a new person. There were lots of changes of staff. Eventually, things settled down and then . . . Well, the abuse began. Rumours started among the children. At first, most didn't believe them. But gradually, more found out the truth – the hard way. I was a bit of an ugly duckling, so I avoided it all until I was twelve. Then . . . Well, to cut a long story short, nothing was done about it officially until an enquiry was started in 2011, long after I'd left. But when I heard they were seeking witnesses, I stepped forward. I was one of twenty-seven victims who ended up testifying. But threats were made. In one or two cases, they were carried out. A witness died. Another disappeared. The rest of us were protected from then on – closed court, remote testifying and all the rest – but afterwards, those of us who could were advised to move away and change all our details, cut ourselves off from our old lives.'

She shrugged. 'It wasn't as if I had any family to cut myself off from, so, with the help of the Crown Prosecution Service and some branch of the police in London, I ended up with a new identity, in a new city, miles from anywhere and anyone I'd known before.' She let out a heavy sigh. 'So, what do you need from me with regard to this case of yours?'

'Can you give us an account of your movements on Tuesday evening of this week, between the hours of eight and eleven?'

She frowned.

The rest of her body had gone completely still.

'Tuesday evening?'

'That's right.'

'I worked late. We had a big case in court on Wednesday. I didn't leave until after nine.'

Pete waited for more, but it wasn't coming. 'And after that?'

'I went home.'

'Did anyone see you? Did you talk to anyone? Make a phone call? Go online? Anything else that's traceable?'

She was shaking her head. 'No. I came in, showered, had a drink and went to bed. Alone.'

'OK. And between leaving work and getting back here: what can you tell us about that period?'

Her eyes narrowed. The frown returned to her brow. 'What do you mean, Detective?'

Pete's lips pressed together as he tired of playing with her. 'What can you tell me about the death of a taxi driver near the junction of Argyll and Pennsylvania Roads between nine-thirty and ten-thirty that night?'

Her eyes flashed wide. 'Death? What do you mean? He . . .' She stopped herself abruptly. Her whole expression closed down. 'I cannot go to court, Detective. You understand that, don't you?'

'There shouldn't be a need, Miss Radcliffe. But I do need to know what happened.'

'Why? If there's no need for it to come out in court, then what's the need for it to come out at all?'

'Corroboration. We have testimony. We need to know if it's reliable.'

'You have testimony of what, Detective?'

Pete shook his head. 'It doesn't work that way, Miss Radcliffe. You're a legal secretary. You know that.'

She closed her eyes, her body almost completely still for several seconds. Then she fixed Pete with an intense stare. 'My car broke down. I called a cab to take me home, rather than waiting for God knows how long on the side of a busy main road. He turned up. I got in. He . . . One moment, he was fine; the next, he was really weird. Then he'd be fine again. When we got close to the end of Argyll Road, he pulled off onto that wide verge in front of the trees and . . .' Her eyes closed again and her jaw clamped tight as she fought with her emotions. Her chest heaving, face scrunched up in a grimace, she finally looked up, this time at Jane. 'He raped me,' she whispered. 'There, in the back of his cab. I tried to fight him off. I even gave him a faceful of pepper spray, but he just wouldn't stop.' She blinked several times. 'Afterwards, I managed to get away and just ran. I went through the woods so he wouldn't see me. I must have spent half an hour or more in the shower afterwards, but I still felt filthy. Soiled. Eventually, I was just so exhausted, I went to sleep, but even then, I had nightmares all night. And sickness. But . . .' She switched her gaze back to Pete. 'You say he died? How? What from? I only had pepper spray. The legal kind. It's in my bag, upstairs.'

Pete dipped his head. 'We'll see about that later. But that's all you know about what happened to the taxi driver? You didn't see anyone else around there? Or hear anything unusual?'

'There were a couple of police cars parked along Argyll Road.

I remember wishing they'd hear me screaming while he was . . .' Her eyes closed again and she shuddered. 'Then, I was just about to come out of the woods onto Pennsylvania when they turned out of the Argyll Road junction. I ducked back into the trees until they'd gone.'

'Why?' *If she was a victim, why wouldn't she jump out and stop them to report it?*

'I didn't want to be seen,' she said incredulously. 'Reporting it, charging him, would have meant a court case. Media coverage. Someone might have seen me, recognised me. Someone from back in Reigate.' She paused. 'What happened to him? You haven't told me.'

'He was stabbed. Actually, he had his throat cut. Right where he'd attacked you. And you're certain you saw or heard nothing?'

'I was running through the wood, Detective. I didn't see or hear anything except my own panic.'

Pete looked at Jane again. They would have to go back up there, see if there were signs of her flight through the little copse, though even that wouldn't prove she didn't do it.

Jane returned his gaze with an expression that said, as plainly as any words – *I believe her.*

Pete nodded his agreement. 'OK, Miss Radcliffe. We'll need to see that pepper spray and you'll need to stay in the city for the next few days and be available if we need to talk to you again. You're sure you've got no idea where Tanya might have gone?'

She stared at him, her brown eyes wide as she processed what he'd just said. Then she shook her head. 'None.'

'And you don't know anyone else who might?'

She shook her head again. 'Her family, perhaps. Other than that, no.'

'OK.' Pete stood up. 'Jane, if you want to go with Miss Radcliffe and check on that spray . . .'

While they went upstairs, he stepped outside and called the squad room.

'Dave,' he said when it was picked up. 'I need you to check something for me.'

'What's that, boss?'

'Reigate. Children's home. An enquiry and court case, five or six years ago. Everything you can find, including transcripts.'

'OK . . . I vaguely remember something about that. Big sexual-abuse case, wasn't it?'

'That's right.'

'And we've got a link?'

'Maybe. We'll see you later.' Pete ended the call and went back inside just in time to meet Jane coming from the other side of the reception area. She nodded. Emma's spray was the legal kind. 'All right. Let's go.'

She waited until they were outside before asking, 'So, what's next?'

Pete sighed. 'If I knew that, this job would be easy.'

Chapter 30

Pete felt the fluttering of butterflies in his stomach and reached out to take Louise's hand. He hadn't felt this nervous in years. Even his driving test hadn't been this bad.

They were seated across from the reception desk in the foyer of Archways Secure Children's Home. It was nine-twenty-three in the morning. As well as arranging the time off work, Pete had had to get written permission to visit the facility from Colin Underhill. The one condition of that was that any contact between him and Tommy was to be supervised at all times by a member of Archways staff.

Pete had readily accepted: it was probably a condition of any parental visit in the facility anyway. If not, then it ought to be, he thought. Not that it was Tommy he was here to see. They had arranged to meet with Dr Brian Letterman at nine-thirty.

He looked at Louise. She looked as nervous as he felt.

What was Brian going to tell them?

He'd called and spoken to Louise the day before, while Pete was out at Emma Radcliffe's place – he still didn't know her real name, and probably never would. The court transcripts were sealed, as were those from the enquiry. Just the results had been published. She'd changed her name legally when she moved down here. That had been the second time she'd changed it since the trial, she'd told him on the phone, the previous afternoon. She had originally moved to Cheltenham, but she'd had to leave there when someone began following her. There had been evidence, but the man had never been caught. So, she'd changed her life again and moved down here.

And now this . . .

Jane had questioned her use of Facebook, but she had pointed out that she did not have any pictures of herself on there. Her profile image was a silhouette of several female graduates jumping up and tossing their mortar boards in the air. The party photos had been put up by a colleague. No one here knew her history or circumstances.

Pete squeezed Louise's hand reassuringly. 'It'll be OK,' he said.

She raised an eyebrow. 'Really? That's the best you can do?'

'What do you want me to say? We don't know what's going on yet, do we? But it will be OK in the end. I'm sure of it. He's a strong kid. Mentally. He might be little for his age, but he's a fighter. Always has been.'

'Yeah, that's part of the problem. They don't like fighters in places like this, do they?'

Pete smiled. 'All right. He's a survivor then. How's that?'

She tipped her head. 'Better.'

Brian came around the corner and hurried over, hand outstretched. 'Hi, Hi. Sorry to keep you. Come on through to my office.' He eagerly shook hands with Pete, then with Louise.

Pete held back a grimace at the quick, clammy grip.

Brian showed them along the corridor. His was the second door along. He held it open for them to enter and offered them seats. 'Can I get you anything? Tea? Coffee?'

Pete shook his head.

'No, thanks,' Louise said.

Brian settled himself behind his desk. 'OK. How are you both? I know it must be difficult, having Tommy in here. You must be having all sorts of awful thoughts and worries. I know you're both professional people. Intelligent. But there has to be an emotional impact in a situation like this.'

He was waffling and none of it was pertinent. Pete's patience began to draw thin. 'We're fine. The question is, how's Tommy?'

'Well, yes.' Brian gave an overexaggerated nodding motion. 'That *is* the question, isn't it?' He clasped his hands together on his desk, fingers entwined. 'I'm afraid that's very much the question. And one that we don't have an easy answer for.'

'So, what's the difficult one?' Pete asked.

'Well, to be perfectly honest, we're not absolutely sure. We thought we were getting there, but . . .' He shrugged, hands spreading wide. 'Then Tommy goes and throws us a curveball, as they say across the pond.'

'What does that mean?'

Brian pursed his lips. 'Honestly – I wish I knew. It seems that every other day he changes in ways we just can't predict. Most recently, he seems to have made a connection with a girl who came to us for her own safety, after making several suicide attempts. She'd shunned every attempt to interact with her until Tommy tried. Why he chose to, I have no idea, but he got through where no one else – staff or young people – could. She seems to be responding well, but . . . I'm worried.'

'Worried?' Louise exclaimed. 'Why?'

Brian grimaced. 'Well, as volatile as he is, if Tommy were to suddenly discard that connection, for whatever reason, I don't think she'd be able to recover from it.'

'So, what are you suggesting?' asked Pete. 'Pull them apart just in case?'

'I don't know. That's why I wanted to talk to you both.'

'I presume you've read Rosie Whitlock's statement?' Louise asked.

'Of course. But Tommy called that into question himself, as far as his motives at the time are concerned.'

321

'What do you mean?'

'He put the notion out there that his actions weren't entirely – or even partially – altruistic.'

'Of course they were,' Louise protested. 'He laid himself open to terrible consequences, to give her the chance to escape.'

'On the face of it, yes. But do we know all the circumstances?'

'What are you suggesting?'

'I'm not suggesting anything. Tommy himself did. That without all the facts, we can't assume motive.'

'He was just messing with you,' Pete asserted.

Brian frowned. 'To what end?'

'He's a kid. Maybe he was just trying to be clever. Who knows what goes on in their heads half the time? It doesn't have to make sense to us, to make sense to them.'

'I'm aware of the vagaries of child psychology, Peter. But I'm not sure I can put the safety of another young person in Tommy's hands.'

Now, we're getting to it, Pete thought. 'So, what are you proposing?'

'I'm tempted to suggest that one of them leaves the facility and goes elsewhere. To separate them before any problem occurs.'

A stab of fear jolted through Pete's chest. When he said "one of them", he obviously meant Tommy. Why else would they be here, now? And where else could Tommy go, as a youth on remand? Certainly, nowhere in Exeter. 'Who's to say there's going to be a problem? If you separate them for no reason, you could set them both back. Why not just take advantage of the progress they've made? Give them the chance to make some more?'

'It would be wonderful if we could. The trouble is, I don't know how reliable Tommy's going to be.'

'It sounds to me like you've already made up your mind,' Louise accused stiffly.

'Not at all. It's a question of exploring options and possibilities.'

'Really?' said Pete. 'What alternatives are there? If you want to move one of them out, which one? And where to?' The answer

322

was obvious: they were here, as opposed to the parents or guardians of this girl he was talking about. But he wanted to force Brian to say it.

'Well, this is the only facility of its type in Devon. The nearest other one would be in Southampton or Bristol. Other than that, we're talking, in Tommy's case, about a secure training centre, the nearest of which would be some distance from here. Or, for Tabitha, it would be a mental health facility. Which means here, Plymouth or Barnstaple.'

'And where's this Tabitha from?'

'Crediton.'

'So, Plymouth would be just as handy as here for any family members wanting to visit her,' Pete said. 'And, if she's suicidal, then mental health professionals would be as well-placed as anyone to give her what she needs. Whereas, Tommy's just on remand for a relatively minor crime. And we both know what those STCs are like nowadays. No kid should be going into that system until it's strictly necessary, no matter what he's accused or suspected of.'

Brian was nodding again. Pete guessed he was trying to look wise and understanding, but it wasn't working. At least, not in Pete's eyes.

'You're quite right, of course,' said the psychiatrist. 'But our mental health facilities are stretched way beyond their limits these days. I'm not at all sure that would be an appropriate environment for Tabitha. And with Tommy's record here . . .'

'His record?' Louise protested. 'One incident of self-defence that wouldn't have been necessary if you people had been doing your jobs properly. Huh! If Tommy's sorted the girl out, she can move on. If he might be able to do more for her, then you should give him the chance. Or take over the job yourself, now he's made the breakthrough, which is what you're supposed to be here for. Between you, surely you can turn her around. How old is she?'

'Fifteen.'

'Has she got family, other than her parents, she could live with until she's got her A-levels?'

'I believe there's an aunt and uncle in Okehampton.'

'Well, there you go then. Talk to them. Talk to her. See if they'll take her in for a couple of years and if she's happy with the idea. If so, you should be able to get her stabilised and out of here. And Tommy's not going to be here long anyway. A couple of months, probably, until the trial he's due to testify in. And by then, the knife issue should have been resolved too. And in the meantime, you could separate them, surely? With the staffing levels in this place, it couldn't be that hard.'

Brian drew a deep breath. 'The whole ethos of this place – the system it's set up around – is one of integration, not segregation.'

Louise's face twisted in disgust. 'This meeting never was about a discussion, was it? It was just your way of pussyfooting around trying to find a way of telling us, without bothering your conscience, that you can't cope with Tommy, so you want rid of him.'

'I am always open to persuasion, Mrs Gayle. Sadly, I've heard nothing, this morning, to offer that persuasion.'

'Well, none of us has got what we wanted then,' Louise said firmly. 'But I shall go back to the hospital from here and see what I can do about it, as a staff member.'

Brian frowned.

'If she wants to cause trouble, trust me – she'll cause a whole damn shitstorm,' Pete told him. 'And you know what I do for a living. You're sure you want to go down this road, are you?'

His frown deepened. 'I don't think there's any need for threats, Mr and Mrs Gayle. This meeting was a courtesy extended to you, in case you could offer any useful insight. And I think you've just done exactly that. I'm afraid my recommendation is going to be that your son is moved out of this establishment at the earliest opportunity.'

Louise came up out of her chair, a noise coming from her throat that Pete couldn't even describe. It was somewhere between a roar and a scream, but very low in volume. Despite his own almost insurmountable need to reach across the desk and strangle the self-righteous little shit, he grabbed Louise and held her back, pushing her down into the chair and holding her there.

'You send my son to jail and I'll finish you, you ineffectual little creep,' she snarled over Pete's shoulder. 'I'll have you struck off every register in Europe before I'm finished.'

She'd do it too, Pete knew. And he'd back her, one hundred per cent. It wouldn't help Tommy, but nothing would, at this stage. Louise was right: Brian's mind had been set before this meeting was even arranged. It had only ever been about assuaging his conscience and maybe some damage-control.

'Come on, Lou,' he said. 'This is getting us nowhere.'

'So, you just want to walk out?'

He met her fierce and desperate gaze and gave her a subtle shake of the head, not wanting to discuss plans in front of Letterman, but she was too distraught to register it.

'You're going to back down to a useless wimp who can't stand the fact that a fourteen-year-old kid can do his job better than he can?'

'No,' he said finally. 'I'm going to do something about it that can't be done in this room. And I'm not leaving you behind to boost his argument by assaulting him. So, come on. Let's go.'

'You're as bad as he is,' she accused. 'This is our son we're talking about. His whole life and future.'

'I know,' he cut in over her. 'And I agree with you. But that's not going to make a difference here. *We're* not going to make a difference here. So, let's go somewhere that we can.' He guided her towards the door.

'What the hell are you doing?' she demanded.

'I'm choosing my fights,' he told her. 'And the battlefield.'

'But . . .'

'Later.' He opened the door behind her, eased her through it, then took her hand and led her briskly away down the corridor.

Pete dropped Louise back at the Royal Devon and Exeter Hospital, where she planned to begin creating as much hell as she possibly could for Dr Brian Letterman.

Finally, outside the secure children's home, he had explained to her that, with Letterman unwilling to listen, there was no point arguing with him. Their time would be far better spent doing something about him. And forewarned was forearmed, which was the last thing they wanted him to be. Far better to hit when and where he wasn't expecting it than to let him prepare his defence in advance.

As he drove out of the hospital, he keyed the hands-free system and called the squad room.

'DC Miles, Exeter CID.'

'Dave, it's Pete. I need you to dig up everything you can on a Dr Brian Letterman for me.'

'Who's he?'

'Someone who works with children and might not be fit to do so.'

'OK . . .' Dave said slowly.

In the background, a phone was ringing. Then it stopped and he thought he heard Jane's voice.

'I want anything and everything, down to neighbour disputes and parking tickets. The works.'

'Right. What's he done, specifically?'

'Most recently – pissed me off. Big-time.'

'Eh? Hold on, boss.' He muffled the mouthpiece for a moment, then was back. 'Jane wants to speak to you.'

'Boss?'

Dave must have passed her the handset.

'What's up, Jane?'

'Tanya Cunliffe. She's been spotted.'

'Excellent. Where?'

'Budleigh Salterton. The Beaches Hotel.'

'Right. I'll pick you up out back in two minutes.'

Chapter 31

Jane was standing outside the back door when he pulled into the car park behind the station. She stepped forward as he swung the car around and climbed in when he got back to her.

'Your meeting didn't go to plan then,' she said as she pulled her seatbelt across and he started back down the side of the station.

'You could say that. The arsehole can't handle the boy, so he wants rid of him before he sullies his reputation. Well, it's too late for that, I can tell you. Time Louise gets through with him, he won't have enough reputation left to get a job as a dustman. Did Dave find anything on him?'

It had to be Dave she'd got the information from.

'No. He's as squeaky-clean as you'd expect, working in a place like that.'

Pete grunted. 'Give him a call, get him to talk to any staff members from Archways who aren't currently on duty, see what they have to say about Letterman. And get Ben to find as many former residents of the place as he can. From within the last twelve months, ideally, but go back two years if need be. We'll talk to them too.'

'You really want to stir that much shit, boss?'

Pete kept his eyes on the road. 'That and more, Jane.'

There was one more source of information he could try when they finished with the task they were on now. When Jane got off the phone, he would call Headquarters and arrange a conversation with Dr Abigail White, the police psychologist who he had been required to see when he came back to work last year, after his extended absence because of Tommy's disappearance.

And round and round we go, he thought. It was weird how things sometimes seemed to go in circles. 'So, how was our girl spotted?'

'The hotel receptionist was watching the news this evening, saw her picture on there and remembered booking her in yesterday. Called us straight away. Well, called the local sergeant, at least, who passed it on to us. He's keeping the place under surveillance until we get there.'

Budleigh Salterton was a small, picturesque town a few miles up the coast from Exmouth and twelve miles from Exeter. It had a long shingle beach with beach huts and fishing boats, a narrow High Street with individual and independent shops rather than the usual chain stores, and a mix of old and ancient houses sprawling up the hills behind and to either side of the bay it was nestled in.

The hotel where Tanya Cunliffe had been spotted was at the end of the main street, where it opened out to overlook the beach. A large old converted house, painted pastel yellow, it stood between the road and the beach.

Pete drove past it and pulled over where space allowed at the edge of the shingle. A uniformed police sergeant was standing in front of the place as they walked back. In his fifties, Pete guessed, he was stocky and weathered-looking with a scar on his right cheek that ran down to his jaw.

Pete showed him his warrant card and held out a hand. 'Pete Gayle, Exeter CID. This is DS Bennett.'

The man nodded and they shook. His grip was firm and dry, the skin hard and work-worn. 'Sid Paxton. She's registered in room six. Don't know if she's up there now but she's not answering the phone.' He tipped his head. 'If not, though, she hasn't left her key at the desk. I've told the lads to keep an eye out for her, in case she's out and about somewhere.'

'Right. We'll go and give her a knock then.'

They went inside. Pete showed his badge to the receptionist as they passed, heading for the carpeted stairs beyond her desk. Signs at the top of the stairs showed rooms one to three to the left and four to six to the right. They turned along a corridor with a tall window at the far end. Room six was on the left, just before that window.

Pete knocked on the door and they listened intently.

Nothing.

They waited, heads close to the thin wooden panel. The silence stretched on until he tried again, louder this time. Still there was no response.

Jane stepped back. 'It's not like we need a warrant, being a hotel. Shall I go and ask for the key?'

Pete nodded and watched her walk away, her long, dark-green coat swirling around her legs, short ginger hair gleaming in the light from the window behind him. She flicked it back with a twist of her head as she turned into the stairway and went from sight.

Moments later she was back, heading towards him with a key held high in her hand, dangling the large fob with its imprinted room number. 'Anything?'

Pete shook his head and stood back as she inserted the key and turned it, pushing the door with her free hand.

The room was stylish, clean and bright, the walls beige up to the picture rail and white above to blend with the ceiling. Long, gold-coloured curtains framed both the side-aspect window and the French doors that led out onto a balcony that was just big enough for two chairs and a tiny table. The French doors stood ajar, admitting the cool sea air and the sounds of seagulls and surf.

There was no one.

Pete stepped forward, heading for the door to the en suite. As he passed the dressing table with its small kettle and tea-making tray, his radio blurted, 'DS Gayle. Sergeant Paxton for DS Gayle. Come in.'

He took the radio, which looked like an old-fashioned mobile phone, from his pocket and pressed the Transmit button. 'We are in. What's up, Sid?'

'She's been spotted. I just got a call from the station. A member of the public recognised her. She's halfway up the cliff path, t'other side of town.'

'We're on the way.' Pete glanced at Jane and they headed quickly out of the room, Jane locking it behind them.

As they passed the front desk, she set the key on it. 'Thanks. Keep it locked, would you? And the cleaner out of it.'

'Why?'

They were almost at the front door. As he reached out to push it open, Pete called back over his shoulder: 'Crime scene.'

'Oh my God! Really?'

But the door was closing behind them by then. Pete nodded to Sid Paxton. 'We'll take my car. Is there room to drive up there?' As close as it was to Exeter, he'd never been to the little town before.

The sergeant grimaced as he stepped forward and they headed for the car. 'No way. Too narrow with the old wall sticking out in places. If you go out on the Exmouth Road, though, then turn down Cliff Road, we might be able to get ahead of her. If not, we'll gain a good bit.'

'OK.' Pete unlocked the silver Ford and they climbed in, Jane taking the back seat so that the local man could provide directions. Pete turned the car around in the narrow street. 'Did the caller say exactly where they saw her or which way she was going?'

'They said she's walking up there, so, presumably, that means away from town, up towards the clifftop. Didn't say exactly how far she'd got, though. I did ask.'

With the car finally facing back into town, Pete flicked on the blue lights and gave the siren a quick 'whoop' as he started as quickly as safety would allow along the narrow, shaded street.

As soon as the road opened out, he switched on the siren and sped up. 'Direct me, will you? I don't know this place.'

'Straight through and up the High Street. There's an estate agent's on the left, then a junction and a pub. We turn left there. It's a wide entrance to a narrow road. I'll point it out. There's bollards at the top so we're on foot from there.'

'Can you get onto your station then? See if they've got the caller's number so we can get them back and get a better idea of where she is?'

Paxton's big hand went to the radio clipped to his upper chest. He pressed the button. 'Mary, this is Sid. Have you got a number for that caller on the Exeter girl?'

'No, Sarge. It was a mobile and it was blocked.'

'Bugger. Why are things never as bloody easy as they ought to be, eh?' he asked, hand dropping back to his lap.

Pete's mind went back to the Archways Secure Children's Home but hadn't formed the thought into words when Jane spoke.

'It's not like our girl to be this easy to spot. All the effort she went to the other night, and now this?'

'Here you go,' Paxton said. 'Left up here.'

Pete glanced in the mirror as he flicked on the indicator. 'We're out of the city. Maybe she doesn't think she needs to hide,' he suggested.

'No. Something isn't right.'

Paxton was right: the road narrowed down considerably a short way up, becoming almost single-track. Pete killed the siren. Then he had another thought. He glanced sideways at the man in the passenger seat. 'Was the caller male or female?'

Paxton looked back at him. The look on his face told Pete that he'd cottoned on immediately. 'That's bold. If it was . . .' He reached for his radio again. 'Mary? Was the caller male or female?'

'Female, Sarge.'

'Received.' He looked at Pete again. 'You reckon we've been had?'

Pete slowed through a narrow section then passed a side road. Two blocks of modern-looking flats stood on the right, a short way beyond, and he could see black bollards across the road in front of him, a stone wall beyond them with shrubs growing up behind it.

'We'll soon find out, I suppose.' He pulled up at the side of the road and they stepped out of the car, heading up between the bollards. 'At least, I hope so.'

Jane looked left and right, up and down the steeply inclined pathway. 'What do you reckon, boss?'

Pete pursed his lips, looking at Paxton. The man was a long way from fit and not far from retirement. Pete didn't want him having a heart attack, especially if this turned out to be a wild goose chase. 'How about you go downhill, we'll go up?'

'Suits me.'

Thought it might. 'Come on then.' He tipped his head at Jane.

Chapter 32

Pete rounded a bend in the path and stopped, panting as he peered ahead, left hand raised to shield his eyes from the sun, which was coming around to reflect back off the sea in a wide swathe of sparkling silver.

There weren't many people this far up the steep cliff path. Not far ahead, the buildings of Budleigh Salterton petered out, giving way to rough grass and bushes – mostly gorse, from the look of them. But near the top, a lone figure walked slowly up the hill as Jane stopped beside him, hands on her knees, breath sawing in and out of her lungs.

At this distance, he wasn't sure, but he thought he could see a hint of colour in the long hair of the figure up ahead. 'What do you reckon?' he gasped.

'I reckon I'm knackered. Any chance of a piggyback?'

He raised an arm to point. 'Up ahead. Has she got red hair?'

'Huh?' She straightened up with an effort and squinted, raising a hand as Pete had done. 'Not sure. Need to be closer.'

Pete swallowed. 'Don't let me stop you, Detective Constable.'

Jane grunted. 'Funny how you bring up my rank when you want me to do something you know I won't like.'

'Go on. You're younger than me,' he grunted, starting forward again himself.

'Yes, boss. Certainly, boss. Whatever you say, boss.' Her hoarse voice matched the rhythm of her reluctantly moving feet.

'If you can waste breath on talking, you can use it to move faster.'

Pete's radio crackled before she could reply. He took it out and heard Sid Paxton saying, '. . . for DS Gayle. She's not on the downhill leg. You got anything?'

Pete pressed the Transmit button and raised the radio slightly. 'Maybe. Not sure yet. We're too far off. Send someone back to the hotel, in the meantime, just in case.'

'Already done.'

'OK. We'll keep you informed.'

'Roger.'

Jane was ten yards ahead of him as he dropped the radio back into his pocket. He pushed on, trying to catch up with her, but she seemed to get her second wind and forged steadfastly ahead, almost at the top of the path now.

Beyond her, he saw the more distant figure step over to the left, towards the tightly packed shrubbery at the top of the high, red cliffs that he knew fell almost straight down to the beach, far below, at the western end of the town.

Jane stopped, hesitated for just an instant, then turned back to face him. 'I reckon it's her,' she said. 'But what's she . . .?' A frown furrowed her brow. 'Do you think she's . . .?'

Pete nodded. 'Accounts for why she didn't worry about being seen.'

'Yeah.' Jane hurried forward, re-energised by a sense of urgency that Pete shared.

Ahead, the young woman had gone from sight among the more than head-high bushes that were sprinkled with bright-yellow flowers. Reaching where she'd disappeared, they saw a wide path going into the shrubbery from the back of a triangular opening that had been invisible from further back.

They ran on, Jane still out in front. The path narrowed, twisting between the thorny bushes, their target still out of sight.

'Tanya,' Jane called. 'Tanya?'

No answer.

In among the high, dense bushes, there was barely any sound from the breeze, but Pete wasn't sure he'd hear a response anyway, over his own hoarse breathing and pounding heart.

'Tanya. That is you, isn't it?'

'Leave me alone.' The shout sounded clearly, from closer than Pete had expected, for some reason. 'I just need some peace.'

'Tanya, come back!'

Pete stepped around yet another twist in the path and stopped on the edge of an area of grass that was around thirty feet wide by ten to fifteen deep, bordered by dense gorse on all sides except the far one, where it dropped abruptly away into nothingness. He was about a third of the way along from the left, eastern end. Tanya Cunliffe was standing at the far western end, just inches from the drop-off at the front of the little arena.

'What are you doing?' Jane was just a step in front of him, partially shielding him from Tanya's view. 'You can't . . . What about your mum and dad? Your auntie? They'd be devastated.'

Pete saw a frown darken her expression. 'Who are you? How do you . . .? You're police,' she realised. 'You must be.' She started to turn away, towards the cliff edge.

'Yes,' Jane said quickly. 'You're right. But that doesn't affect the impact this would have on your family. The people you love. I know you were with your mum and dad only a couple of days ago. You don't want to put them through something like this.'

'It'd be better than putting them through a trial,' she argued. 'Making them sit there and listen to me being called a murderer. Going through all the sordid details of what I did and why.'

'Why, would the reason be so terrible for them to learn?' Jane asked, Pete staying quiet and unobtrusive behind her. 'Surely it must have been valid, or you wouldn't be here.'

'Of course it was valid,' she snapped. 'I was raped. I was fifteen. I'd gone out into the city. My dad had insisted I get a cab home, to make sure I was safe, and the bloody driver attacked me! How's that going to make him feel, eh? Knowing he put me in harm's way.'

'Yes, but not deliberately. He was trying to look out for you.'

'And how's that going to help the way he feels when he finds out?'

'But . . . you were fifteen. You were doing as you were told. And anyway, if that's the reason, why wait until now to . . .? That's what – twelve years ago? What suddenly made you start now?'

'Dumb luck,' she said. 'I saw what that bastard did to Emma. At least, the aftermath. I was going up to her flat, to return a DVD I'd borrowed. I saw her get into the cab, down by the Old Mill, but I was too far away to get her attention so I followed. I got held up by some of your lot, halfway along the back lane, trying to arrest a couple of guys. By the time I got past and saw the taxi parked up on the grass, she was just running for the trees on the far side, so . . .' She shrugged. '. . . I made sure he didn't go after her.'

'And we've got forensics that support all that,' Jane said. 'So good luck to you, I say. But what about the other two, after that? What did they do?'

Tanya seemed to slump. Her head dropped forward, her shoulders dipped. She said nothing for what seemed like a long time until, finally, she looked up, her eyes haunted. 'I'm sorry,' she said in a tiny voice.

'For what?' Jane asked.

'Mr Randrashan. I'm . . .' She shook her head. 'So sorry.'

'Why? Was it a mistake of some sort?'

Well done, Pete thought. *Keep her talking. Calm her down. She'll step back in a bit.*

Tanya held Jane's gaze. 'He . . . the things he said. I thought he was going to attack me. After Emma and then that other one molesting me a couple of days later, I . . .' Her voice choked off. She swallowed and paused, gathering herself. 'I didn't know about his daughter until I saw it in the paper at Mum and Dad's at the weekend.'

Hardeep Randrashan's daughter had been raped at the age of fourteen, Pete knew from the background checks they'd done on him after he was found.

'All the work he's done since then,' Tanya went on. 'Trying to stamp out such things. Obviously, I jumped the gun and I was wrong and I can't face his little girl or his wife, knowing what I've done. Or my parents. The other two deserved all they got, but he didn't. I wish so much I could take it back. Turn back the clock. But I can't, so here I am. Now, just go away, will you?' Her voice got stronger as she finished.

'I can't and you know it,' Jane said. 'I'm a police officer. My whole career is based on helping and protecting the public. Every member of the public, good, bad or indifferent. And you're not a bad person, Tanya. You wouldn't have come up here if you were. And you're certainly not indifferent, are you?'

'Well, I'm not good, am I?' she argued. 'I'm not good at avoiding you, or you wouldn't be here. And I've killed three people, one of them entirely innocent, so how can that allow me to be classified as good? Thou shalt not kill. Isn't that one of the Ten Commandments?'

'Yes, but it includes thyself,' Jane pointed out. 'Suicide's also a sin and two wrongs don't make a right.'

Tanya's face twisted in disgust. 'If all you can do is come out with clichés, you might as well just go away.' She started to unbutton her coat.

Sensing that Jane was losing her, Pete stepped forward into clear view. 'Clichés only got be clichés because they're repeated so often. And that's because they're right. You talk about your parents. I am one and I can tell you, they'll get over any disappointment that you made a mistake. They'd never get over the fact that you'd died for it. That you'd died for any reason. It's not the way things are meant to be. We're not designed to cope with burying our own kids.' He took another step forward along the edge of the grass.

'Of course we are,' Tanya argued. 'Why else do people in the third world have ten kids or more? It's so that at least a few will survive to look after them in their old age.'

'And they've got more to help them recover from the loss of any that don't make it: to distract them from it. Yours haven't. They've only got you. You go, that leaves them nothing. No one. They'll be completely bereft.'

Tanya shed her beige wool coat and dropped it on the ground. 'Stay where you are.' Beneath the coat, she wore all black. Blouse, skirt, tights and low-heeled shoes that Pete knew from his daughter were called ballet flats.

He raised his hands, palms out. 'All right. You're in charge here. I'm just saying this isn't the answer. I've lived longer than you. I've seen a lot more than you have, of the worst things society can produce as well as some of the best, and I'm telling you, it's a fact: there are better ways to deal with this situation. Better for everyone. You. Your family. Hardeep Randrashan's. Even mine and Jane's, here.'

She frowned. 'What the hell have your families got to do with it?'

'What, you think we wouldn't be affected by seeing you jump off and splatter on those rocks down there?' Pete nodded towards the drop behind her.

'I didn't ask you to come here. In fact, I told you to go away. You refused. That's not my fault.'

'We refused because it's what we do. We try to save lives. To keep people safe. All people, no matter what mistakes they might have made in life. You're young. You've got your whole life ahead of you. You've got people who love you. You don't want to waste that. To end it in a mess of blood and gore that'll give the kids

338

playing down there nightmares for the rest of their lives. What have they done to deserve that, eh?'

For the first time, he saw a hint of doubt creep into her eyes.

No, she didn't want to do that to innocent children. But were there any down there? Pete didn't know and neither did she. Her eyes flicked sideways and down, towards the drop just inches from her feet. Then she looked back at Pete. Straightened her back. 'Life isn't perfect. Sometimes there are unintended consequences.'

'That only counts if we don't know about them beforehand,' he said quickly. Behind his back, he waved to Jane, trying to get her to move out across the grass, towards the clifftop, so that Tanya would focus on her, allowing Pete to close in on her. 'If we do, then we're guilty of them, whether we wanted to cause them or not.'

'Just as I'm guilty of killing Hardeep Randrashan. An innocent man. Not just an innocent man, but one who was fighting the same issues as me. A man who was on my side, effectively. There's a note in my pocket, there.' She pointed to her coat, on the ground between them.

'We don't need a note. We need you,' Pete said, a wave of fear sweeping through his innards.

To his left, Jane moved outward from the bushes.

Tanya's head turned towards her. 'No. Don't come any closer.'

'I'm not. I'm just checking down there.'

Pete moved as soon as Tanya's attention was off him. A wide step sideways, then he leapt forward. Landed and dove, arms outstretched, trying to reach her before she could react.

'No!' she shrieked, spinning away from him, towards the cliff edge. Her body tilted out over the abyss. Pete sensed Jane coming in from his side, striving to reach them. One of Tanya's feet left the ground, stepping out into nothingness. Pete's right arm went around her lower legs as his left went up to grab her skirt, near the waistband. She screamed, falling backwards, away from him. He clasped her ankles to his chest, his grip firming on the front of her skirt as he hit the ground on his side, legs lifting as his head and shoulders hung out over the vertiginous drop.

'Come here,' he snarled, twisting his body in an effort to stop them both from falling.

Tanya's feet dug into his chest, her weight taking her beyond the point of no return.

Shafts of agony ran through Pete's torso. Inches further and he'd have broken his back on the edge of the cliff. His left hand locked into the material of her skirt and whatever she wore under it, her weight pulling his arm back over his shoulder so that he cried out in pain as Jane's body came down hard over his legs, anchoring him to the ground and safety. He struggled to hold on, but then Tanya wriggled, trying to kick out.

'Jane, roll me over,' he said. 'Quick, before I lose her.'

'I can't. You'll slip.'

'Do it!'

Jane's body lifted off him. He felt her hands at his thigh and flank. She began to lift and push.

'No!' Tanya screamed. 'Let me go!'

She twisted and writhed, legs jerking in his grasp. Jane got him over onto his side, rolling him so he could hold on to Tanya better and haul her back up, but Tanya realised what was happening and changed the way she was fighting him. Suddenly, one of her legs jerked up, bending sharply at the knee to slide it free of his arms, leaving her shoe behind for his to roll onto. Her heel slammed into his chest. Pete grunted, but held onto the foot he still gripped. Jane got him turned fully over. The shoe was a minor discomfort under his body, but the relief in his back was incredible.

Tanya's free foot, wrapped in black nylon, came hard and fast at his face. He ducked to the side, digging his knees into the ground for purchase.

'Let me go!' she yelled. Her free foot came at him again, but this time from an angle. He had nowhere to go. It hit the side of his head like a hammer.

'Ow! Damn it.' He straightened his legs. 'Drag me back, Jane.'

Tanya bucked upwards, bending from the waist, then dropped back, trying to free his grip on her skirt, but Pete hung on, focused on not losing her. Her foot hit him again. This time, he hadn't seen it coming. It slammed into his face. Pain exploded in his nose. Every instinct drove him to let go of her and protect his face, but he fought against it. Then her foot got purchase on the edge of the cliff, pushing away from him as Jane tried to drag him backwards by the ankles. He couldn't see anything but sparkling lights. Blood was pouring from his smashed nose. The two women were pulling him in both directions at once as if he was on a medieval torture rack. He dropped his face onto Tanya's leg, holding on for all he was worth. The pressure eased abruptly from her direction and he slid backwards a few inches, only for her heel to slam into his back. He grunted. She tried the same move again.

'Tanya, pack it in,' Jane gasped. 'We're trying to save you, for God's sake.'

'I don't want you to,' she cried. 'Let me go!'

Her foot came down on the back of Pete's head and she bent up from the waist again, hands reaching for his face. He could still see nothing, but the shift in her weight and the pressure on his left hand, just below her waist, shifted enough that he could sense she was about to try something new. He felt her fingers on his hand. Her other hand fumbled around his face, seeking purchase. Pete squeezed his eyes shut defensively but her other hand did its work, slender fingers wrapping around his little finger, prying it loose.

Shit, he thought. *She's going to try and break it.*

He twisted his hand, but her skirt was too tight over her stomach to allow much movement that way. Then her other hand got a grip at an angle across his face. Her little finger hooked into his still-tender nose, thumb pressing into the notch of his temple while the sharp nail of another finger pushed into the corner of his eye.

He twisted his head away but, in doing so, allowed her the purchase she needed on his hand. She gripped his little finger firmly and wrenched it backwards. Pete yelled, trying to fight her. He felt Jane's grip vanish from his ankles. He bellowed, forced to release Tanya's skirt and twist his hand away as Jane's weight landed across his lower legs.

'Shit,' she swore as she missed whatever she'd been trying to do. Grab the girl's free leg, he imagined. But at the same time, he felt Tanya's weight swing back away from him. He shook his head and opened his eyes. They were still blurry with tears, but he could see. Tanya had swung her free leg back in an upside-down high-kick. Then, with her backside resting against the red stone of the cliff, inches from his face, she jerked her other leg away from him, her powerful thigh muscle far stronger than his arm. He almost lost his grip on her, just his weight holding her ankle in place beneath his torso. Then her other leg came back up, bending at the knee, the foot driving in once more at his face. He tucked his head down so that he took the blow on the crown of his head, but it was finally enough. With a jerk and a twist, her ankle went from under him.

'No!' he shouted as she fell away, arms wide, legs spread like an upside-down free-falling parachutist. She looked back at him and actually waved and smiled as she sailed downwards as if in slow motion, her clothes fluttering around her. He held her gaze, his emotions raw, for what seemed like for ever but could only have been a couple of seconds, until she hit the roughly heaped rocks at the base of the cliffs.

'Oh, God!'

It was only when she spoke that he realised Jane's weight was gone from on top of him. He rolled over and sat up.

Jane turned away, head hanging. 'Shit,' she said softly. 'Shit, shit, shit, shit, shit. I'm so sorry, boss. I thought if I could grab her free leg while it was waving about like that, I could help pull her back, but she must have seen me coming. She snatched it away before I could get hold of it.'

Pete stood up and wrapped an arm around her shoulders.

'Not your fault. She was determined to go. We did all we could.'

'Yeah, but if I'd . . .'

'Ifs and buts mean nothing,' he broke in. 'We tried. She won.' *End of*, he thought, but managed not to say. It was way too soon. 'Have you got any gloves?'

'Yes. Only my size, though.'

'Do the coat up and fold the collar into the middle of it.' He nodded to Tanya's coat, which she'd dropped on the ground, signalling her intention to jump. 'It's not like we need it for forensics.'

Jane looked up at him and her eyes flashed with horror. 'Jeez, you look terrible.'

'Thanks.' He glanced down. The front of his shirt and jacket were splashed with blood. He could feel it congealing around his nose, mouth and chin. 'A kick in the face'll do that for you.'

'Are you OK?'

'Better than I look.' He sighed. 'What really pisses me off is that she won. She got away with three murders.'

'Hardly got away with them. She died for them, didn't she?'

'Yeah, but that was her choice. I'm not saying it's the coward's way out, because dying like that took some guts, but at the end of the day, she got to choose her fate, and that's more than she allowed her victims.'

Jane grimaced and crouched over Tanya's coat, pulling on a pair of pale-blue nitrile gloves.

'Is the note there?' Pete asked.

She checked the coat. Pete heard the rustle of paper and she reached into one of the pockets.

'Leave it there,' he said. 'I don't want to read it. Not now, at least.'

He drew a deep breath. He didn't want to think about Tanya's excuses. The fact was, she'd got what she wanted. A clean death. A family that would grieve for her – that would forget the mistakes

343

she'd made and invent some kind of fiction about how noble she'd been. Because, as parents, that's what they were bound to do. It's what he would have done. Maybe what he was already doing, in a way, with Tommy – clinging to the possibility that he was just a victim who was coping in the only way he could.

And, like Tanya, Brian Letterman would probably win, at least in the short-term. He would get his way on Tommy's relocation because he had the ear of whoever would make the decision. But what would the consequences of that be – for himself, for Louise, and especially for Tommy? Tommy would no doubt withdraw even more than ever. Louise, unable to see him every day, might even sink back into the depression that she'd only recently climbed out of. And how would Annie cope? Pete felt physically sick. His jaw muscles bunched as he fought to retain control. He glanced down at Jane, who had fastened and folded the beige coat and was about to stand up with it. 'Ready?'

She nodded.

'Let's go then. I need to get out of here.'

Nowhere To Run

A missing child. A dead body. A killer on the loose.

Returning to Exeter CID after his son's unsolved disappearance, Detective Sergeant Peter Gayle's first day back was supposed to be gentle. Until a young girl is reported missing and the clock begins to tick.

Rosie Whitlock was abducted from outside her school. There are no clues, but Peter isn't letting another child disappear.

When the body of another young victim is found, the hunt escalates. Someone is abducting young girls and now they have a murderer on their hands. Time could well be running out for Rosie, and when evidence in the case relating to his own son's disappearance is discovered, the stakes get even higher . . .

No Place to Hide

A house fire. A suspicious death. A serial killer to catch.

When a body is found in a house fire DS Peter Gayle
is called to the scene. It looks like an accidental death,
but the evidence just doesn't add up.

With only one murder victim they can't make any calls,
but it looks like a serial killer is operating in Exeter
and it's up to Pete to track him down.

But with his wife still desperate for news on their missing son
and his boss watching his every move, the pressure is on for
Pete to bring the murderer to justice before it is too late.

Acknowledgements

Thanks once again to former Thames Valley Police Officer Rick Ell and his wife Christine for their invaluable advice on technical matters and to my wife Pru for . . . too much to list here.

Also to Charlotte Mursell and everyone else at HQ Digital for their hard work and insight and to Kathy Gale, who suggested I step onto this road in the first place. Although it's a detour from the direction I was going in, it has been a joy getting to know Pete Gayle and his team and sharing their adventures and adversities.

Which brings me to you – the readers who have come along for the ride. Without you, there would be no point to this journey, so thank you for the interest you have taken in my work and all the messages of support I've received. I really appreciate you all. This last year has been a hell of a ride – long may it continue.

Dear Reader,

We hope you enjoyed reading this book. If you did, we'd be so appreciative if you left a review. It really helps us and the author to bring more books like this to you.

Here at HQ Digital we are dedicated to publishing fiction that will keep you turning the pages into the early hours. Don't want to miss a thing? To find out more about our books, promotions, discover exclusive content and enter competitions you can keep in touch in the following ways:

JOIN OUR COMMUNITY:

Sign up to our new email newsletter: http://smarturl.it/SignUpHQ

Read our new blog www.hqstories.co.uk

https://twitter.com/HQStories

www.facebook.com/HQStories

BUDDING WRITER?

We're also looking for authors to join the HQ Digital family! Find out more here:

https://www.hqstories.co.uk/want-to-write-for-us/

Thanks for reading, from the HQ Digital team

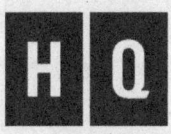